SOUPY LEAVES HOME

SOUPY LEAVES HOME

Written by **Cecil Castellucci**

Illustrated by **Jose Pimienta**

Lettered by **Nate Piekos of Blambot®**

DARK HORSE BOOKS

Special thanks to Sierra Hahn, Kel McDonald, Joe Infurnari, the MacDowell Colony, and all the mentors who've taken us under their wings.

President & Publisher **Mike Richardson**
Editor **Shantel LaRocque** | Assistant Editor **Katii O'Brien**
Designer **Sarah Terry** | Digital Art Technician **Christianne Goudreau**

Published by Dark Horse Books
A division of Dark Horse Comics, Inc.
10956 SE Main Street | Milwaukie, OR 97222

DarkHorse.com
First edition: April 2017 | ISBN 978-1-61655-431-6

1 3 5 7 9 10 8 6 4 2
Printed in China

To find a comics shop in your area, call the Comic Shop Locator Service toll-free at
1-888-266-4226. International Licensing: (503) 905-2377

Neil Hankerson Executive Vice President | **Tom Weddle** Chief Financial Officer | **Randy Stradley** Vice President of Publishing | **Matt Parkinson** Vice President of Marketing **David Scroggy** Vice President of Product Development | **Dale LaFountain** Vice President of Information Technology | **Cara Niece** Vice President of Production and Scheduling **Nick McWhorter** Vice President of Media Licensing | **Mark Bernardi** Vice President of Digital and Book Trade Sales | **Ken Lizzi** General Counsel | **Dave Marshall** Editor in Chief **Davey Estrada** Editorial Director | **Scott Allie** Executive Senior Editor | **Chris Warner** Senior Books Editor | **Cary Grazzini** Director of Specialty Projects | **Lia Ribacchi** Art Director | **Vanessa Todd** Director of Print Purchasing | **Matt Dryer** Director of Digital Art and Prepress | **Sarah Robertson** Director of Product Sales | **Michael Gombos** Director of International Publishing and Licensing

Library of Congress Cataloging-in-Publication Data

Names: Castellucci, Cecil, 1969- author. | Pimienta, Jose, illustrator. |
 Piekos, Nate, letterer.
Title: Soupy leaves home / written by Cecil Castellucci ; illustrated by Jose
 Pimienta ; lettered by Nate Piekos of Blambot.
Description: First edition. | Milwaukie, OR : Dark Horse Books, 2017.
Identifiers: LCCN 2016052804 | ISBN 9781616554316 (paperback)
Subjects: LCSH: Graphic novels. | BISAC: JUVENILE FICTION / Comics & Graphic
 Novels / General. | JUVENILE FICTION / Historical / General.
Classification: LCC PN6727.C389 S68 2017 | DDC 741.5/973--dc23
LC record available at https://lccn.loc.gov/2016052804

For all the Pearls in the world.
—Cecil Castellucci

To Tita, the kindest person I've known.
—Jose Pimienta

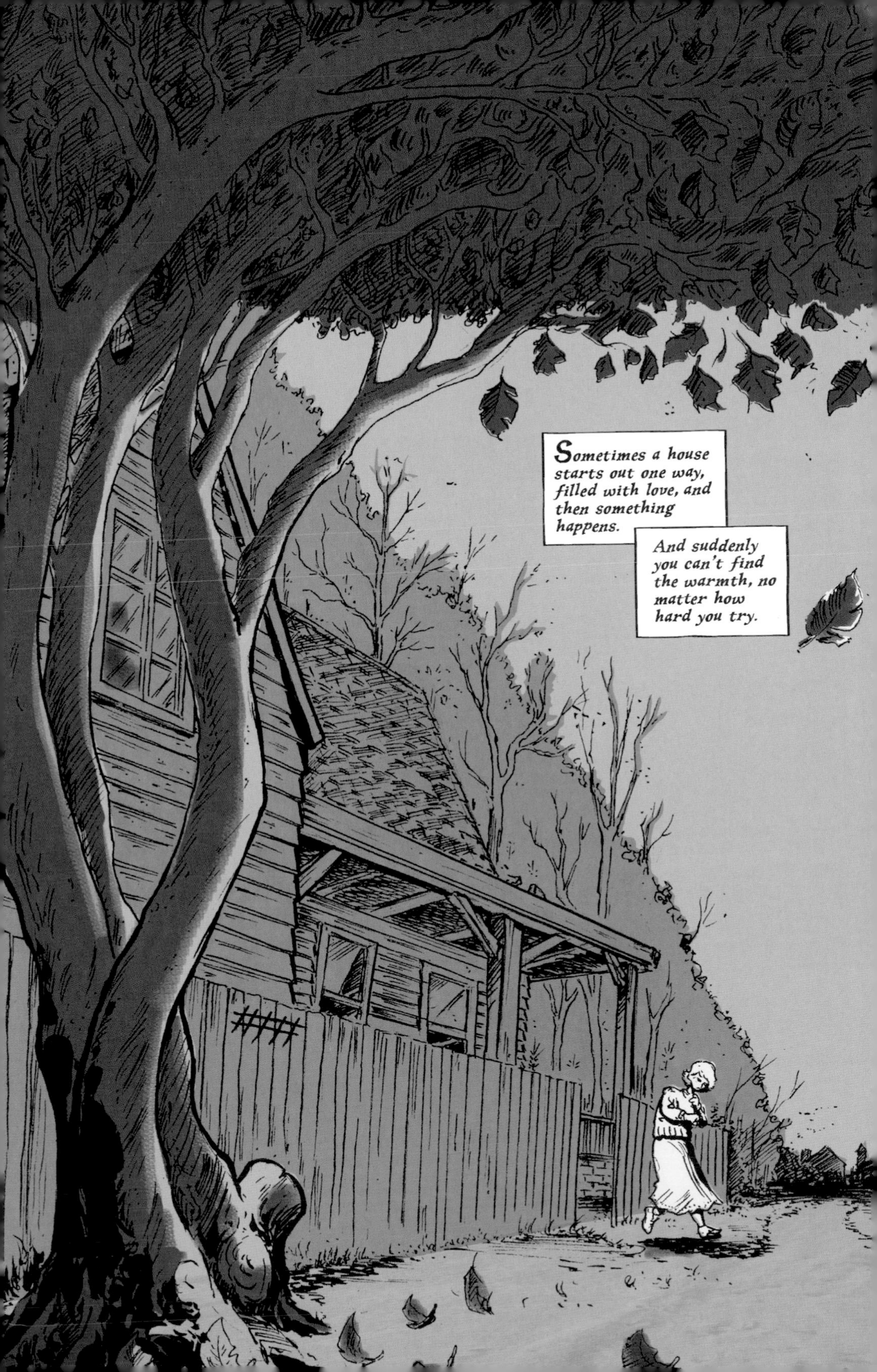
Sometimes a house starts out one way, filled with love, and then something happens.
And suddenly you can't find the warmth, no matter how hard you try.

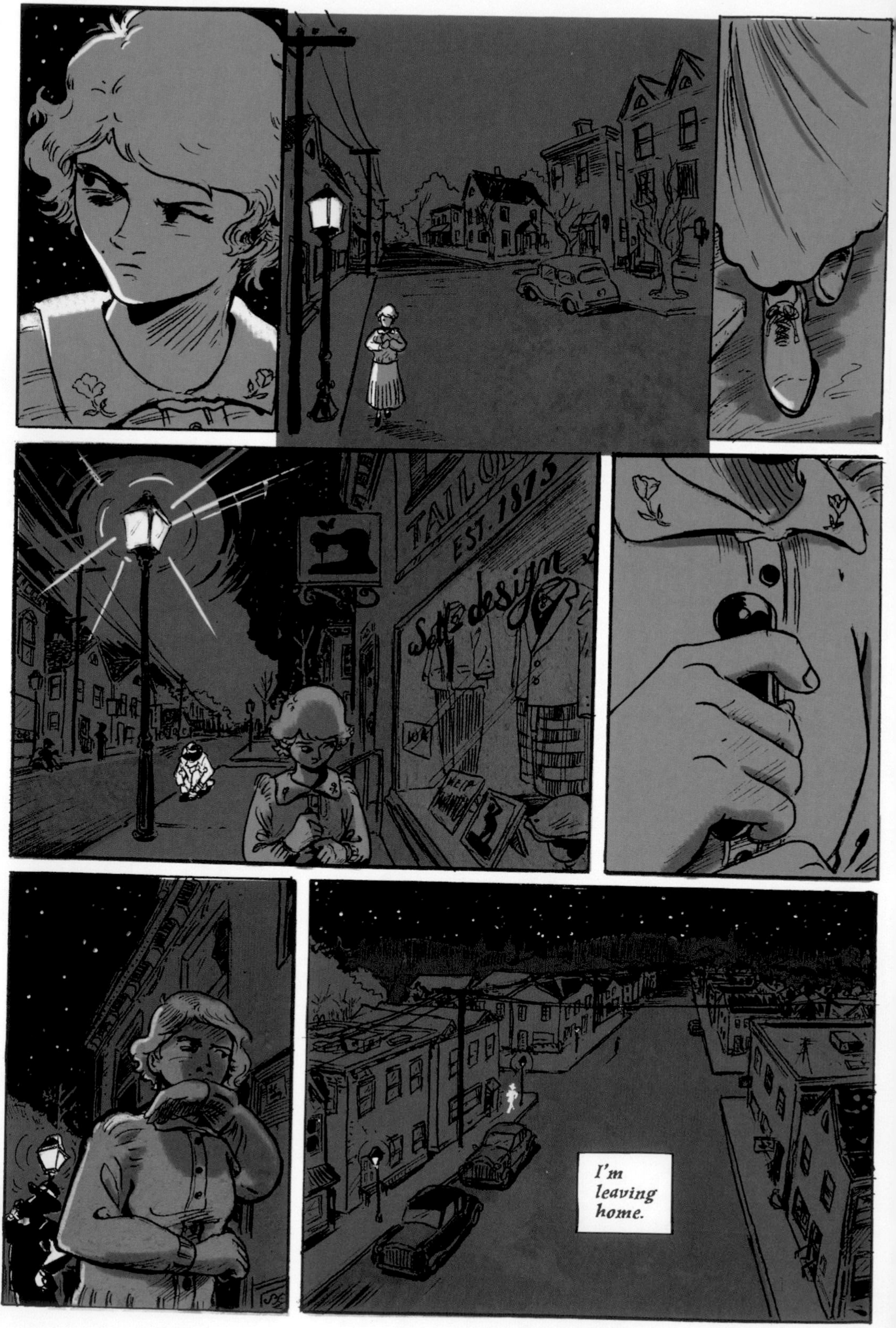
EST. 1875
I'm leaving home.

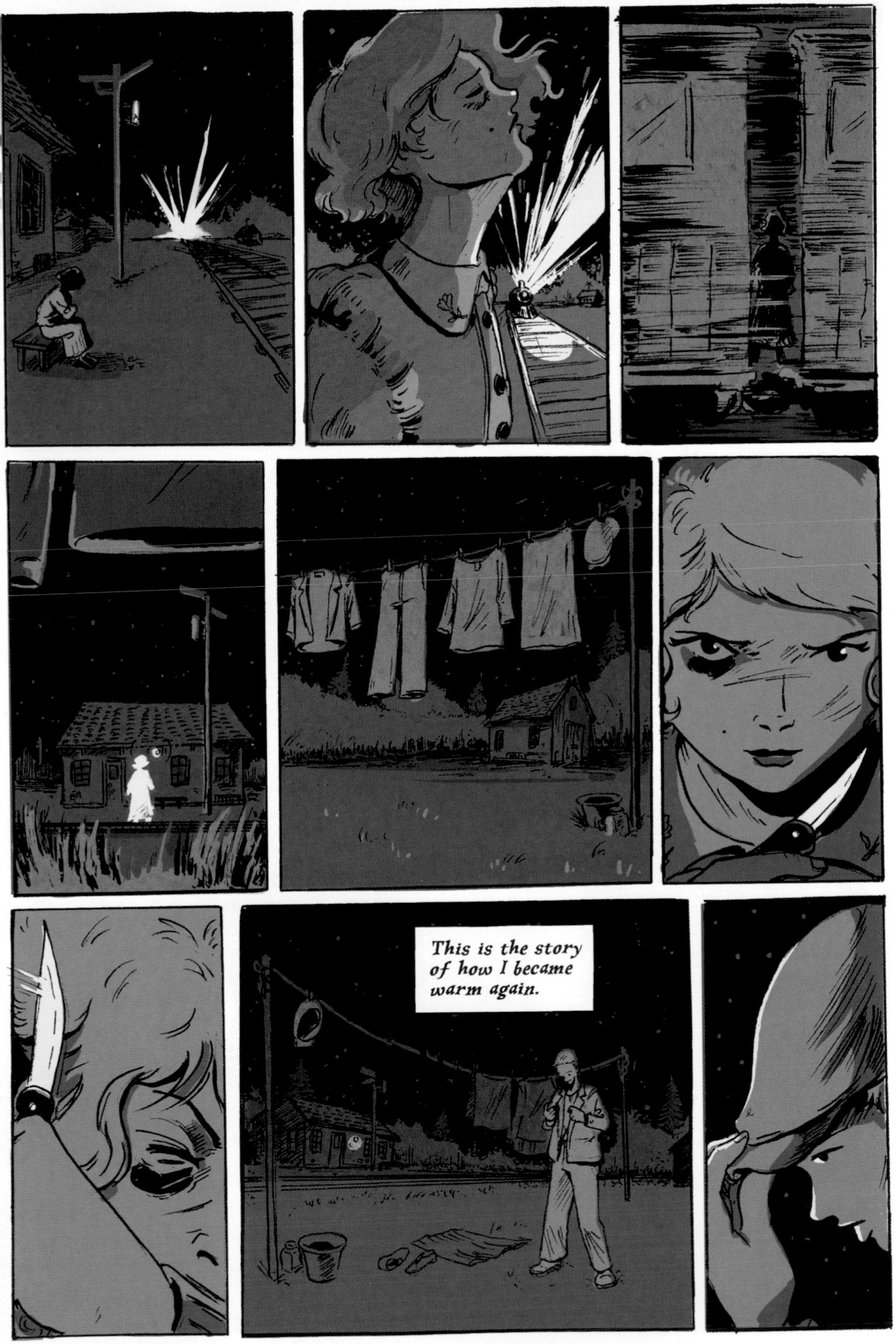
This is the story of how I became warm again.

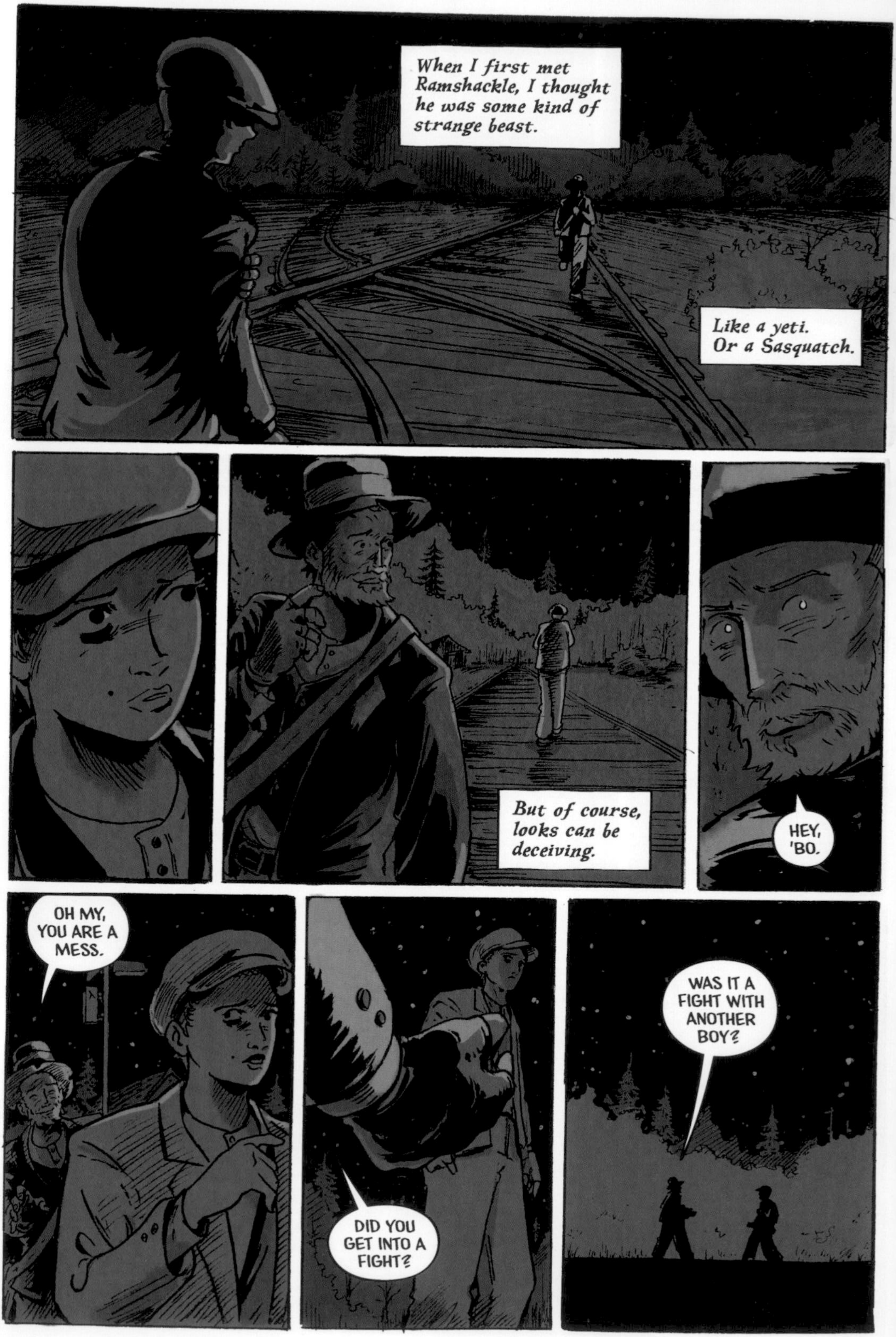
When I first met Ramshackle, I thought he was some kind of strange beast.
Like a yeti. Or a Sasquatch.
But of course, looks can be deceiving.
HEY, 'BO.
OH MY, YOU ARE A MESS.
DID YOU GET INTO A FIGHT?
WAS IT A FIGHT WITH ANOTHER BOY?

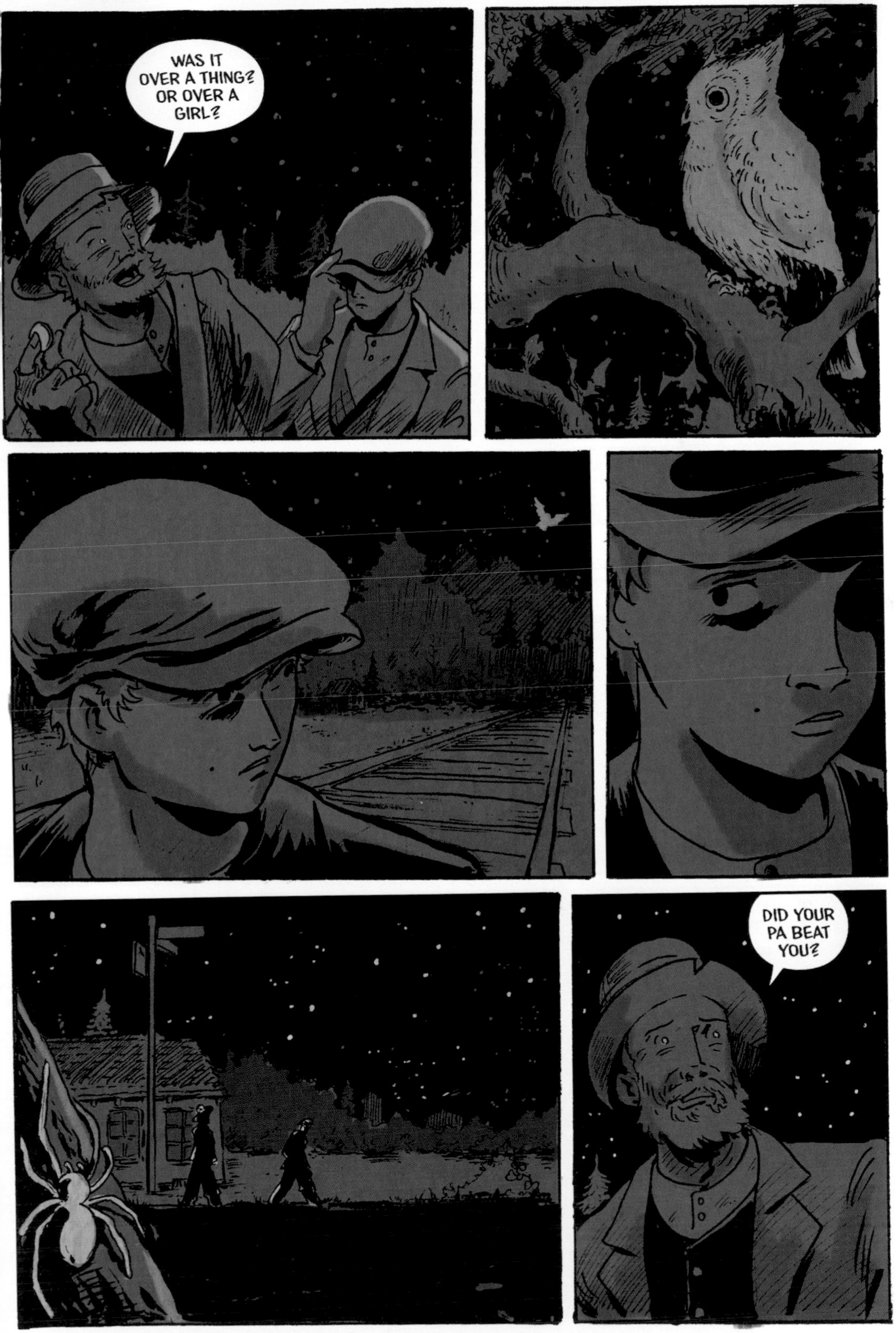
WAS IT OVER A THING? OR OVER A GIRL?
DID YOUR PA BEAT YOU?

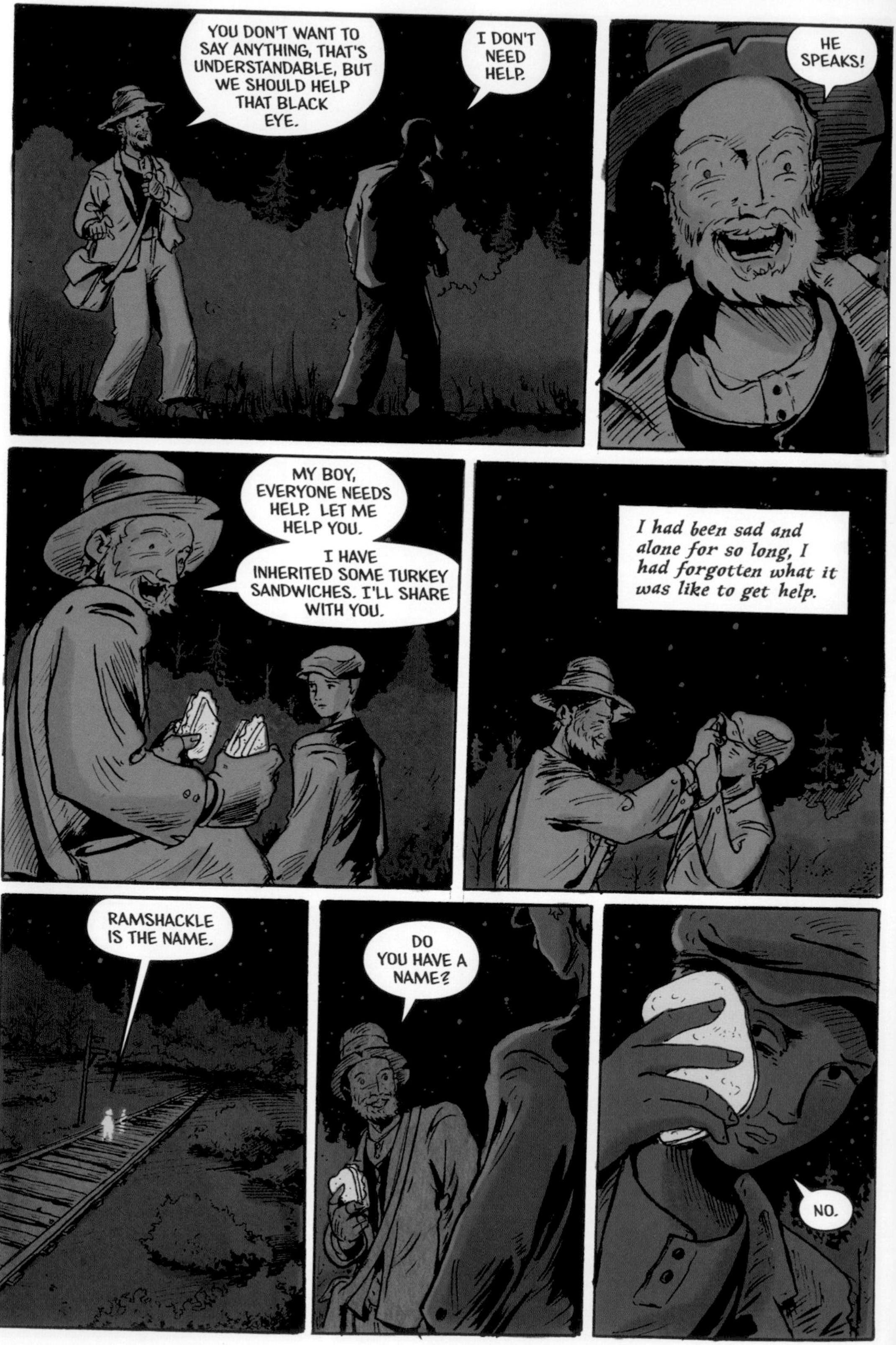
YOU DON'T WANT TO SAY ANYTHING, THAT'S UNDERSTANDABLE, BUT WE SHOULD HELP THAT BLACK EYE.
I DON'T NEED HELP.
HE SPEAKS!
MY BOY, EVERYONE NEEDS HELP. LET ME HELP YOU.
I HAVE INHERITED SOME TURKEY SANDWICHES. I'LL SHARE WITH YOU.
I had been sad and alone for so long, I had forgotten what it was like to get help.
RAMSHACKLE IS THE NAME.
DO YOU HAVE A NAME?
NO.

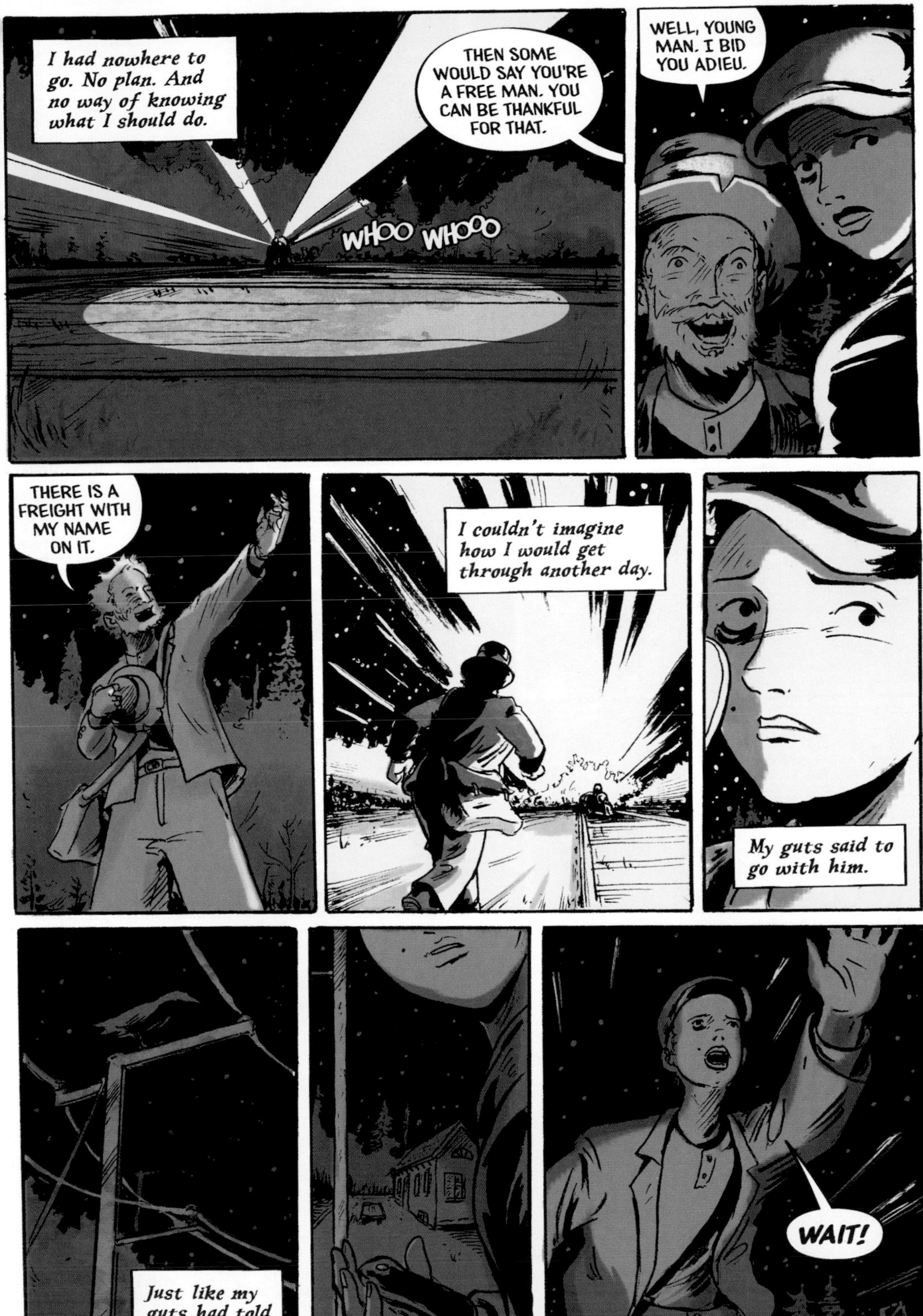
I had nowhere to go. No plan. And no way of knowing what I should do.
THEN SOME WOULD SAY YOU'RE A FREE MAN. YOU CAN BE THANKFUL FOR THAT.
WHOO WHOOO
WELL, YOUNG MAN. I BID YOU ADIEU.
THERE IS A FREIGHT WITH MY NAME ON IT.
I couldn't imagine how I would get through another day.
My guts said to go with him.
Just like my guts had told me to run.
WAIT!

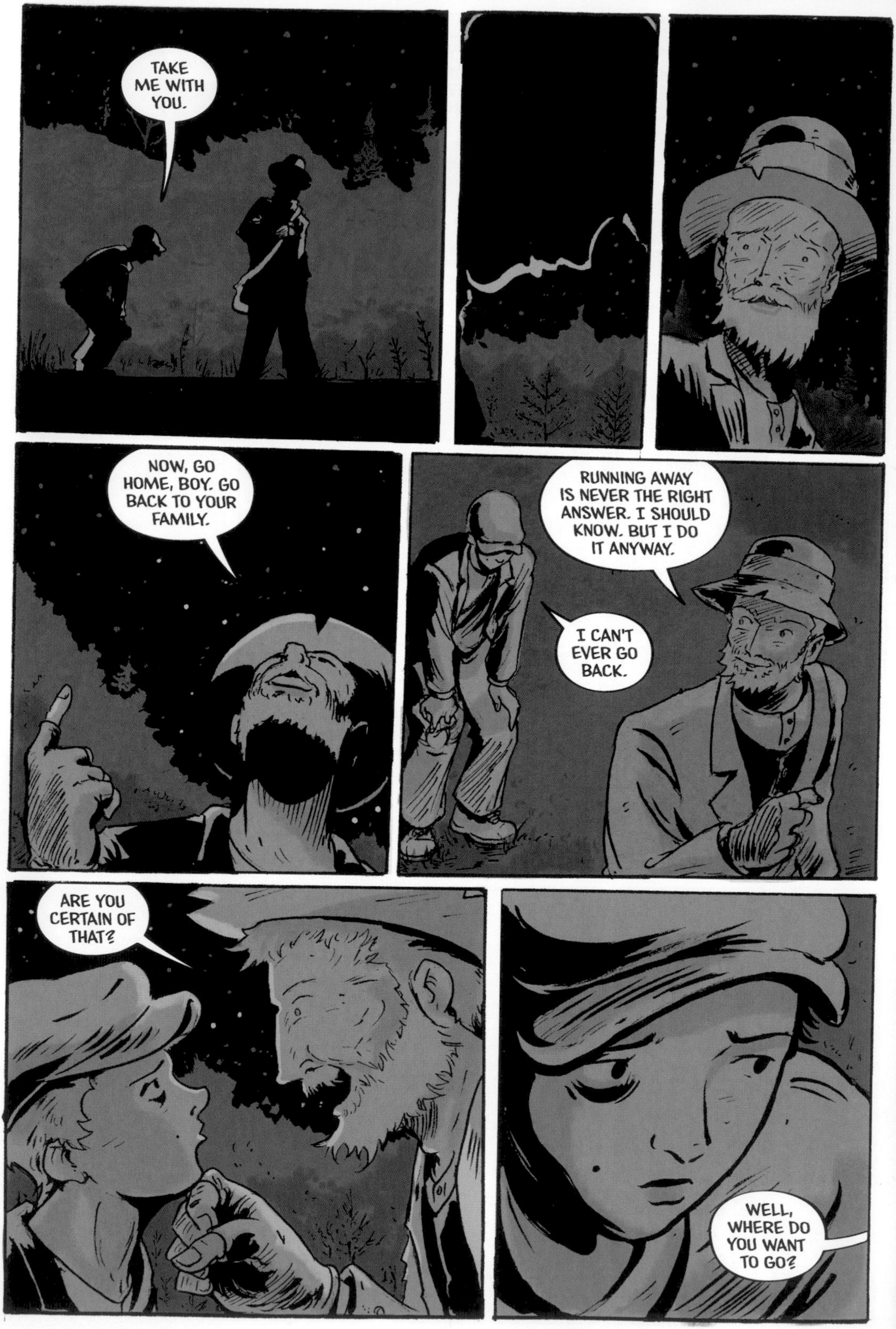
TAKE ME WITH YOU.
NOW, GO HOME, BOY. GO BACK TO YOUR FAMILY.
RUNNING AWAY IS NEVER THE RIGHT ANSWER. I SHOULD KNOW. BUT I DO IT ANYWAY.
I CAN'T EVER GO BACK.
ARE YOU CERTAIN OF THAT?
WELL, WHERE DO YOU WANT TO GO?

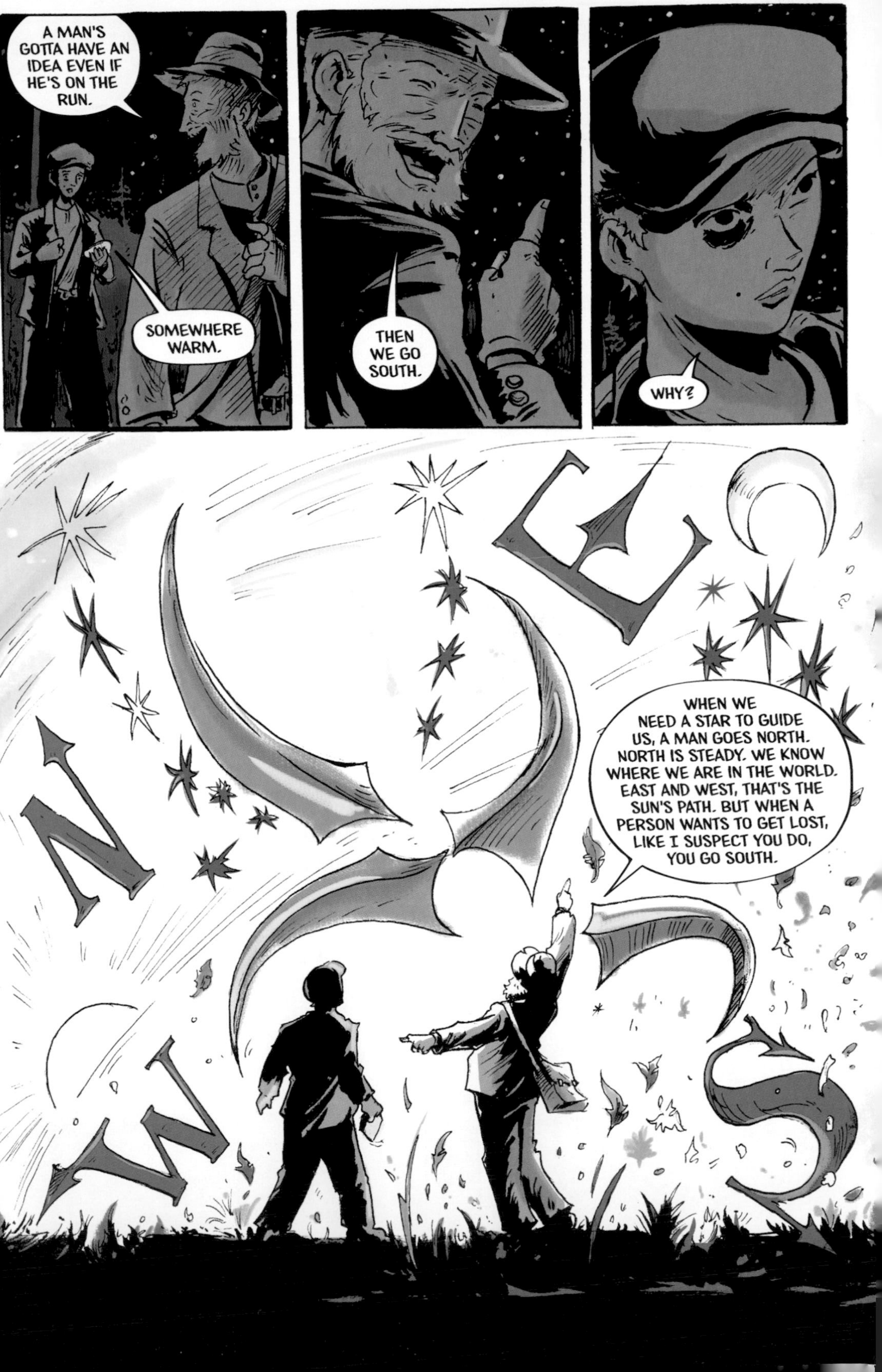
A MAN'S GOTTA HAVE AN IDEA EVEN IF HE'S ON THE RUN.
SOMEWHERE WARM.
THEN WE GO SOUTH.
WHY?
WHEN WE NEED A STAR TO GUIDE US, A MAN GOES NORTH. NORTH IS STEADY. WE KNOW WHERE WE ARE IN THE WORLD. EAST AND WEST, THAT'S THE SUN'S PATH. BUT WHEN A PERSON WANTS TO GET LOST, LIKE I SUSPECT YOU DO, YOU GO SOUTH.
N
E
W
S

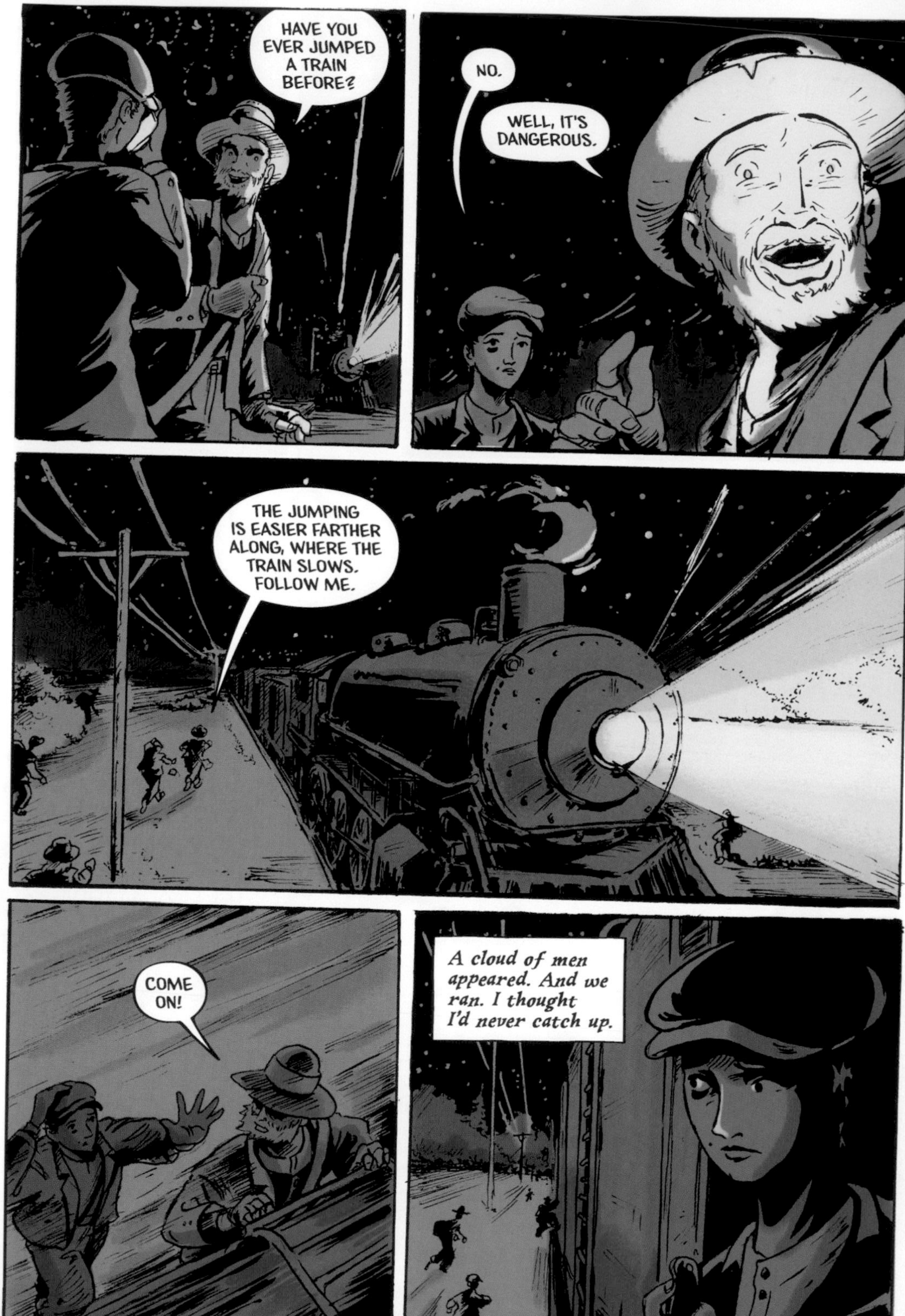
HAVE YOU EVER JUMPED A TRAIN BEFORE?
NO.
WELL, IT'S DANGEROUS.
THE JUMPING IS EASIER FARTHER ALONG, WHERE THE TRAIN SLOWS. FOLLOW ME.
COME ON!
A cloud of men appeared. And we ran. I thought I'd never catch up.

The wind cut my cheeks.

My heart beat like a wild thing.

NOW CAREFUL YOU DON'T GET SUCKED OFF. SEE THIS HERE HANDLE-LIKE THING? HOOK IN THERE.

I drank in all the beauty I could.

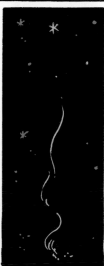

17

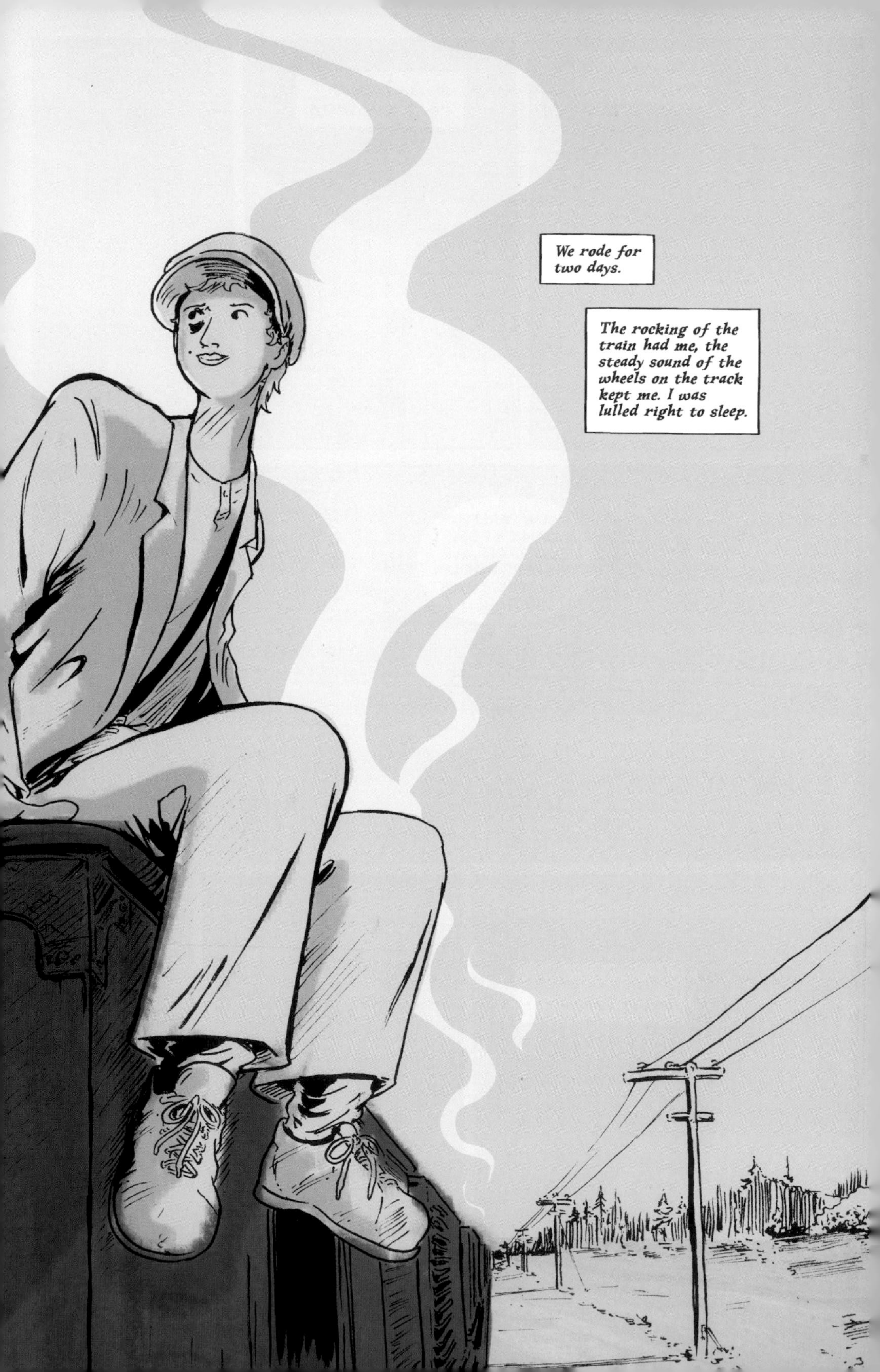
We rode for two days.
The rocking of the train had me, the steady sound of the wheels on the track kept me. I was lulled right to sleep.

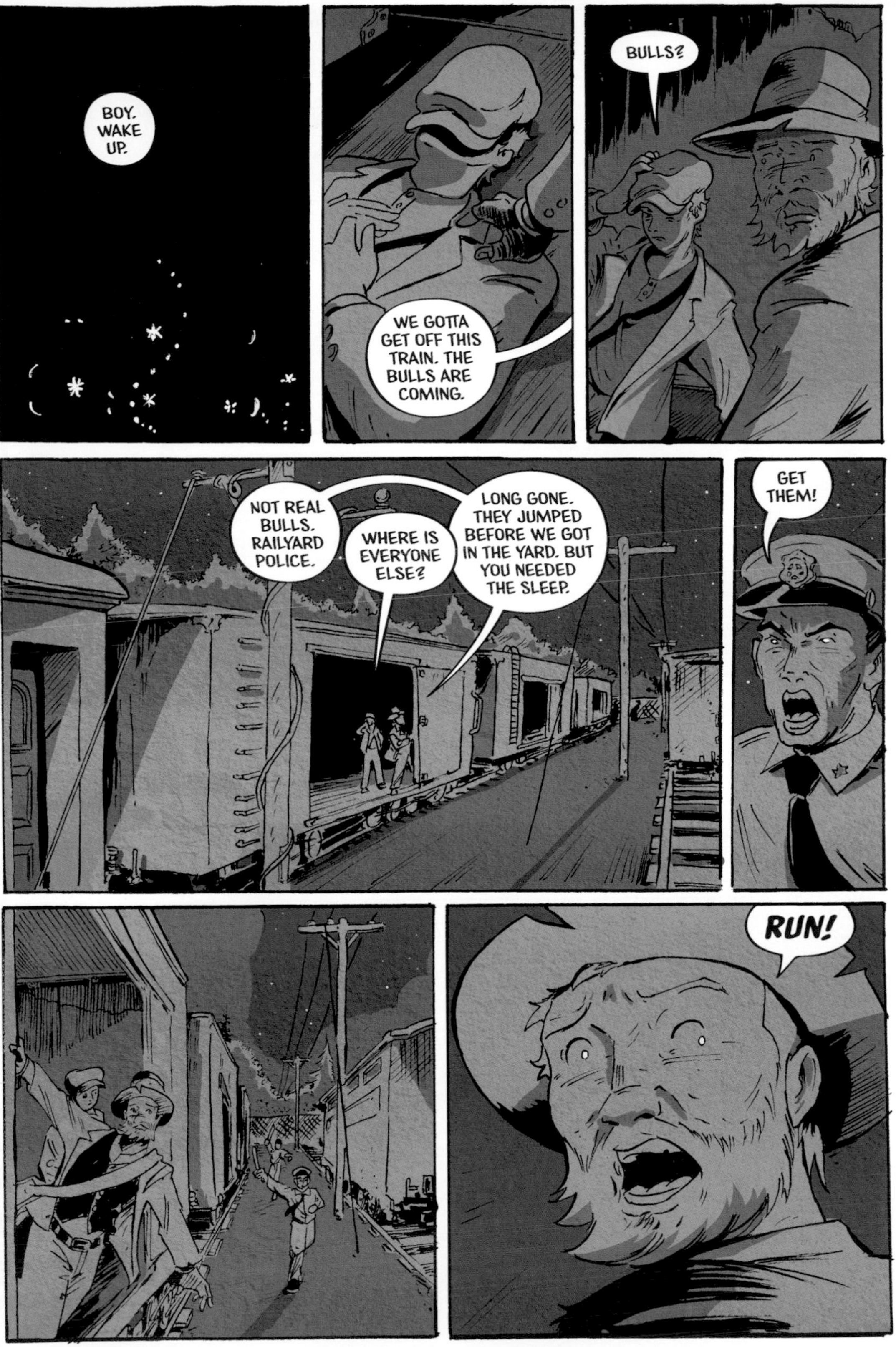
BOY. WAKE UP.
WE GOTTA GET OFF THIS TRAIN. THE BULLS ARE COMING.
BULLS?
NOT REAL BULLS. RAILYARD POLICE.
WHERE IS EVERYONE ELSE?
LONG GONE. THEY JUMPED BEFORE WE GOT IN THE YARD. BUT YOU NEEDED THE SLEEP.
GET THEM!
RUN!

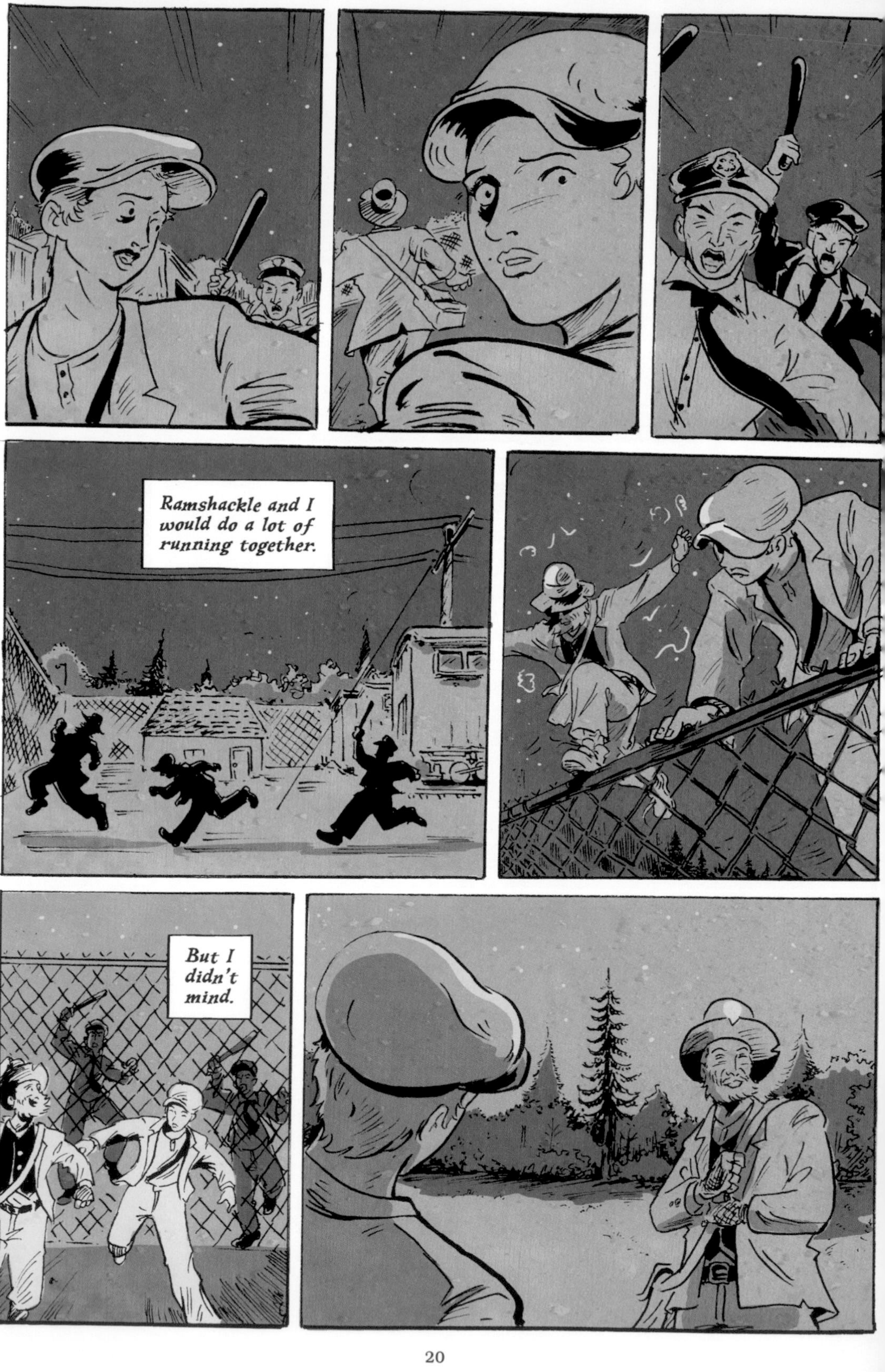
Ramshackle and I would do a lot of running together.
But I didn't mind.

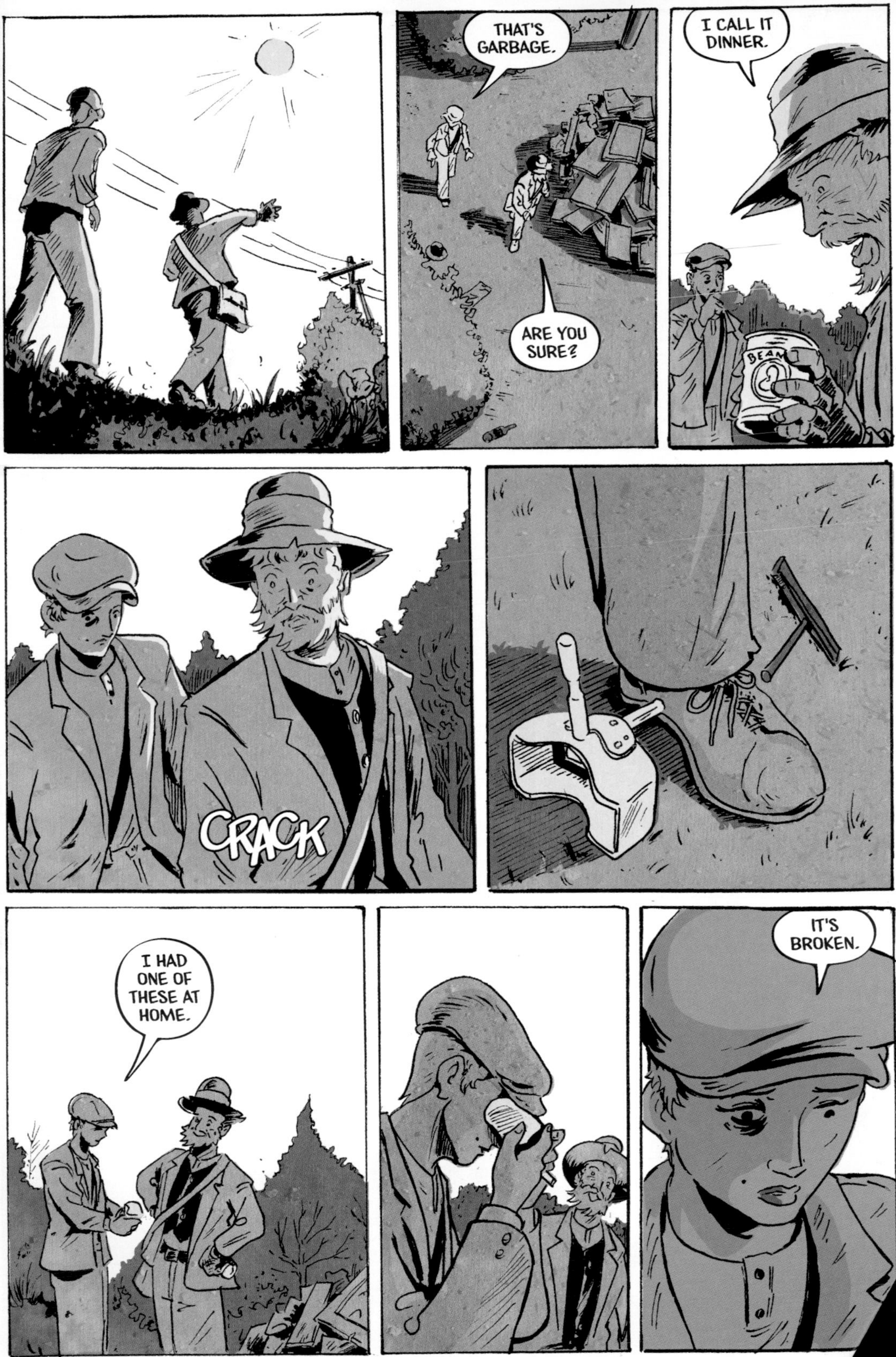
THAT'S GARBAGE.
ARE YOU SURE?
I CALL IT DINNER.
BEAM
CRACK
I HAD ONE OF THESE AT HOME.
IT'S BROKEN.

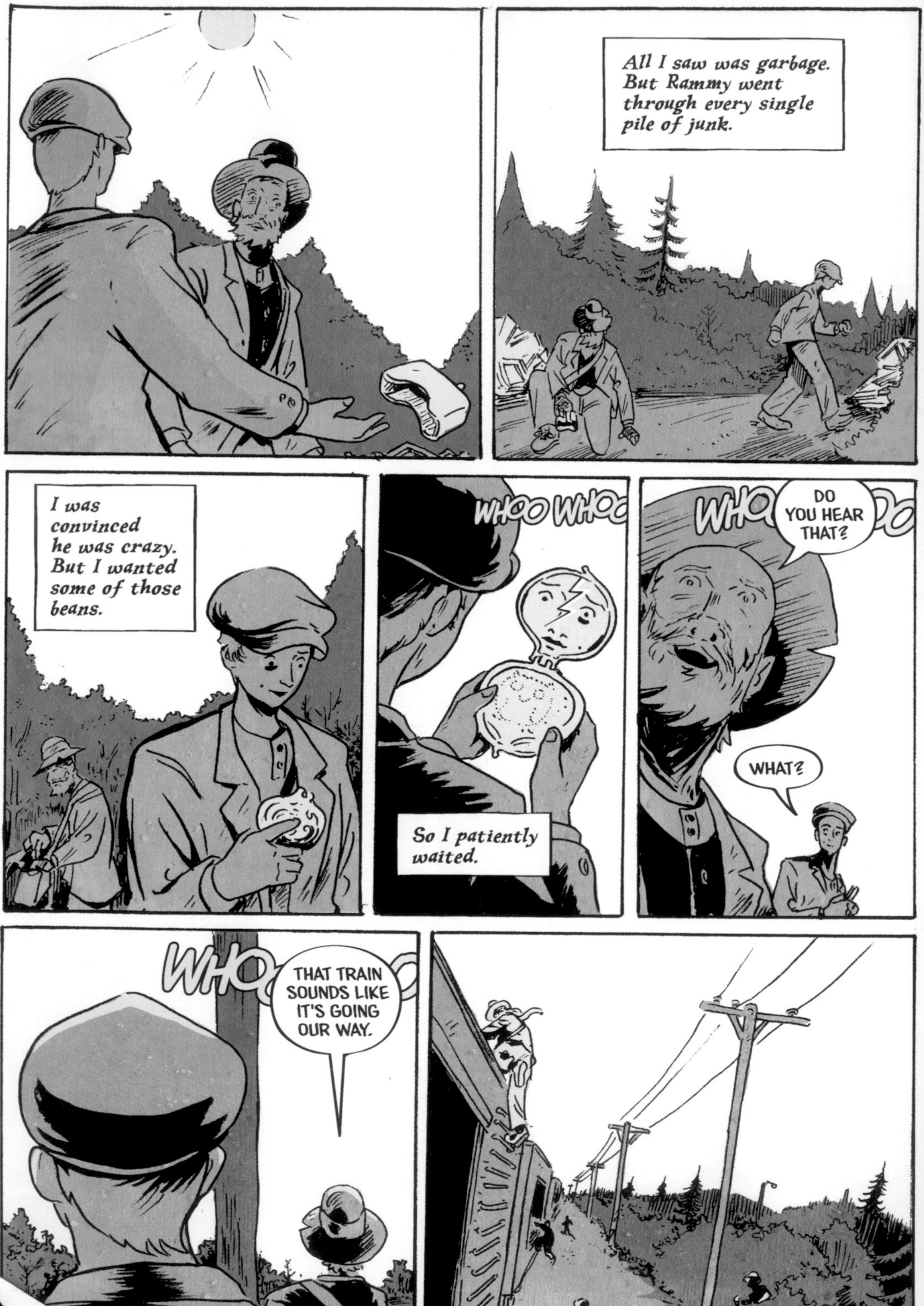
All I saw was garbage. But Rammy went through every single pile of junk.
I was convinced he was crazy. But I wanted some of those beans.
WHOO WHOO
So I patiently waited.
WHO
DO YOU HEAR THAT?
WHAT?
WHOO
THAT TRAIN SOUNDS LIKE IT'S GOING OUR WAY.

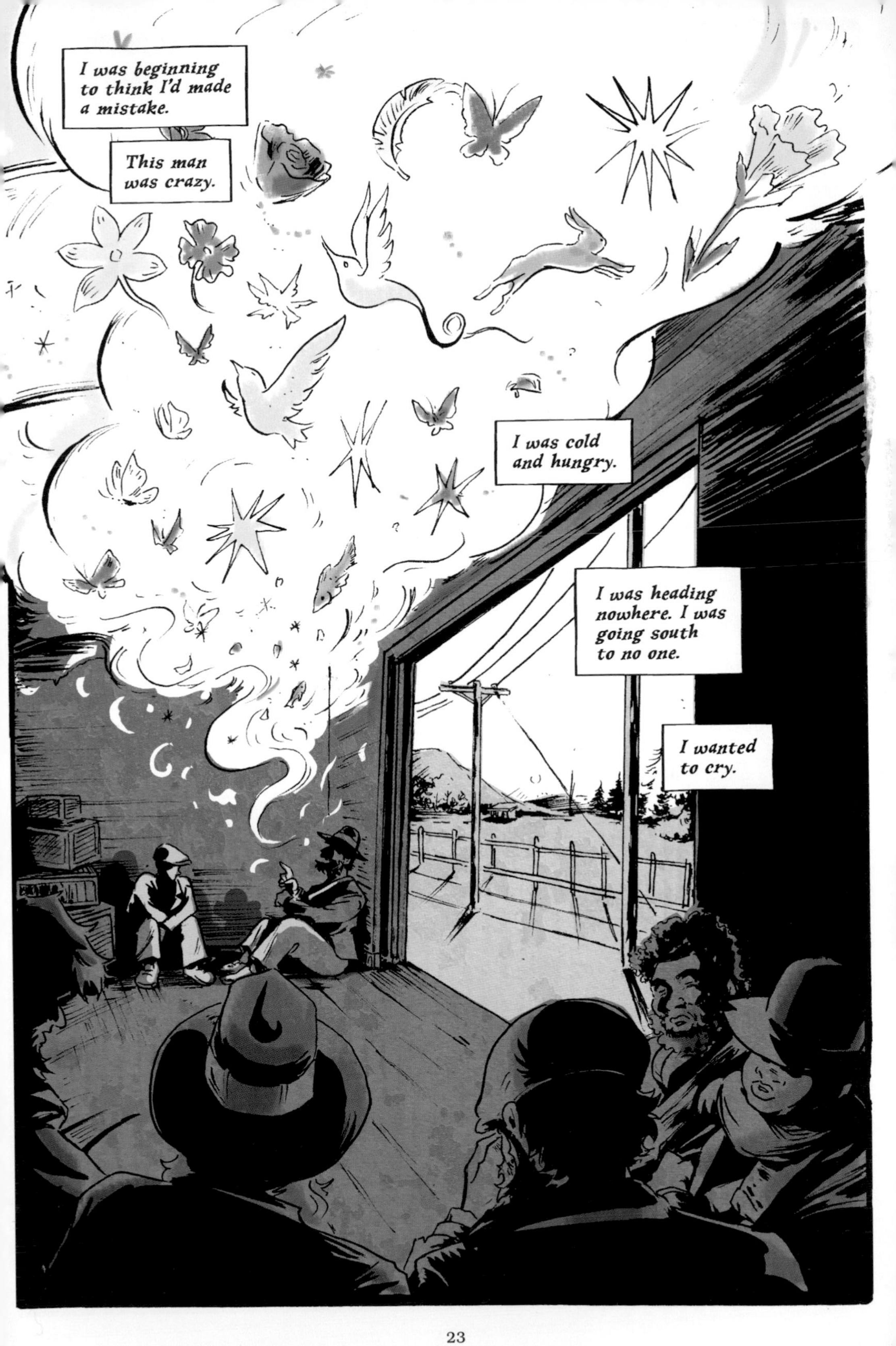
I was beginning to think I'd made a mistake.
This man was crazy.
I was cold and hungry.
I was heading nowhere. I was going south to no one.
I wanted to cry.

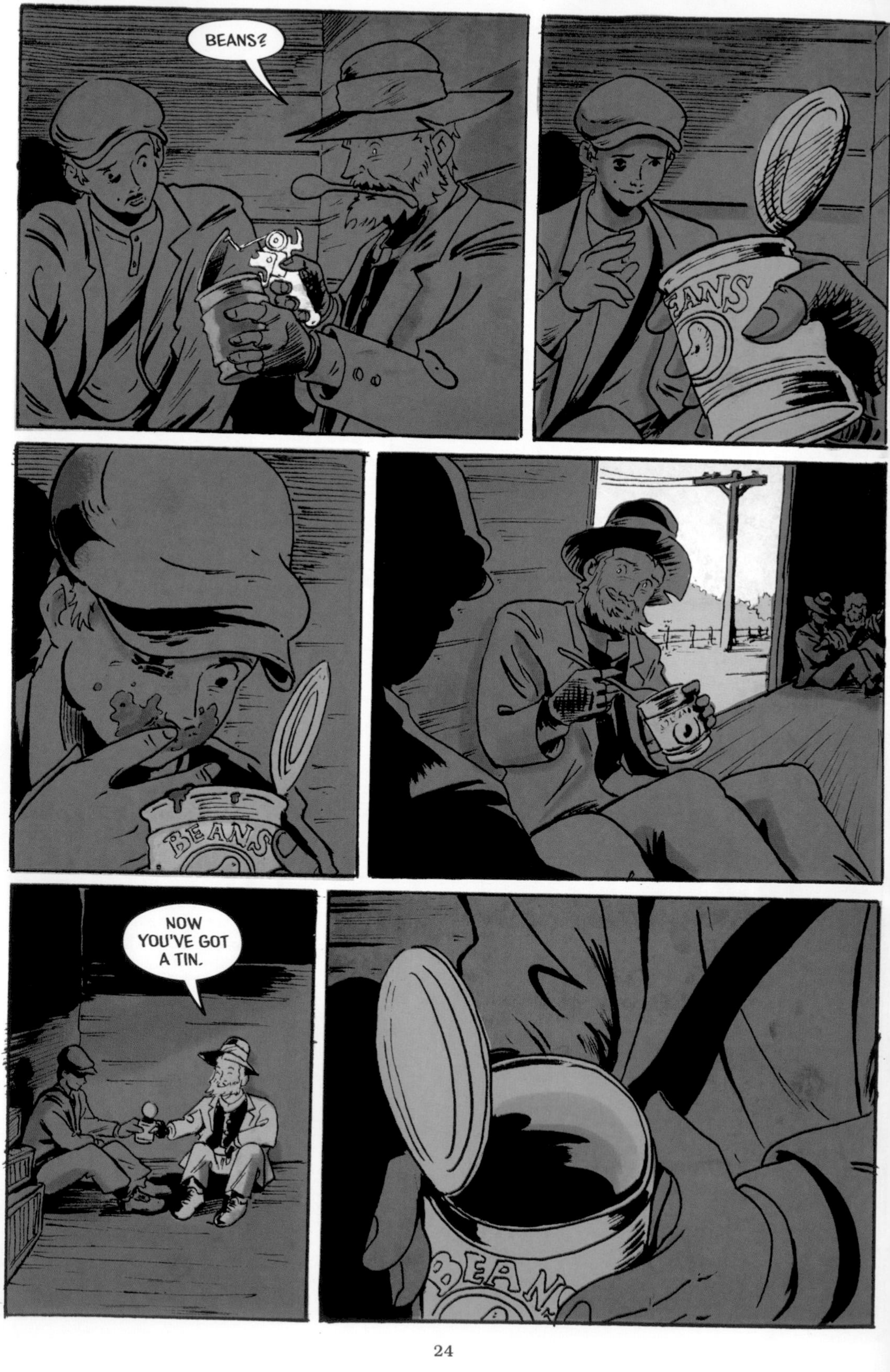
BEANS?
BEANS
BEANS
NOW YOU'VE GOT A TIN.
BEAN

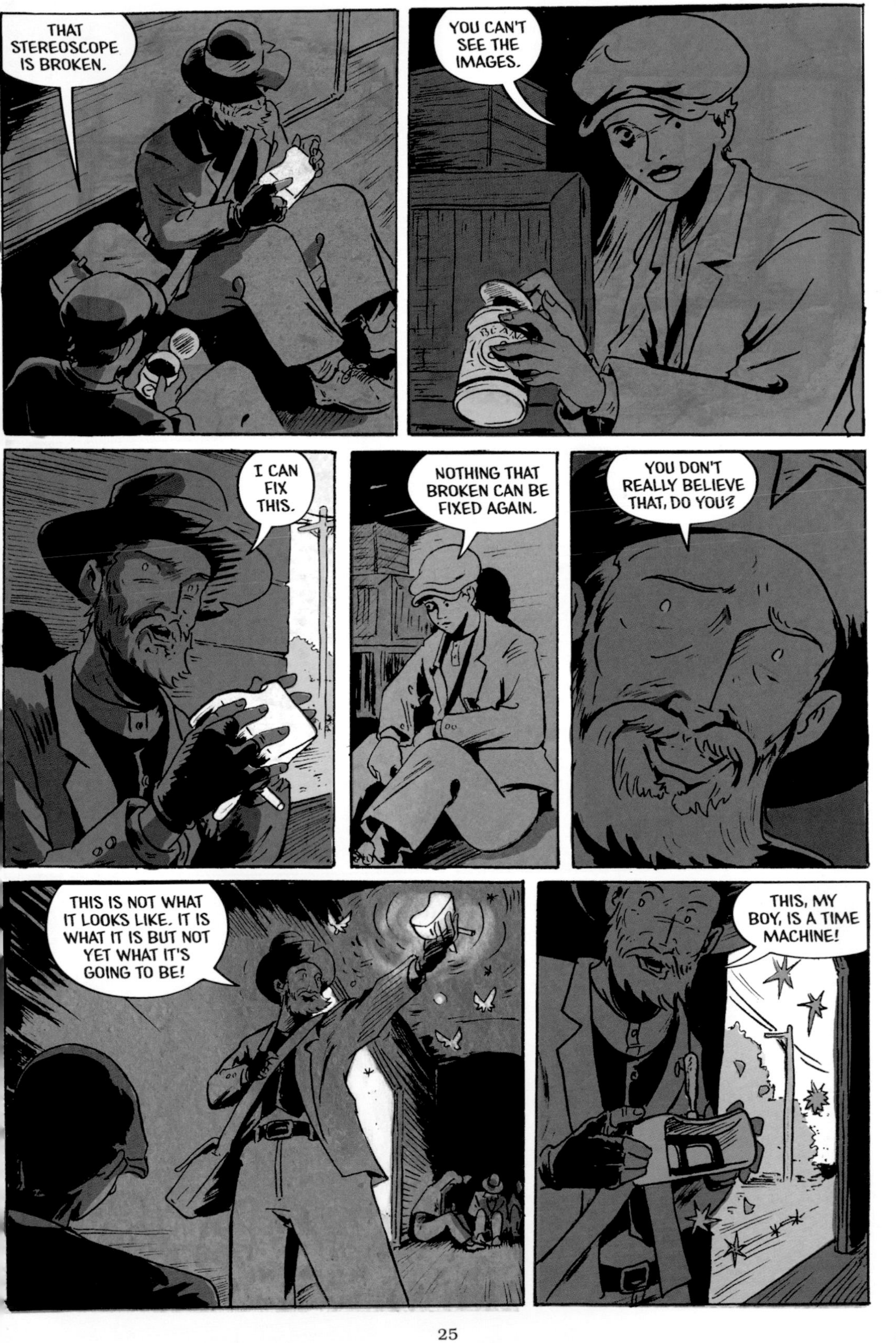
THAT STEREOSCOPE IS BROKEN.
YOU CAN'T SEE THE IMAGES.
BEANS
I CAN FIX THIS.
NOTHING THAT BROKEN CAN BE FIXED AGAIN.
YOU DON'T REALLY BELIEVE THAT, DO YOU?
THIS IS NOT WHAT IT LOOKS LIKE. IT IS WHAT IT IS BUT NOT YET WHAT IT'S GOING TO BE!
THIS, MY BOY, IS A TIME MACHINE!

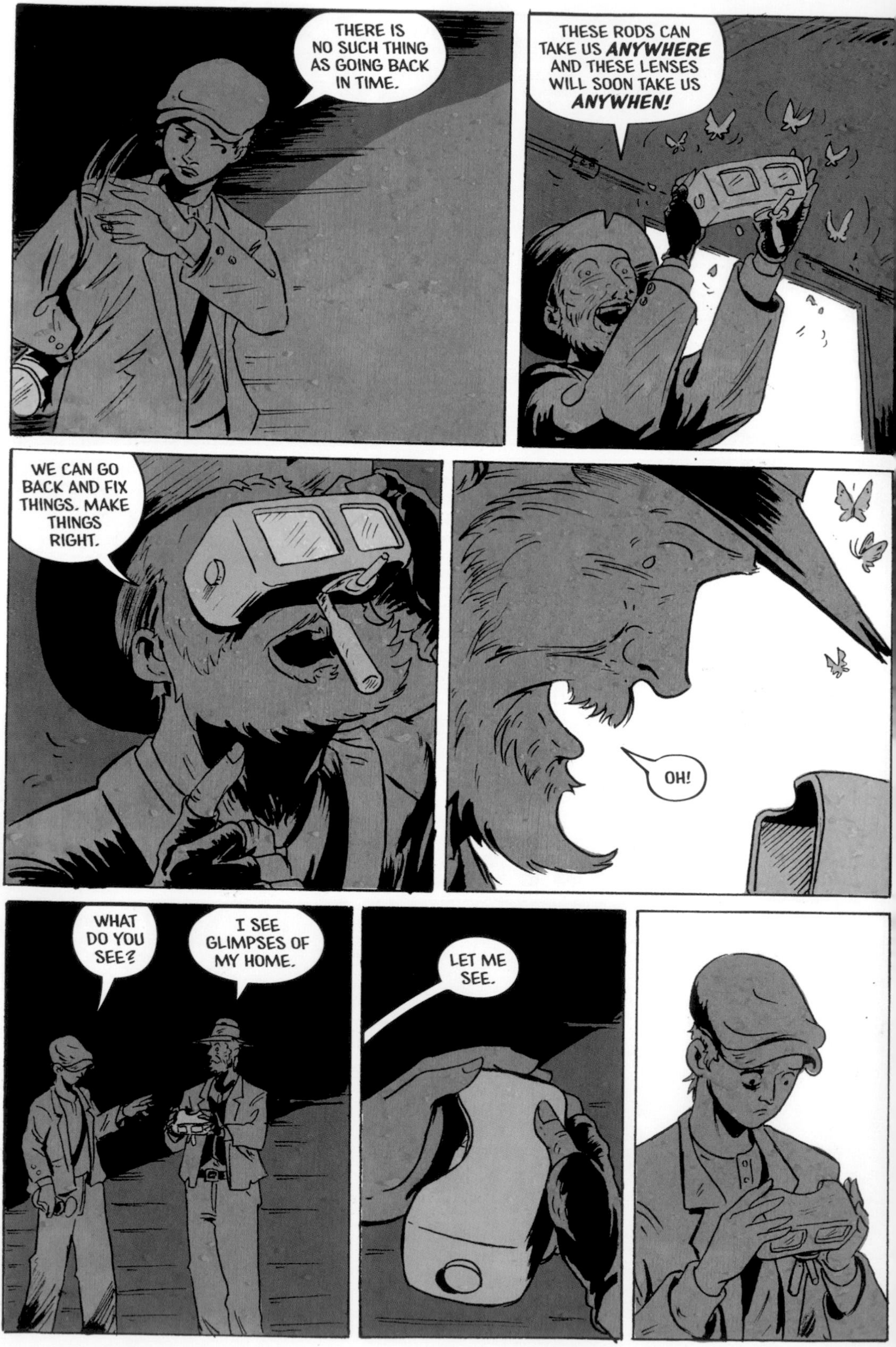
THERE IS NO SUCH THING AS GOING BACK IN TIME.
THESE RODS CAN TAKE US ANYWHERE AND THESE LENSES WILL SOON TAKE US ANYWHEN!
WE CAN GO BACK AND FIX THINGS. MAKE THINGS RIGHT.
OH!
WHAT DO YOU SEE?
I SEE GLIMPSES OF MY HOME.
LET ME SEE.

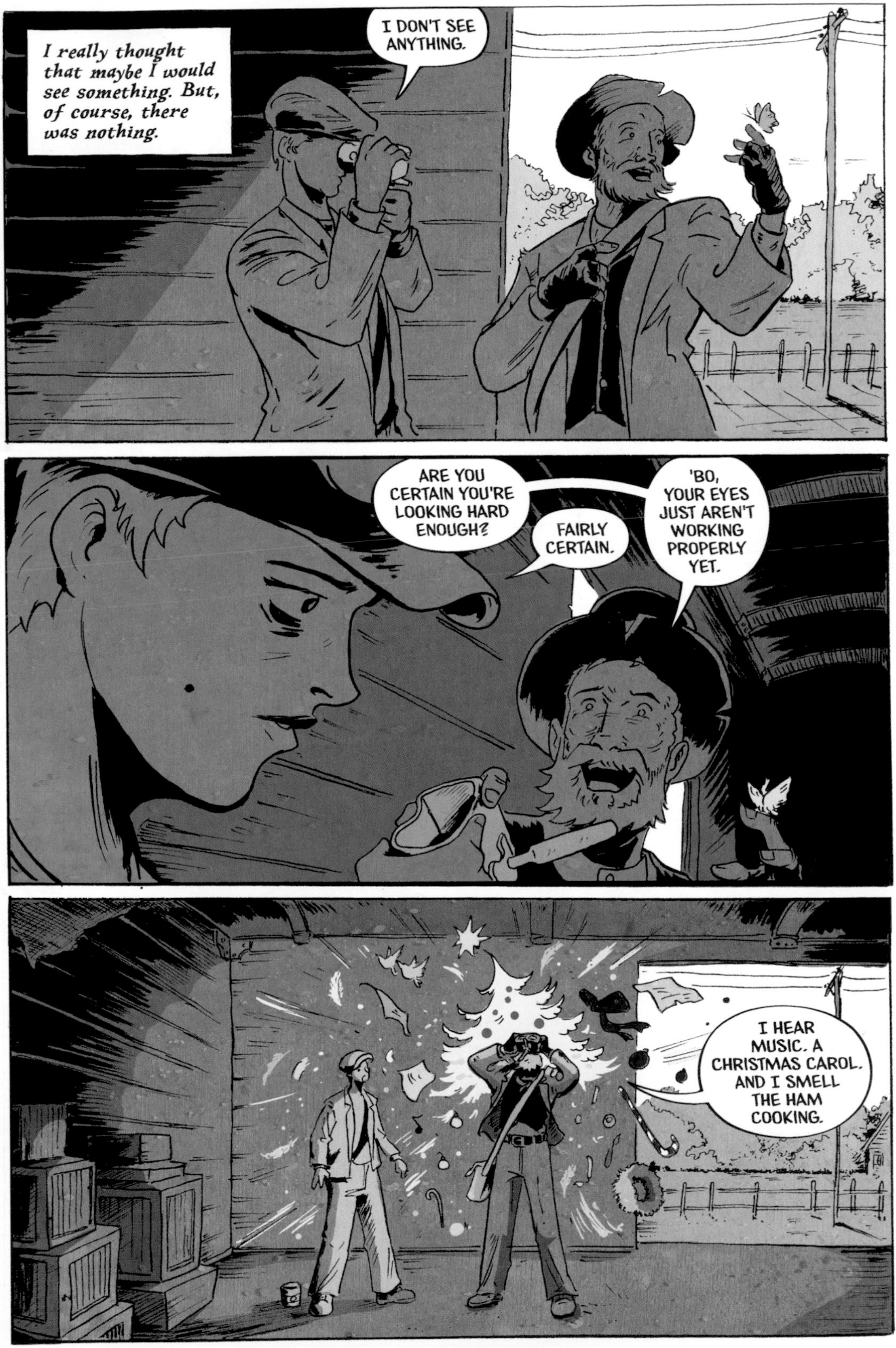
I really thought that maybe I would see something. But, of course, there was nothing.
I DON'T SEE ANYTHING.
ARE YOU CERTAIN YOU'RE LOOKING HARD ENOUGH?
FAIRLY CERTAIN.
'BO, YOUR EYES JUST AREN'T WORKING PROPERLY YET.
I HEAR MUSIC. A CHRISTMAS CAROL. AND I SMELL THE HAM COOKING.

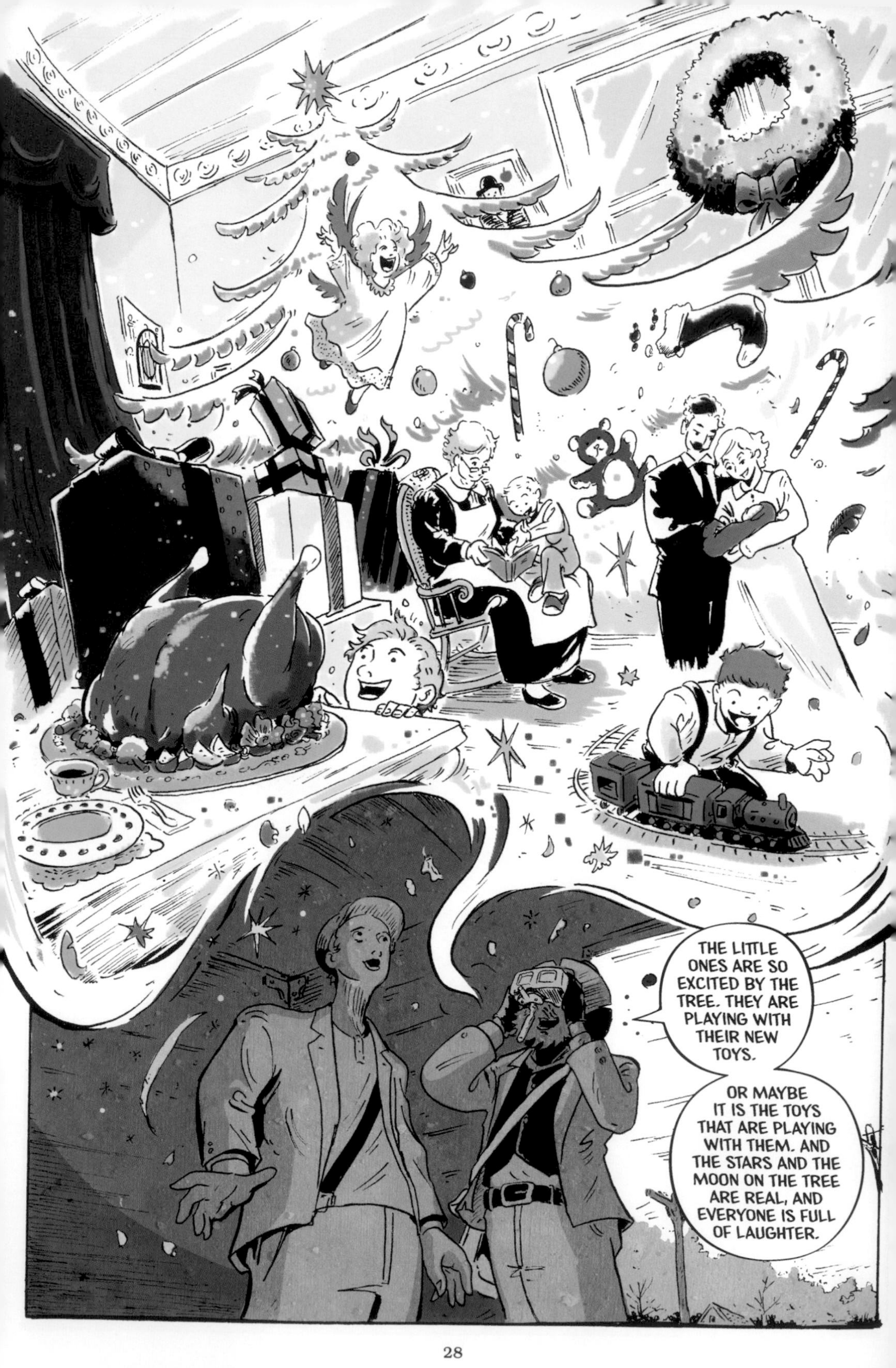
THE LITTLE ONES ARE SO EXCITED BY THE TREE. THEY ARE PLAYING WITH THEIR NEW TOYS.
OR MAYBE IT IS THE TOYS THAT ARE PLAYING WITH THEM. AND THE STARS AND THE MOON ON THE TREE ARE REAL, AND EVERYONE IS FULL OF LAUGHTER.

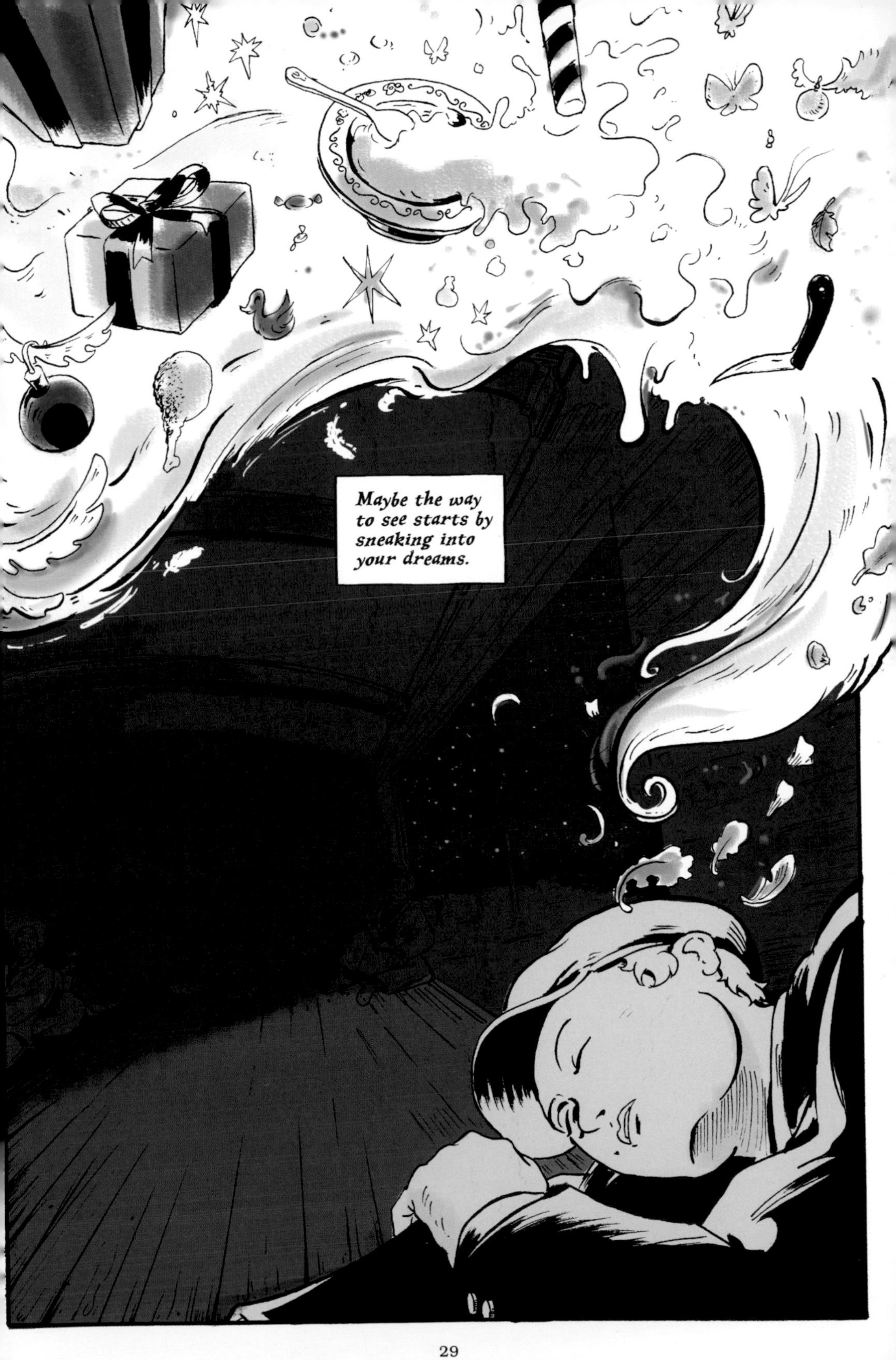
Maybe the way to see starts by sneaking into your dreams.

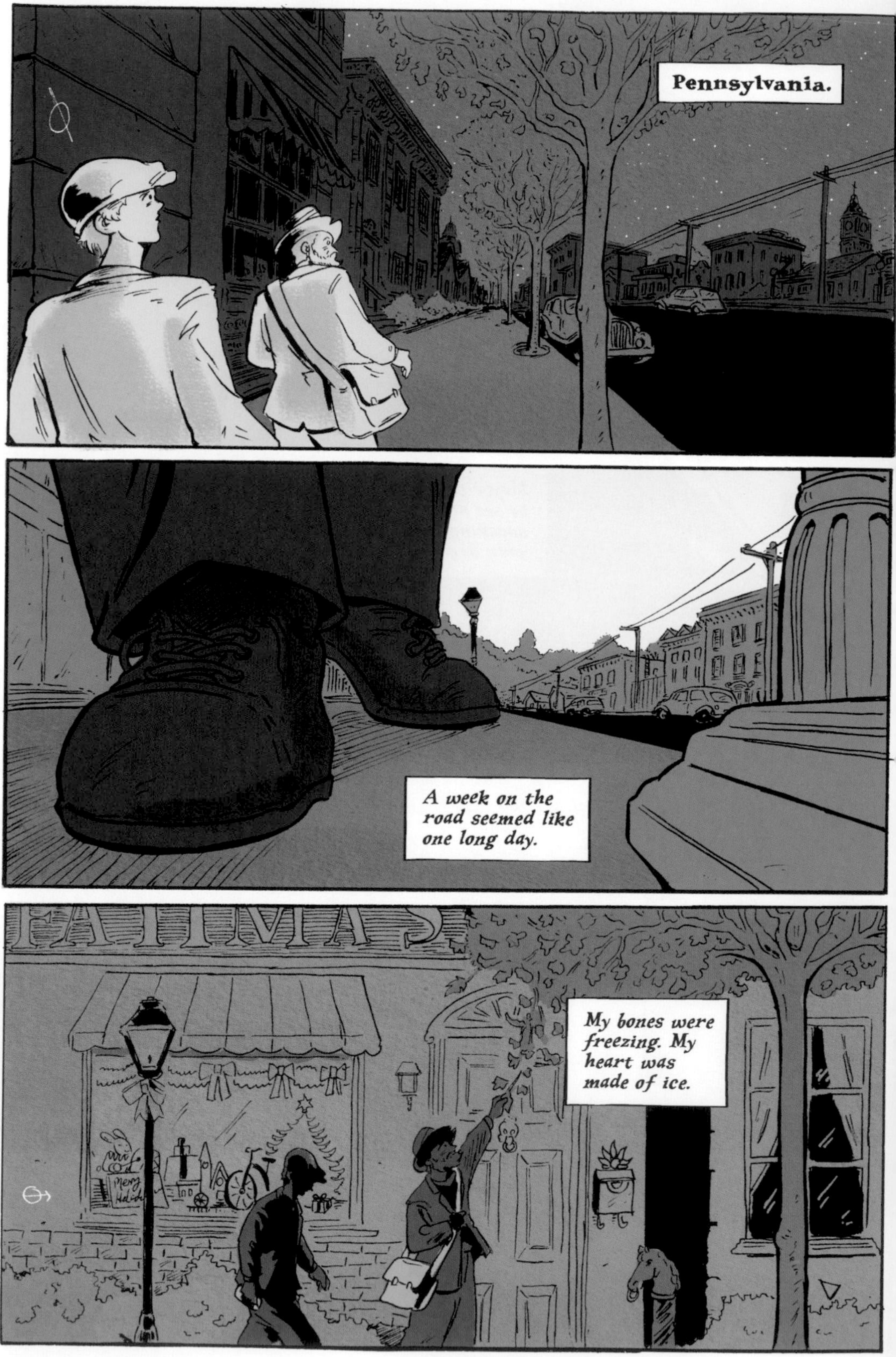
Pennsylvania.
A week on the road seemed like one long day.
My bones were freezing. My heart was made of ice.

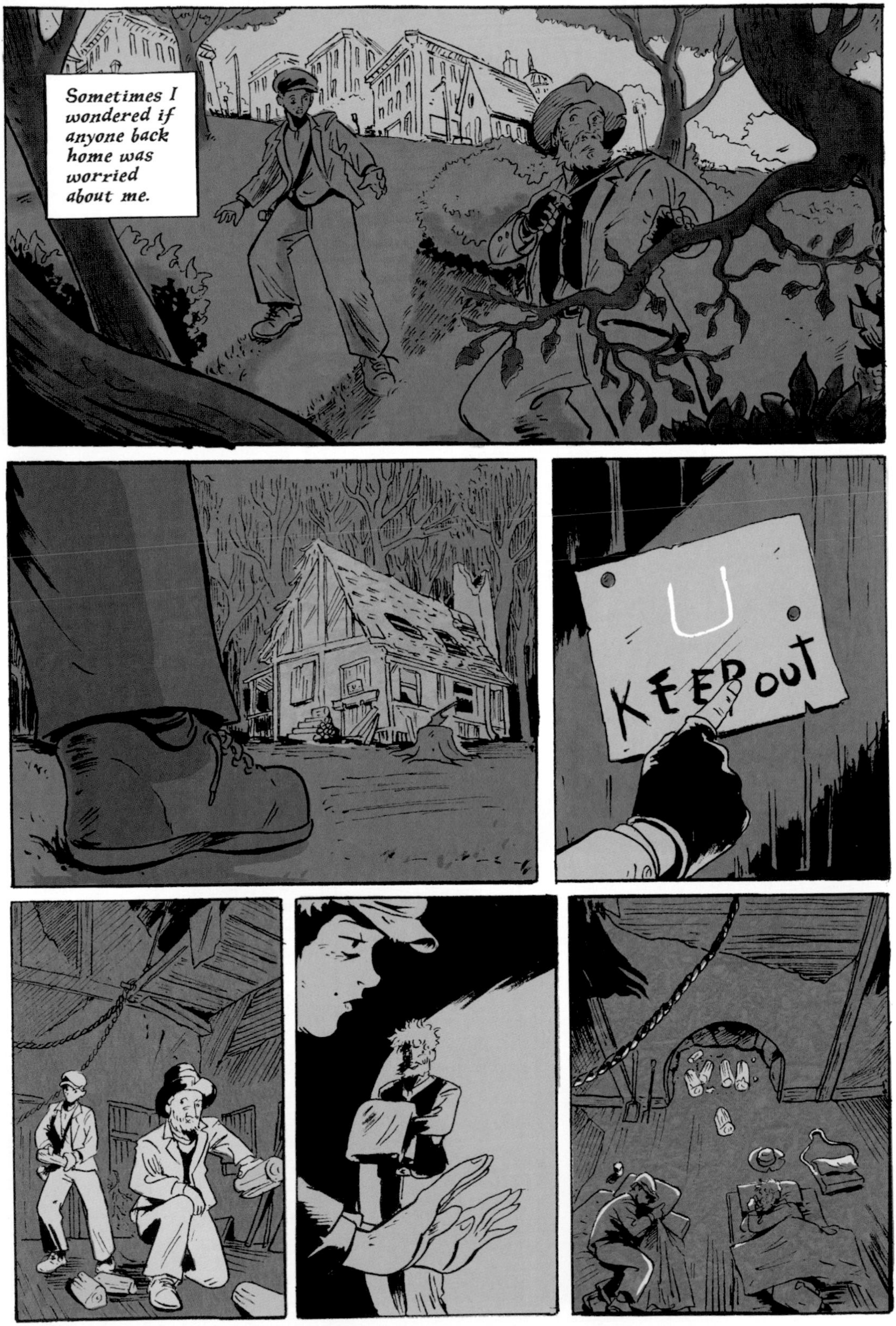
Sometimes I wondered if anyone back home was worried about me.
U
KEEP OUT

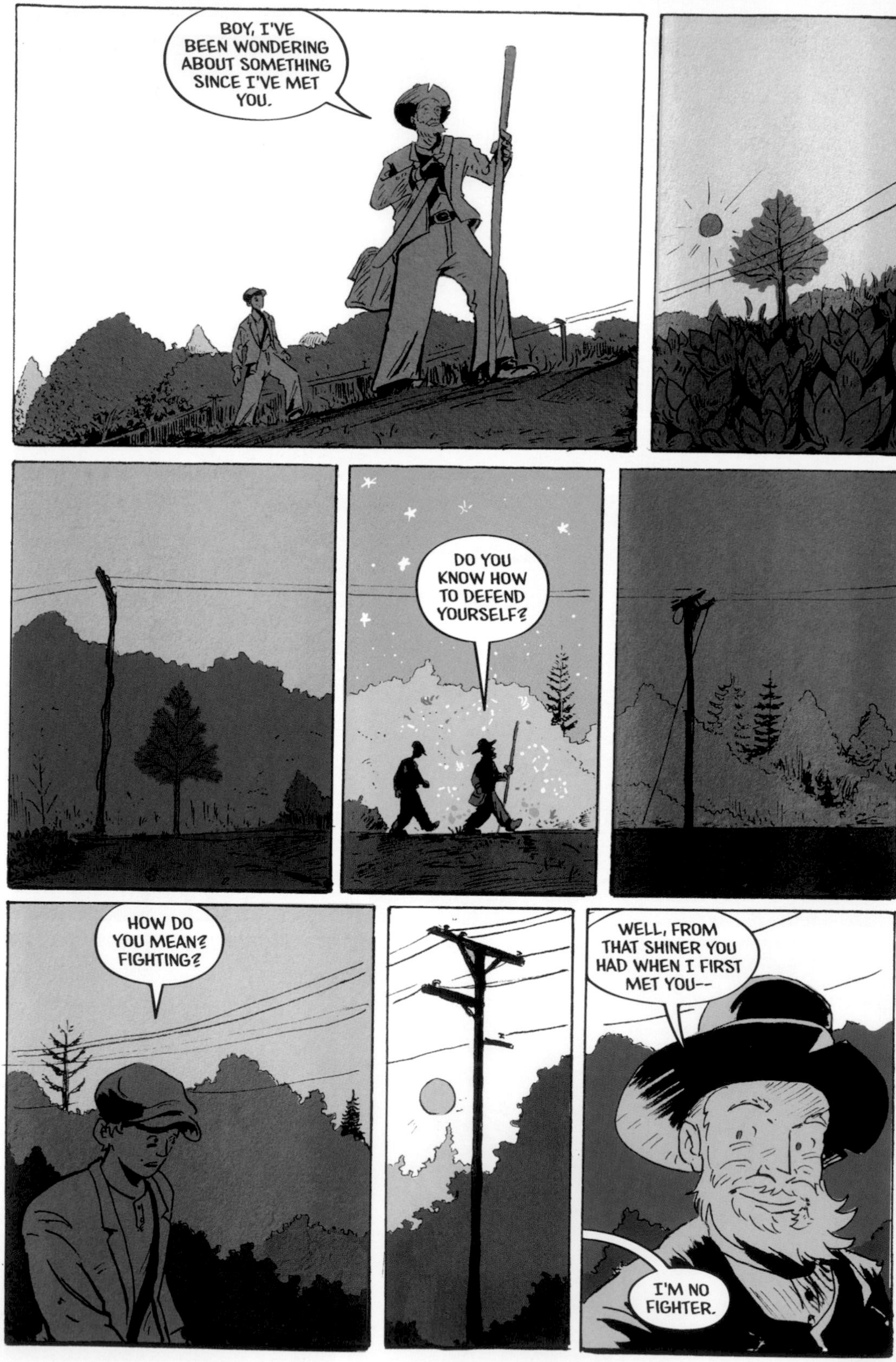
BOY, I'VE BEEN WONDERING ABOUT SOMETHING SINCE I'VE MET YOU.
DO YOU KNOW HOW TO DEFEND YOURSELF?
HOW DO YOU MEAN? FIGHTING?
WELL, FROM THAT SHINER YOU HAD WHEN I FIRST MET YOU--
I'M NO FIGHTER.

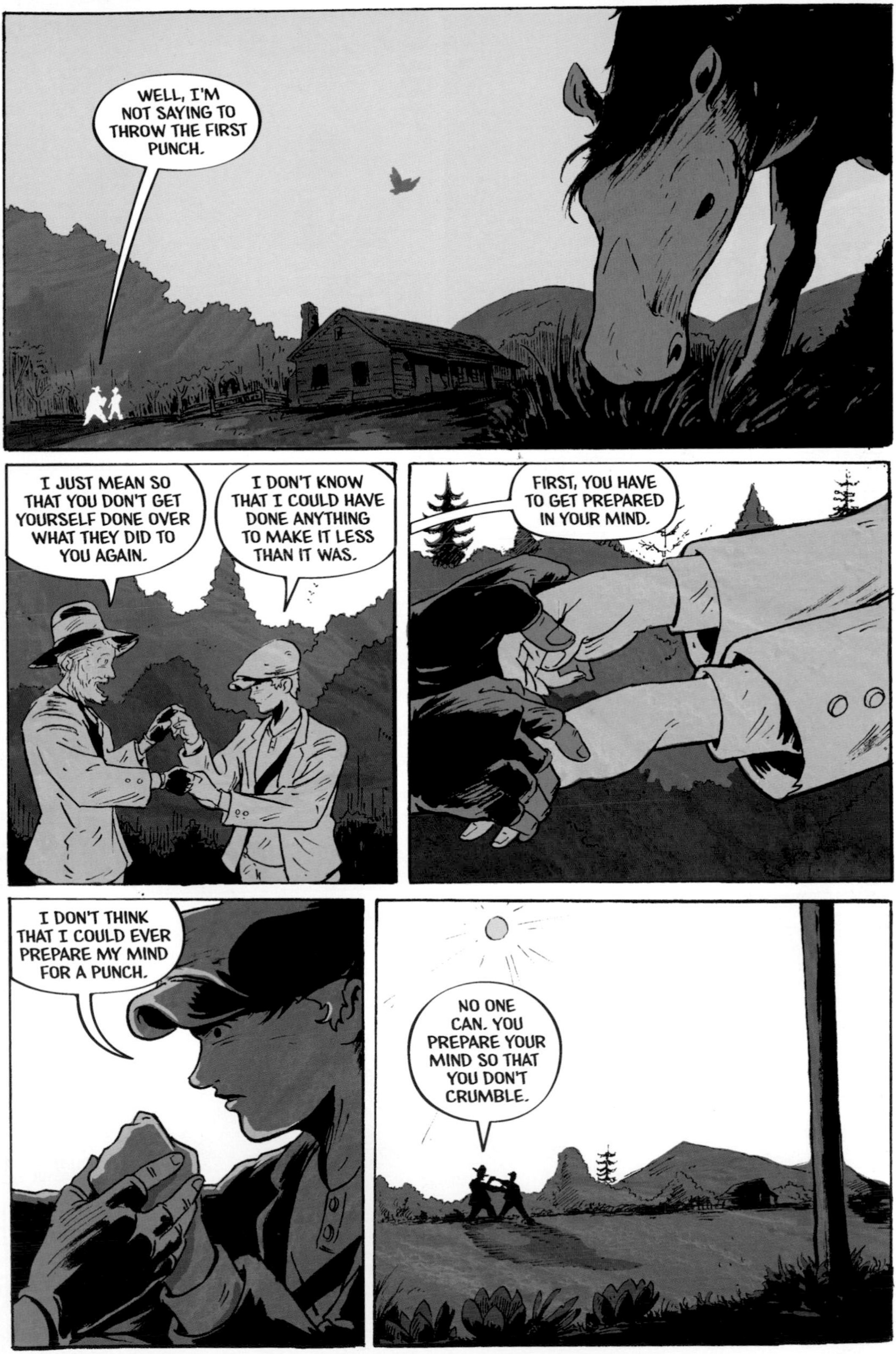
WELL, I'M NOT SAYING TO THROW THE FIRST PUNCH.
I JUST MEAN SO THAT YOU DON'T GET YOURSELF DONE OVER WHAT THEY DID TO YOU AGAIN.
I DON'T KNOW THAT I COULD HAVE DONE ANYTHING TO MAKE IT LESS THAN IT WAS.
FIRST, YOU HAVE TO GET PREPARED IN YOUR MIND.
I DON'T THINK THAT I COULD EVER PREPARE MY MIND FOR A PUNCH.
NO ONE CAN. YOU PREPARE YOUR MIND SO THAT YOU DON'T CRUMBLE.

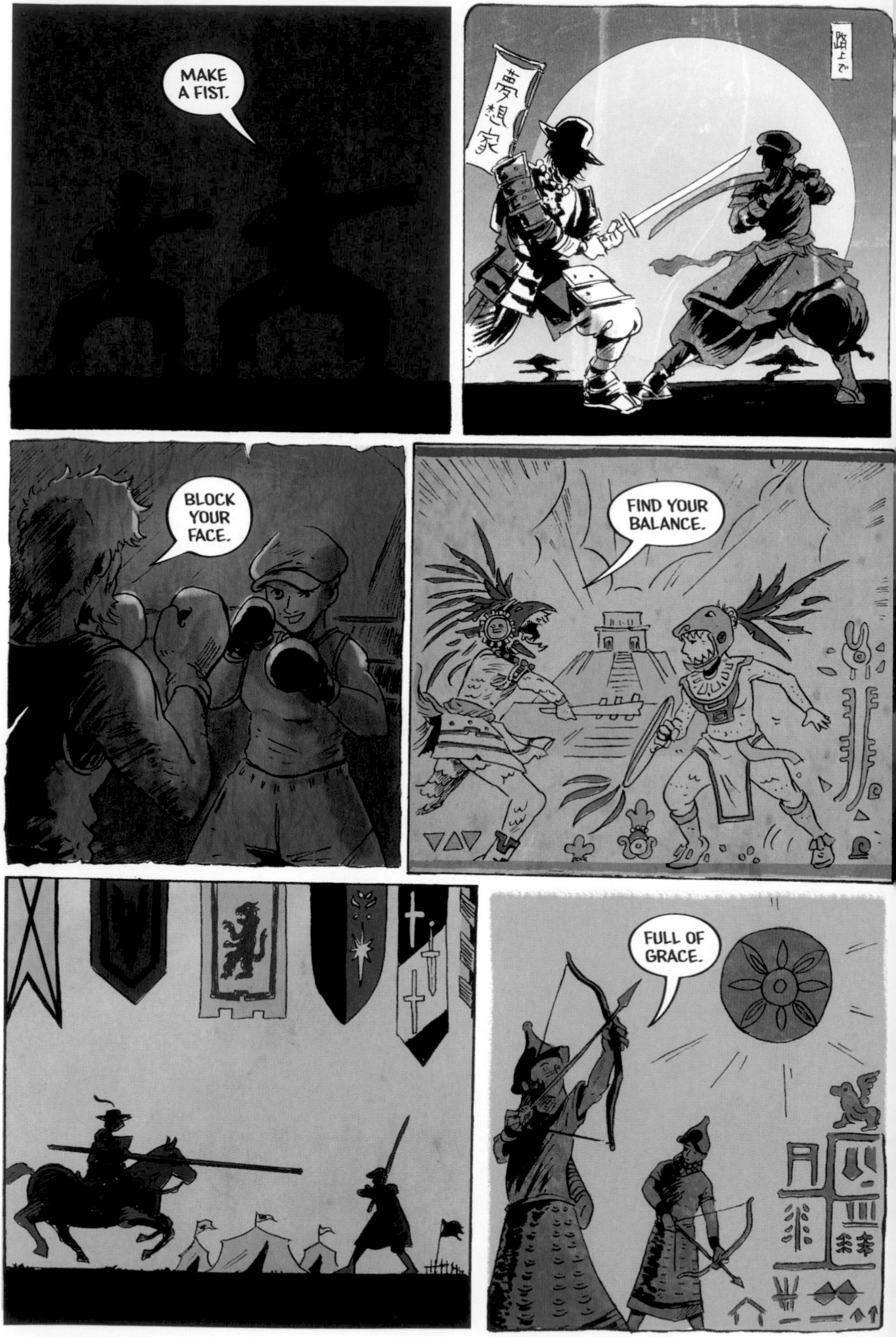
MAKE A FIST.
路上で
夢想家
BLOCK YOUR FACE.
FIND YOUR BALANCE.
FULL OF GRACE.

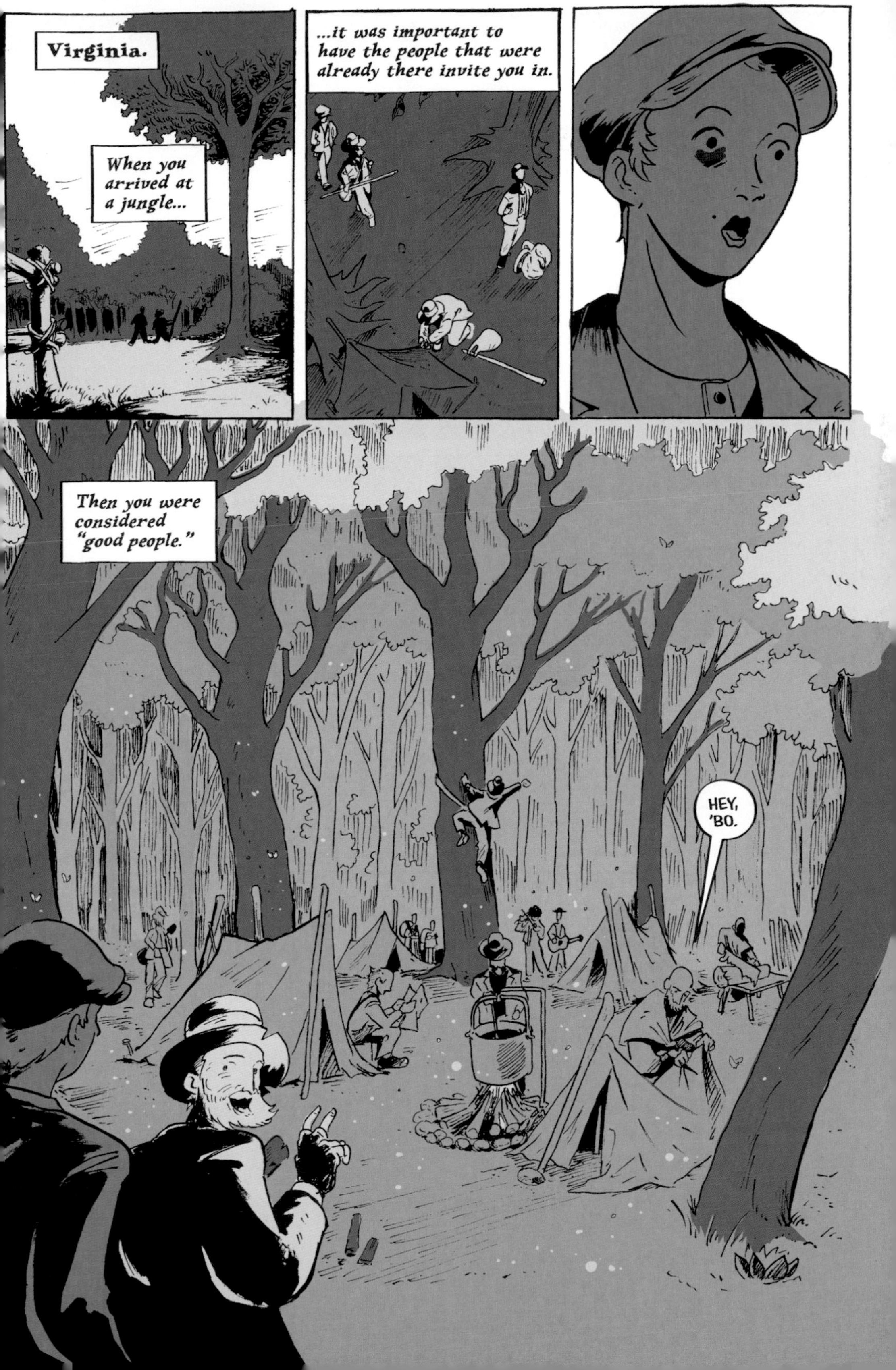
Virginia.
When you arrived at a jungle...
...it was important to have the people that were already there invite you in.
Then you were considered "good people."
HEY, 'BO.

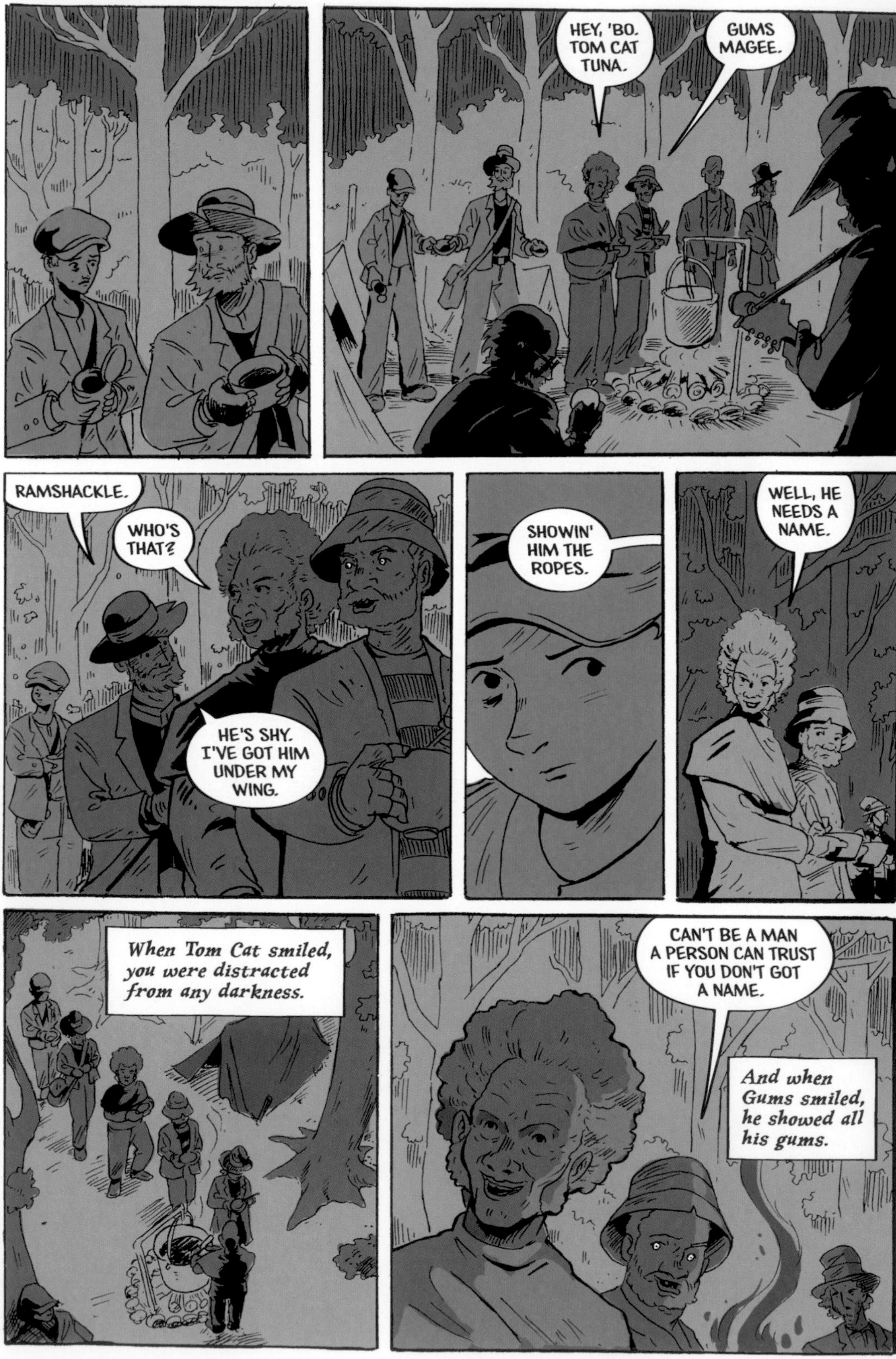
HEY, 'BO. TOM CAT TUNA.
GUMS MAGEE.
RAMSHACKLE.
WHO'S THAT?
HE'S SHY. I'VE GOT HIM UNDER MY WING.
SHOWIN' HIM THE ROPES.
WELL, HE NEEDS A NAME.
When Tom Cat smiled, you were distracted from any darkness.
CAN'T BE A MAN A PERSON CAN TRUST IF YOU DON'T GOT A NAME.
And when Gums smiled, he showed all his gums.

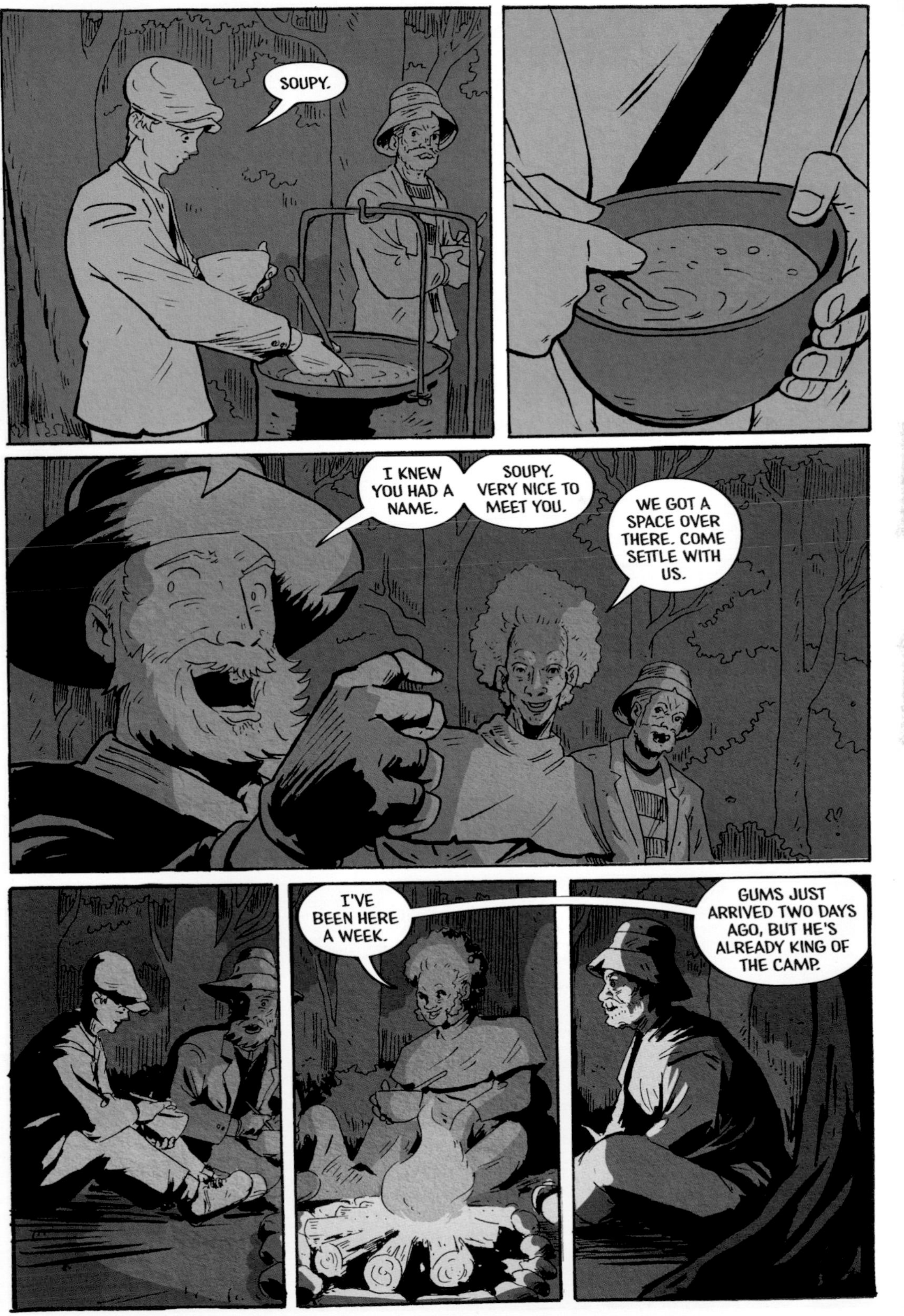
SOUPY.
I KNEW YOU HAD A NAME.
SOUPY. VERY NICE TO MEET YOU.
WE GOT A SPACE OVER THERE. COME SETTLE WITH US.
I'VE BEEN HERE A WEEK.
GUMS JUST ARRIVED TWO DAYS AGO, BUT HE'S ALREADY KING OF THE CAMP.

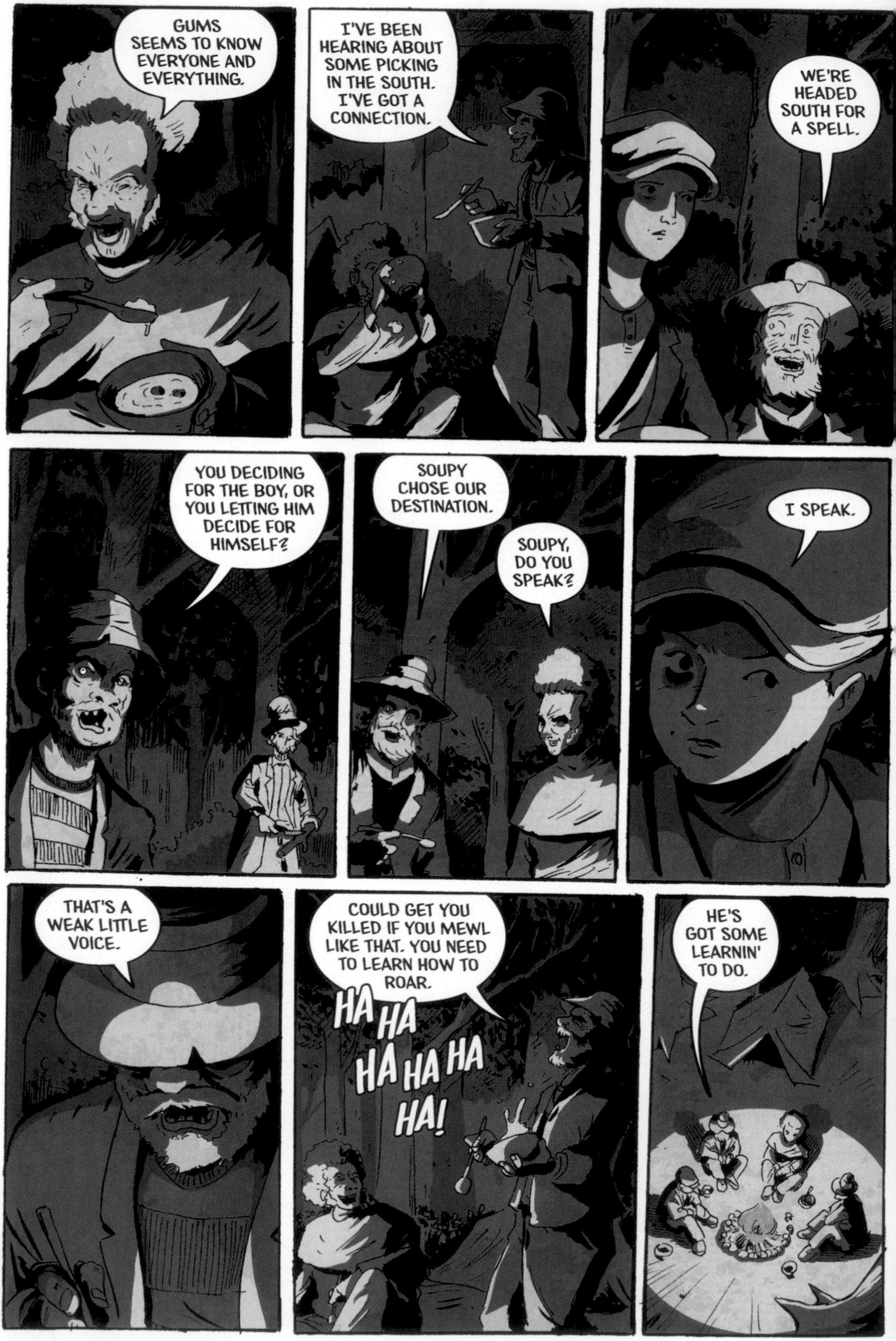
GUMS SEEMS TO KNOW EVERYONE AND EVERYTHING.
I'VE BEEN HEARING ABOUT SOME PICKING IN THE SOUTH. I'VE GOT A CONNECTION.
WE'RE HEADED SOUTH FOR A SPELL.
YOU DECIDING FOR THE BOY, OR YOU LETTING HIM DECIDE FOR HIMSELF?
SOUPY CHOSE OUR DESTINATION.
SOUPY, DO YOU SPEAK?
I SPEAK.
THAT'S A WEAK LITTLE VOICE.
COULD GET YOU KILLED IF YOU MEWL LIKE THAT. YOU NEED TO LEARN HOW TO ROAR.
HA HA HA HA HA HA!
HE'S GOT SOME LEARNIN' TO DO.

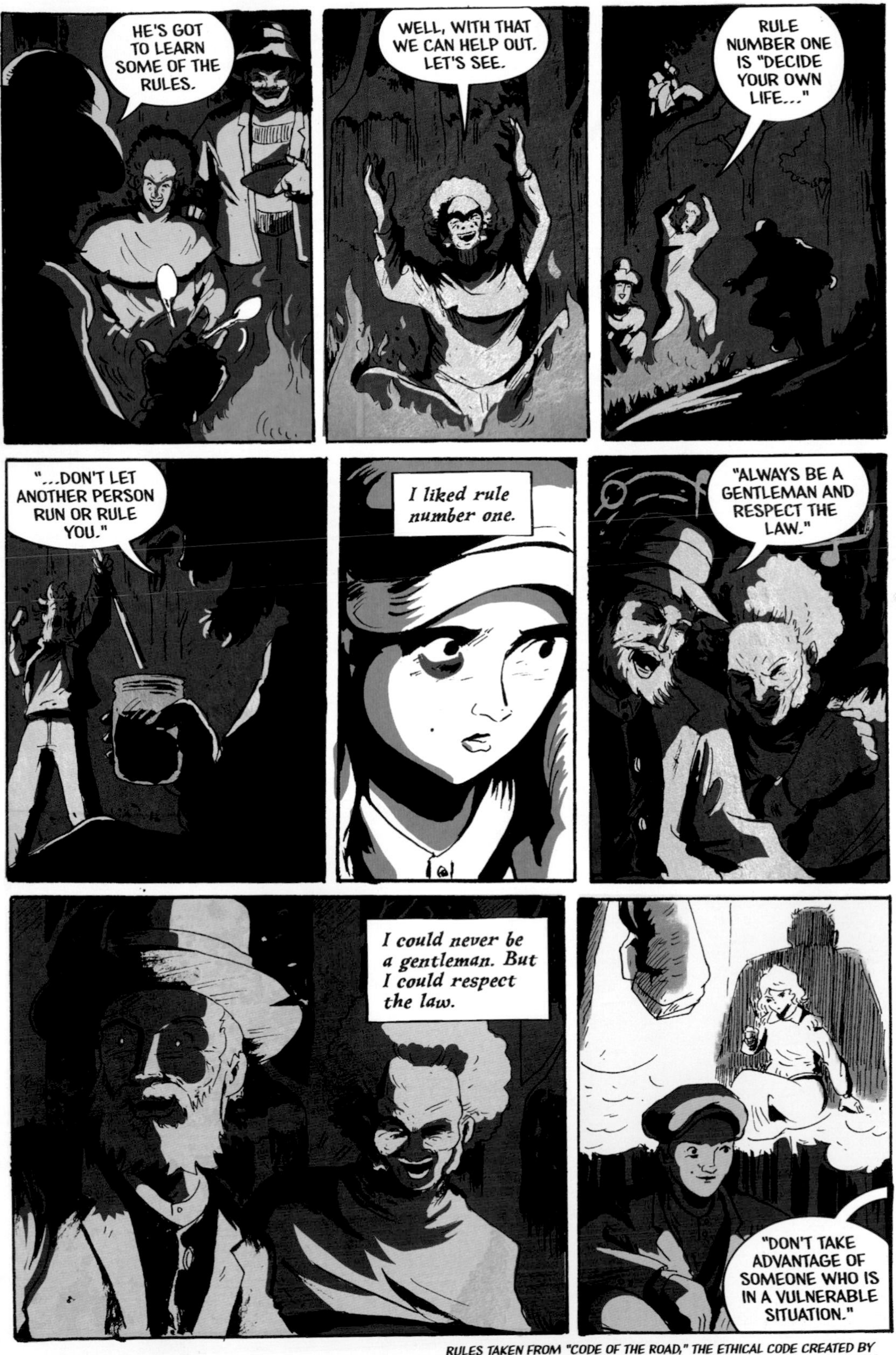
HE'S GOT TO LEARN SOME OF THE RULES.
WELL, WITH THAT WE CAN HELP OUT. LET'S SEE.
RULE NUMBER ONE IS "DECIDE YOUR OWN LIFE..."
"...DON'T LET ANOTHER PERSON RUN OR RULE YOU."
I liked rule number one.
"ALWAYS BE A GENTLEMAN AND RESPECT THE LAW."
I could never be a gentleman. But I could respect the law.
"DON'T TAKE ADVANTAGE OF SOMEONE WHO IS IN A VULNERABLE SITUATION."

RULES TAKEN FROM "CODE OF THE ROAD," THE ETHICAL CODE CREATED BY TOURIST UNION #63 AT THE ANNUAL HOBO CONVENTION IN THE LATE 1880'S.

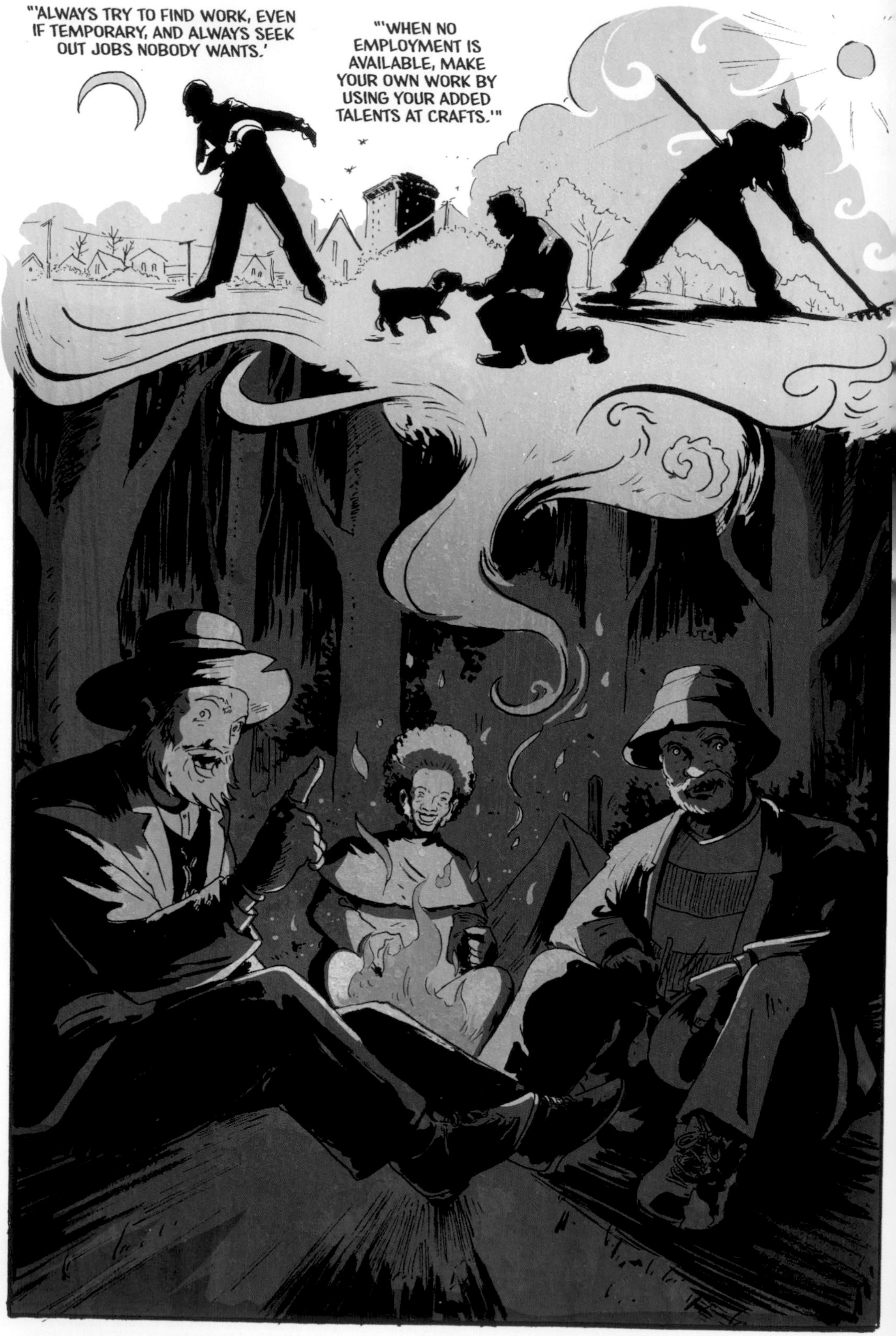
"'ALWAYS TRY TO FIND WORK, EVEN IF TEMPORARY, AND ALWAYS SEEK OUT JOBS NOBODY WANTS.'
"'WHEN NO EMPLOYMENT IS AVAILABLE, MAKE YOUR OWN WORK BY USING YOUR ADDED TALENTS AT CRAFTS.'"

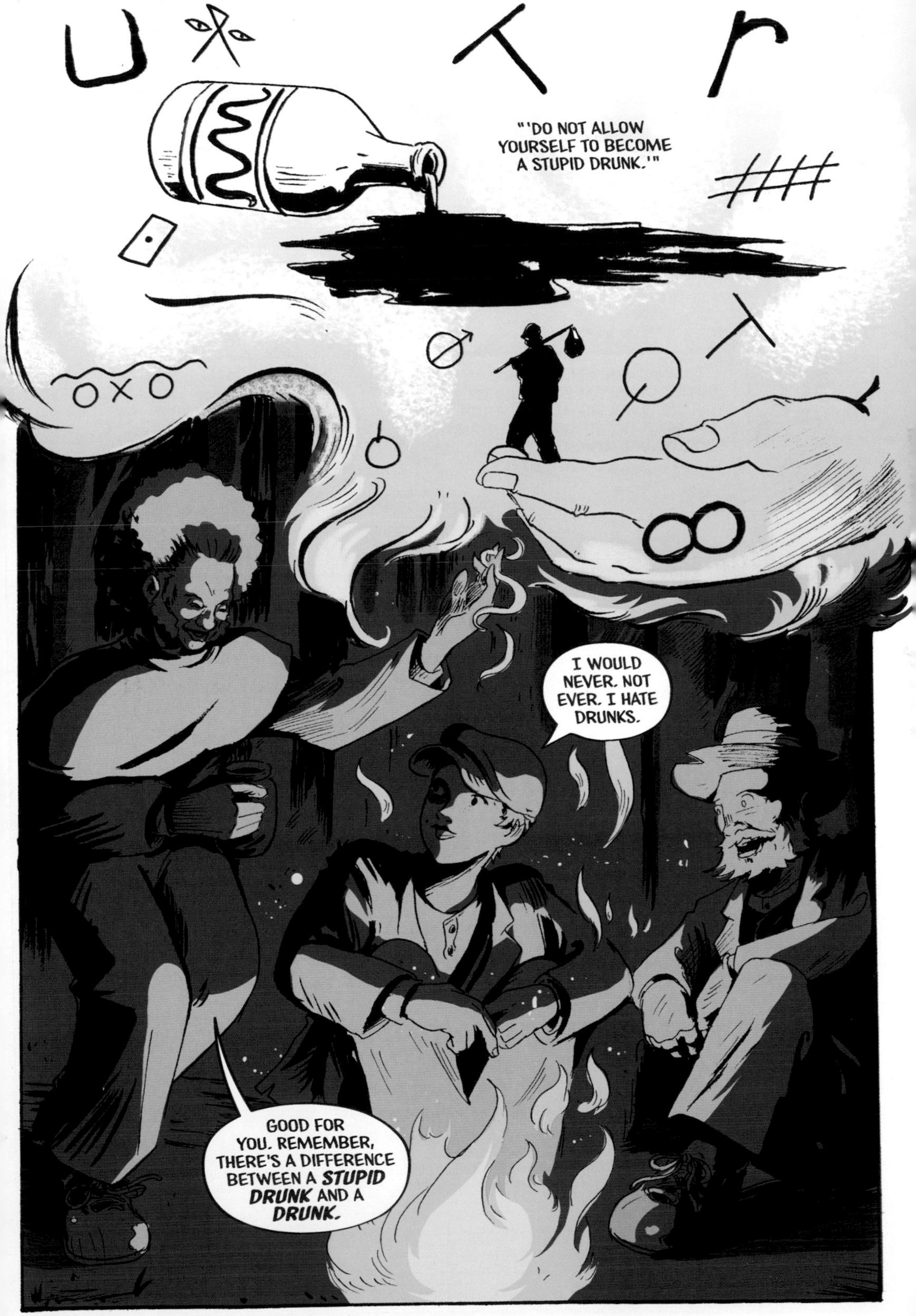
"'DO NOT ALLOW YOURSELF TO BECOME A STUPID DRUNK.'"
I WOULD NEVER. NOT EVER. I HATE DRUNKS.
GOOD FOR YOU. REMEMBER, THERE'S A DIFFERENCE BETWEEN A *STUPID DRUNK* AND A *DRUNK.*

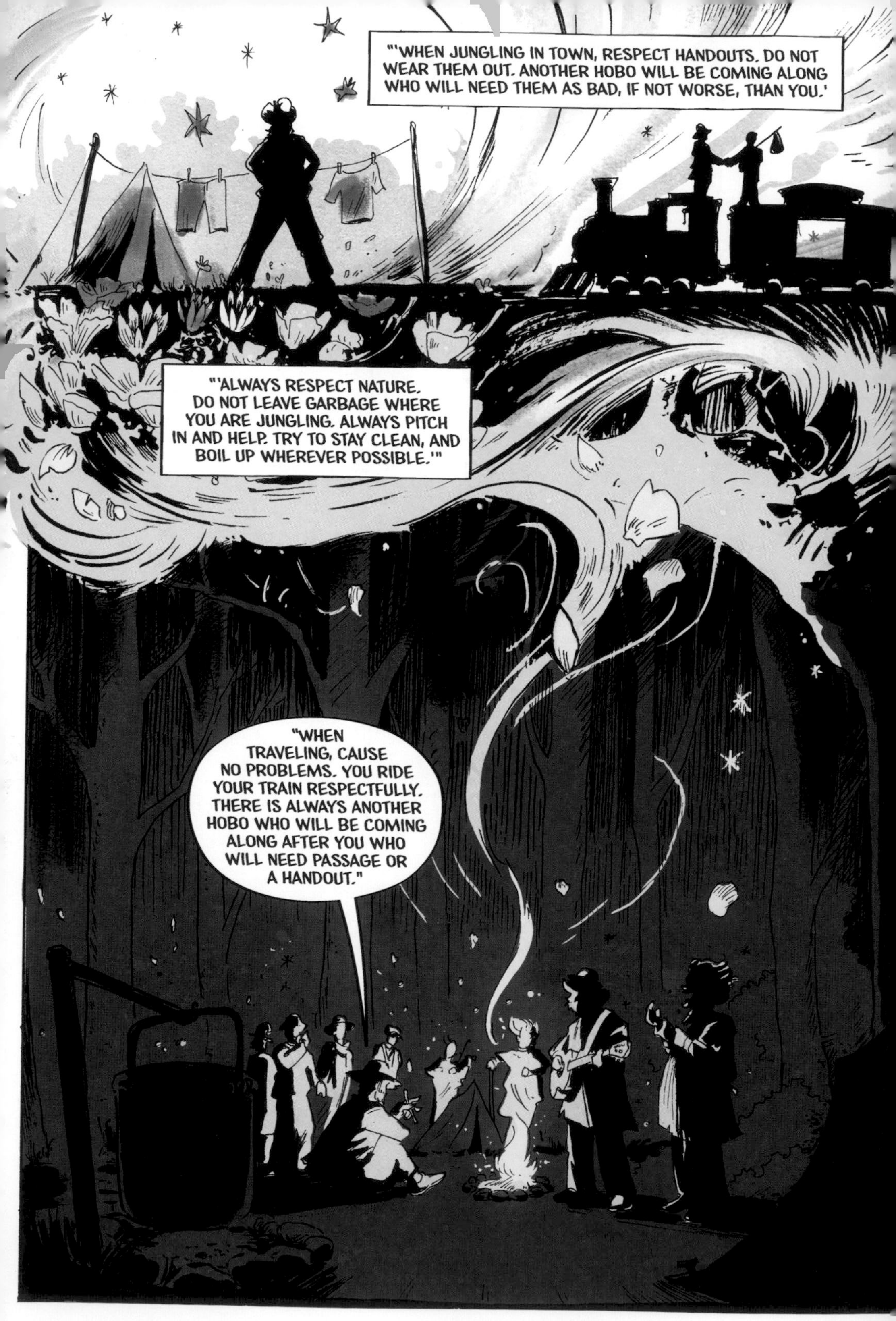
"'WHEN JUNGLING IN TOWN, RESPECT HANDOUTS. DO NOT WEAR THEM OUT. ANOTHER HOBO WILL BE COMING ALONG WHO WILL NEED THEM AS BAD, IF NOT WORSE, THAN YOU.'
"'ALWAYS RESPECT NATURE. DO NOT LEAVE GARBAGE WHERE YOU ARE JUNGLING. ALWAYS PITCH IN AND HELP. TRY TO STAY CLEAN, AND BOIL UP WHEREVER POSSIBLE.'"
"WHEN TRAVELING, CAUSE NO PROBLEMS. YOU RIDE YOUR TRAIN RESPECTFULLY. THERE IS ALWAYS ANOTHER HOBO WHO WILL BE COMING ALONG AFTER YOU WHO WILL NEED PASSAGE OR A HANDOUT."

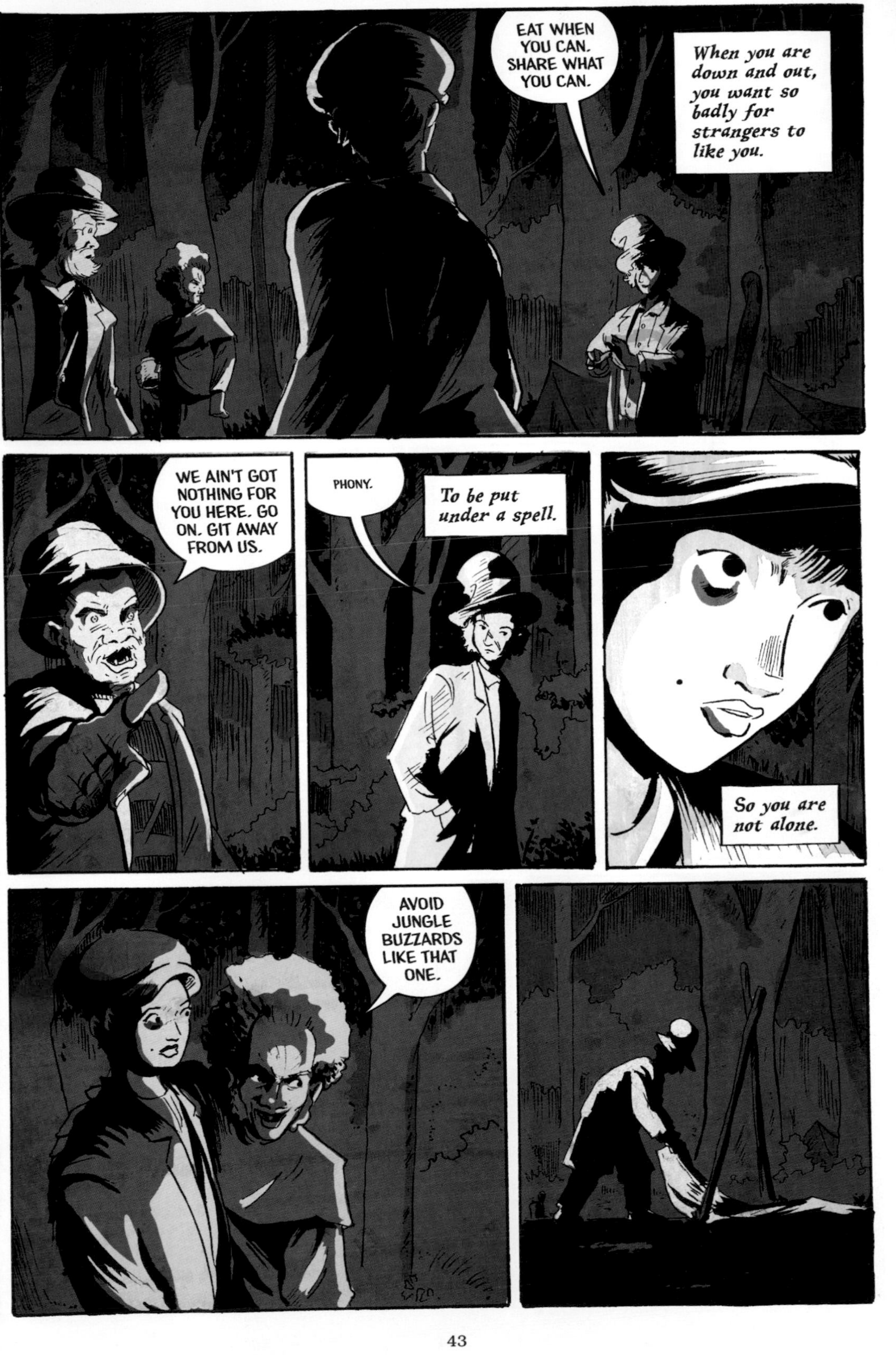
EAT WHEN YOU CAN. SHARE WHAT YOU CAN.
When you are down and out, you want so badly for strangers to like you.
WE AIN'T GOT NOTHING FOR YOU HERE. GO ON. GIT AWAY FROM US.
PHONY.
To be put under a spell.
So you are not alone.
AVOID JUNGLE BUZZARDS LIKE THAT ONE.

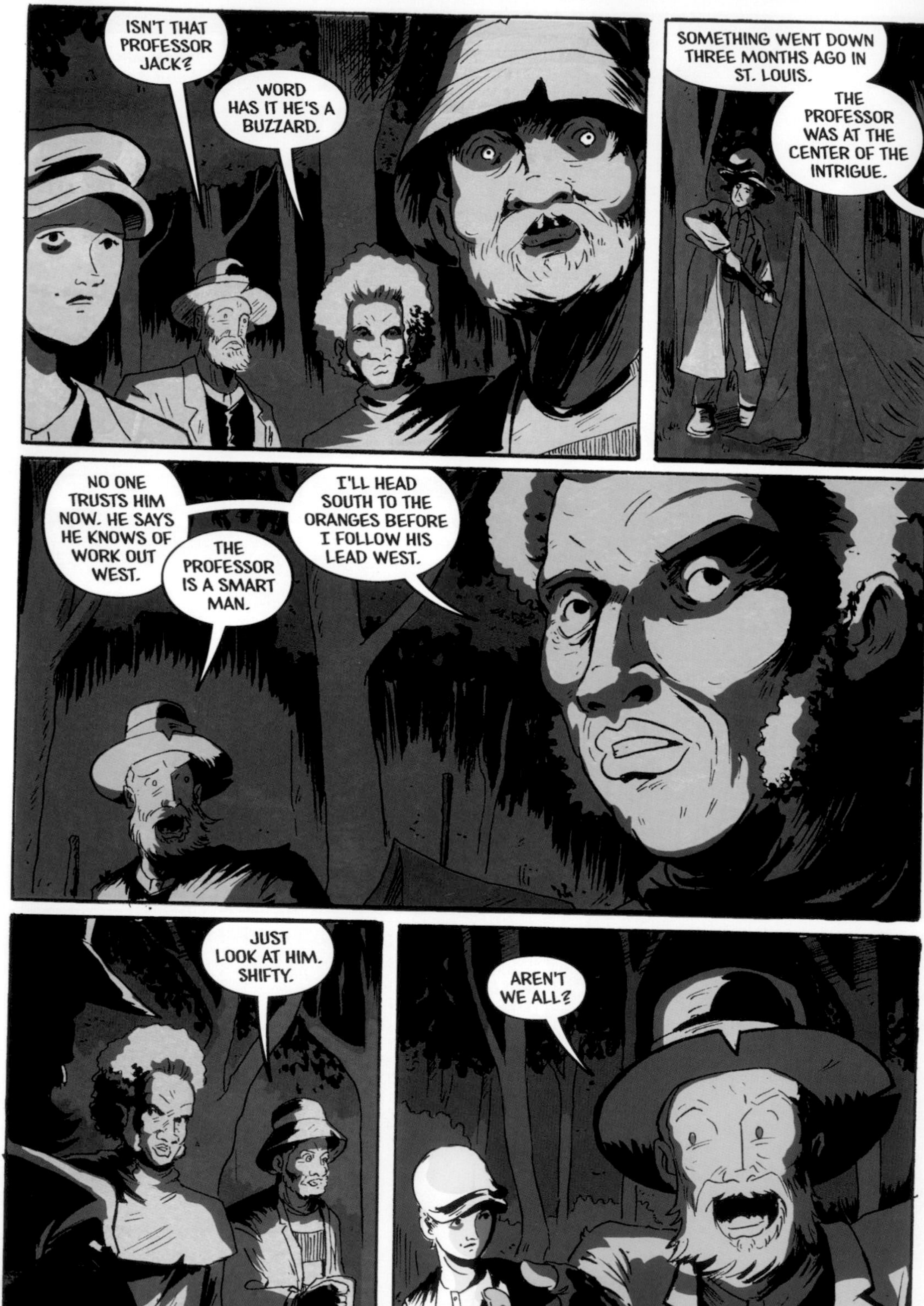
ISN'T THAT PROFESSOR JACK?
WORD HAS IT HE'S A BUZZARD.
SOMETHING WENT DOWN THREE MONTHS AGO IN ST. LOUIS.
THE PROFESSOR WAS AT THE CENTER OF THE INTRIGUE.
NO ONE TRUSTS HIM NOW. HE SAYS HE KNOWS OF WORK OUT WEST.
THE PROFESSOR IS A SMART MAN.
I'LL HEAD SOUTH TO THE ORANGES BEFORE I FOLLOW HIS LEAD WEST.
JUST LOOK AT HIM. SHIFTY.
AREN'T WE ALL?

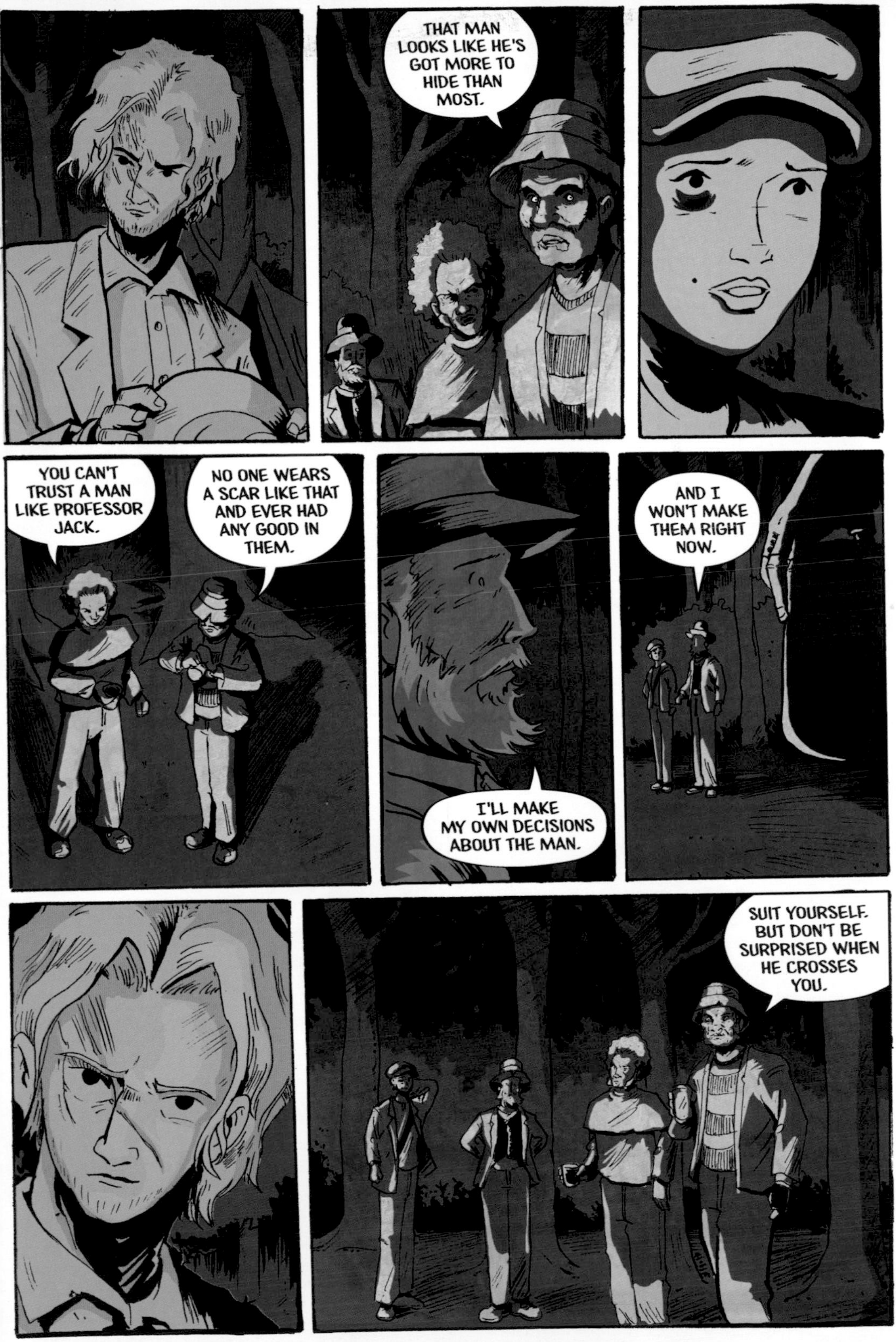
THAT MAN LOOKS LIKE HE'S GOT MORE TO HIDE THAN MOST.
YOU CAN'T TRUST A MAN LIKE PROFESSOR JACK.
NO ONE WEARS A SCAR LIKE THAT AND EVER HAD ANY GOOD IN THEM.
I'LL MAKE MY OWN DECISIONS ABOUT THE MAN.
AND I WON'T MAKE THEM RIGHT NOW.
SUIT YOURSELF. BUT DON'T BE SURPRISED WHEN HE CROSSES YOU.

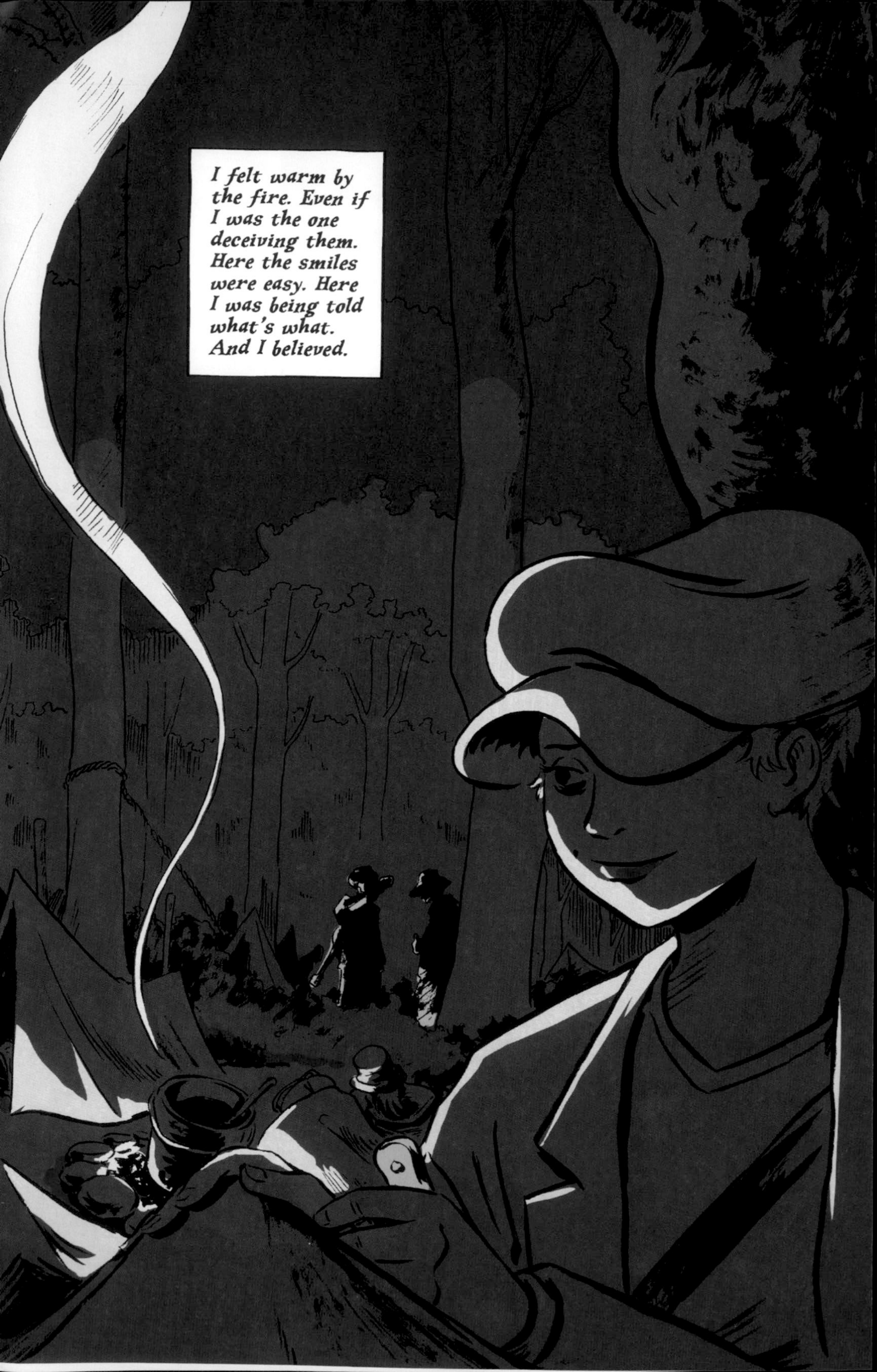
I felt warm by the fire. Even if I was the one deceiving them. Here the smiles were easy. Here I was being told what's what. And I believed.

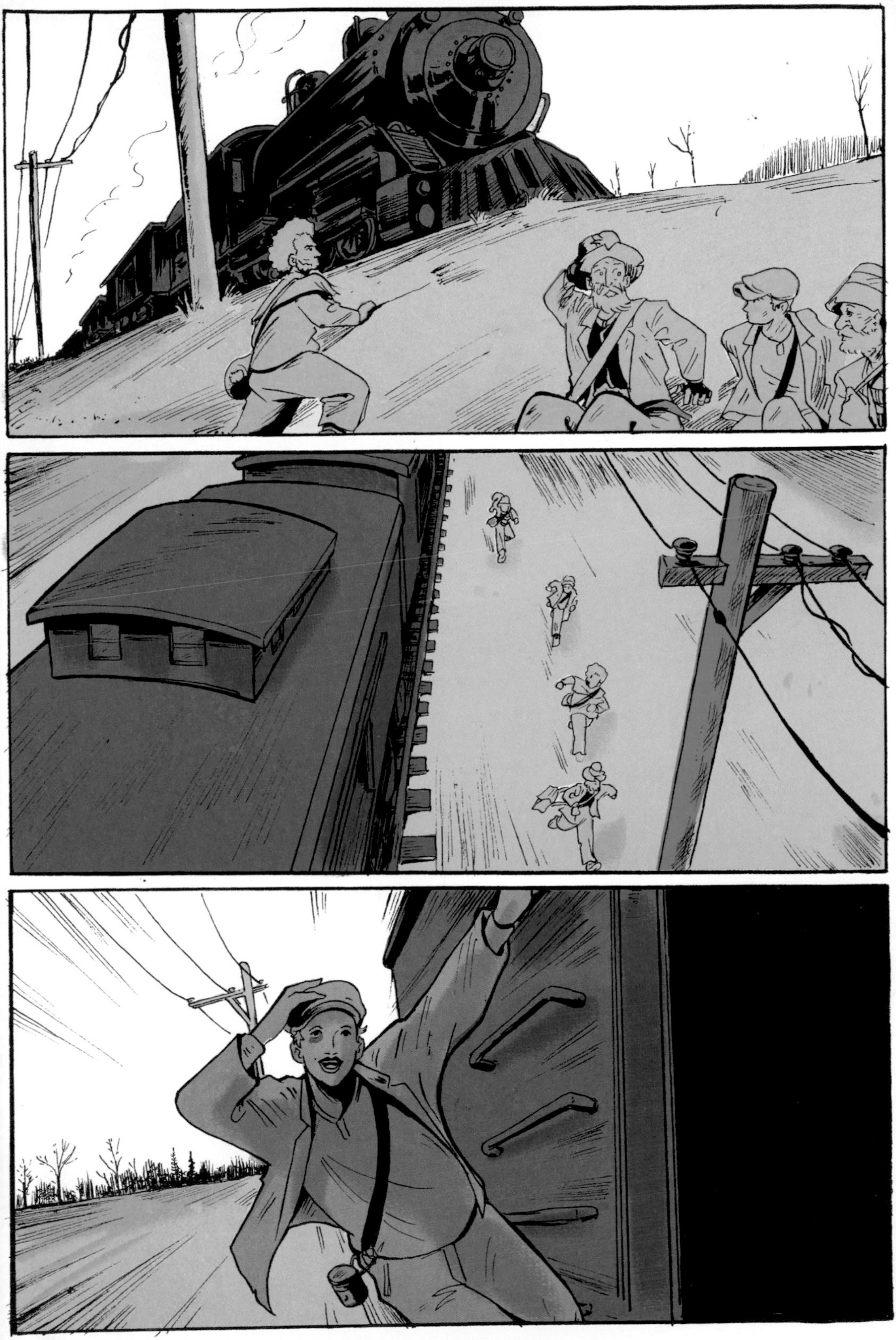

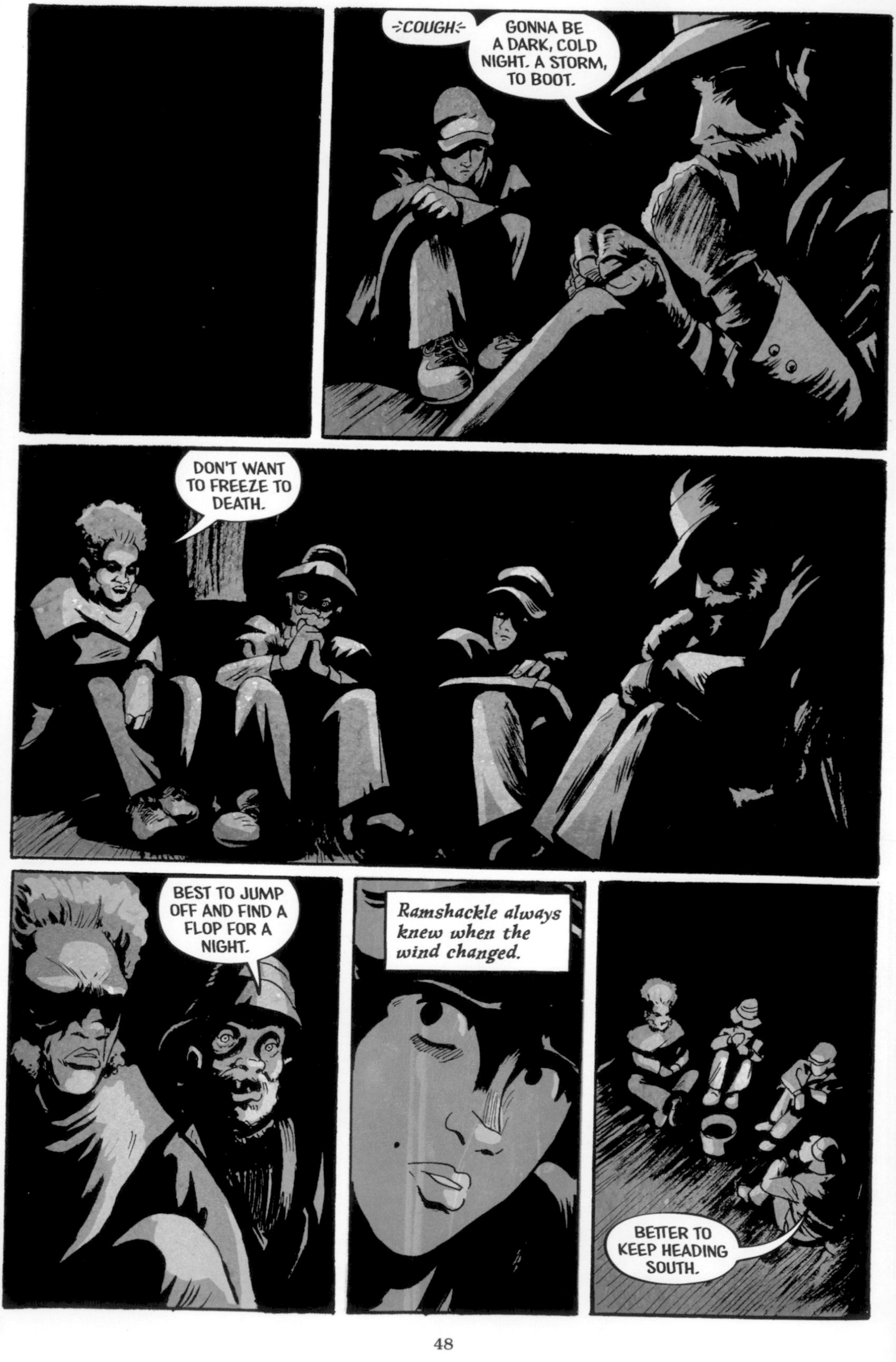

-COUGH-
GONNA BE A DARK, COLD NIGHT. A STORM, TO BOOT.
DON'T WANT TO FREEZE TO DEATH.
BEST TO JUMP OFF AND FIND A FLOP FOR A NIGHT.
Ramshackle always knew when the wind changed.
BETTER TO KEEP HEADING SOUTH.

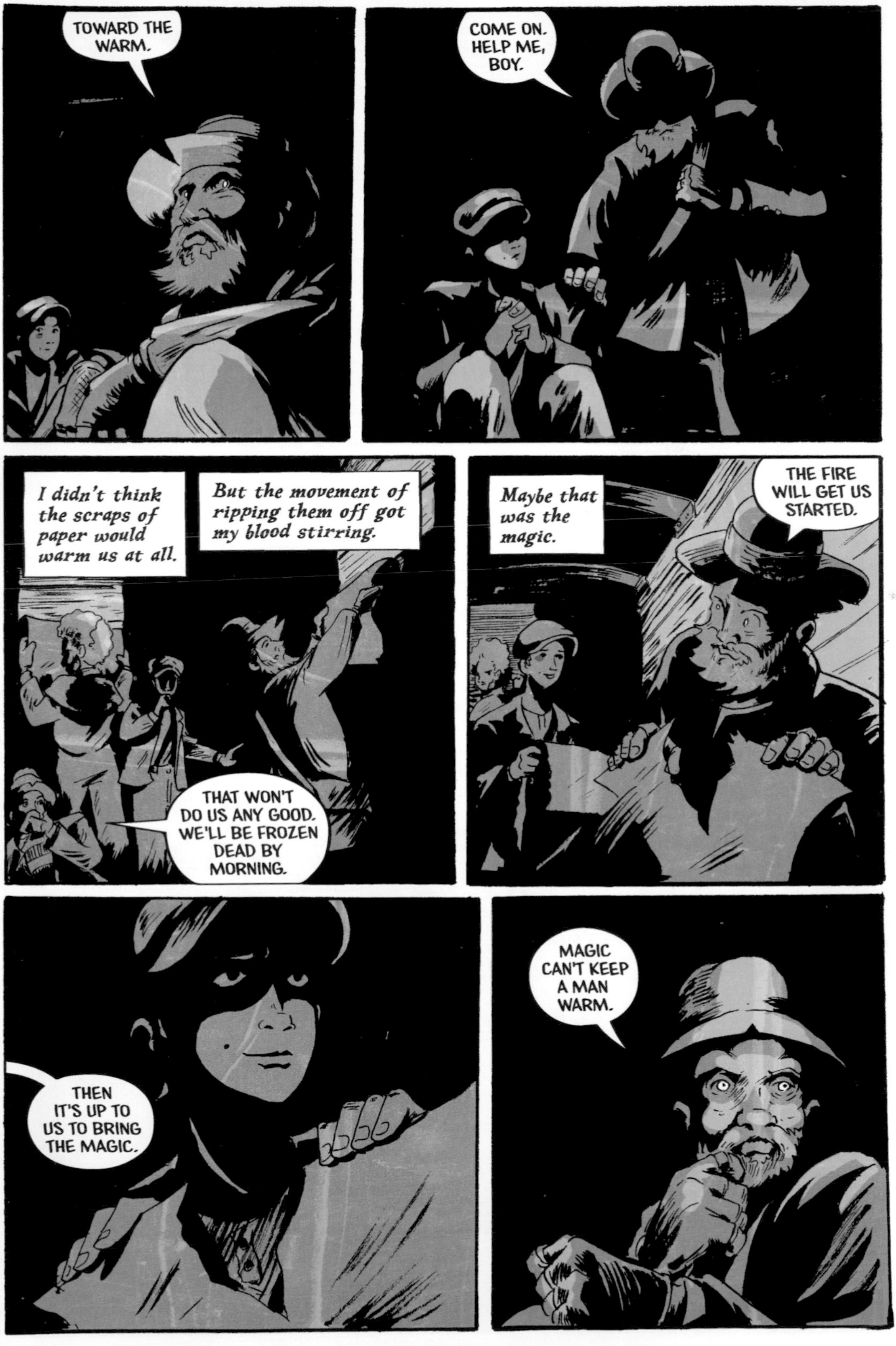
TOWARD THE WARM.
COME ON. HELP ME, BOY.
I didn't think the scraps of paper would warm us at all.
But the movement of ripping them off got my blood stirring.
THAT WON'T DO US ANY GOOD. WE'LL BE FROZEN DEAD BY MORNING.
Maybe that was the magic.
THE FIRE WILL GET US STARTED.
THEN IT'S UP TO US TO BRING THE MAGIC.
MAGIC CAN'T KEEP A MAN WARM.

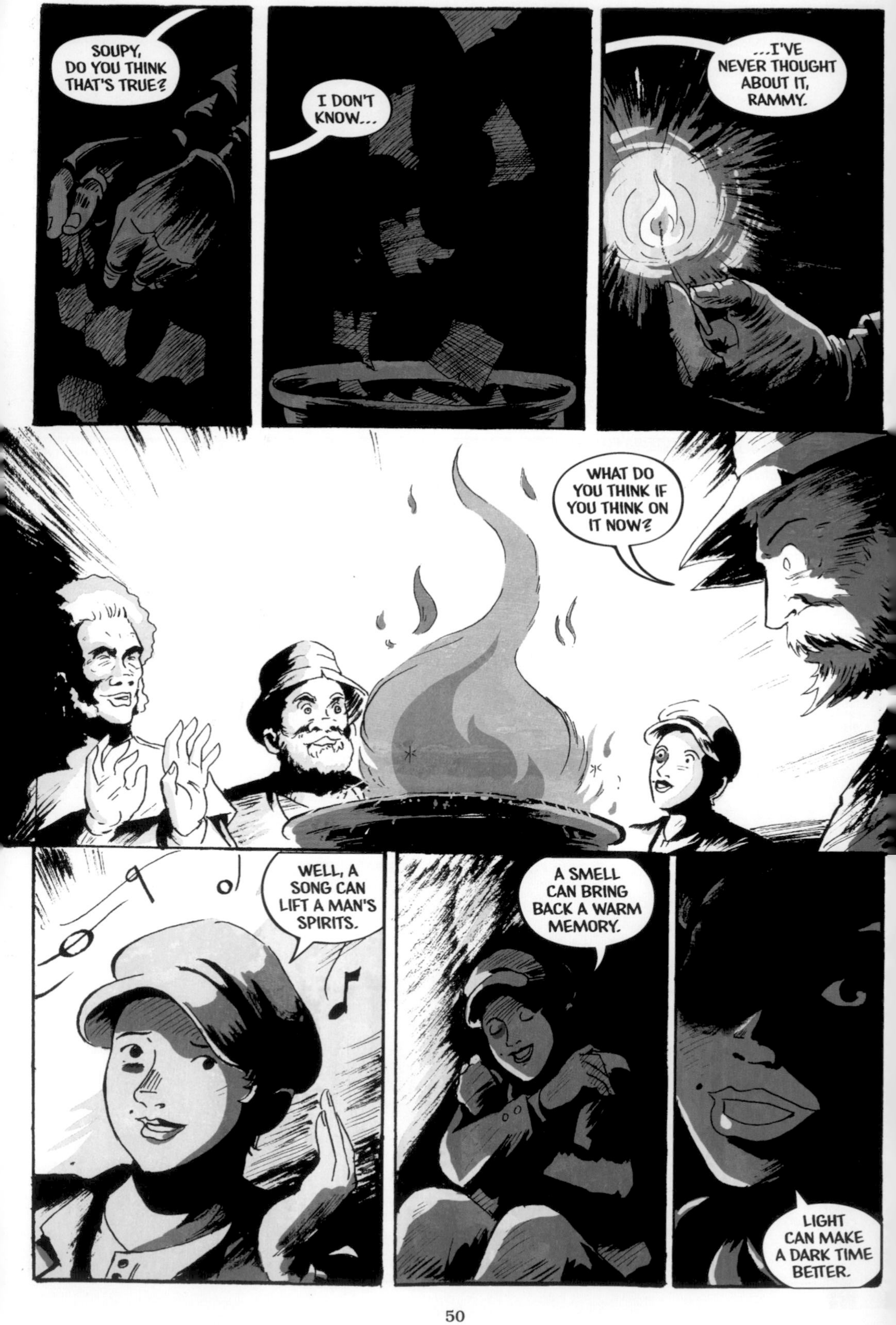
SOUPY, DO YOU THINK THAT'S TRUE?
I DON'T KNOW...
...I'VE NEVER THOUGHT ABOUT IT, RAMMY.
WHAT DO YOU THINK IF YOU THINK ON IT NOW?
WELL, A SONG CAN LIFT A MAN'S SPIRITS.
A SMELL CAN BRING BACK A WARM MEMORY.
LIGHT CAN MAKE A DARK TIME BETTER.

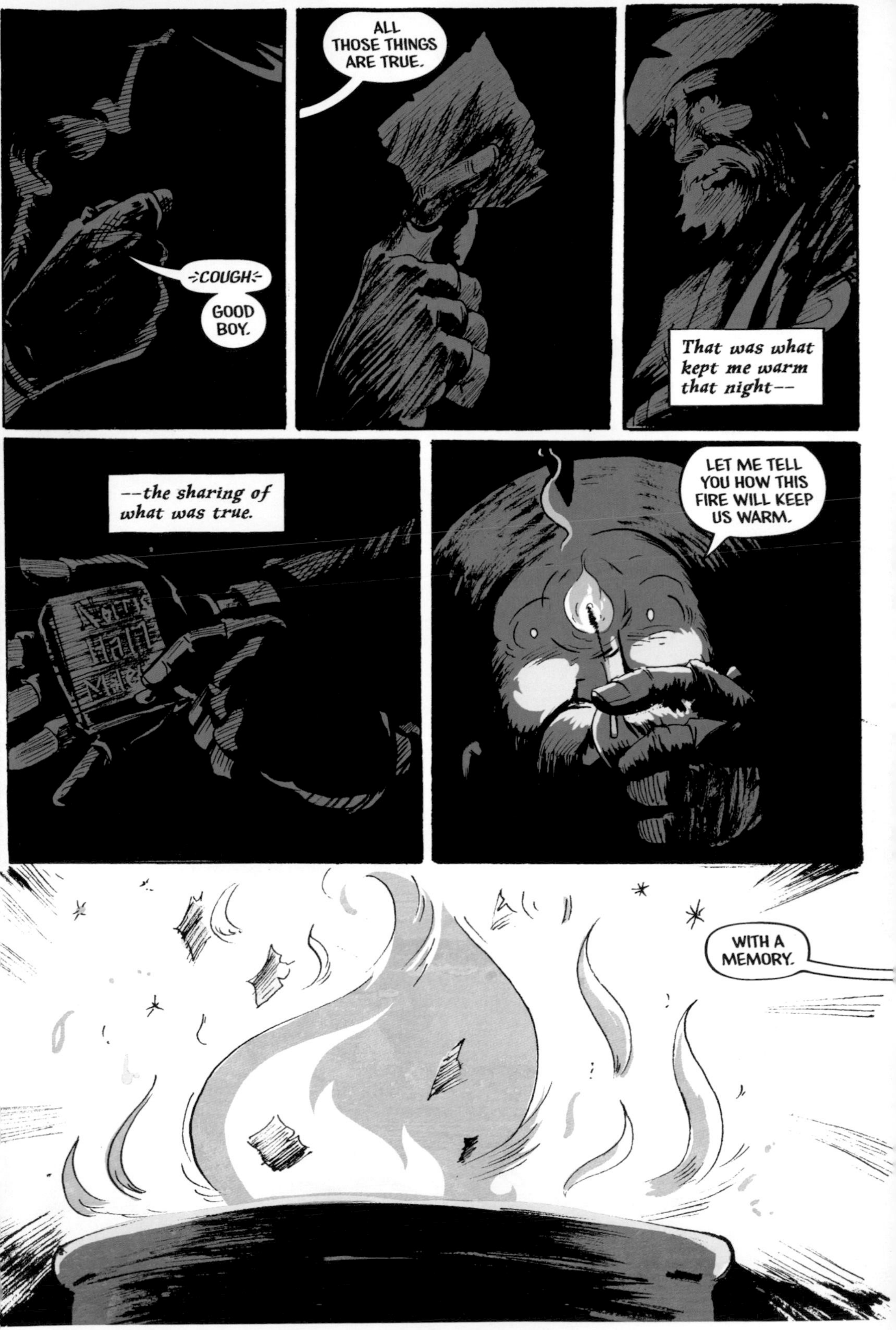

ALL THOSE THINGS ARE TRUE.
COUGH
GOOD BOY.
That was what kept me warm that night--
--the sharing of what was true.
LET ME TELL YOU HOW THIS FIRE WILL KEEP US WARM.
WITH A MEMORY.

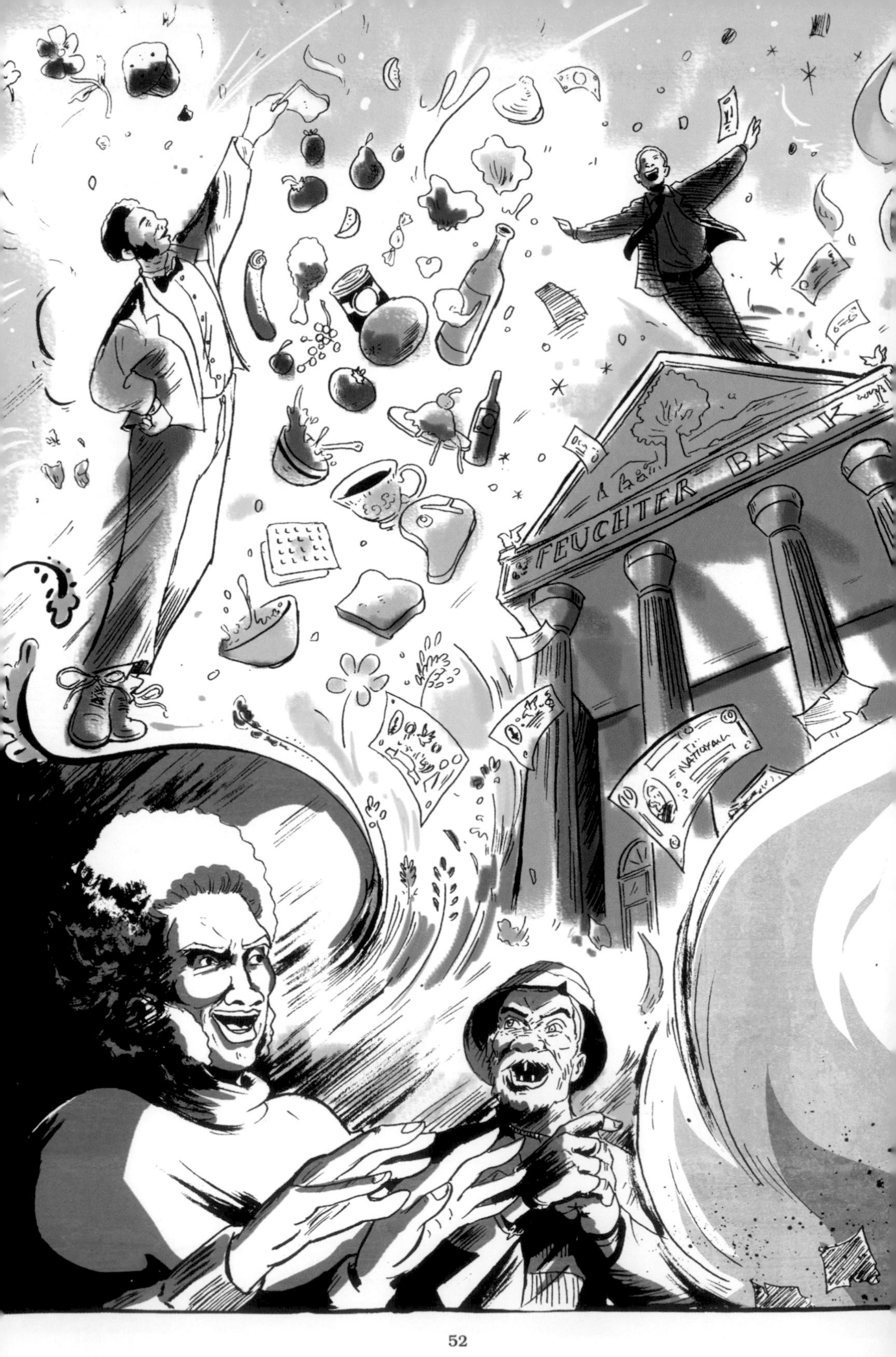
FEUCHTER BANK

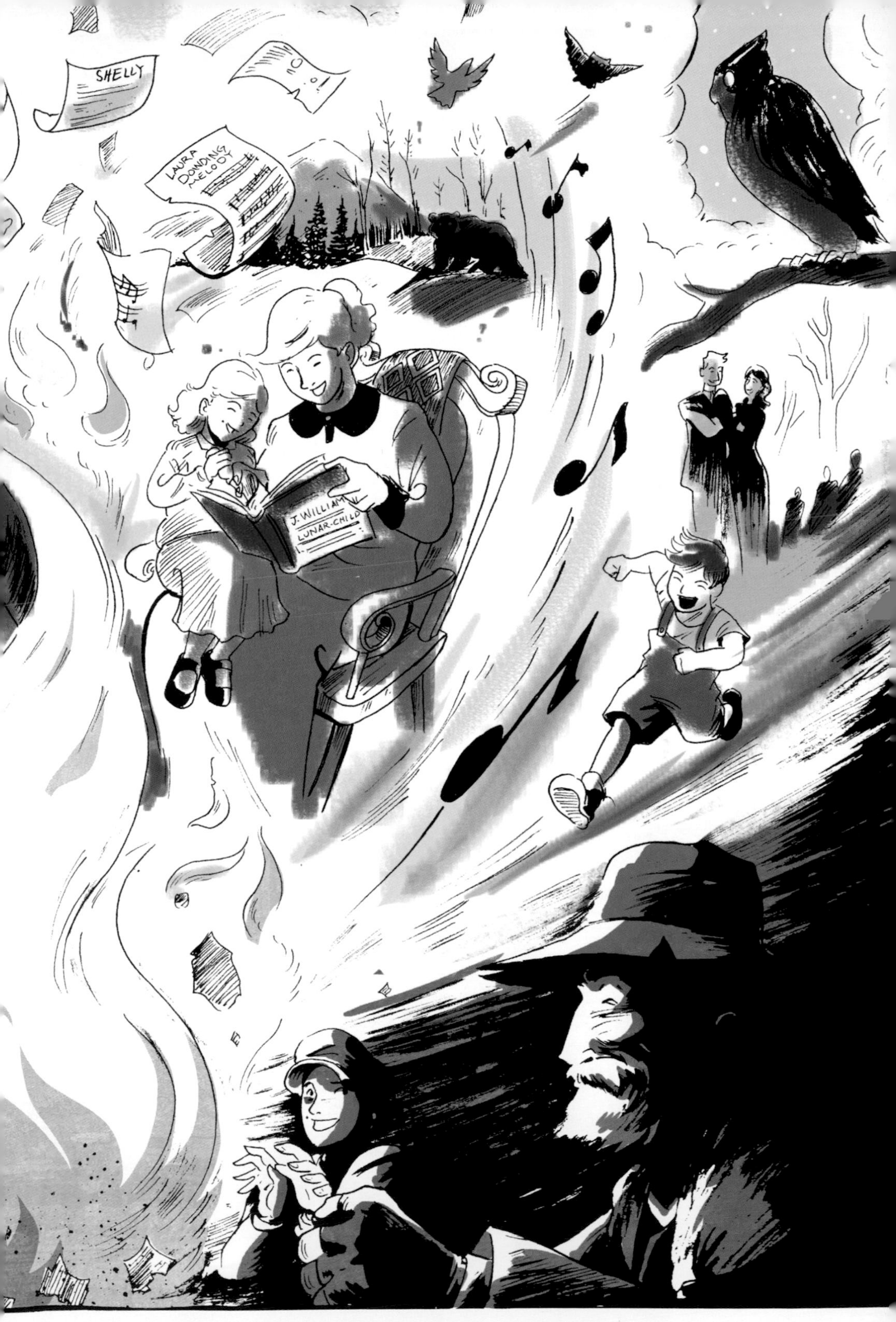
SHELLY
LAURA DOWDING MELODY
J. WILLIAM LUNAR-CHILD

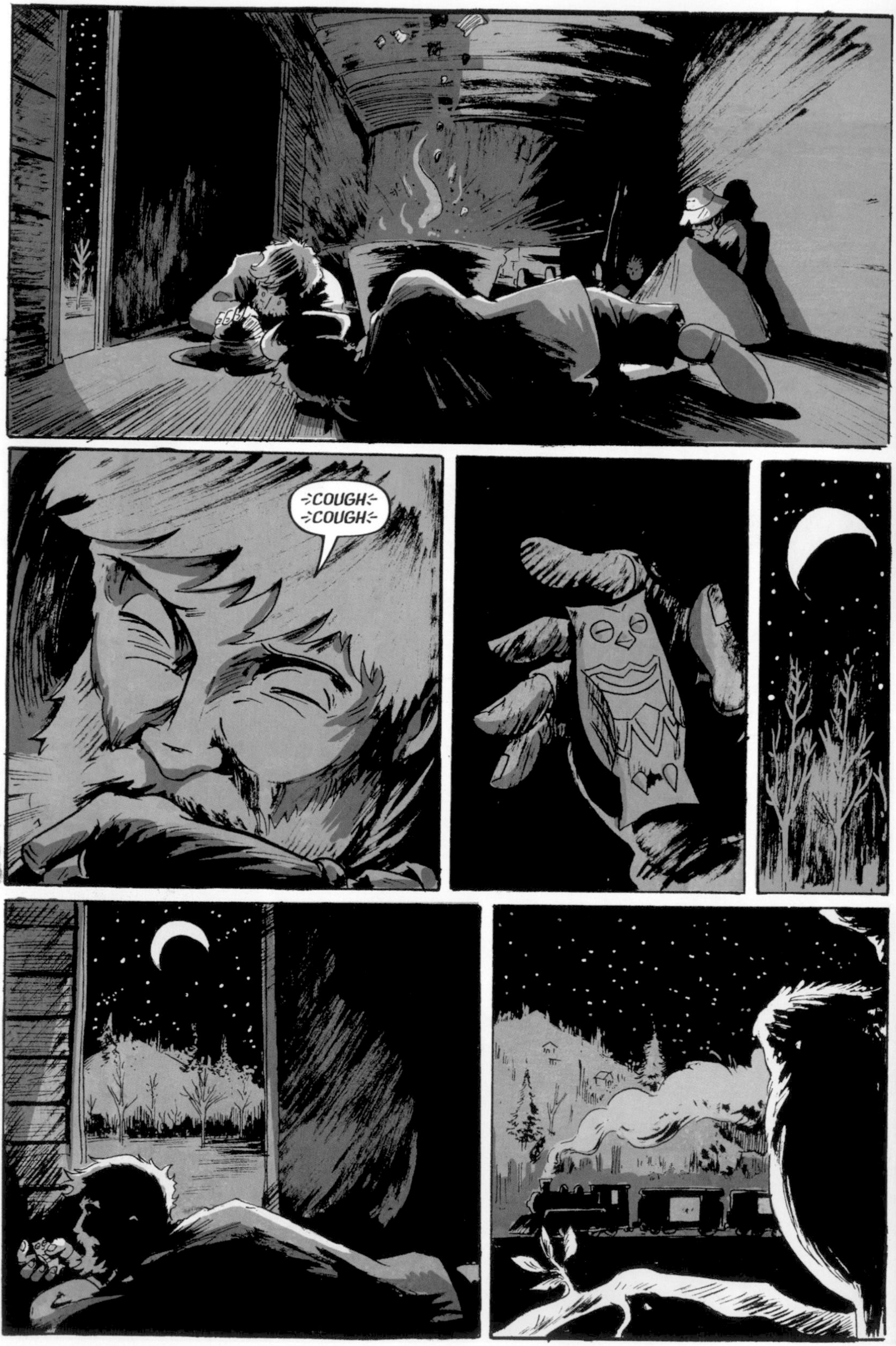
COUGH COUGH

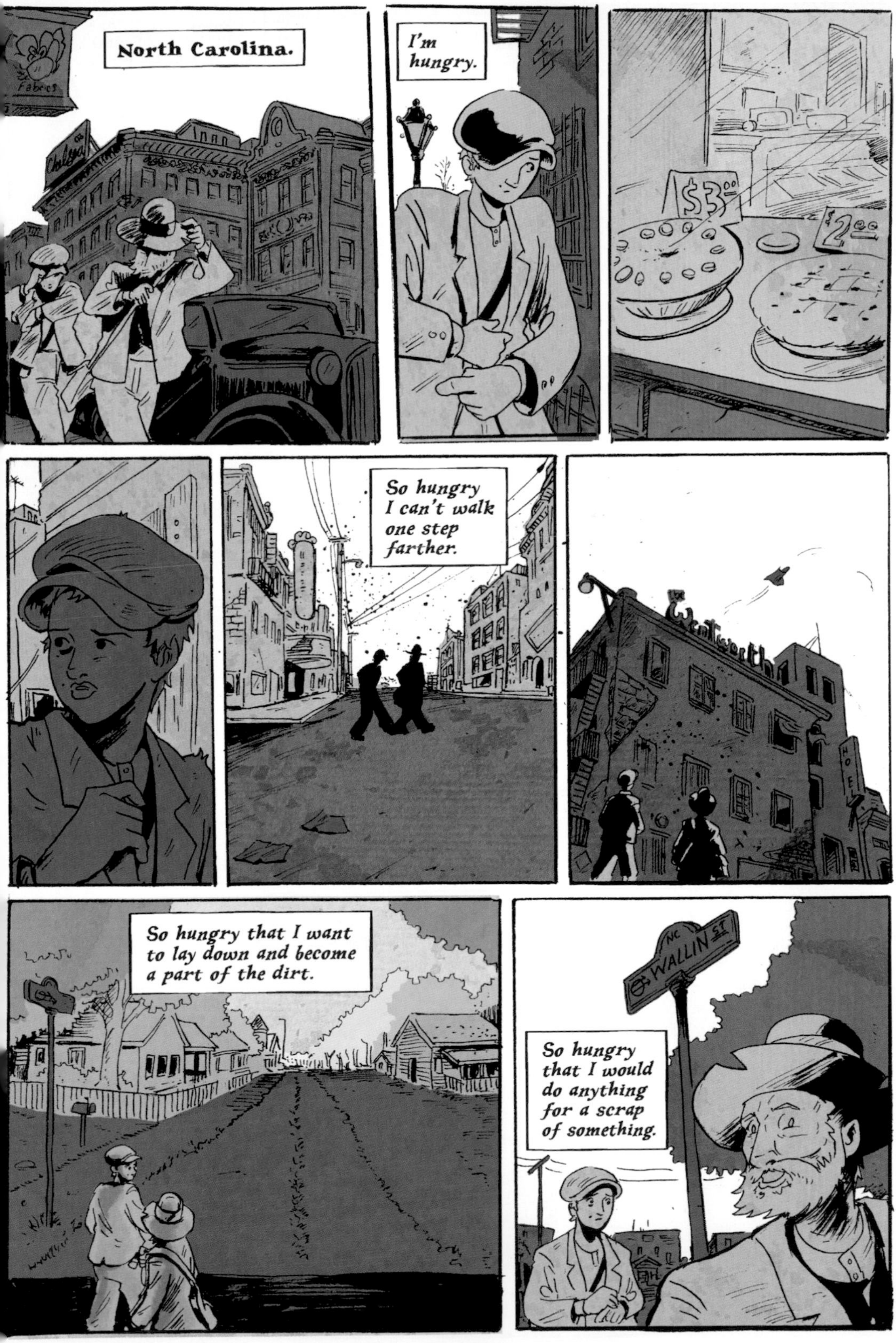
North Carolina.
I'm hungry.
$3.00
$2.00
So hungry I can't walk one step farther.
Wentworth
HOTEL
So hungry that I want to lay down and become a part of the dirt.
NC WALLIN ST
So hungry that I would do anything for a scrap of something.

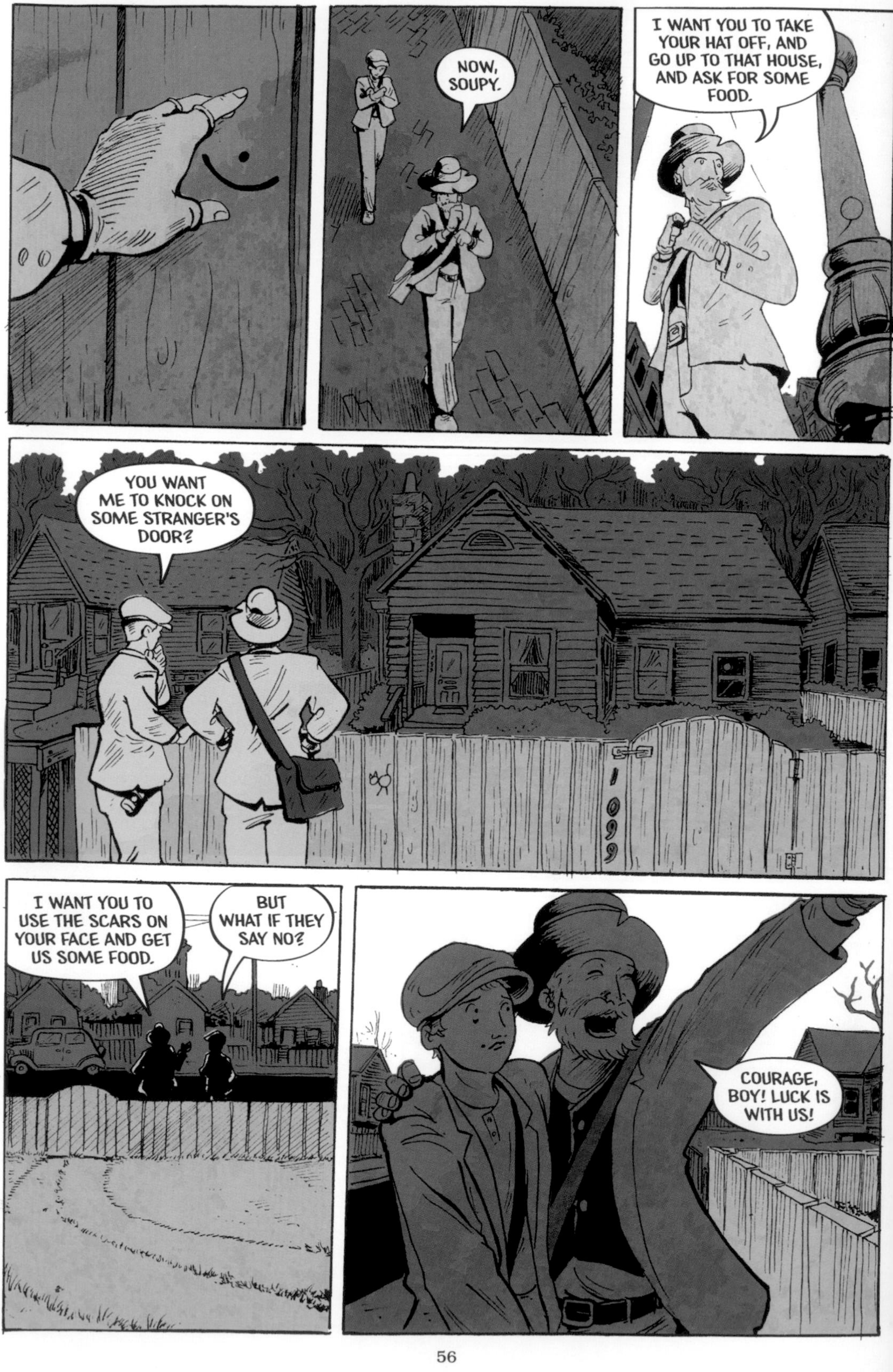
NOW, SOUPY.
I WANT YOU TO TAKE YOUR HAT OFF, AND GO UP TO THAT HOUSE, AND ASK FOR SOME FOOD.
YOU WANT ME TO KNOCK ON SOME STRANGER'S DOOR?
1099
I WANT YOU TO USE THE SCARS ON YOUR FACE AND GET US SOME FOOD.
BUT WHAT IF THEY SAY NO?
COURAGE, BOY! LUCK IS WITH US!

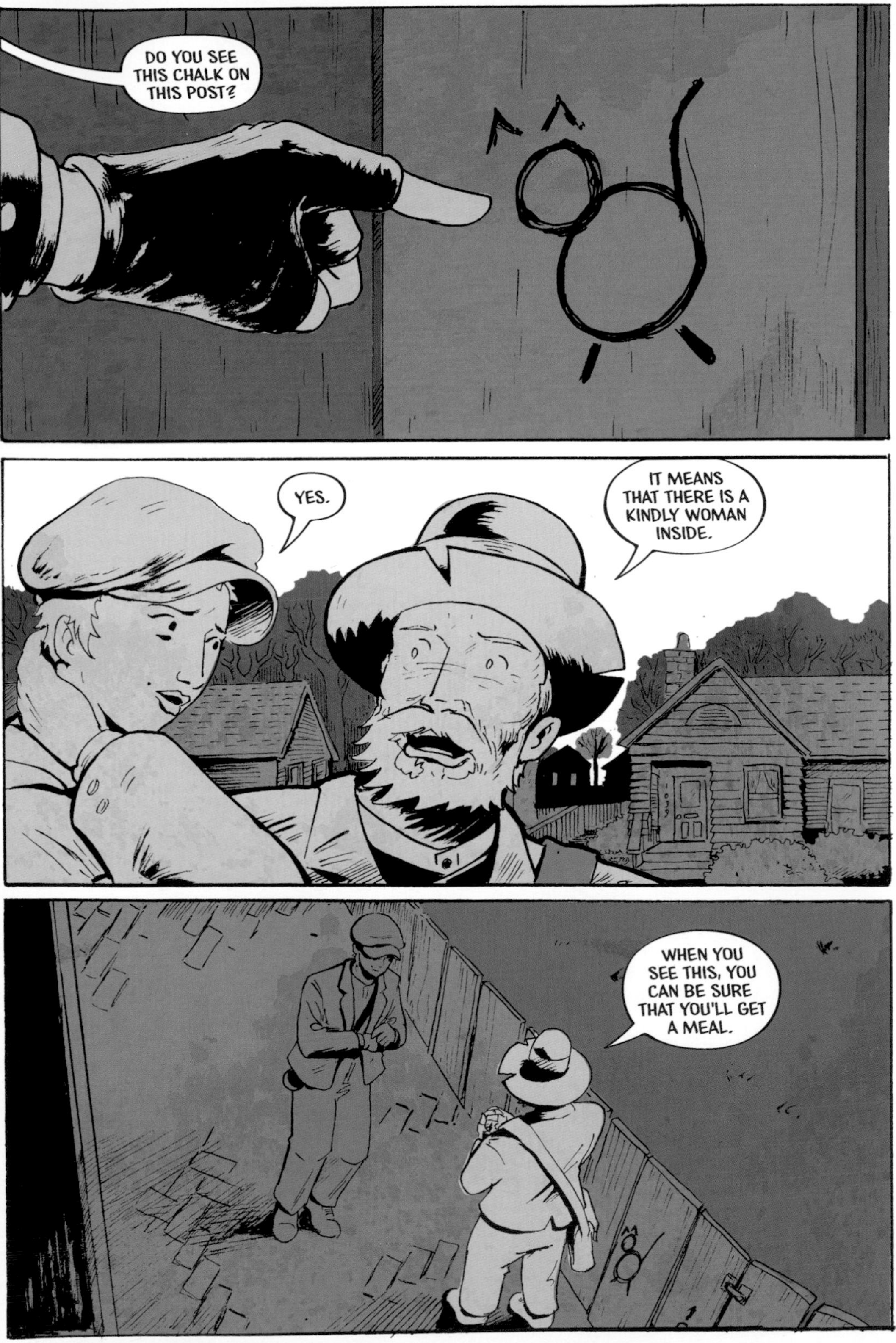
DO YOU SEE THIS CHALK ON THIS POST?
YES.
IT MEANS THAT THERE IS A KINDLY WOMAN INSIDE.
WHEN YOU SEE THIS, YOU CAN BE SURE THAT YOU'LL GET A MEAL.

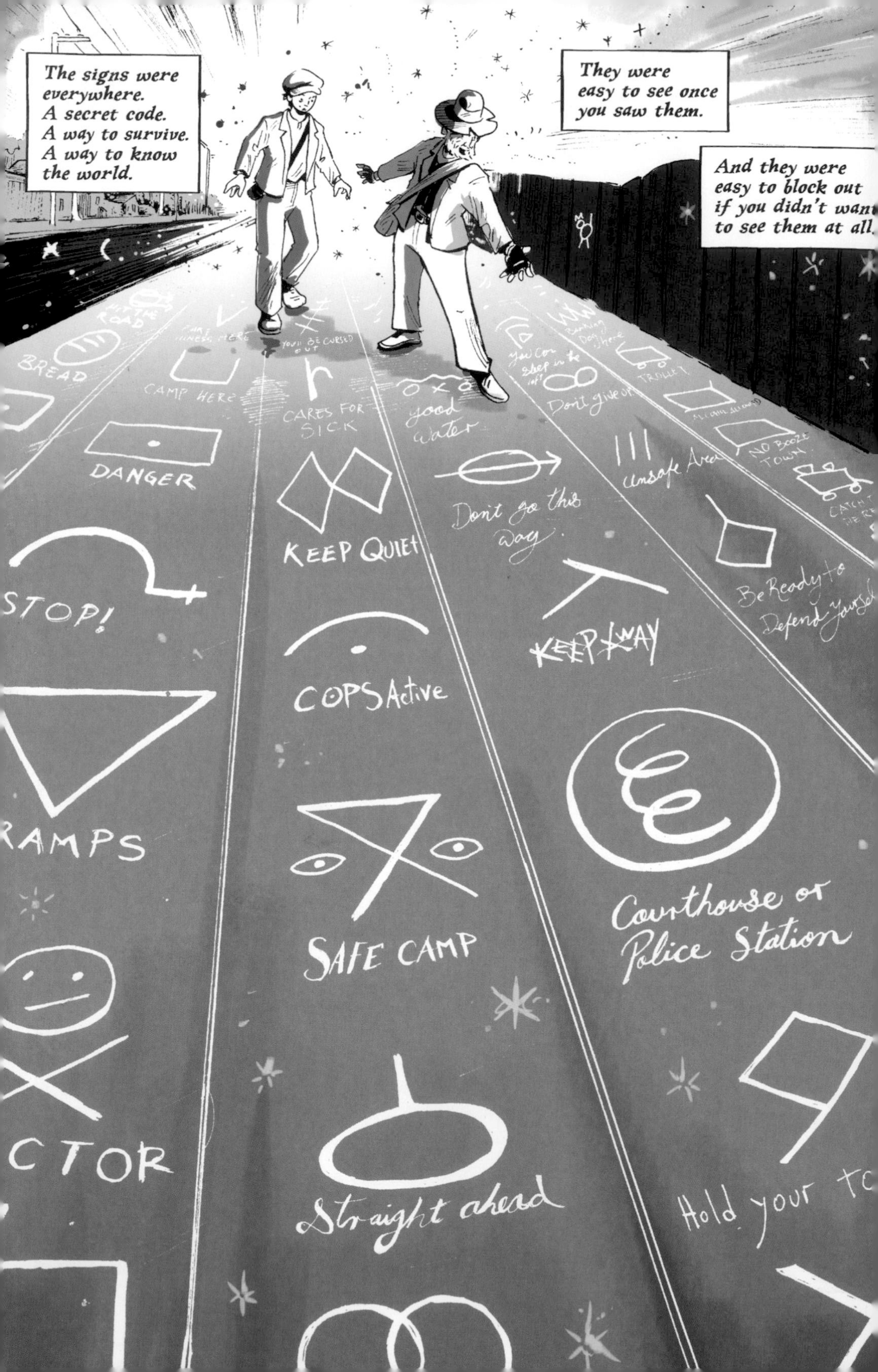

The signs were everywhere. A secret code. A way to survive. A way to know the world.
They were easy to see once you saw them.
And they were easy to block out if you didn't want to see them at all.
HIT THE ROAD
You'll be cursed out
BREAD
Barking Dog here
You can sleep in the loft
TROLLEY
CAMP HERE
CARES FOR SICK
good Water
Don't give up
NO BOOZE TOWN
DANGER
Unsafe Area
KEEP QUIET
Don't go this way
STOP!
Be Ready to Defend Yourself
KEEP AWAY
COPS Active
RAMPS
SAFE CAMP
Courthouse or Police Station
CTOR
Straight ahead
Hold your t

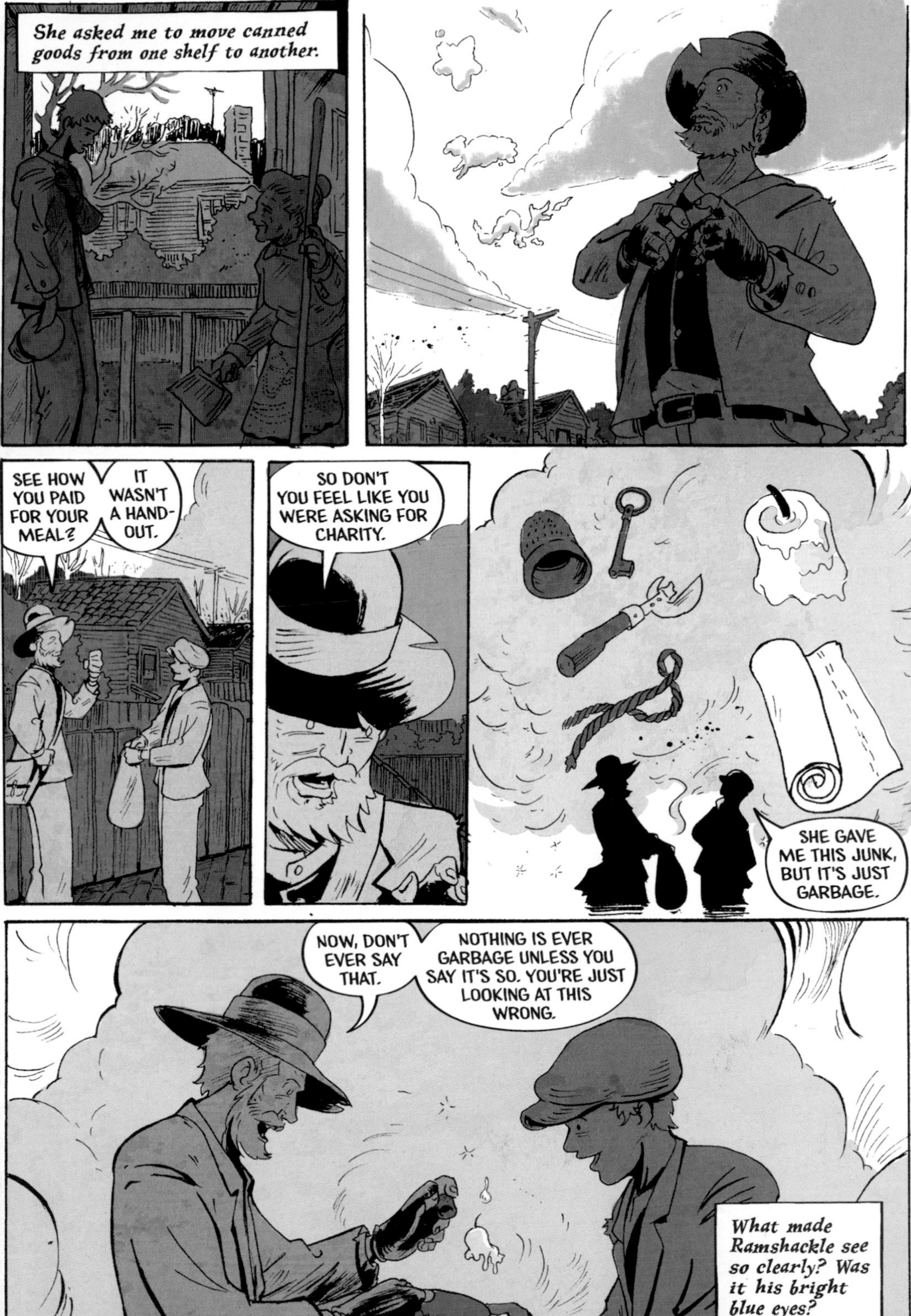
She asked me to move canned goods from one shelf to another.
SEE HOW YOU PAID FOR YOUR MEAL?
IT WASN'T A HAND-OUT.
SO DON'T YOU FEEL LIKE YOU WERE ASKING FOR CHARITY.
SHE GAVE ME THIS JUNK, BUT IT'S JUST GARBAGE.
NOW, DON'T EVER SAY THAT.
NOTHING IS EVER GARBAGE UNLESS YOU SAY IT'S SO. YOU'RE JUST LOOKING AT THIS WRONG.
What made Ramshackle see so clearly? Was it his bright blue eyes?

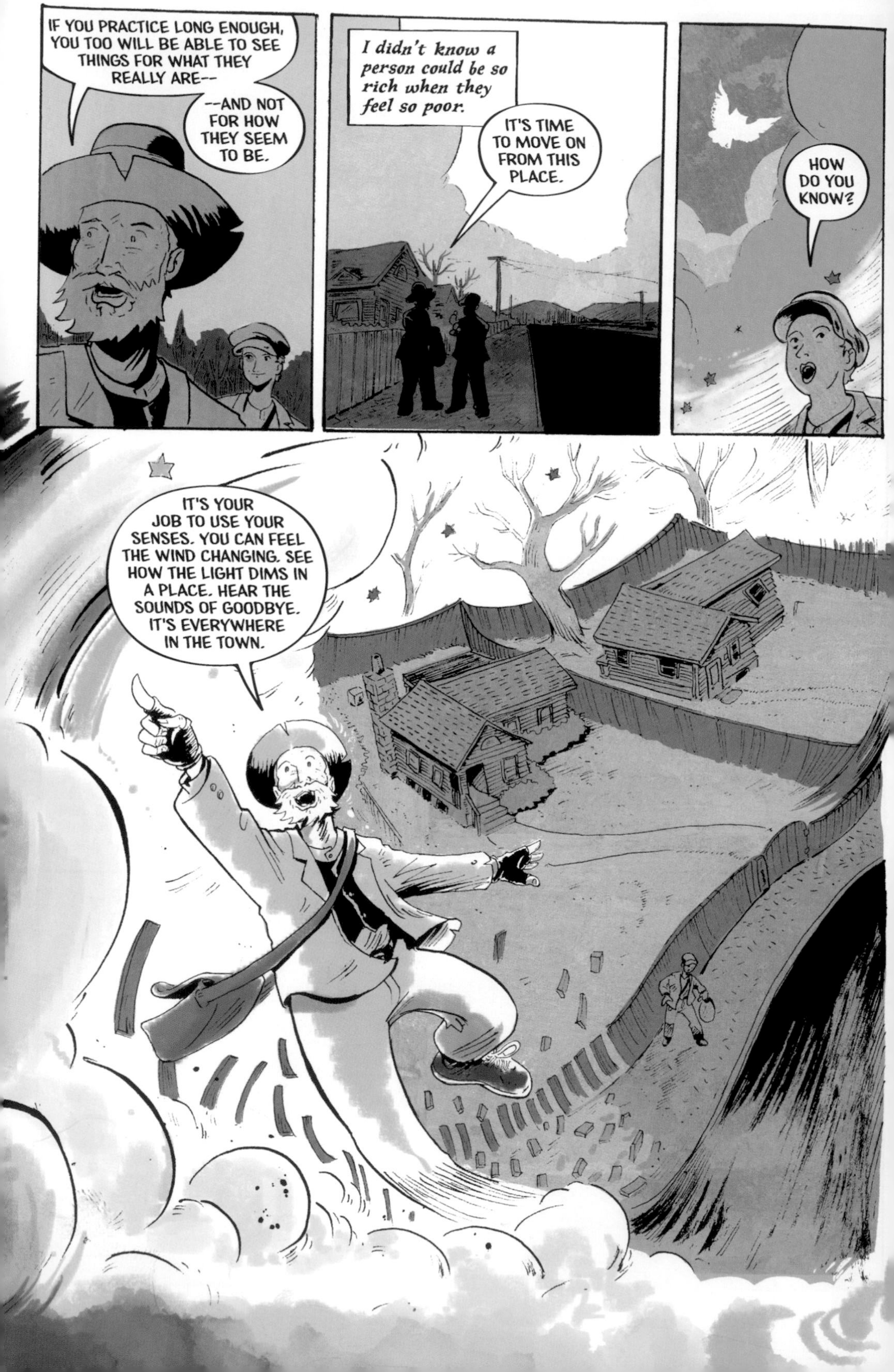
IF YOU PRACTICE LONG ENOUGH, YOU TOO WILL BE ABLE TO SEE THINGS FOR WHAT THEY REALLY ARE--
--AND NOT FOR HOW THEY SEEM TO BE.
I didn't know a person could be so rich when they feel so poor.
IT'S TIME TO MOVE ON FROM THIS PLACE.
HOW DO YOU KNOW?
IT'S YOUR JOB TO USE YOUR SENSES. YOU CAN FEEL THE WIND CHANGING. SEE HOW THE LIGHT DIMS IN A PLACE. HEAR THE SOUNDS OF GOODBYE. IT'S EVERYWHERE IN THE TOWN.

"IT'S THE SAME WHEN A FEELING HAS BEEN STUCK INSIDE OF YOU AND MADE YOU SICK WITH FEELING BAD. IT'LL TELL YOU, THAT WOUND, THAT IT IS TIME TO GO. OR ELSE THE FEELING WILL STAY THERE AND MAKE YOU FEEL EVEN WORSE."

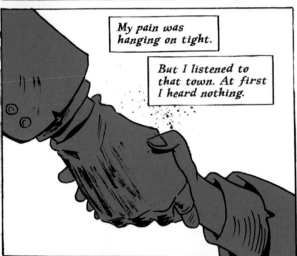

My pain was hanging on tight.

But I listened to that town. At first I heard nothing.

And then, I swear, I heard it saying goodbye.

Georgia.

YOU CAN HOP A TRAIN WHEN IT'S STOPPED, OR FIFTEEN MILES AN HOUR...

BUT ANY FASTER THAN TWENTY-FIVE AND YOU ARE INVITING A GRISLY DEATH.

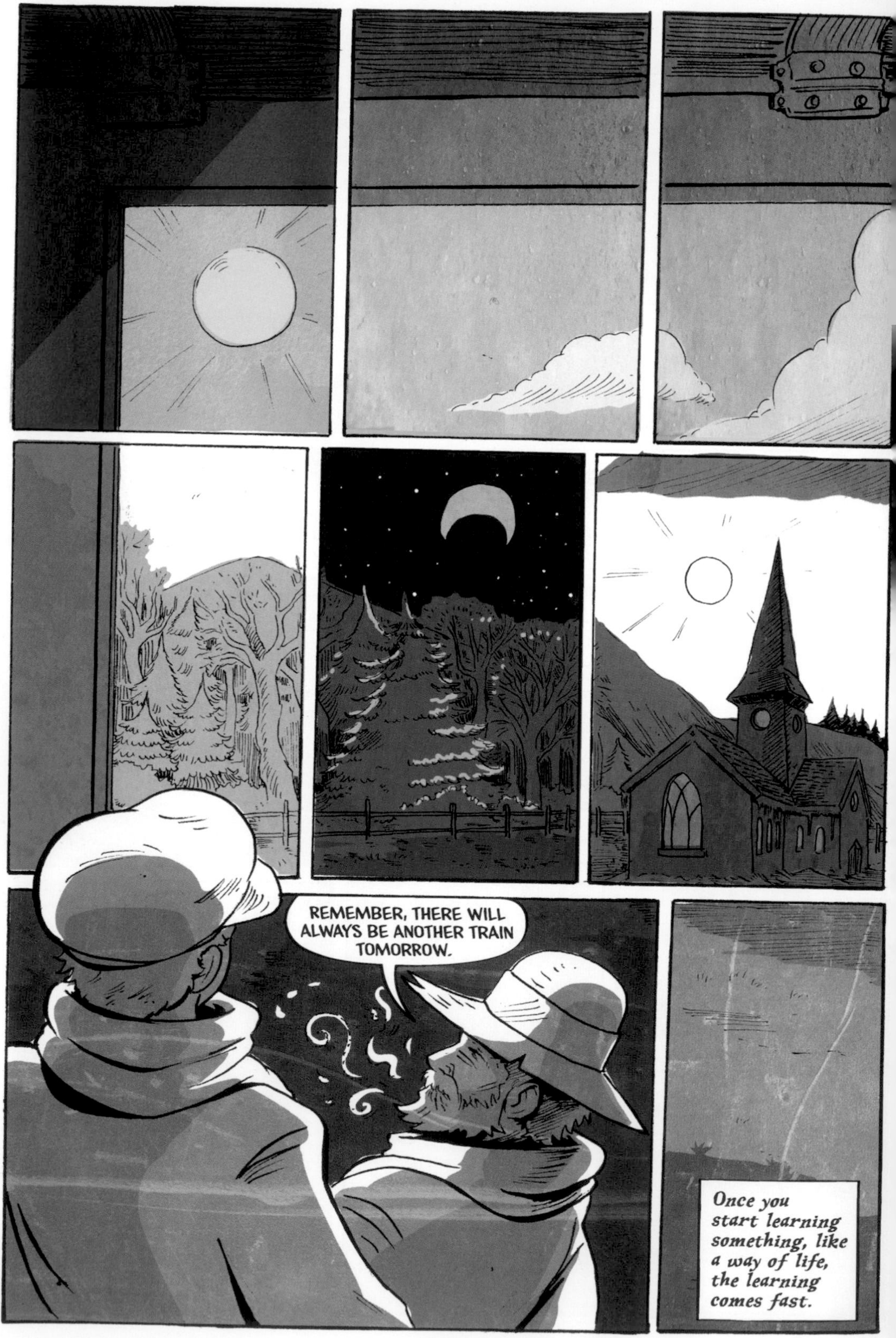
REMEMBER, THERE WILL ALWAYS BE ANOTHER TRAIN TOMORROW.
Once you start learning something, like a way of life, the learning comes fast.

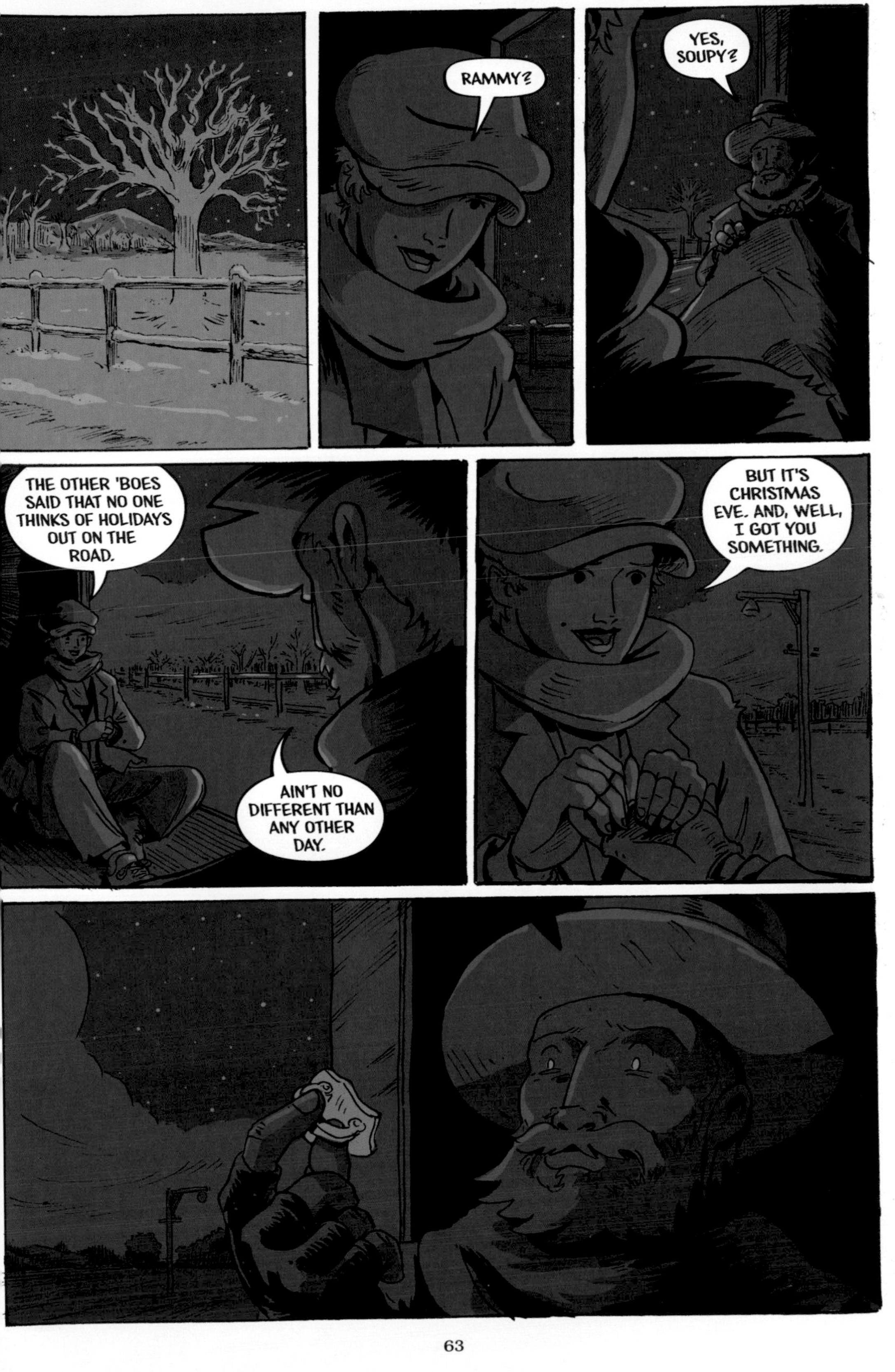
RAMMY?
YES, SOUPY?
THE OTHER 'BOES SAID THAT NO ONE THINKS OF HOLIDAYS OUT ON THE ROAD.
AIN'T NO DIFFERENT THAN ANY OTHER DAY.
BUT IT'S CHRISTMAS EVE. AND, WELL, I GOT YOU SOMETHING.

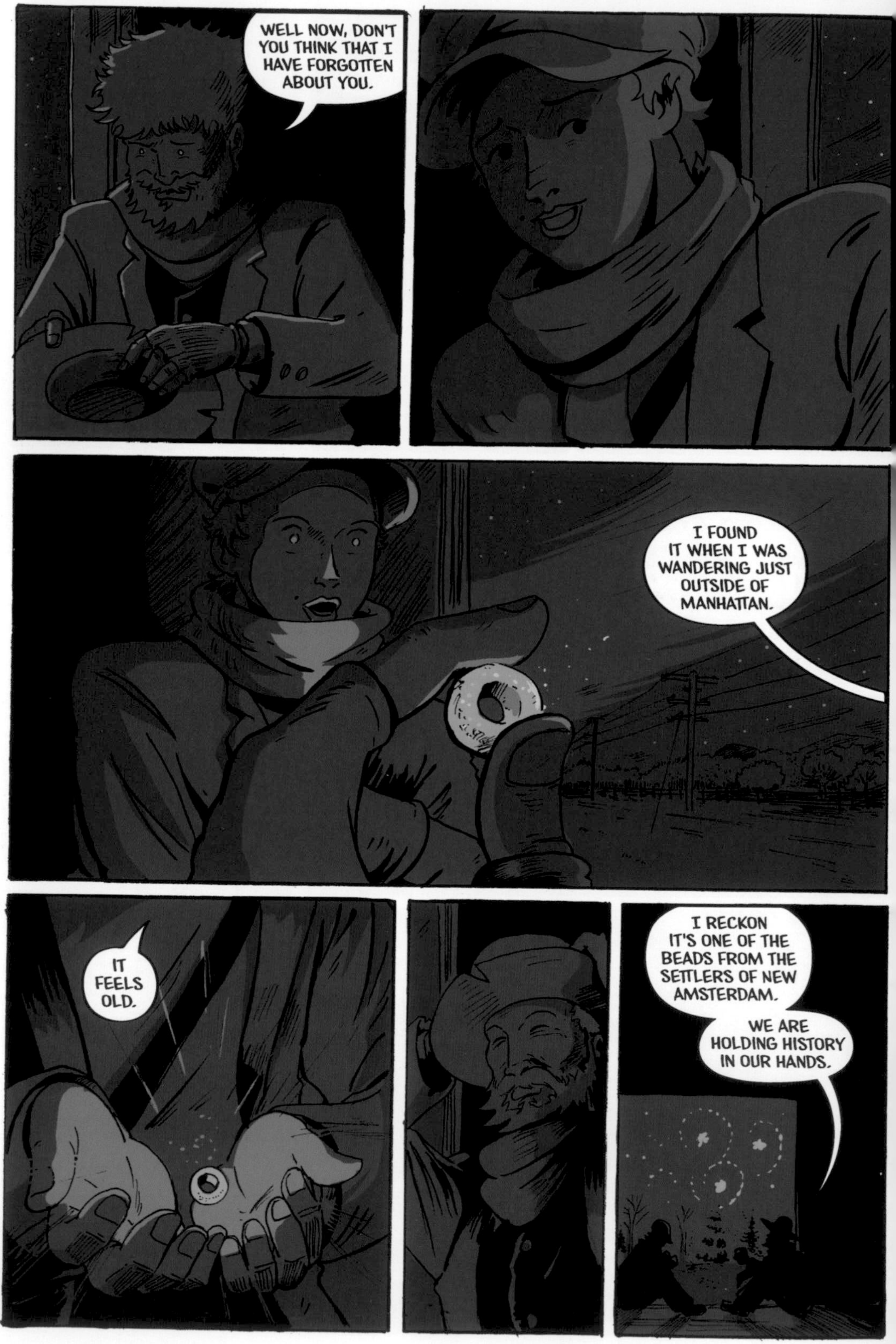
WELL NOW, DON'T YOU THINK THAT I HAVE FORGOTTEN ABOUT YOU.
I FOUND IT WHEN I WAS WANDERING JUST OUTSIDE OF MANHATTAN.
IT FEELS OLD.
I RECKON IT'S ONE OF THE BEADS FROM THE SETTLERS OF NEW AMSTERDAM.
WE ARE HOLDING HISTORY IN OUR HANDS.

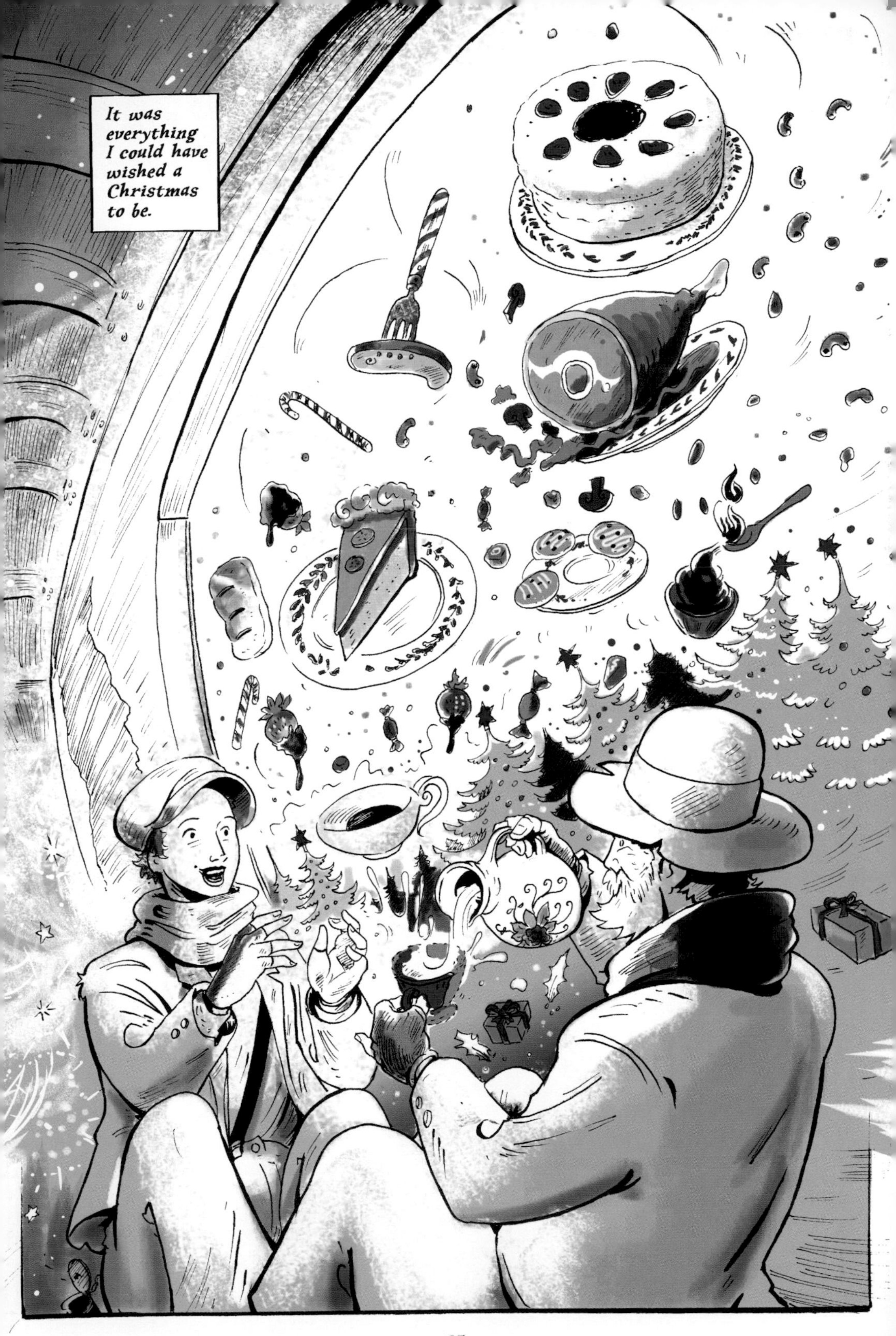
It was everything I could have wished a Christmas to be.

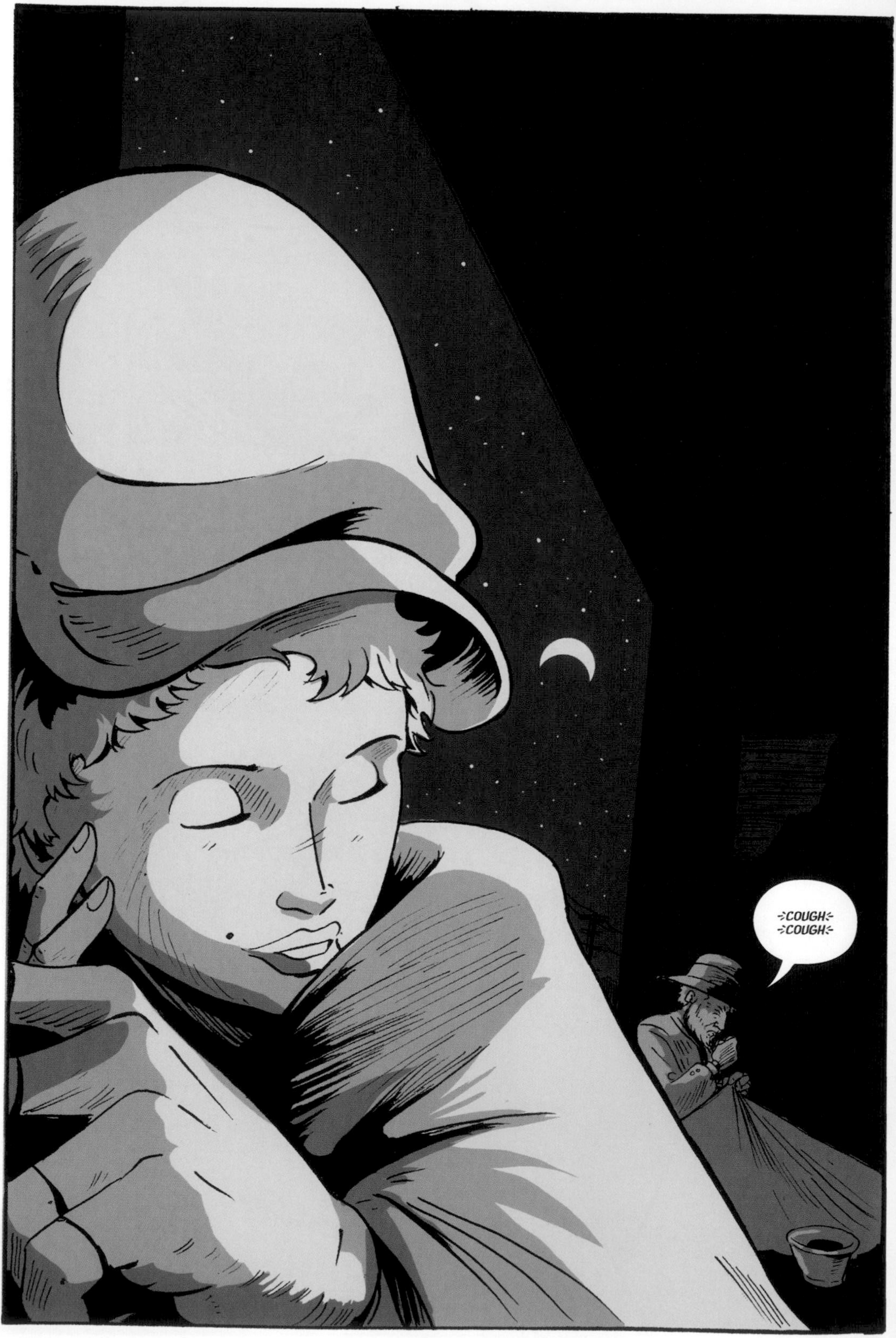
COUGH COUGH

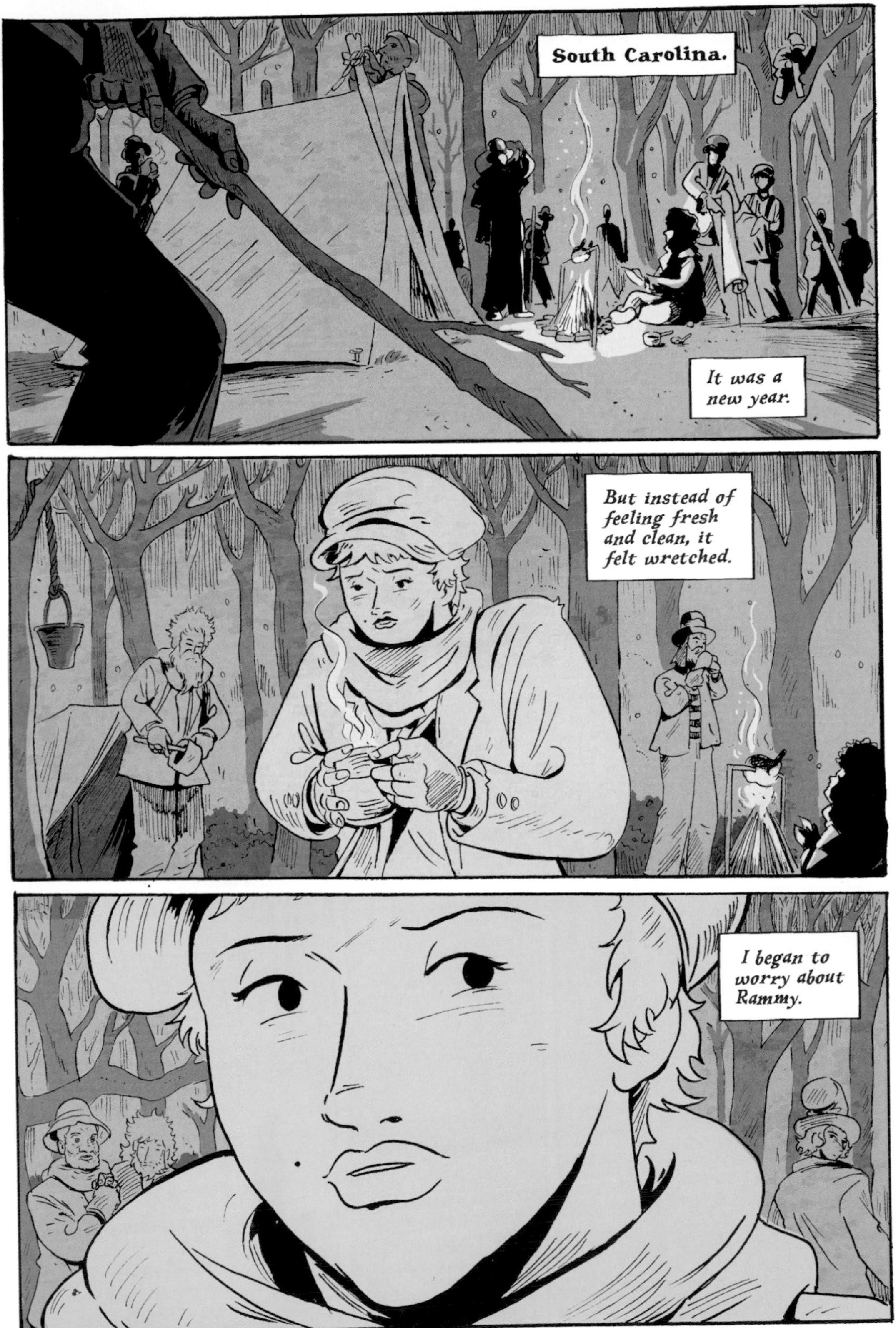
South Carolina.
It was a new year.
But instead of feeling fresh and clean, it felt wretched.
I began to worry about Rammy.

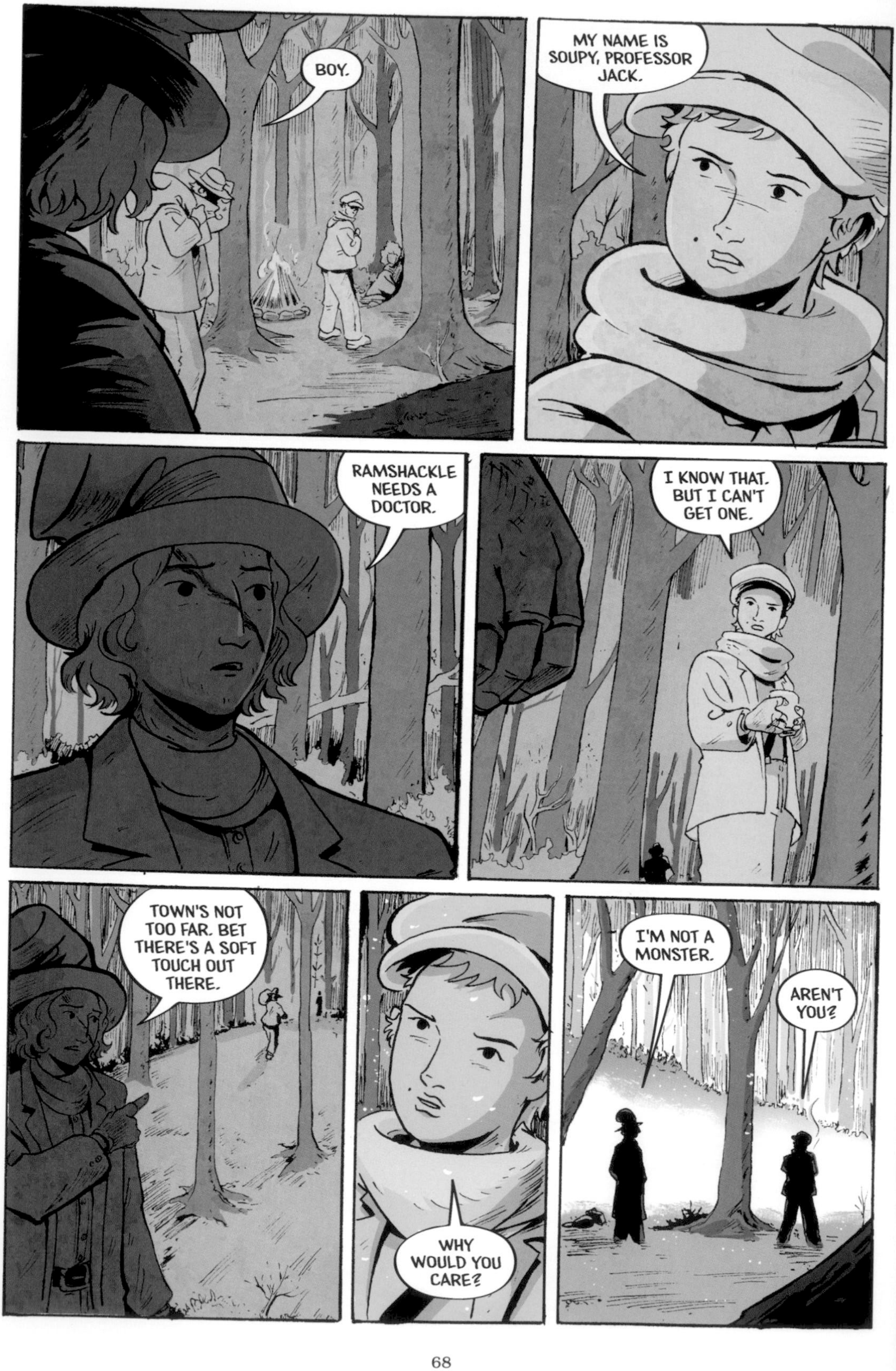
BOY.
MY NAME IS SOUPY, PROFESSOR JACK.
RAMSHACKLE NEEDS A DOCTOR.
I KNOW THAT. BUT I CAN'T GET ONE.
TOWN'S NOT TOO FAR. BET THERE'S A SOFT TOUCH OUT THERE.
WHY WOULD YOU CARE?
I'M NOT A MONSTER.
AREN'T YOU?

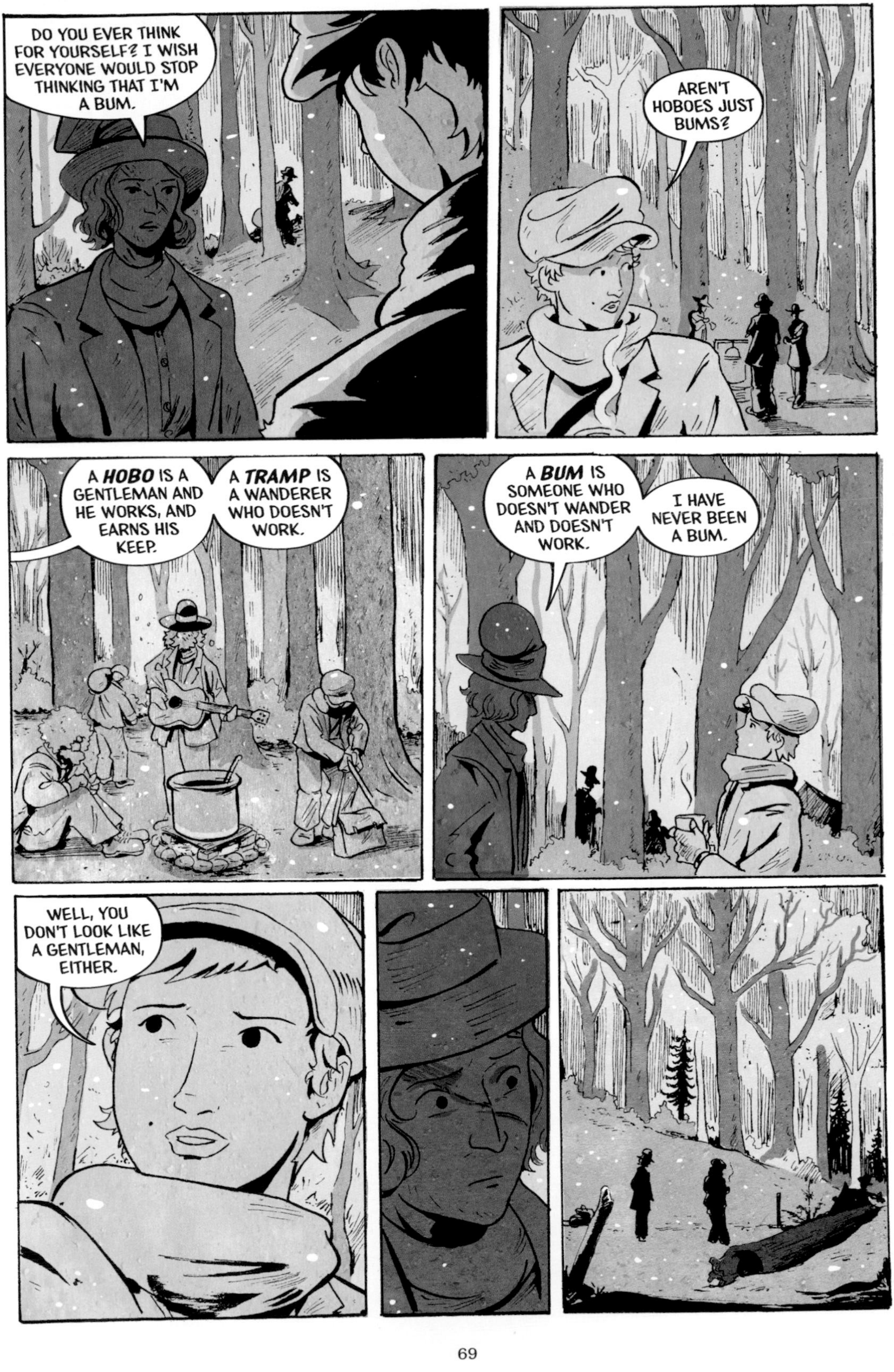
DO YOU EVER THINK FOR YOURSELF? I WISH EVERYONE WOULD STOP THINKING THAT I'M A BUM.
AREN'T HOBOES JUST BUMS?
A HOBO IS A GENTLEMAN AND HE WORKS, AND EARNS HIS KEEP.
A TRAMP IS A WANDERER WHO DOESN'T WORK.
A BUM IS SOMEONE WHO DOESN'T WANDER AND DOESN'T WORK.
I HAVE NEVER BEEN A BUM.
WELL, YOU DON'T LOOK LIKE A GENTLEMAN, EITHER.

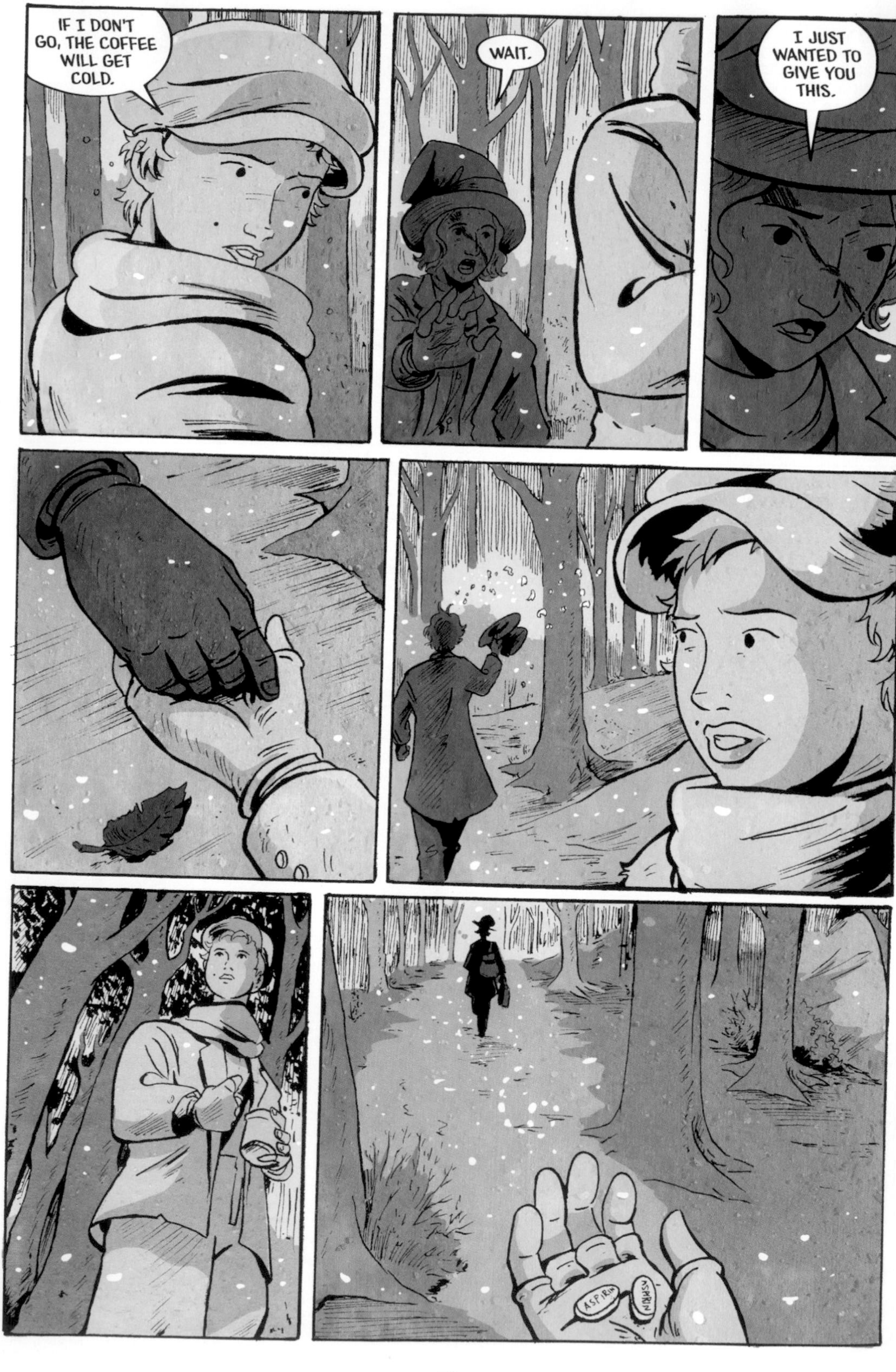
IF I DON'T GO, THE COFFEE WILL GET COLD.
WAIT.
I JUST WANTED TO GIVE YOU THIS.
ASPIRIN
ASPIRIN

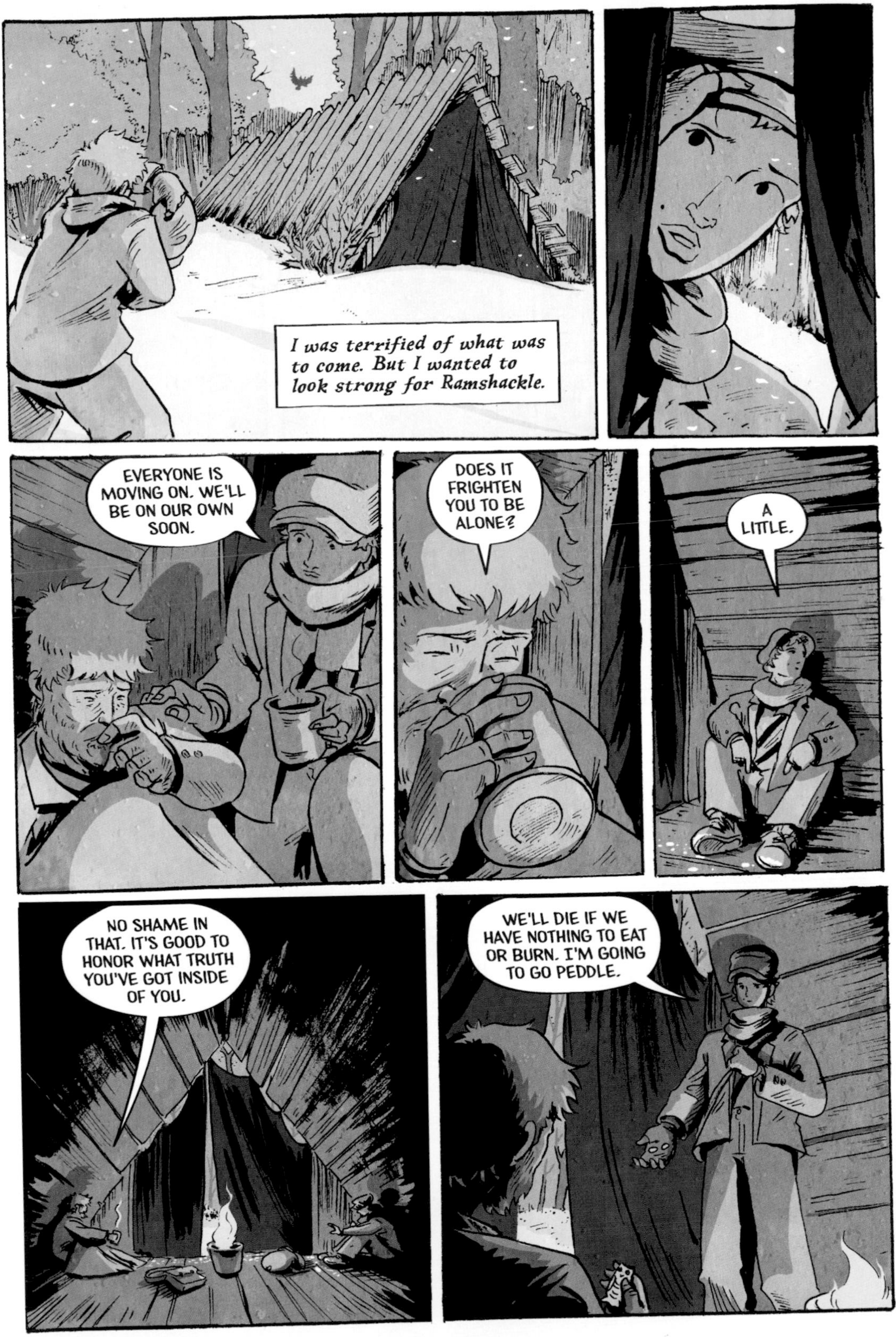
I was terrified of what was to come. But I wanted to look strong for Ramshackle.
EVERYONE IS MOVING ON. WE'LL BE ON OUR OWN SOON.
DOES IT FRIGHTEN YOU TO BE ALONE?
A LITTLE.
NO SHAME IN THAT. IT'S GOOD TO HONOR WHAT TRUTH YOU'VE GOT INSIDE OF YOU.
WE'LL DIE IF WE HAVE NOTHING TO EAT OR BURN. I'M GOING TO GO PEDDLE.

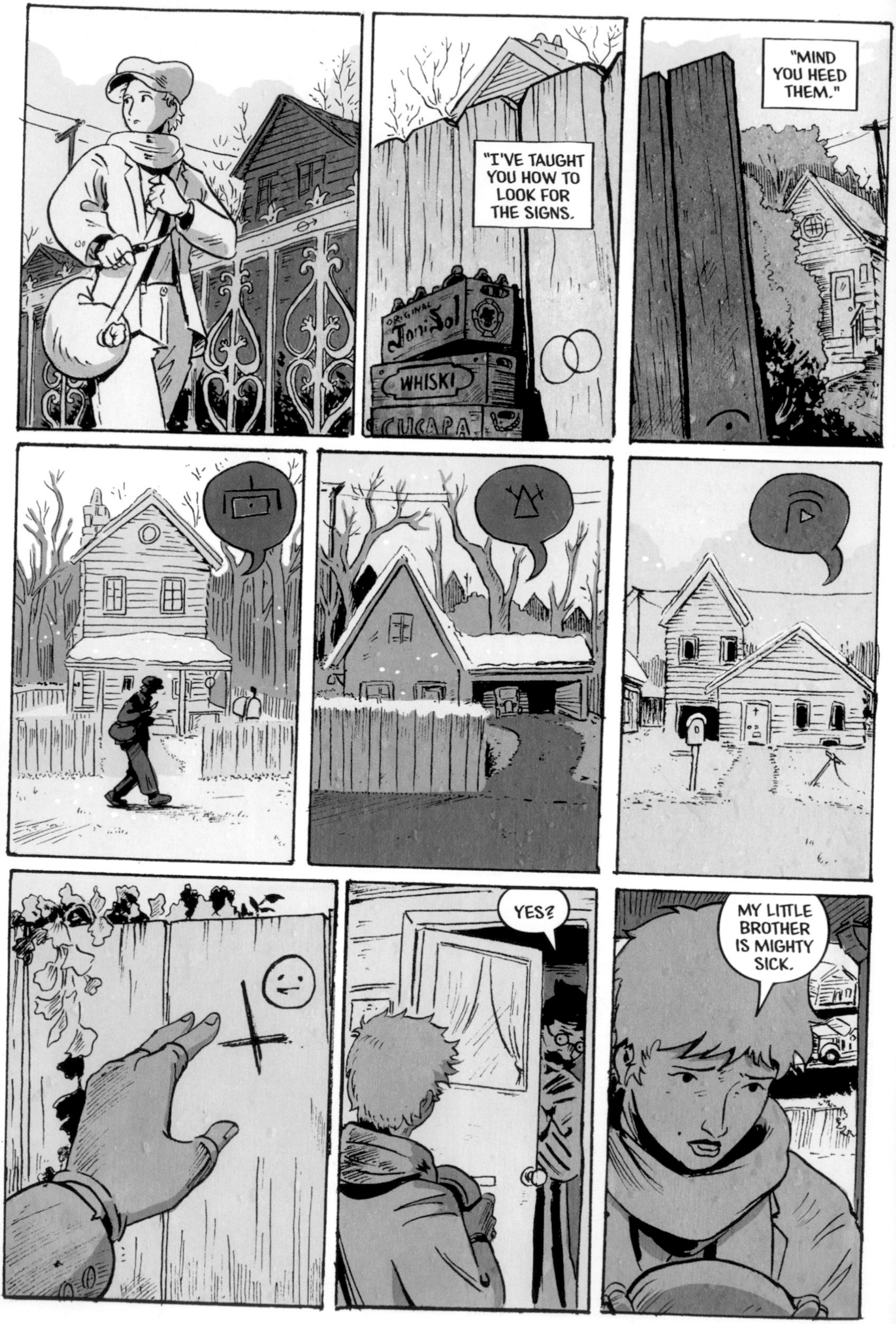
"I'VE TAUGHT YOU HOW TO LOOK FOR THE SIGNS.
ORIGINAL
JoniSol
WHISKI
CUCAPA
"MIND YOU HEED THEM."
YES?
MY LITTLE BROTHER IS MIGHTY SICK.

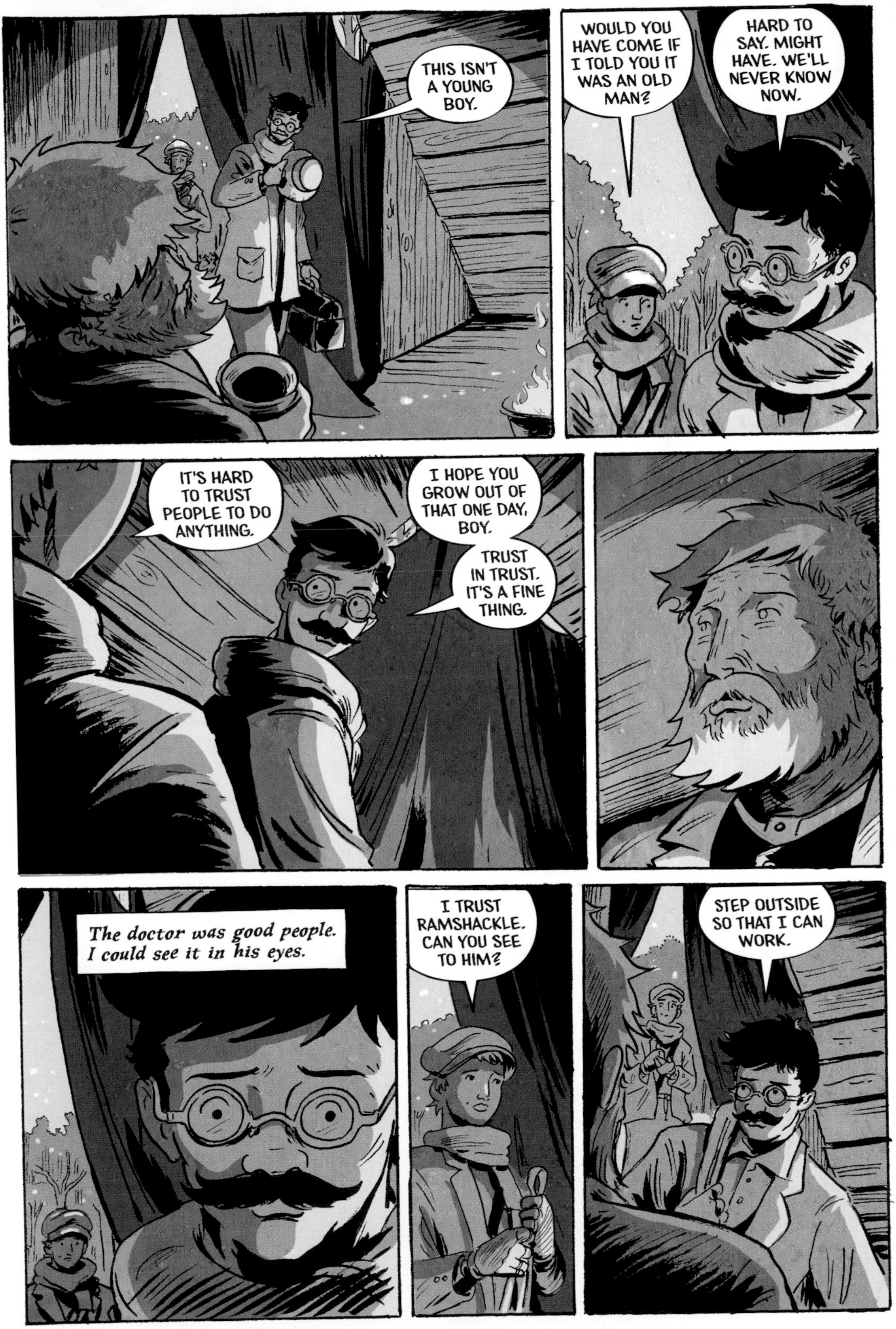
THIS ISN'T A YOUNG BOY.
WOULD YOU HAVE COME IF I TOLD YOU IT WAS AN OLD MAN?
HARD TO SAY. MIGHT HAVE. WE'LL NEVER KNOW NOW.
IT'S HARD TO TRUST PEOPLE TO DO ANYTHING.
I HOPE YOU GROW OUT OF THAT ONE DAY, BOY.
TRUST IN TRUST. IT'S A FINE THING.
The doctor was good people. I could see it in his eyes.
I TRUST RAMSHACKLE. CAN YOU SEE TO HIM?
STEP OUTSIDE SO THAT I CAN WORK.

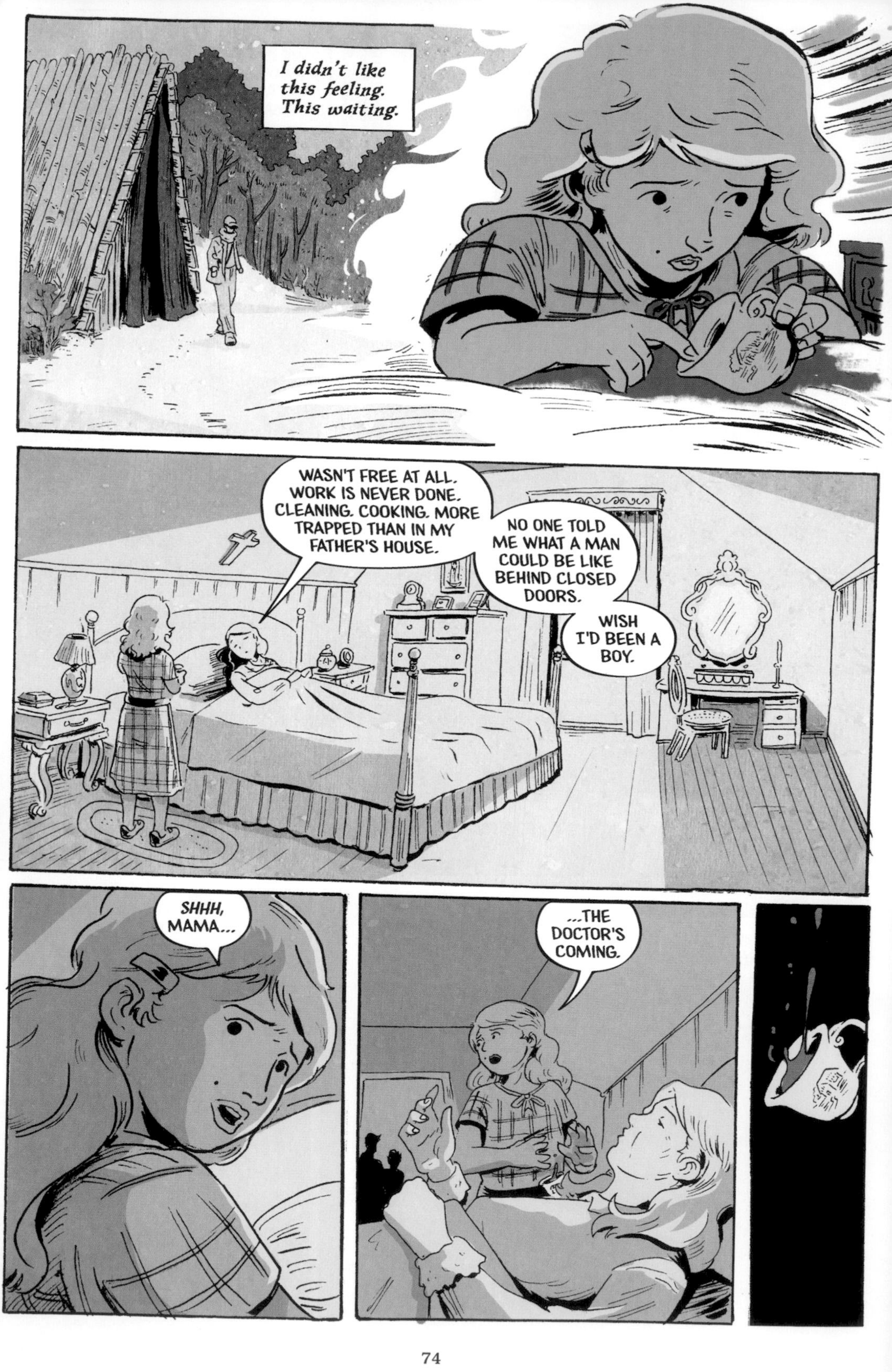
I didn't like this feeling. This waiting.
WASN'T FREE AT ALL. WORK IS NEVER DONE. CLEANING. COOKING. MORE TRAPPED THAN IN MY FATHER'S HOUSE.
NO ONE TOLD ME WHAT A MAN COULD BE LIKE BEHIND CLOSED DOORS.
WISH I'D BEEN A BOY.
SHHH, MAMA...
...THE DOCTOR'S COMING.

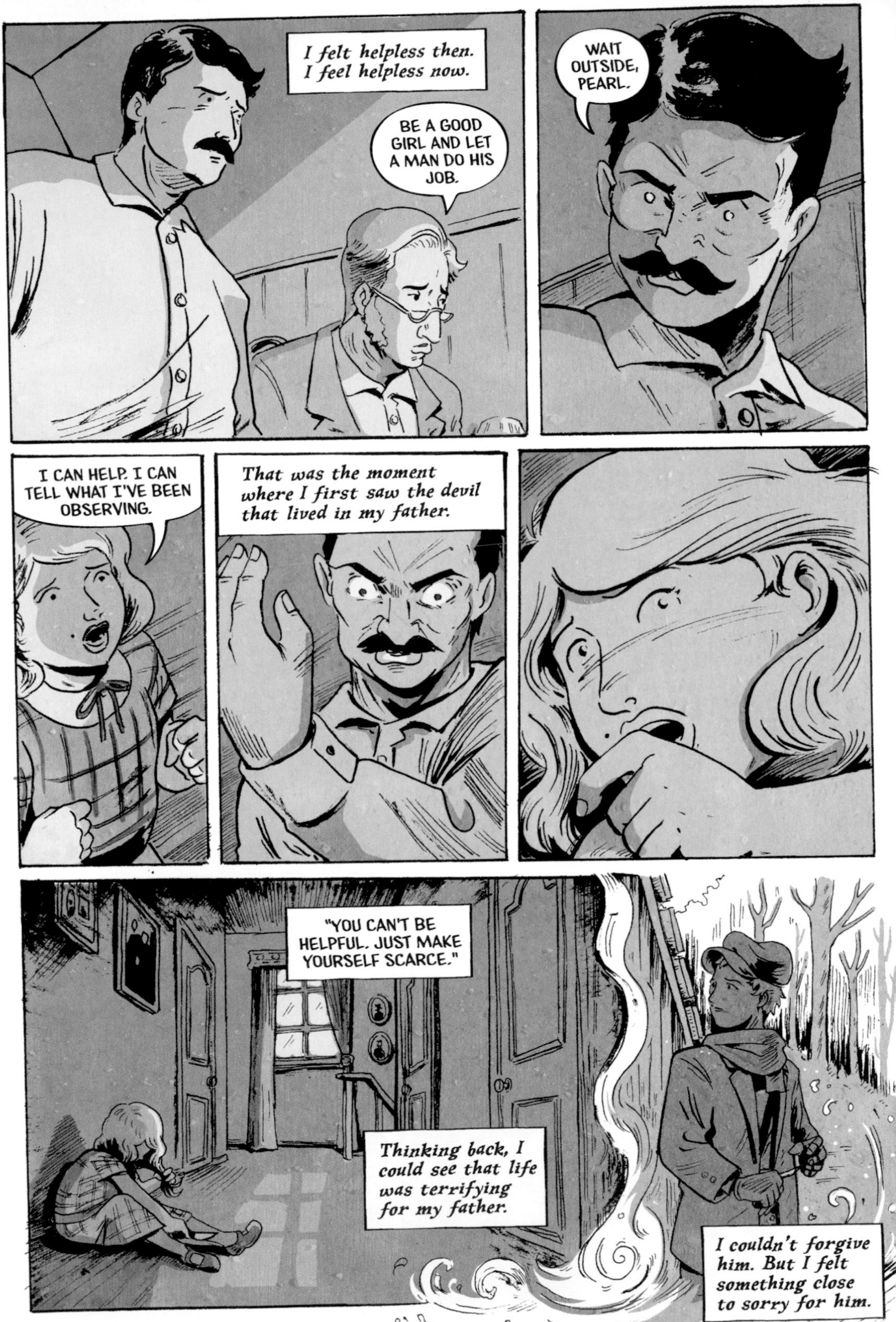
I felt helpless then. I feel helpless now.
BE A GOOD GIRL AND LET A MAN DO HIS JOB.
WAIT OUTSIDE, PEARL.
I CAN HELP. I CAN TELL WHAT I'VE BEEN OBSERVING.
That was the moment where I first saw the devil that lived in my father.
"YOU CAN'T BE HELPFUL. JUST MAKE YOURSELF SCARCE."
Thinking back, I could see that life was terrifying for my father.
I couldn't forgive him. But I felt something close to sorry for him.

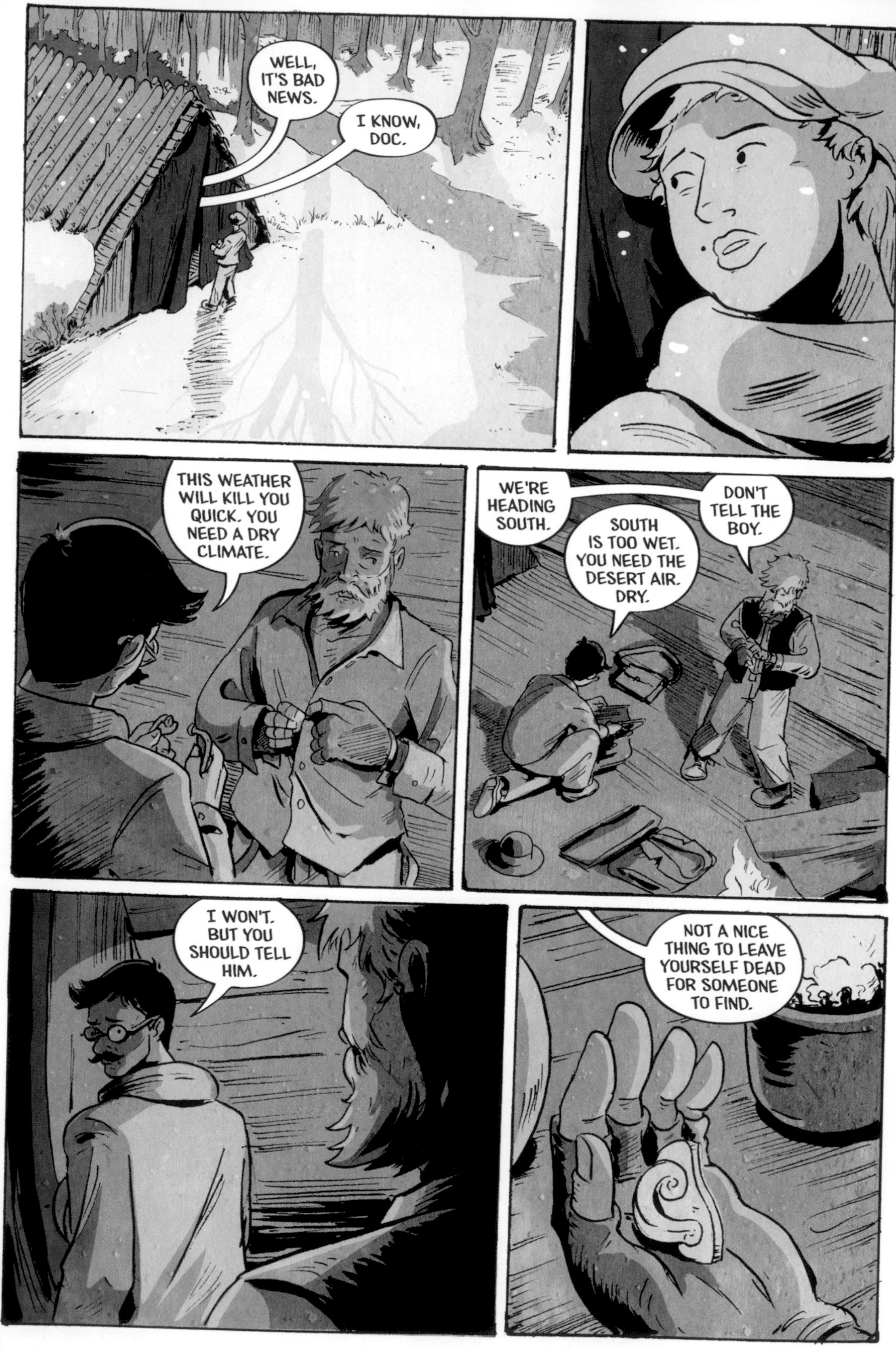
WELL, IT'S BAD NEWS.
I KNOW, DOC.
THIS WEATHER WILL KILL YOU QUICK. YOU NEED A DRY CLIMATE.
WE'RE HEADING SOUTH.
DON'T TELL THE BOY.
SOUTH IS TOO WET. YOU NEED THE DESERT AIR. DRY.
I WON'T. BUT YOU SHOULD TELL HIM.
NOT A NICE THING TO LEAVE YOURSELF DEAD FOR SOMEONE TO FIND.

HE'S BROKEN. WON'T TELL ME HIS STORY, BUT IT'S A SAD ONE, THAT'S FOR SURE.

GOTTA GO SLOW. HE'S SKITTISH. HE WON'T LAST WITHOUT SOMEONE LOOKING AFTER HIM.

MY COUSIN HAS A SANATORIUM IN LOS ANGELES.

I DON'T TAKE CHARITY. I'LL PAY FOR MY BED.

I'VE GOT SOME TUCKED AWAY.

IF THAT'S TRUE, YOU SHOULDN'T BE LIVING ON THE ROAD.

THIS LIFE IS TOO HARD FOR SOMEONE IN YOUR CONDITION.

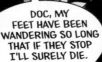

DOC, MY FEET HAVE BEEN WANDERING SO LONG THAT IF THEY STOP I'LL SURELY DIE.

STONY BROOK RETREAT. I'LL WRITE TO OPEN UP A BED FOR YOU. YOU CAN ARRANGE PAYMENT WITH HIM. THAT'S YOUR BUSINESS.

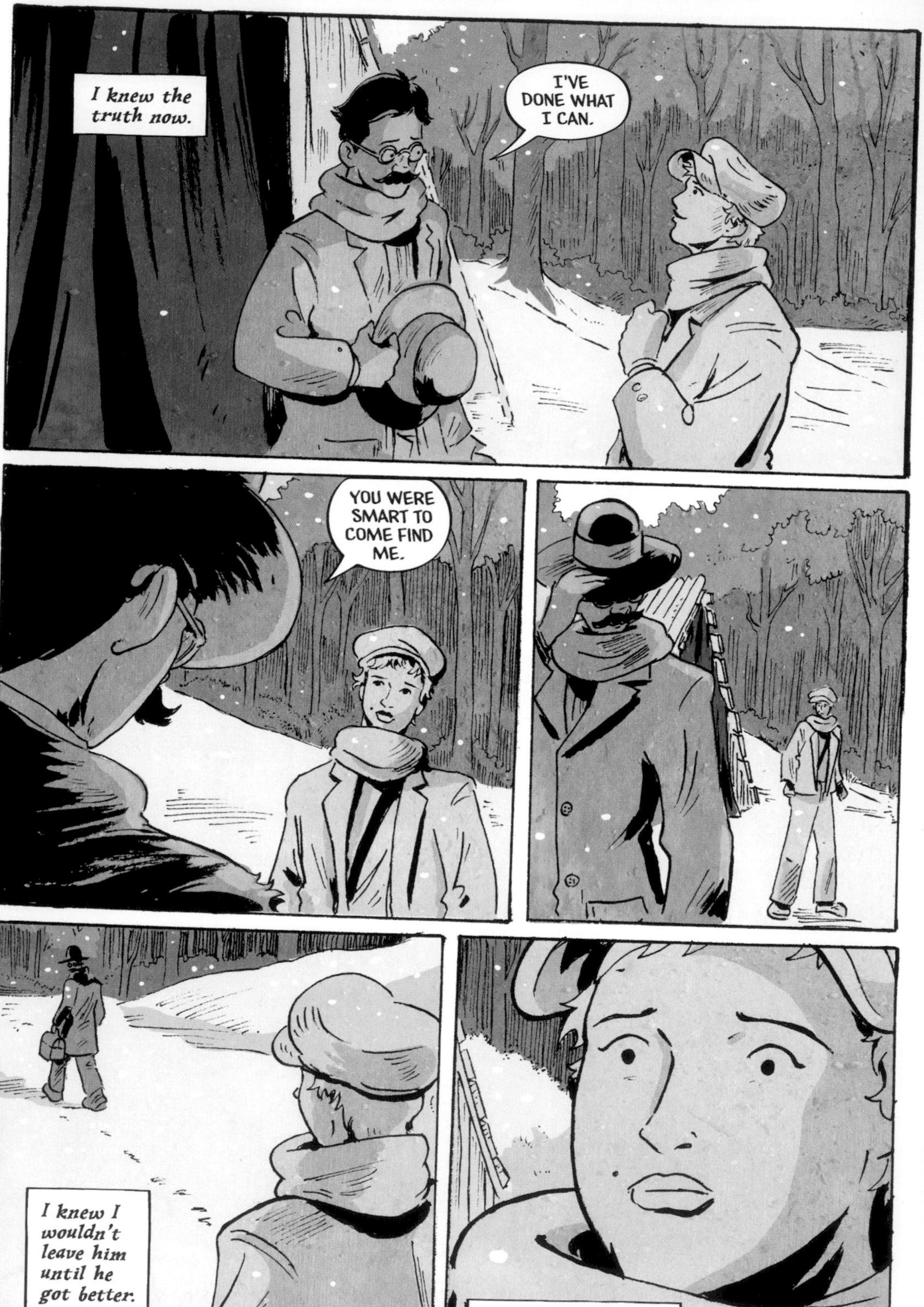
I knew the truth now.
I'VE DONE WHAT I CAN.
YOU WERE SMART TO COME FIND ME.
I knew I wouldn't leave him until he got better.
I would go wherever Ramshackle went.

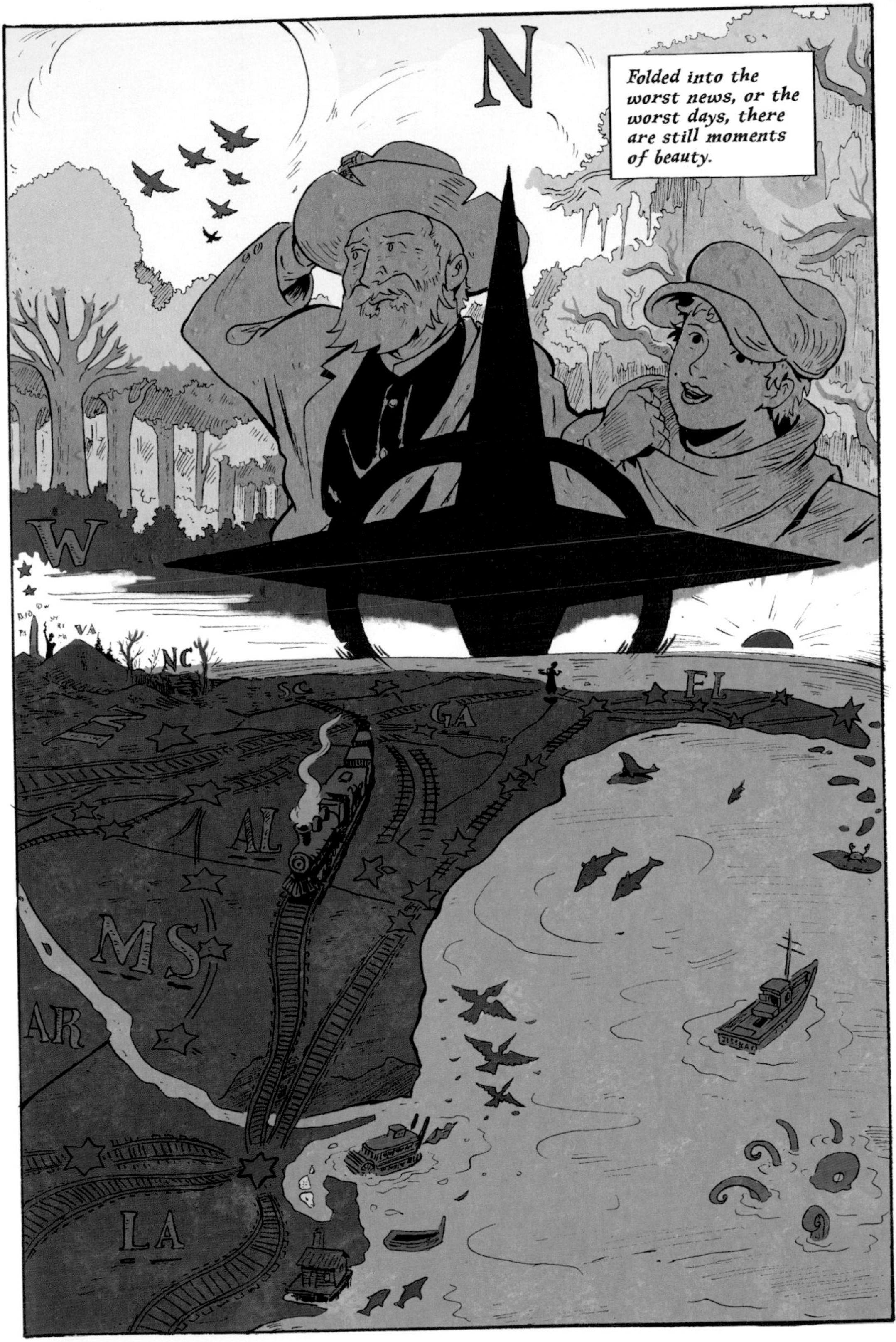
N
Folded into the worst news, or the worst days, there are still moments of beauty.
W
VA
NC
SC
GA
FL
TN
AL
MS
AR
LA

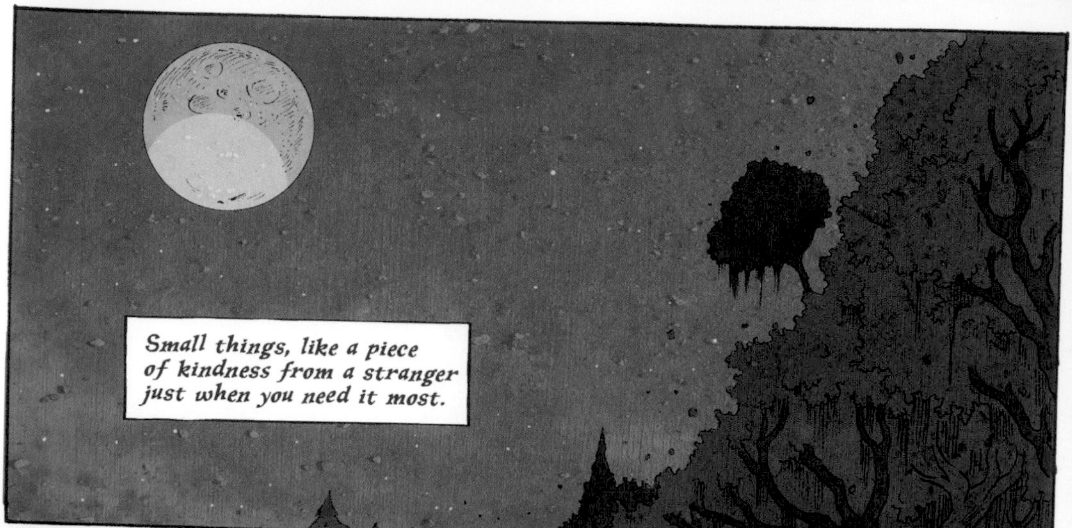
Small things, like a piece of kindness from a stranger just when you need it most.

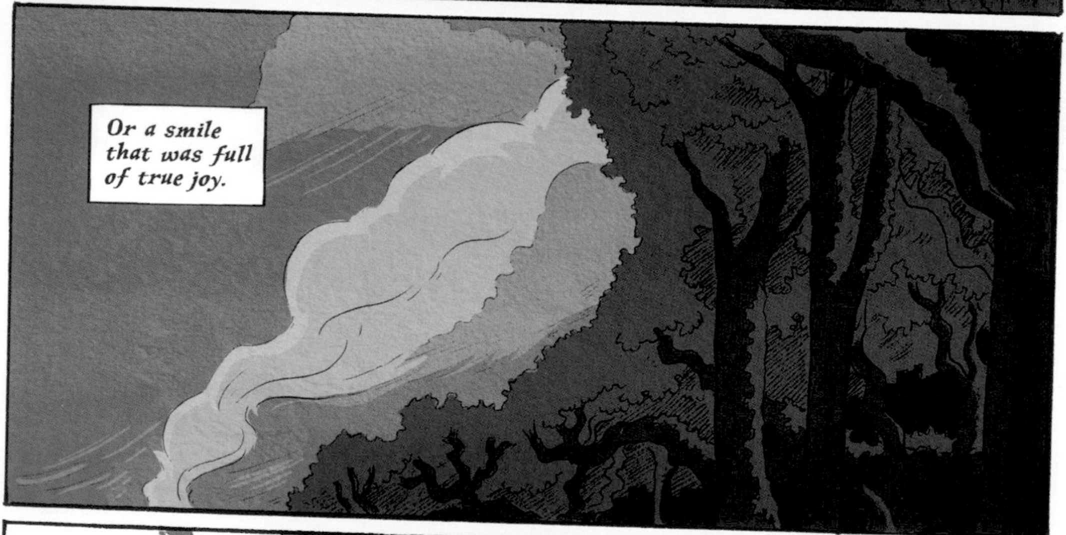
Or a smile that was full of true joy.

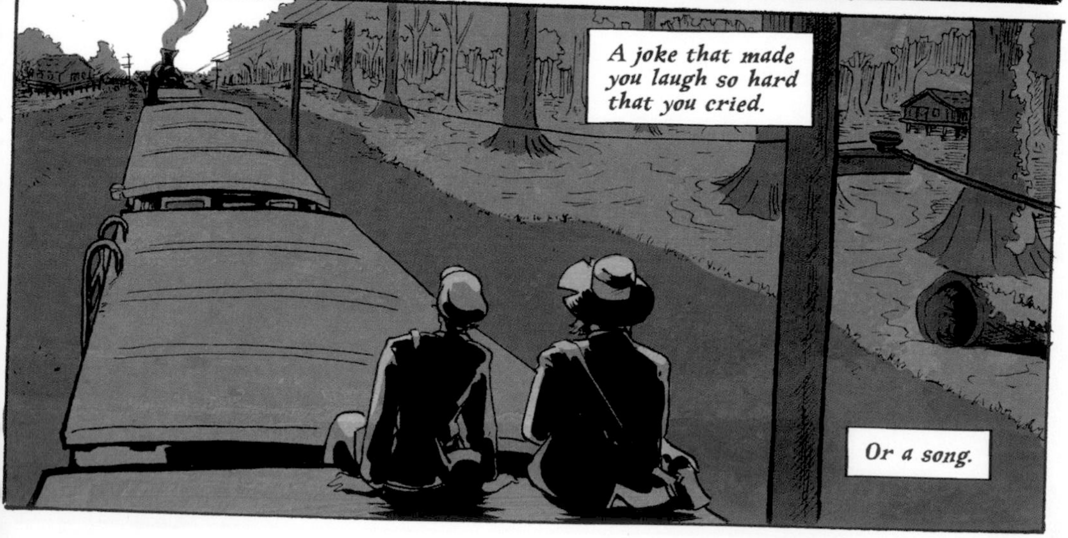
A joke that made you laugh so hard that you cried.
Or a song.

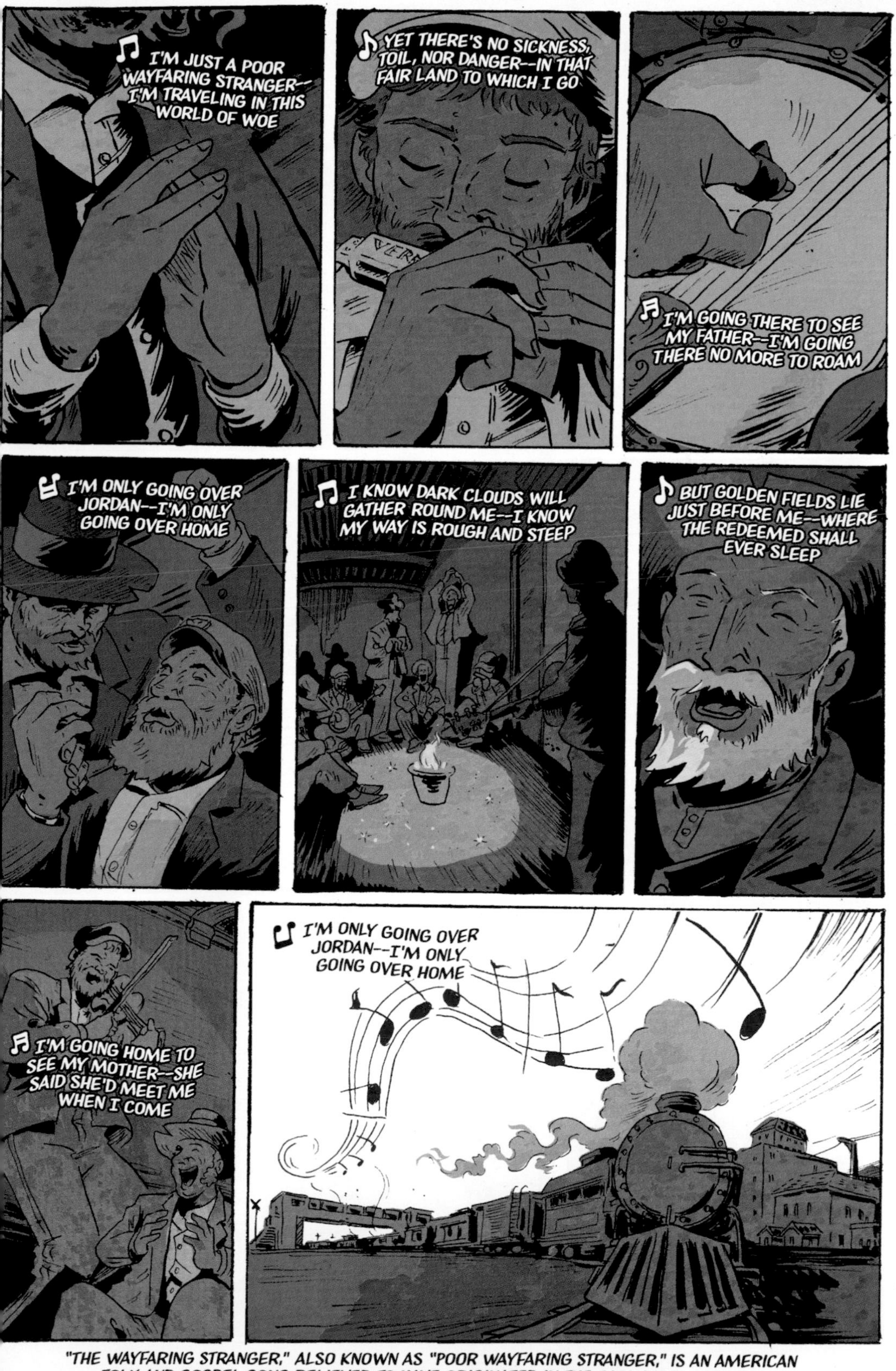
I'M JUST A POOR WAYFARING STRANGER--I'M TRAVELING IN THIS WORLD OF WOE
YET THERE'S NO SICKNESS, TOIL, NOR DANGER--IN THAT FAIR LAND TO WHICH I GO
I'M GOING THERE TO SEE MY FATHER--I'M GOING THERE NO MORE TO ROAM
I'M ONLY GOING OVER JORDAN--I'M ONLY GOING OVER HOME
I KNOW DARK CLOUDS WILL GATHER ROUND ME--I KNOW MY WAY IS ROUGH AND STEEP
BUT GOLDEN FIELDS LIE JUST BEFORE ME--WHERE THE REDEEMED SHALL EVER SLEEP
I'M GOING HOME TO SEE MY MOTHER--SHE SAID SHE'D MEET ME WHEN I COME
I'M ONLY GOING OVER JORDAN--I'M ONLY GOING OVER HOME

"THE WAYFARING STRANGER," ALSO KNOWN AS "POOR WAYFARING STRANGER," IS AN AMERICAN FOLK AND GOSPEL SONG BELIEVED TO HAVE ORIGINATED IN THE EARLY 19TH CENTURY.

I think that back then all the living parts of Rammy were attaching themselves to me.

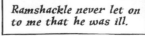

Ramshackle never let on to me that he was ill.

We just concentrated on the basic things that got us from place to place--

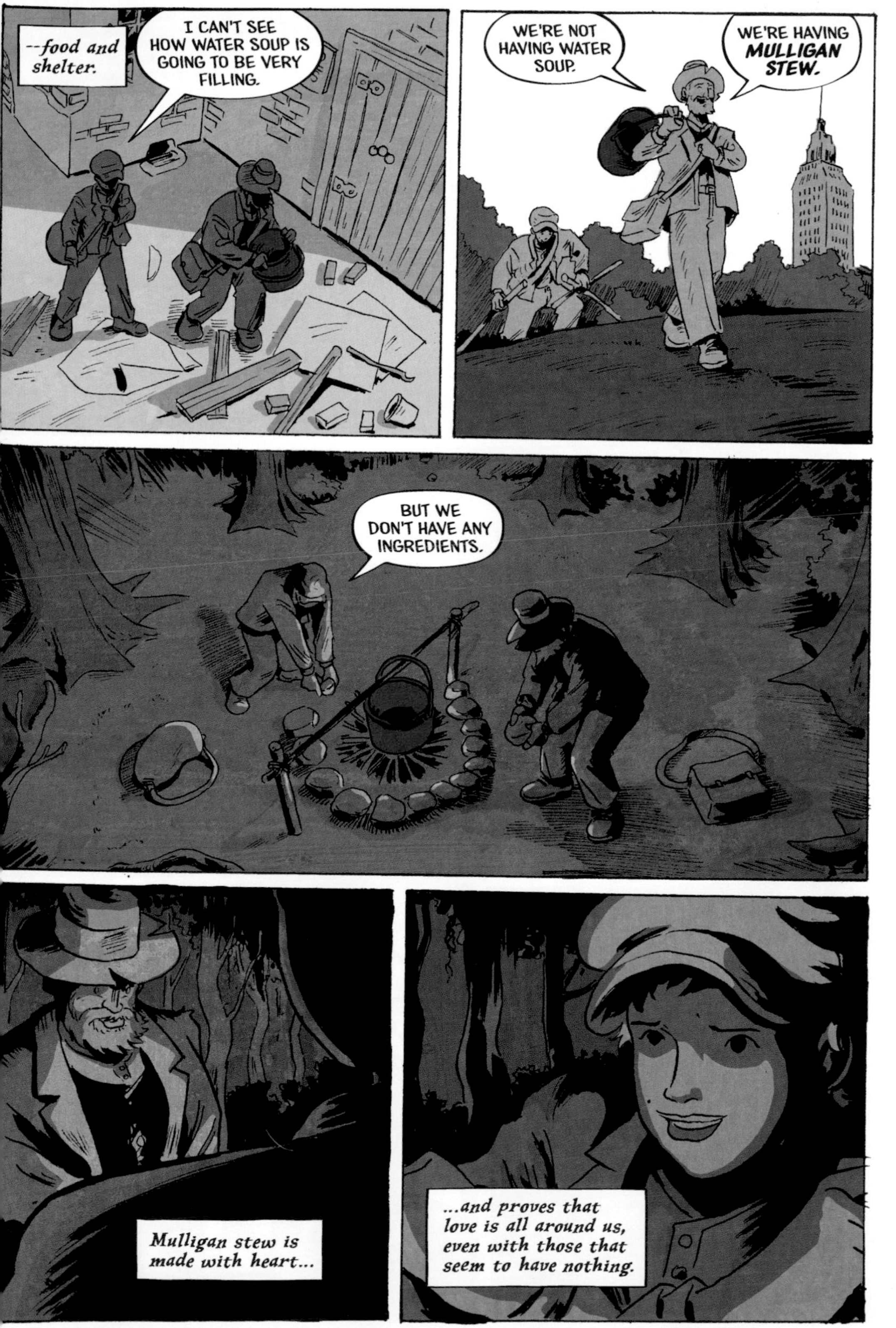
--food and shelter.
I CAN'T SEE HOW WATER SOUP IS GOING TO BE VERY FILLING.
WE'RE NOT HAVING WATER SOUP.
WE'RE HAVING MULLIGAN STEW.
BUT WE DON'T HAVE ANY INGREDIENTS.
Mulligan stew is made with heart...
...and proves that love is all around us, even with those that seem to have nothing.

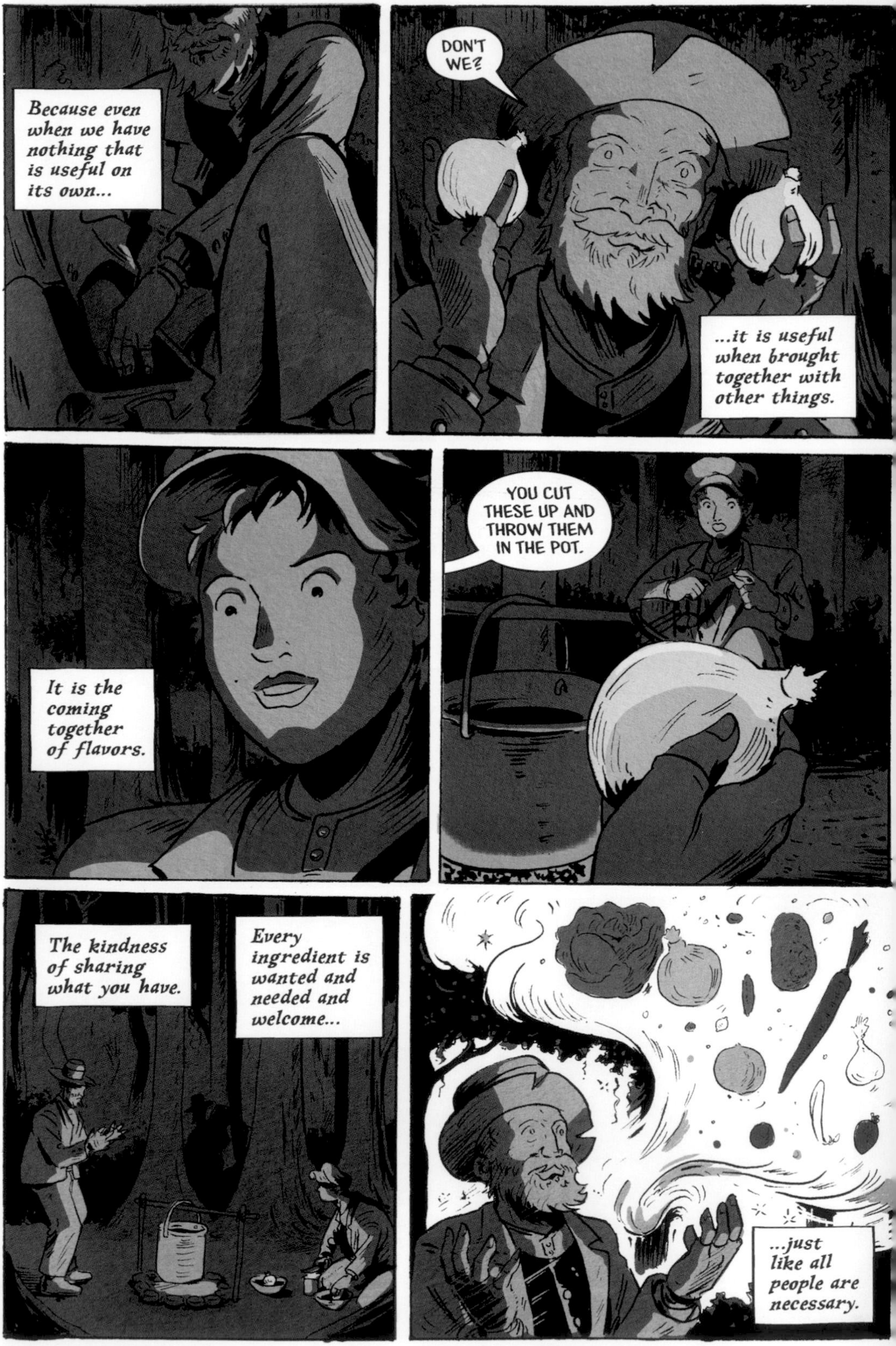
Because even when we have nothing that is useful on its own...
DON'T WE?
...it is useful when brought together with other things.
It is the coming together of flavors.
YOU CUT THESE UP AND THROW THEM IN THE POT.
The kindness of sharing what you have.
Every ingredient is wanted and needed and welcome...
...just like all people are necessary.

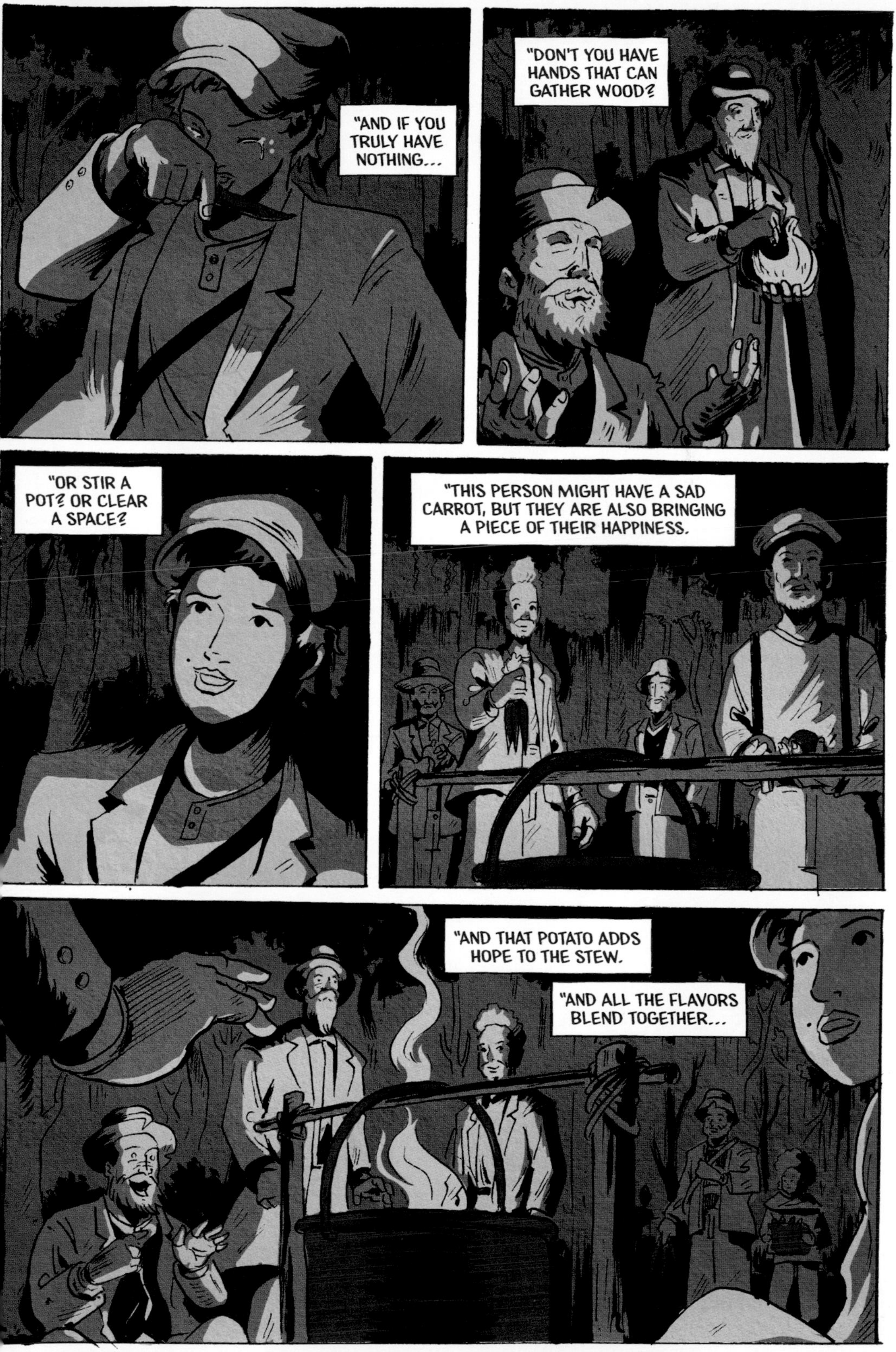
"AND IF YOU TRULY HAVE NOTHING...
"DON'T YOU HAVE HANDS THAT CAN GATHER WOOD?
"OR STIR A POT? OR CLEAR A SPACE?
"THIS PERSON MIGHT HAVE A SAD CARROT, BUT THEY ARE ALSO BRINGING A PIECE OF THEIR HAPPINESS.
"AND THAT POTATO ADDS HOPE TO THE STEW.
"AND ALL THE FLAVORS BLEND TOGETHER...

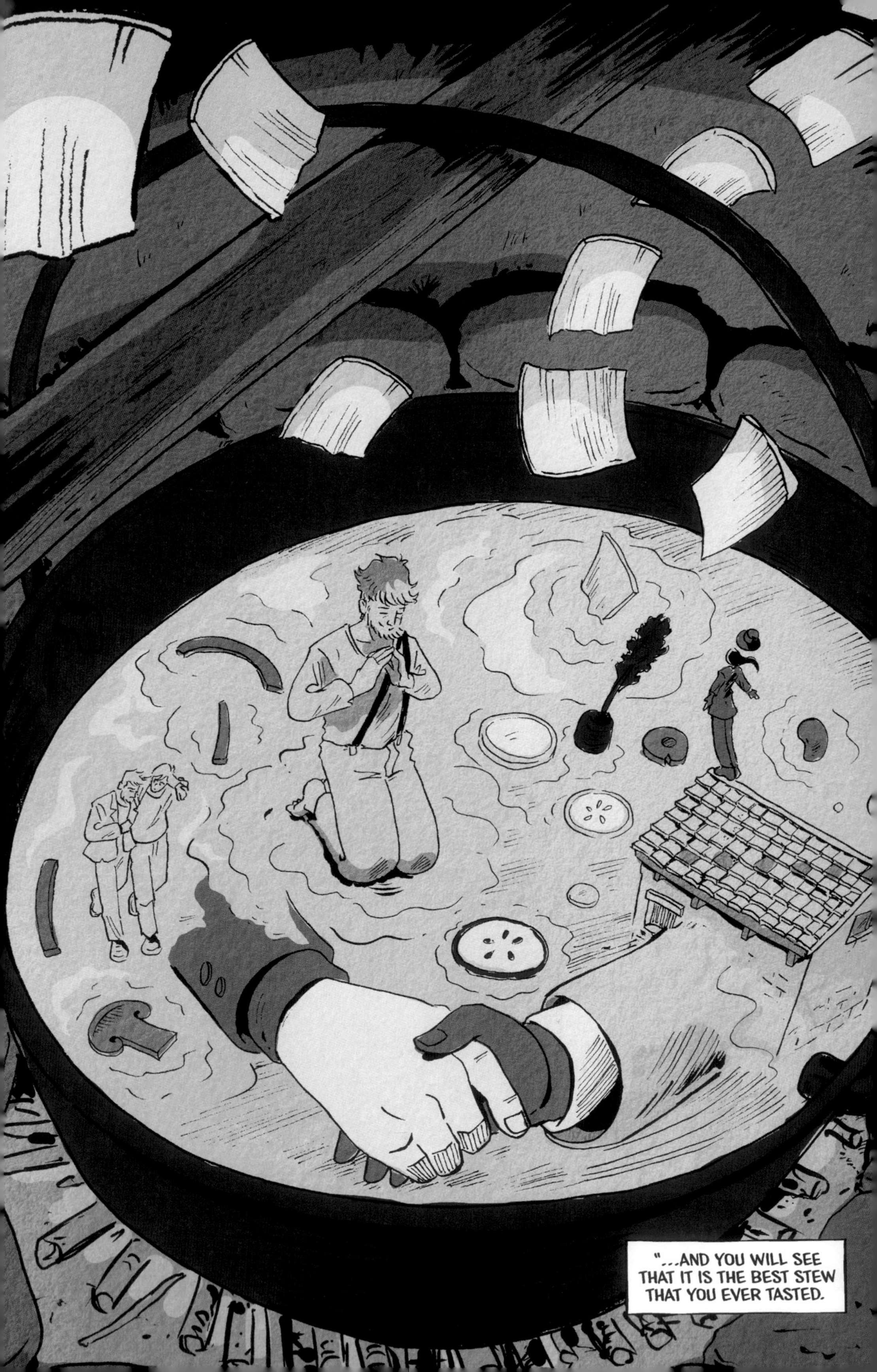
"...AND YOU WILL SEE THAT IT IS THE BEST STEW THAT YOU EVER TASTED.

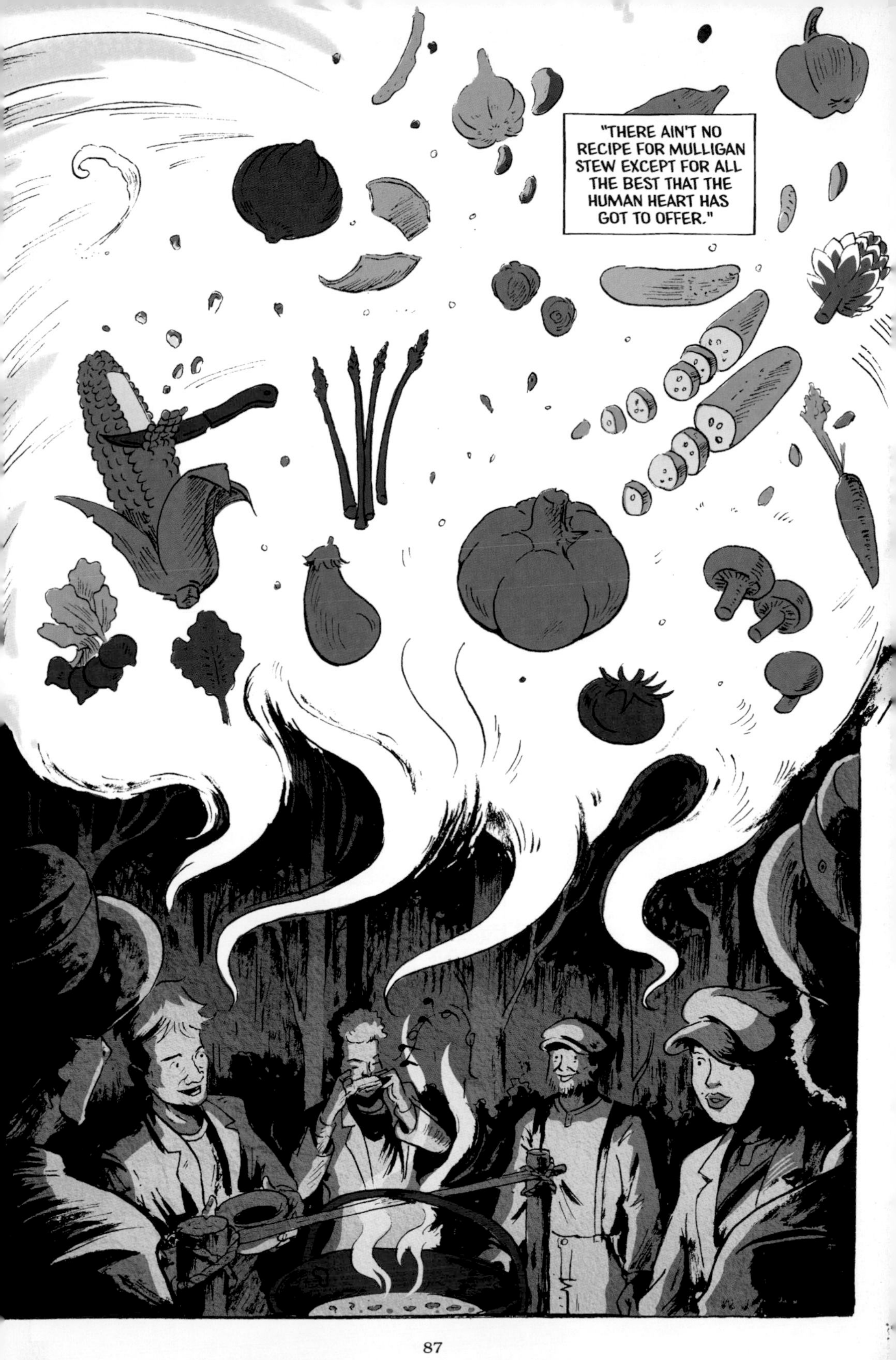
"THERE AIN'T NO RECIPE FOR MULLIGAN STEW EXCEPT FOR ALL THE BEST THAT THE HUMAN HEART HAS GOT TO OFFER."

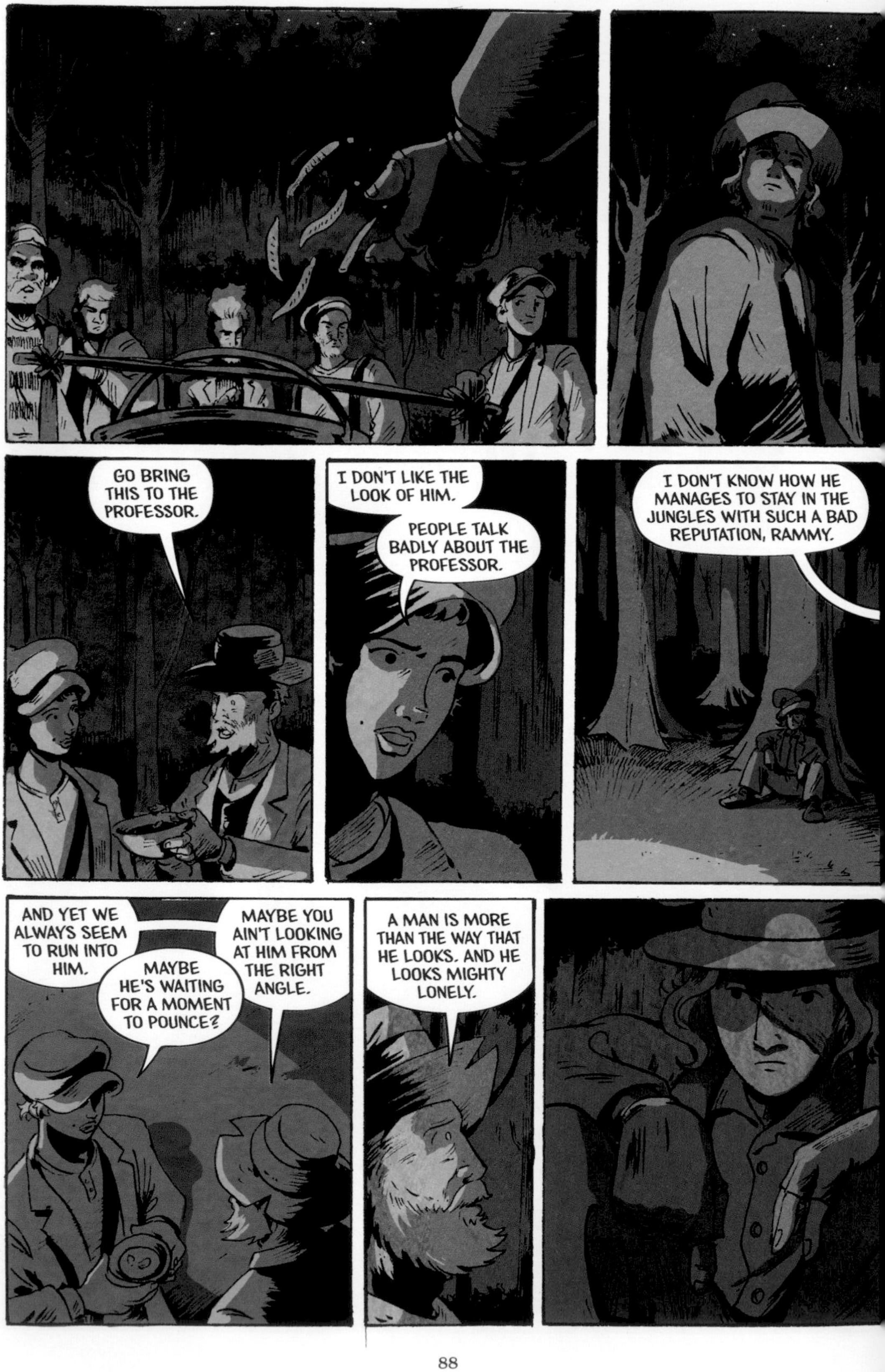
GO BRING THIS TO THE PROFESSOR.
I DON'T LIKE THE LOOK OF HIM.
PEOPLE TALK BADLY ABOUT THE PROFESSOR.
I DON'T KNOW HOW HE MANAGES TO STAY IN THE JUNGLES WITH SUCH A BAD REPUTATION, RAMMY.
AND YET WE ALWAYS SEEM TO RUN INTO HIM.
MAYBE YOU AIN'T LOOKING AT HIM FROM THE RIGHT ANGLE.
MAYBE HE'S WAITING FOR A MOMENT TO POUNCE?
A MAN IS MORE THAN THE WAY THAT HE LOOKS. AND HE LOOKS MIGHTY LONELY.

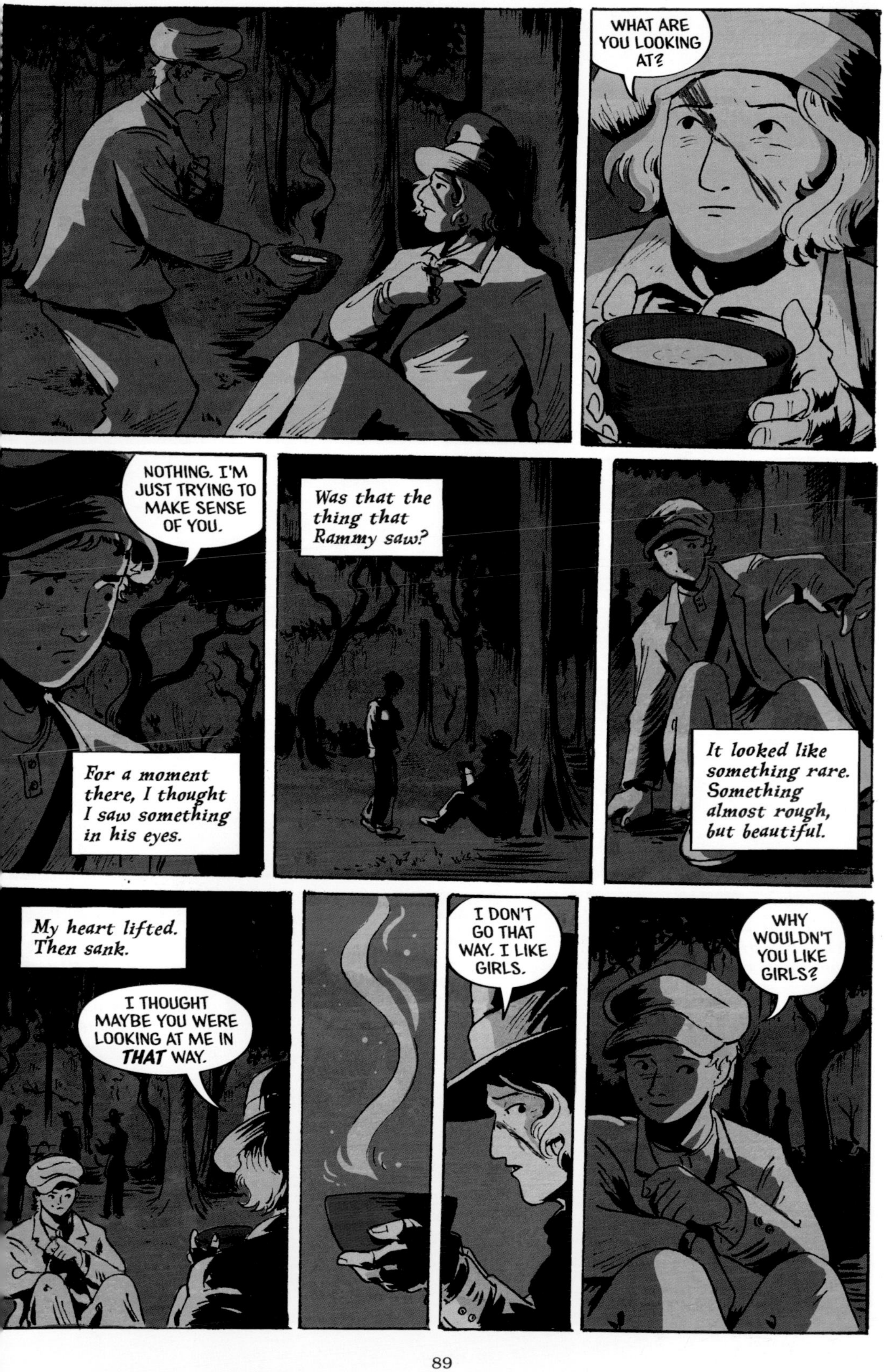

WHAT ARE YOU LOOKING AT?
NOTHING. I'M JUST TRYING TO MAKE SENSE OF YOU.
For a moment there, I thought I saw something in his eyes.
Was that the thing that Rammy saw?
It looked like something rare. Something almost rough, but beautiful.
My heart lifted. Then sank.
I THOUGHT MAYBE YOU WERE LOOKING AT ME IN THAT WAY.
I DON'T GO THAT WAY. I LIKE GIRLS.
WHY WOULDN'T YOU LIKE GIRLS?

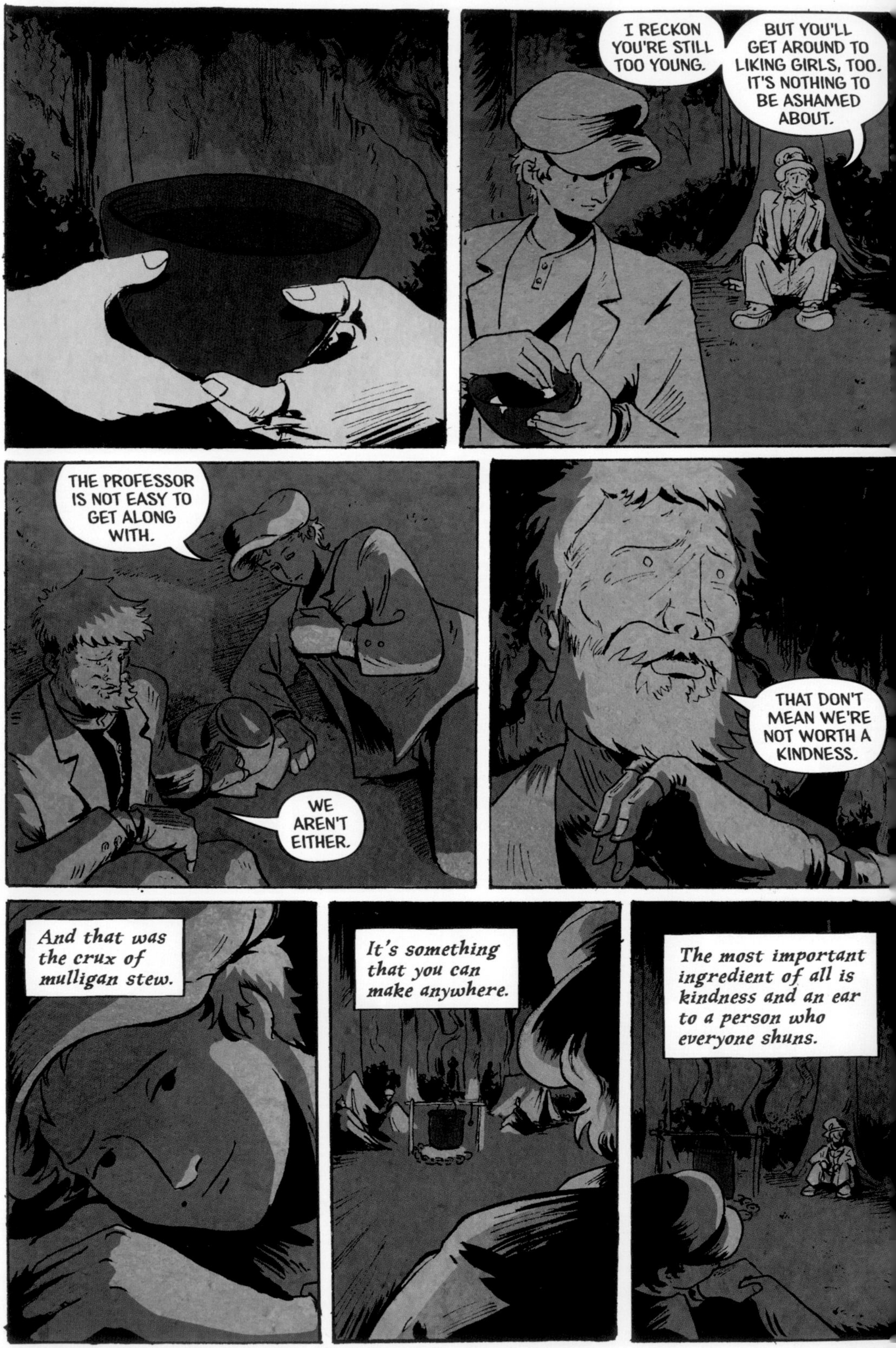
I RECKON YOU'RE STILL TOO YOUNG.
BUT YOU'LL GET AROUND TO LIKING GIRLS, TOO. IT'S NOTHING TO BE ASHAMED ABOUT.
THE PROFESSOR IS NOT EASY TO GET ALONG WITH.
WE AREN'T EITHER.
THAT DON'T MEAN WE'RE NOT WORTH A KINDNESS.
And that was the crux of mulligan stew.
It's something that you can make anywhere.
The most important ingredient of all is kindness and an ear to a person who everyone shuns.

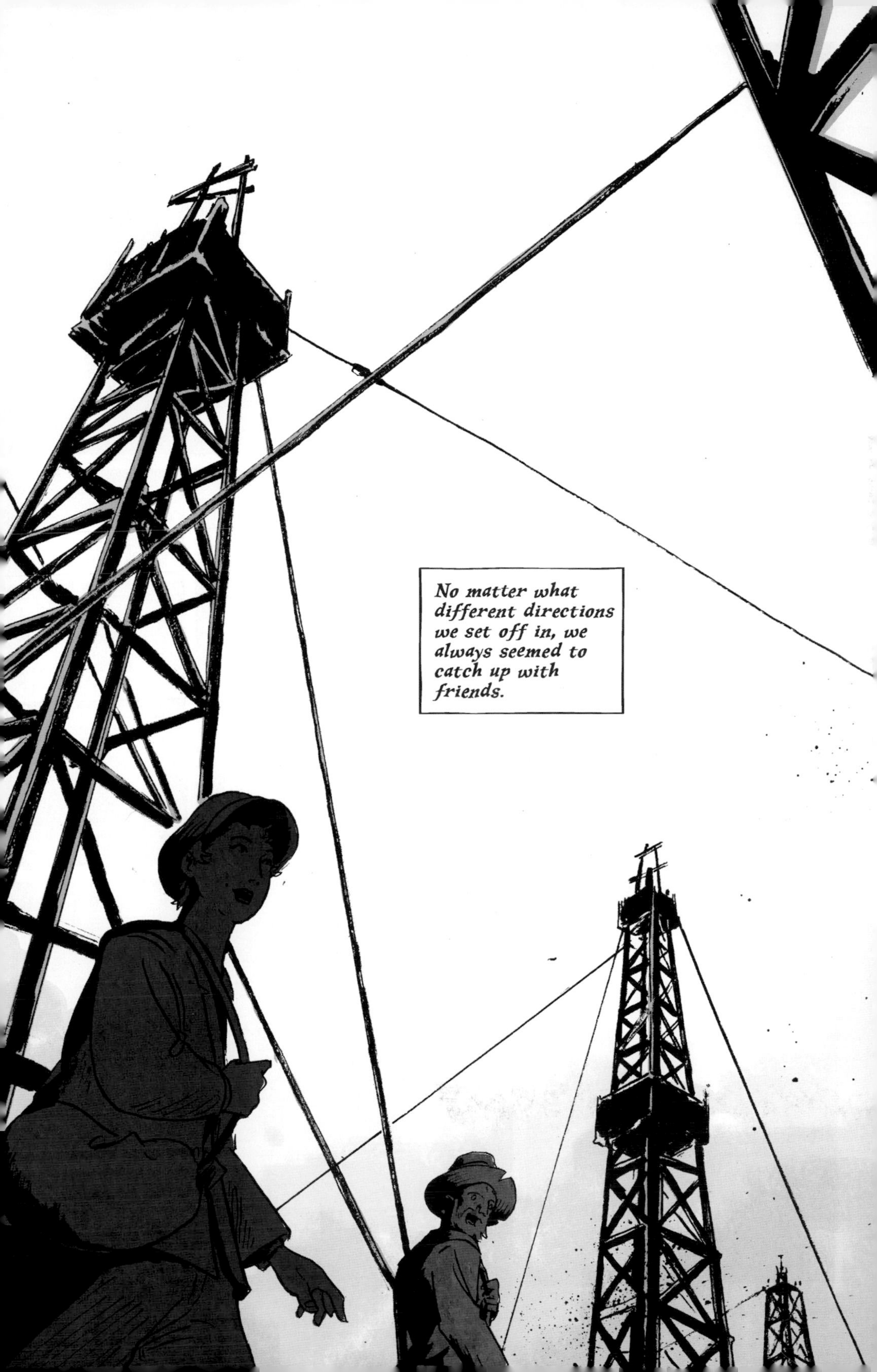
No matter what different directions we set off in, we always seemed to catch up with friends.

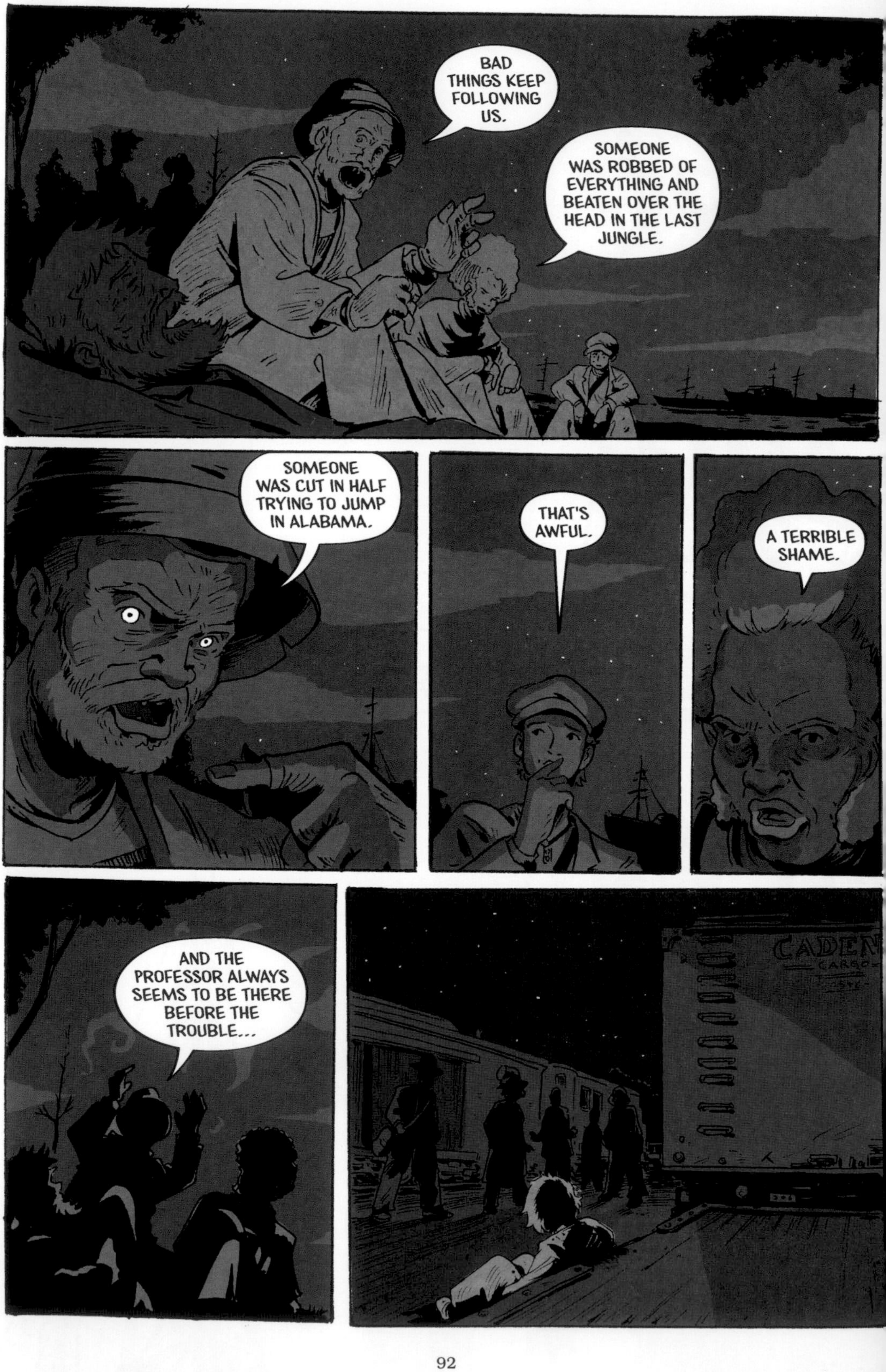
BAD THINGS KEEP FOLLOWING US.
SOMEONE WAS ROBBED OF EVERYTHING AND BEATEN OVER THE HEAD IN THE LAST JUNGLE.
SOMEONE WAS CUT IN HALF TRYING TO JUMP IN ALABAMA.
THAT'S AWFUL.
A TERRIBLE SHAME.
AND THE PROFESSOR ALWAYS SEEMS TO BE THERE BEFORE THE TROUBLE...

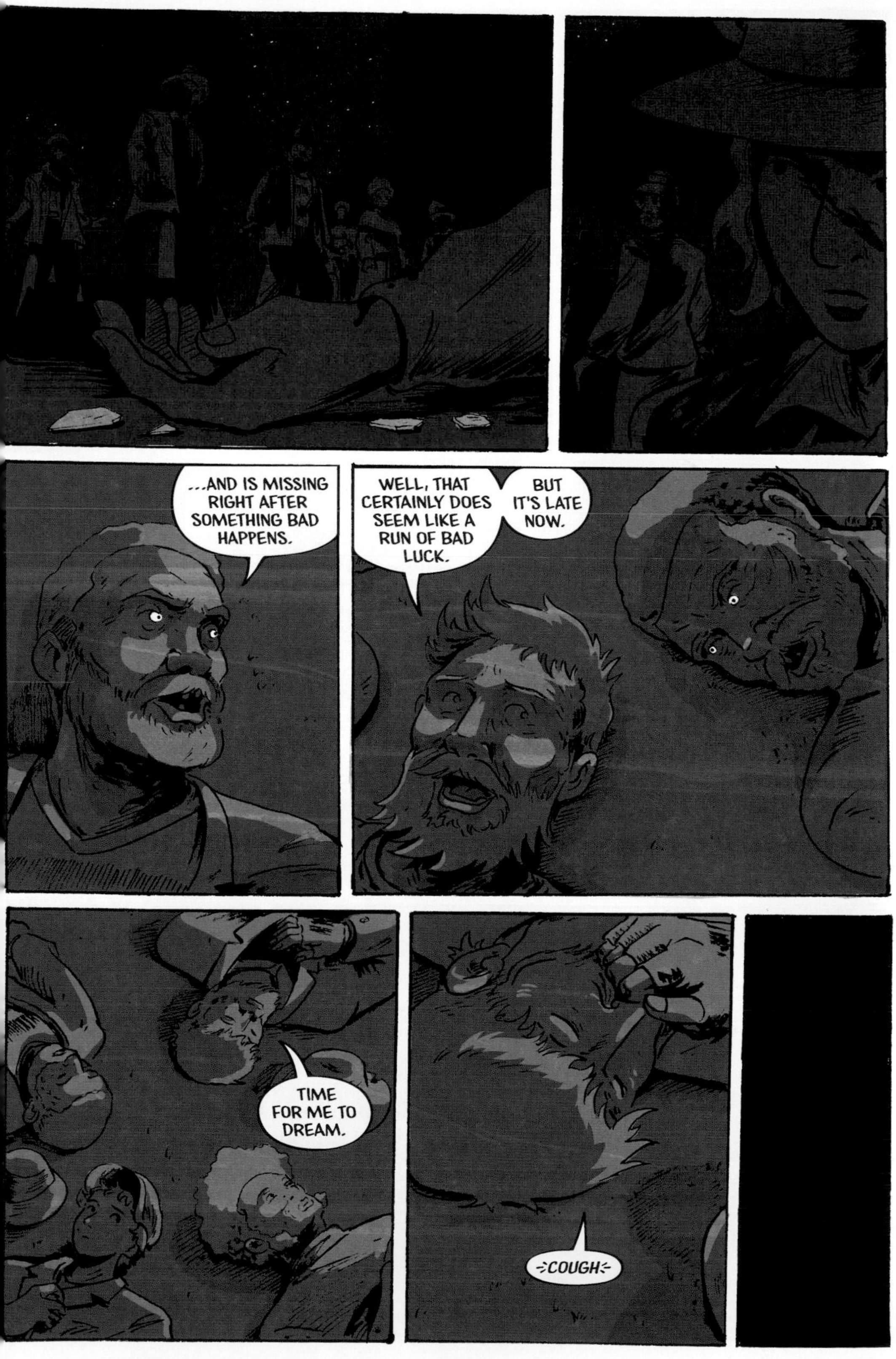
...AND IS MISSING RIGHT AFTER SOMETHING BAD HAPPENS.
WELL, THAT CERTAINLY DOES SEEM LIKE A RUN OF BAD LUCK.
BUT IT'S LATE NOW.
TIME FOR ME TO DREAM.
COUGH

AAAIIIIEEE!

WHAT'S THAT?

MAYBE A COUGAR.

SOUNDS BAD.

I'LL GO CHECK.

STAY HERE.

THE PROFESSOR...THE PROFESSOR...

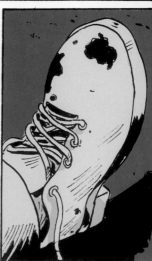

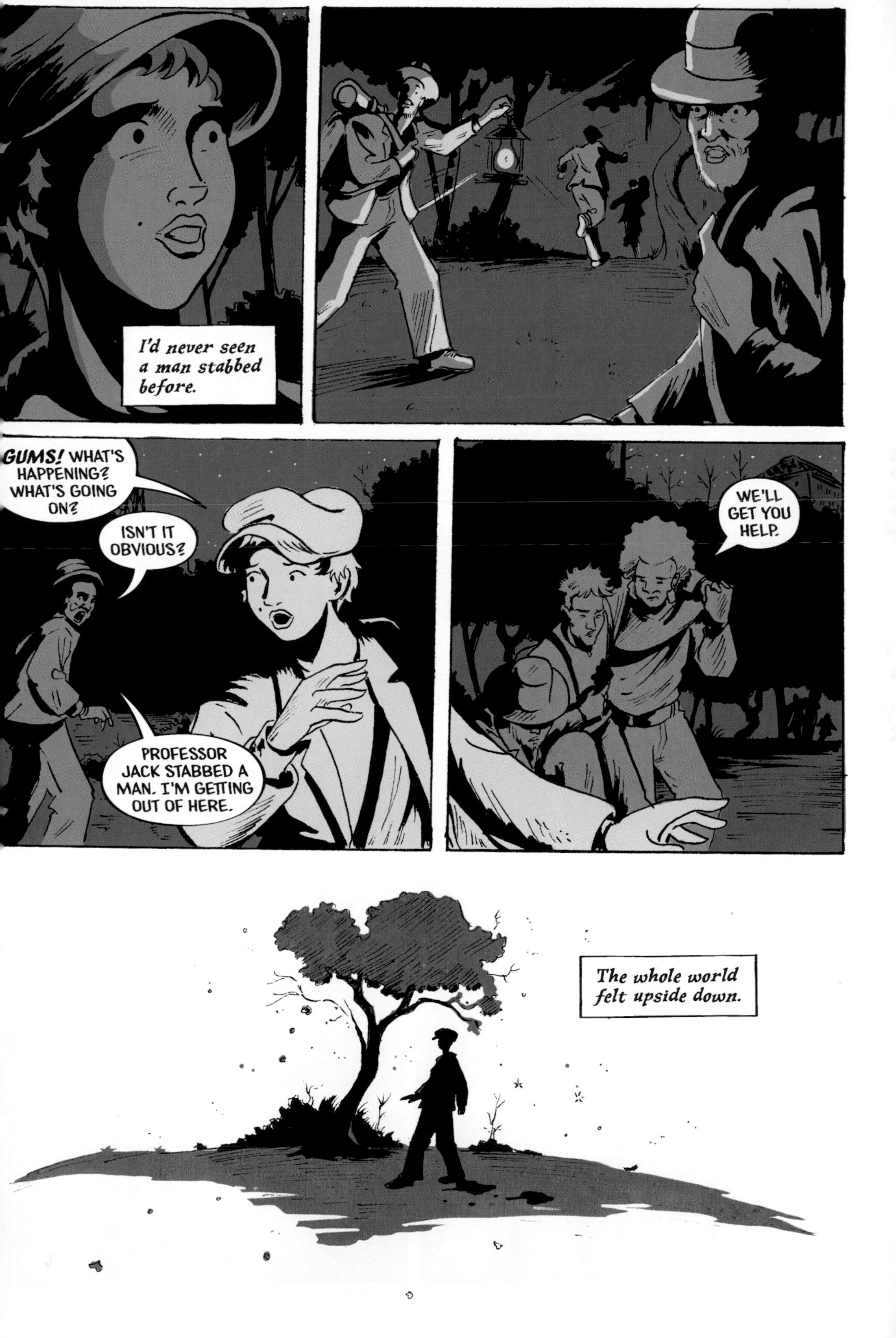
I'd never seen a man stabbed before.
GUMS! WHAT'S HAPPENING? WHAT'S GOING ON?
ISN'T IT OBVIOUS?
PROFESSOR JACK STABBED A MAN. I'M GETTING OUT OF HERE.
WE'LL GET YOU HELP.
The whole world felt upside down.

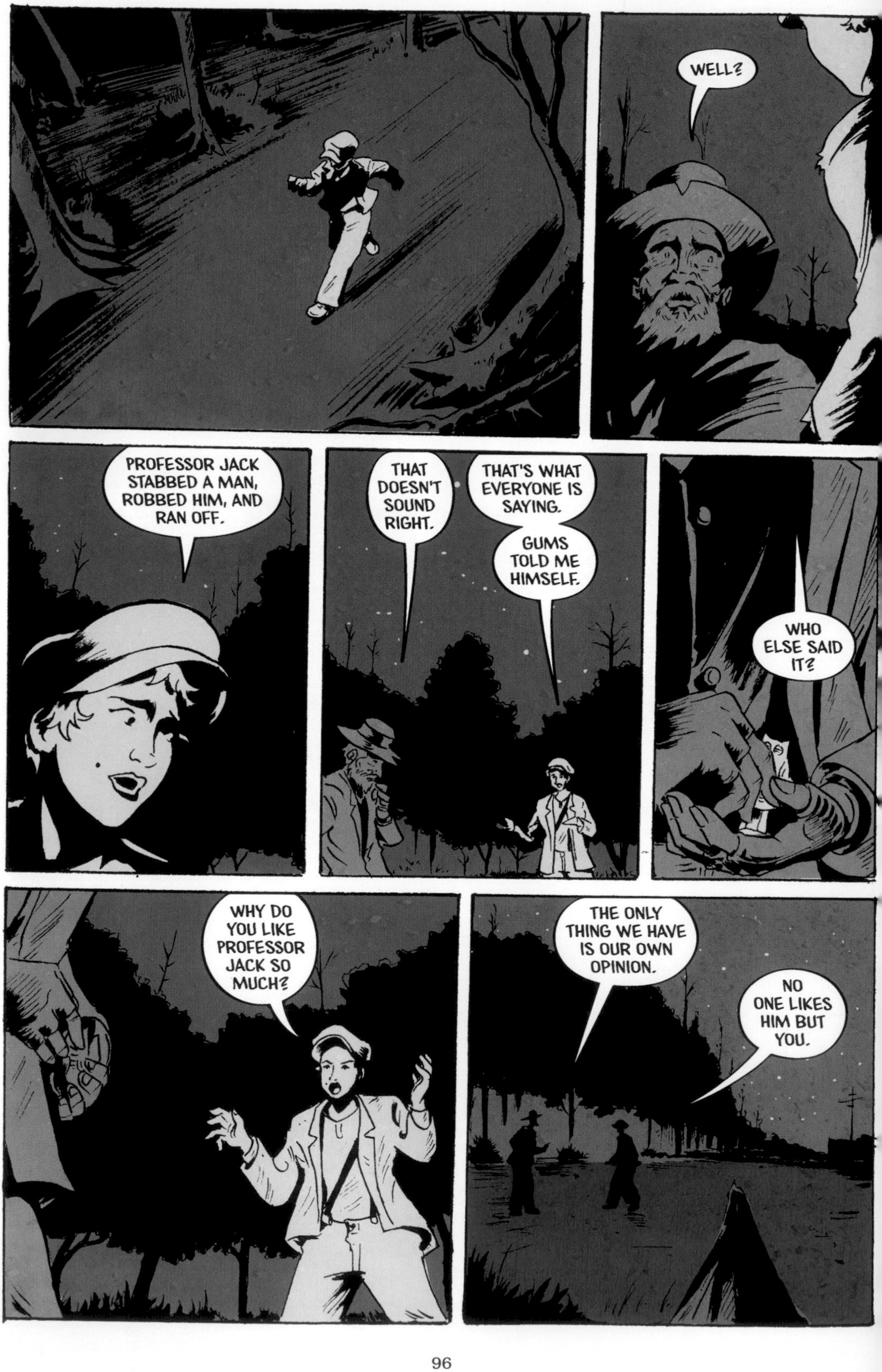
WELL?
PROFESSOR JACK STABBED A MAN, ROBBED HIM, AND RAN OFF.
THAT DOESN'T SOUND RIGHT.
THAT'S WHAT EVERYONE IS SAYING.
GUMS TOLD ME HIMSELF.
WHO ELSE SAID IT?
WHY DO YOU LIKE PROFESSOR JACK SO MUCH?
THE ONLY THING WE HAVE IS OUR OWN OPINION.
NO ONE LIKES HIM BUT YOU.

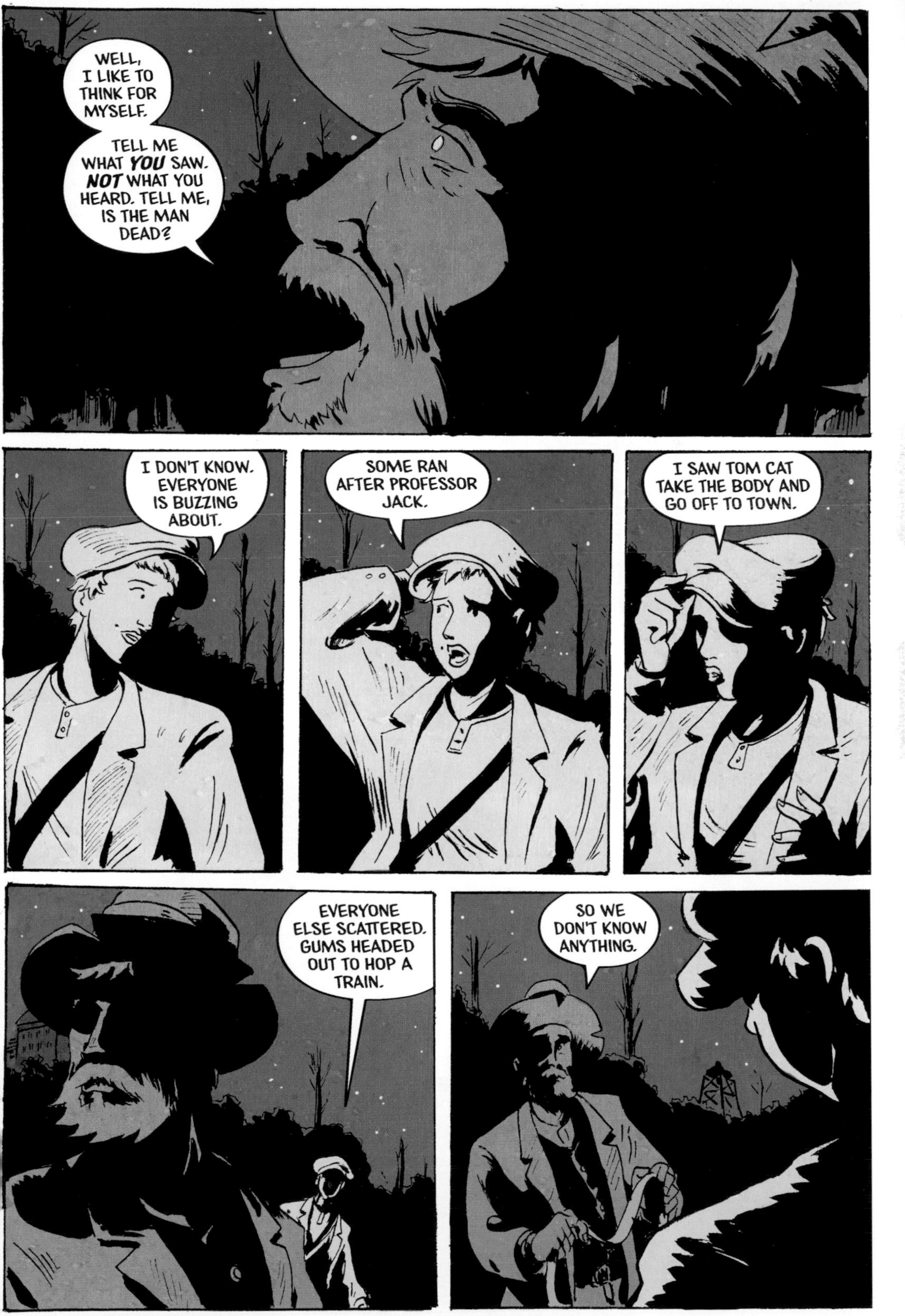
WELL, I LIKE TO THINK FOR MYSELF.
TELL ME WHAT YOU SAW. NOT WHAT YOU HEARD. TELL ME, IS THE MAN DEAD?
I DON'T KNOW. EVERYONE IS BUZZING ABOUT.
SOME RAN AFTER PROFESSOR JACK.
I SAW TOM CAT TAKE THE BODY AND GO OFF TO TOWN.
EVERYONE ELSE SCATTERED. GUMS HEADED OUT TO HOP A TRAIN.
SO WE DON'T KNOW ANYTHING.

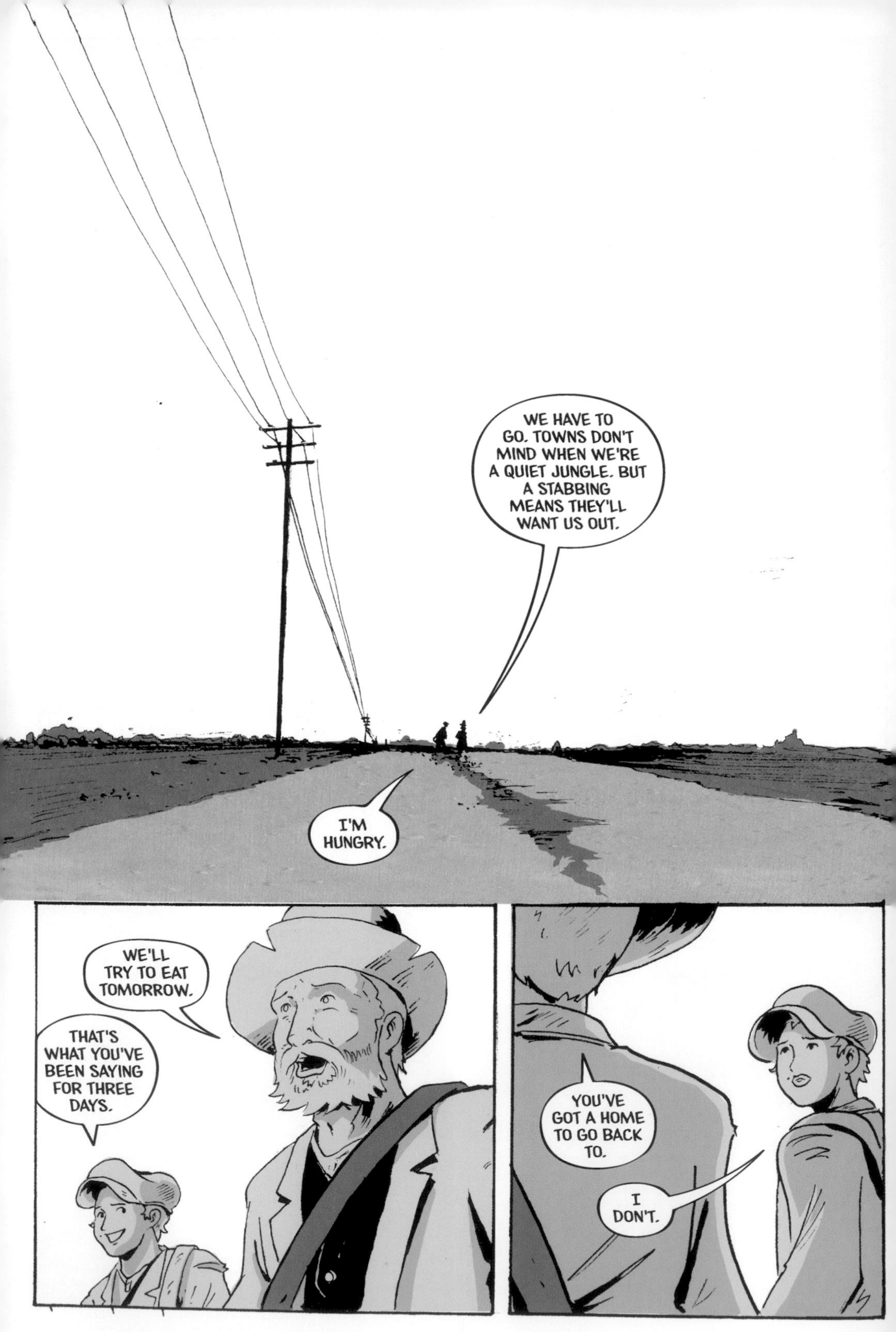

WE HAVE TO GO. TOWNS DON'T MIND WHEN WE'RE A QUIET JUNGLE. BUT A STABBING MEANS THEY'LL WANT US OUT.
I'M HUNGRY.
WE'LL TRY TO EAT TOMORROW.
THAT'S WHAT YOU'VE BEEN SAYING FOR THREE DAYS.
YOU'VE GOT A HOME TO GO BACK TO.
I DON'T.

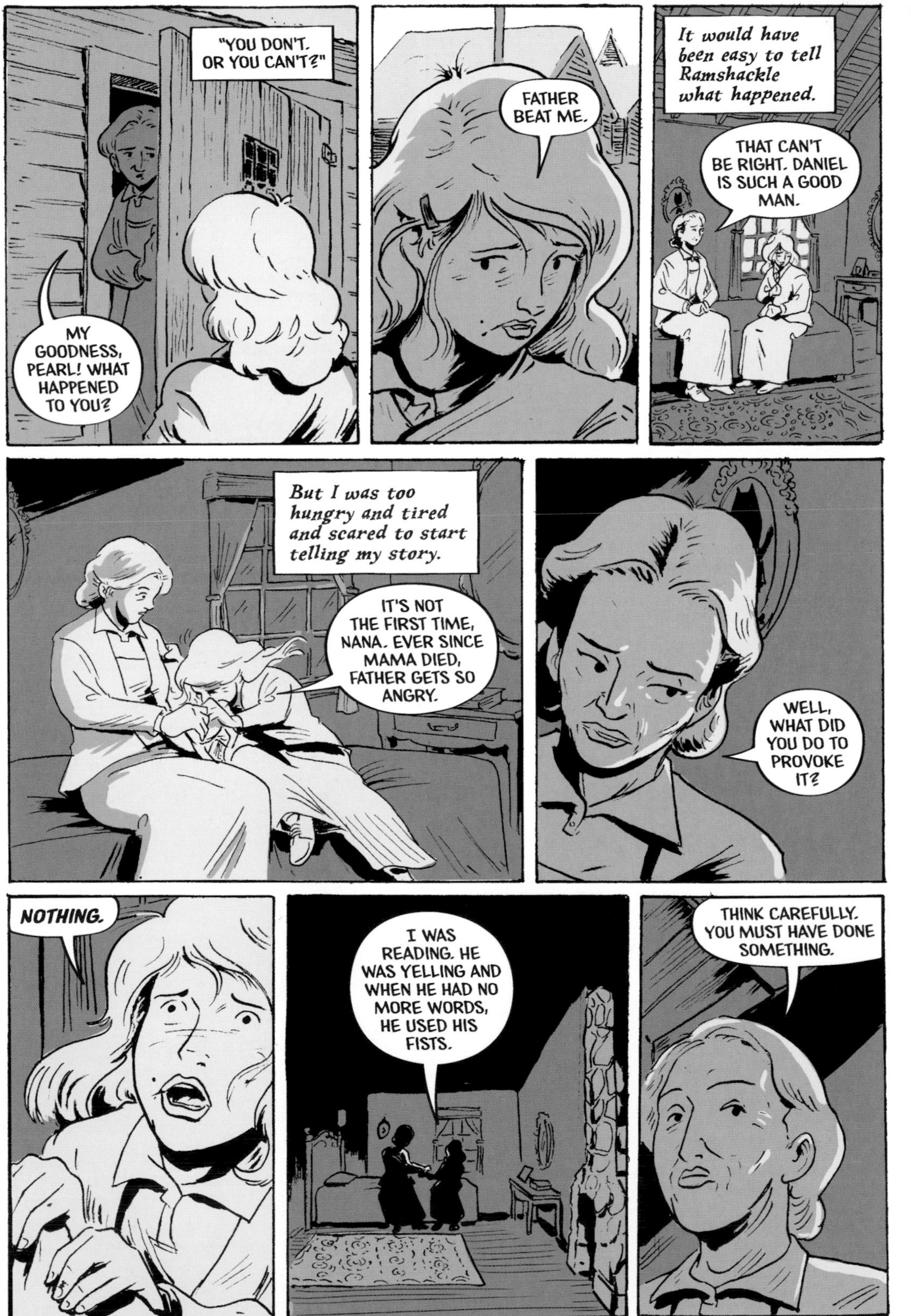
"YOU DON'T. OR YOU CAN'T?"
MY GOODNESS, PEARL! WHAT HAPPENED TO YOU?
FATHER BEAT ME.
It would have been easy to tell Ramshackle what happened.
THAT CAN'T BE RIGHT. DANIEL IS SUCH A GOOD MAN.
But I was too hungry and tired and scared to start telling my story.
IT'S NOT THE FIRST TIME, NANA. EVER SINCE MAMA DIED, FATHER GETS SO ANGRY.
WELL, WHAT DID YOU DO TO PROVOKE IT?
NOTHING.
I WAS READING. HE WAS YELLING AND WHEN HE HAD NO MORE WORDS, HE USED HIS FISTS.
THINK CAREFULLY. YOU MUST HAVE DONE SOMETHING.

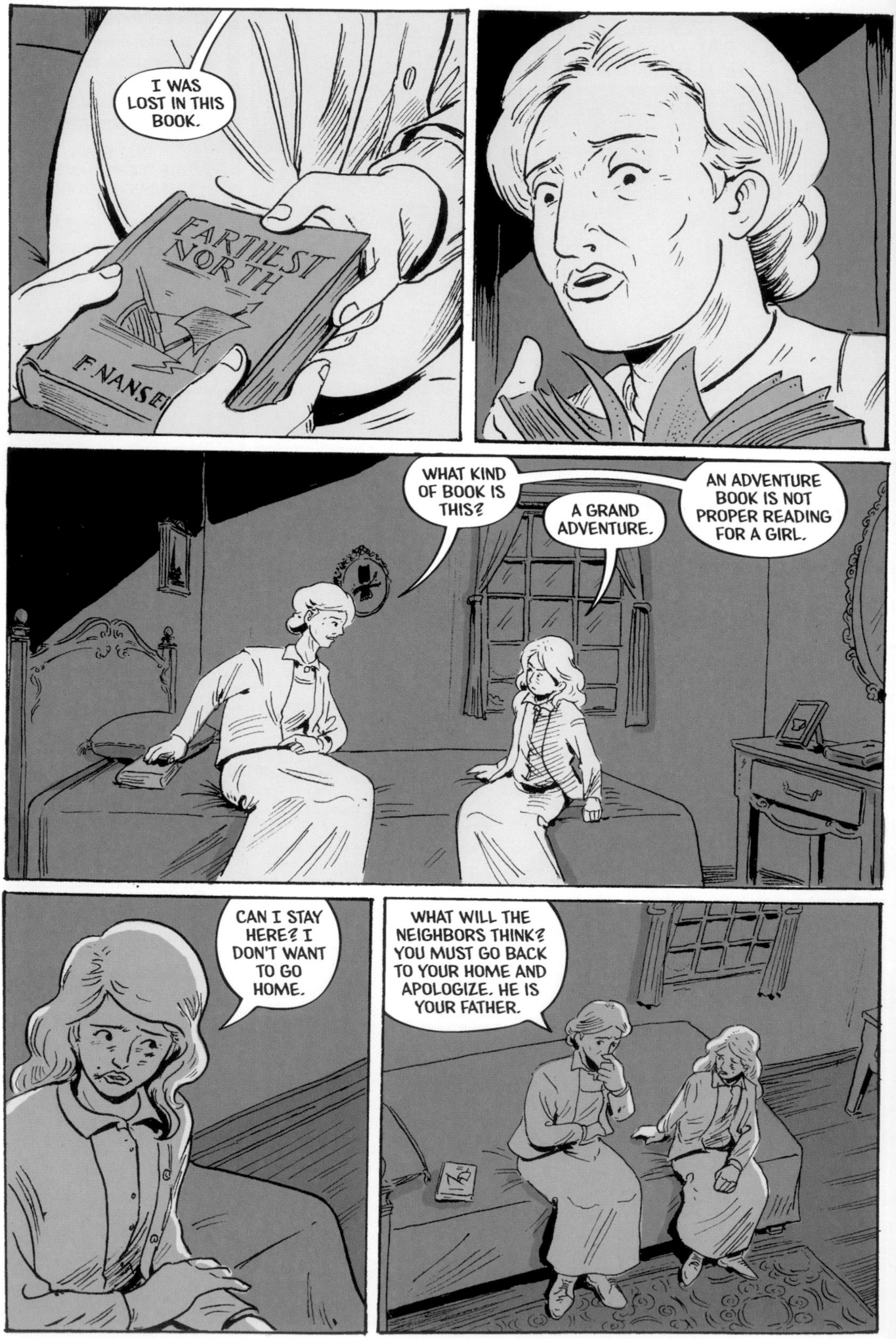
I WAS LOST IN THIS BOOK.
FARTHEST NORTH
F. NANSEN
WHAT KIND OF BOOK IS THIS?
A GRAND ADVENTURE.
AN ADVENTURE BOOK IS NOT PROPER READING FOR A GIRL.
CAN I STAY HERE? I DON'T WANT TO GO HOME.
WHAT WILL THE NEIGHBORS THINK? YOU MUST GO BACK TO YOUR HOME AND APOLOGIZE. HE IS YOUR FATHER.

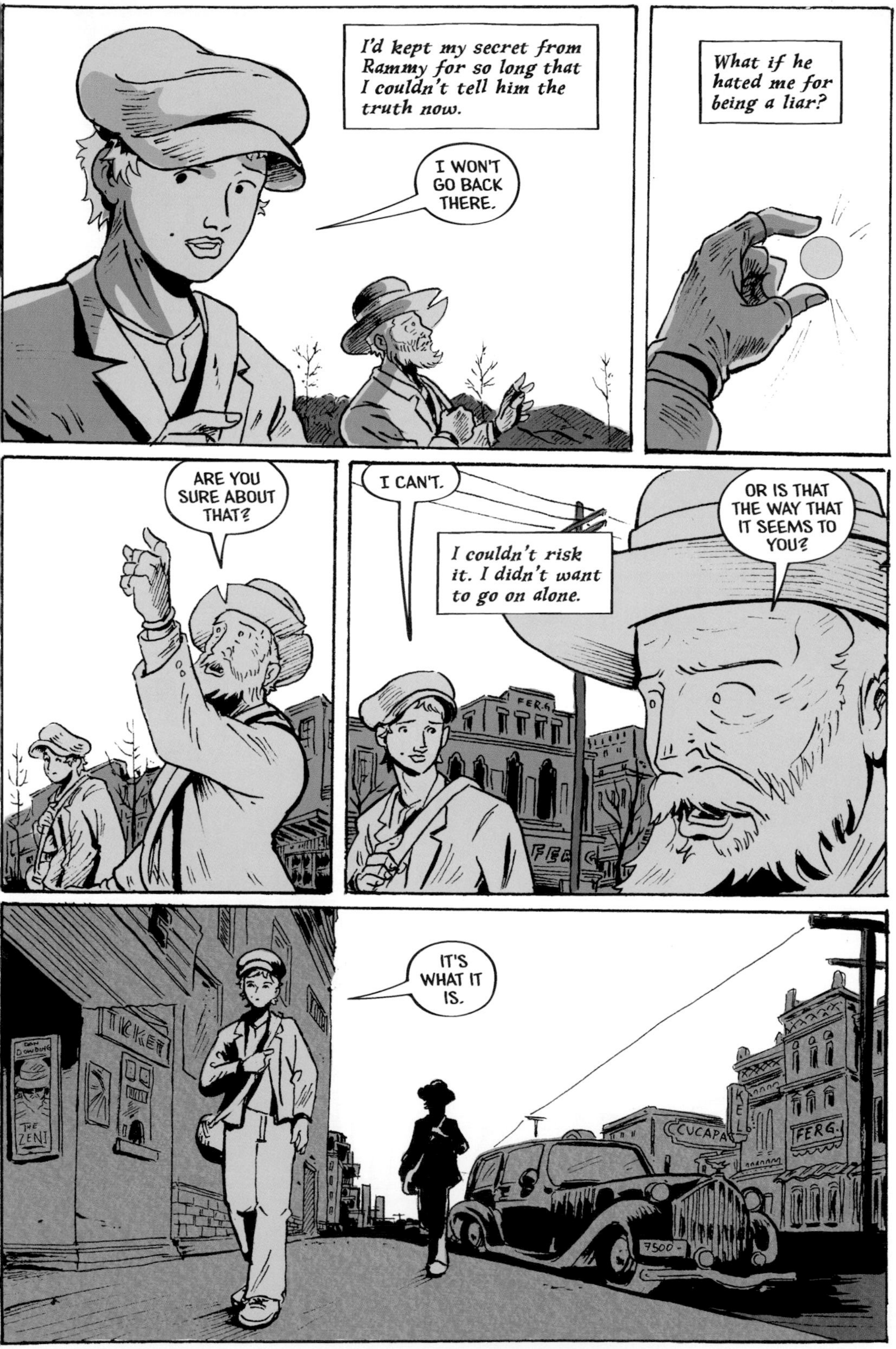
I'd kept my secret from Rammy for so long that I couldn't tell him the truth now.
I WON'T GO BACK THERE.
What if he hated me for being a liar?
ARE YOU SURE ABOUT THAT?
I CAN'T.
I couldn't risk it. I didn't want to go on alone.
OR IS THAT THE WAY THAT IT SEEMS TO YOU?
IT'S WHAT IT IS.
TICKET
CUCAPA
FERG.

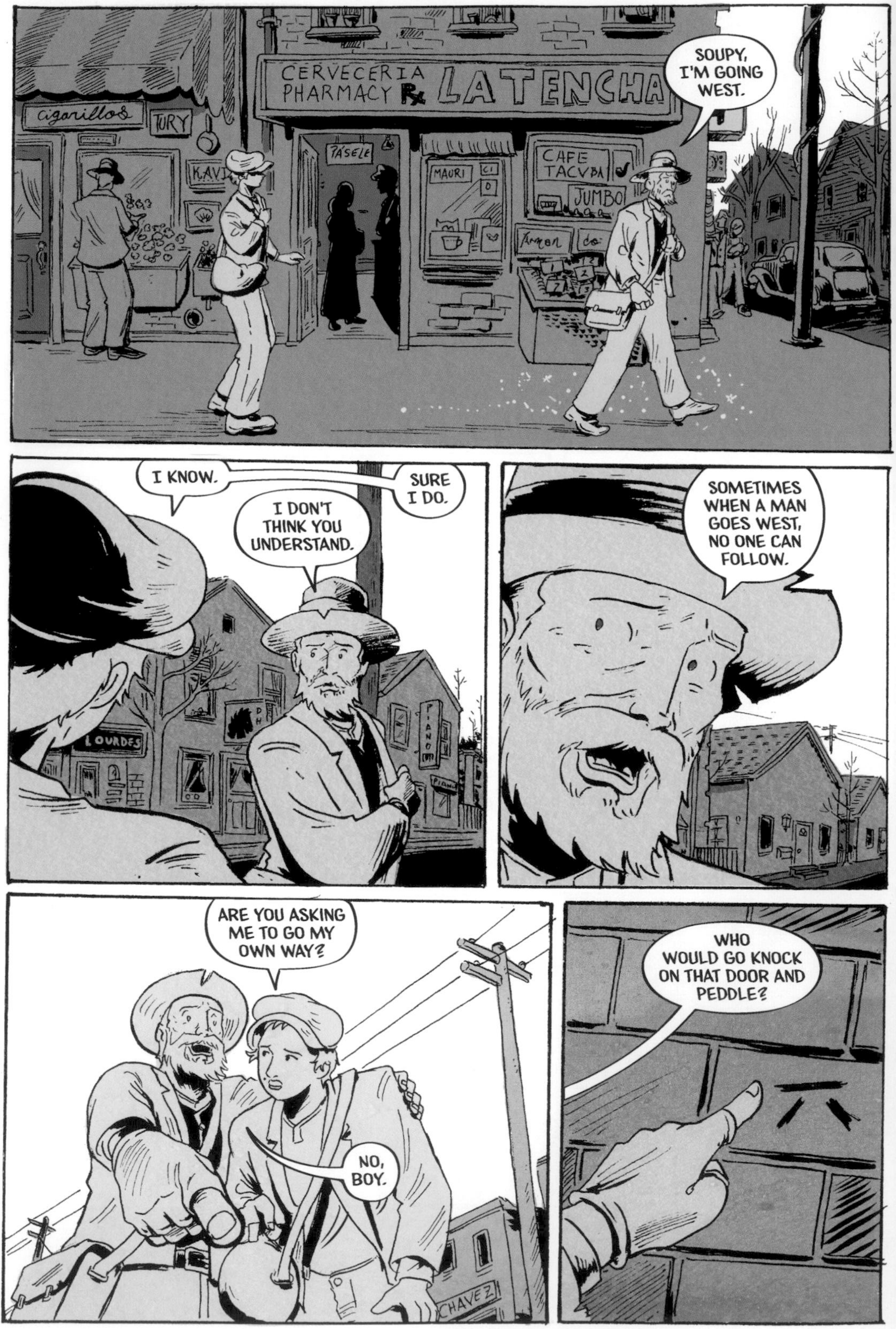
CERVECERIA
PHARMACY ℞
LA TENCHA
cigarillos
TURY
KAVI
PÁSELE
MAURI
CAFE TACUBA
JUMBO
SOUPY, I'M GOING WEST.
I KNOW.
SURE I DO.
I DON'T THINK YOU UNDERSTAND.
LOURDES
PIANO
SOMETIMES WHEN A MAN GOES WEST, NO ONE CAN FOLLOW.
ARE YOU ASKING ME TO GO MY OWN WAY?
NO, BOY.
CHAVEZ
WHO WOULD GO KNOCK ON THAT DOOR AND PEDDLE?

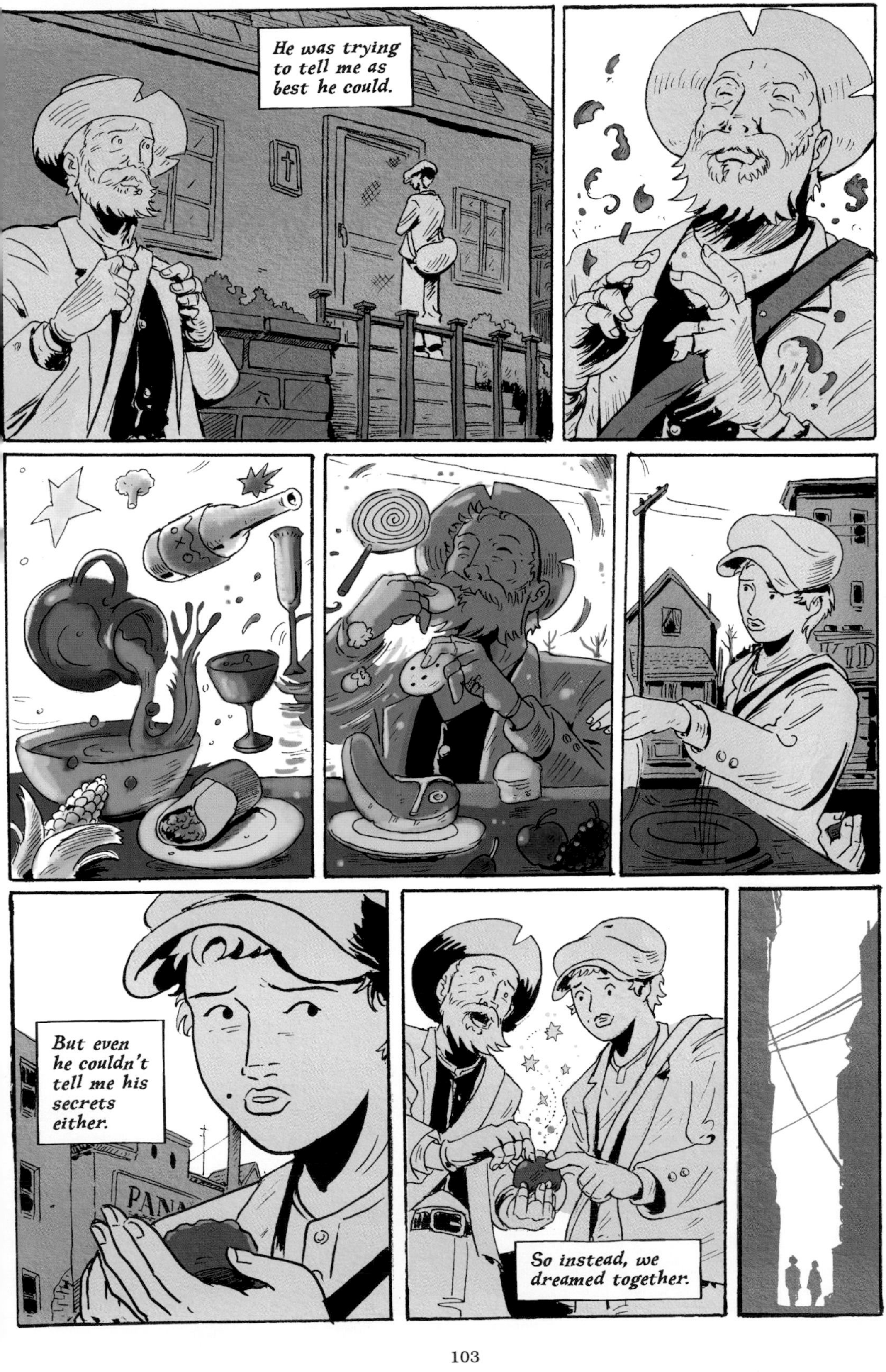
He was trying to tell me as best he could.
But even he couldn't tell me his secrets either.
So instead, we dreamed together.

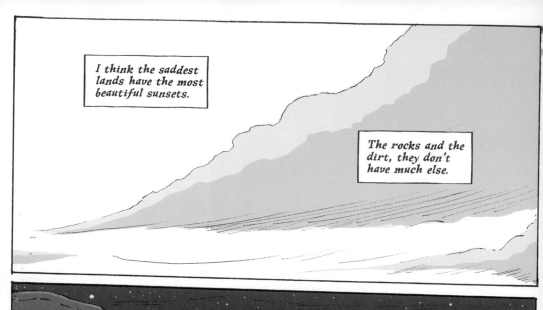

I think the saddest lands have the most beautiful sunsets.

The rocks and the dirt, they don't have much else.

Just like the saddest hearts are warmed by the tiniest and brightest of moments, just to get through to the next one.

So that heart can keep beating.

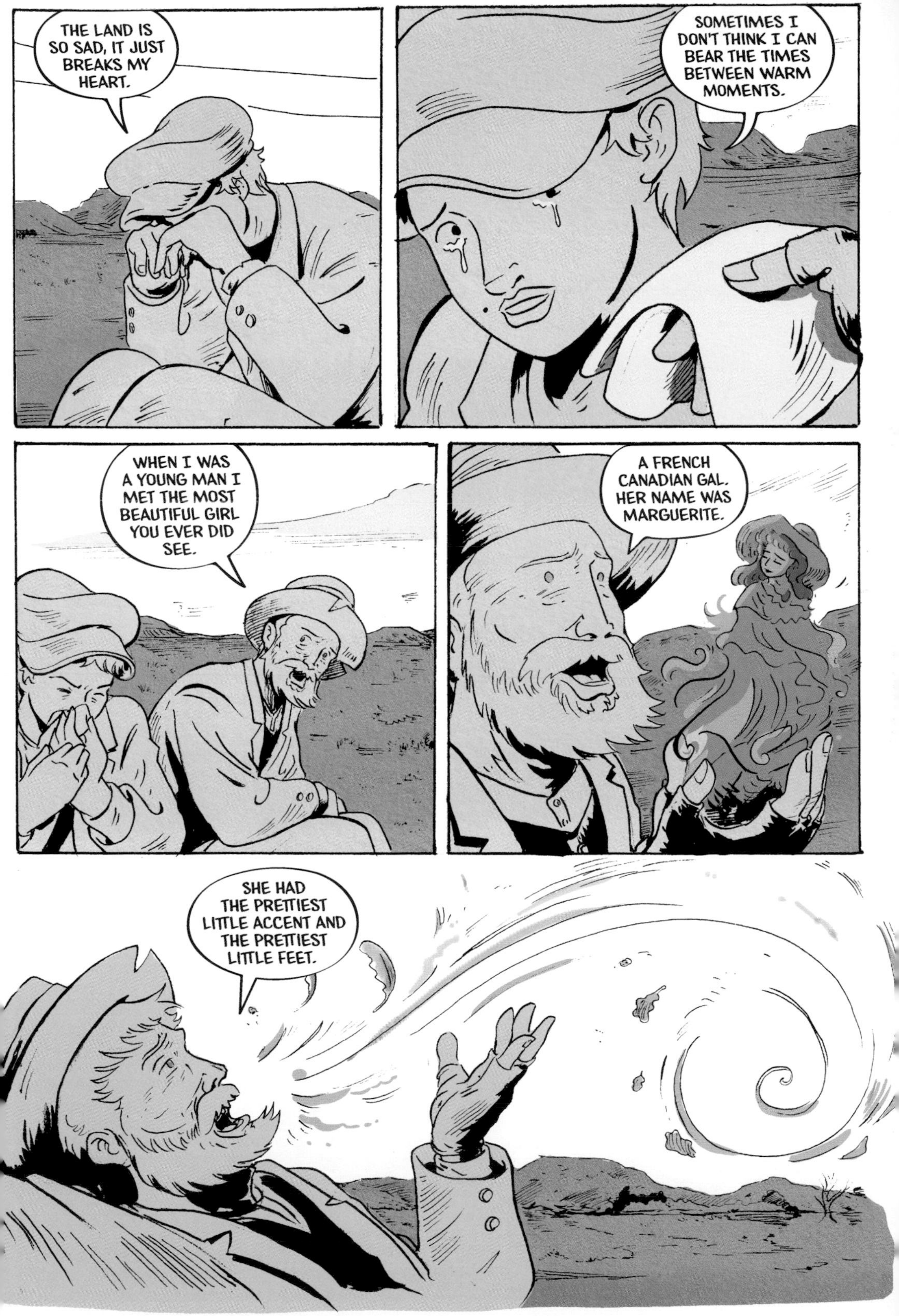
THE LAND IS SO SAD, IT JUST BREAKS MY HEART.
SOMETIMES I DON'T THINK I CAN BEAR THE TIMES BETWEEN WARM MOMENTS.
WHEN I WAS A YOUNG MAN I MET THE MOST BEAUTIFUL GIRL YOU EVER DID SEE.
A FRENCH CANADIAN GAL. HER NAME WAS MARGUERITE.
SHE HAD THE PRETTIEST LITTLE ACCENT AND THE PRETTIEST LITTLE FEET.

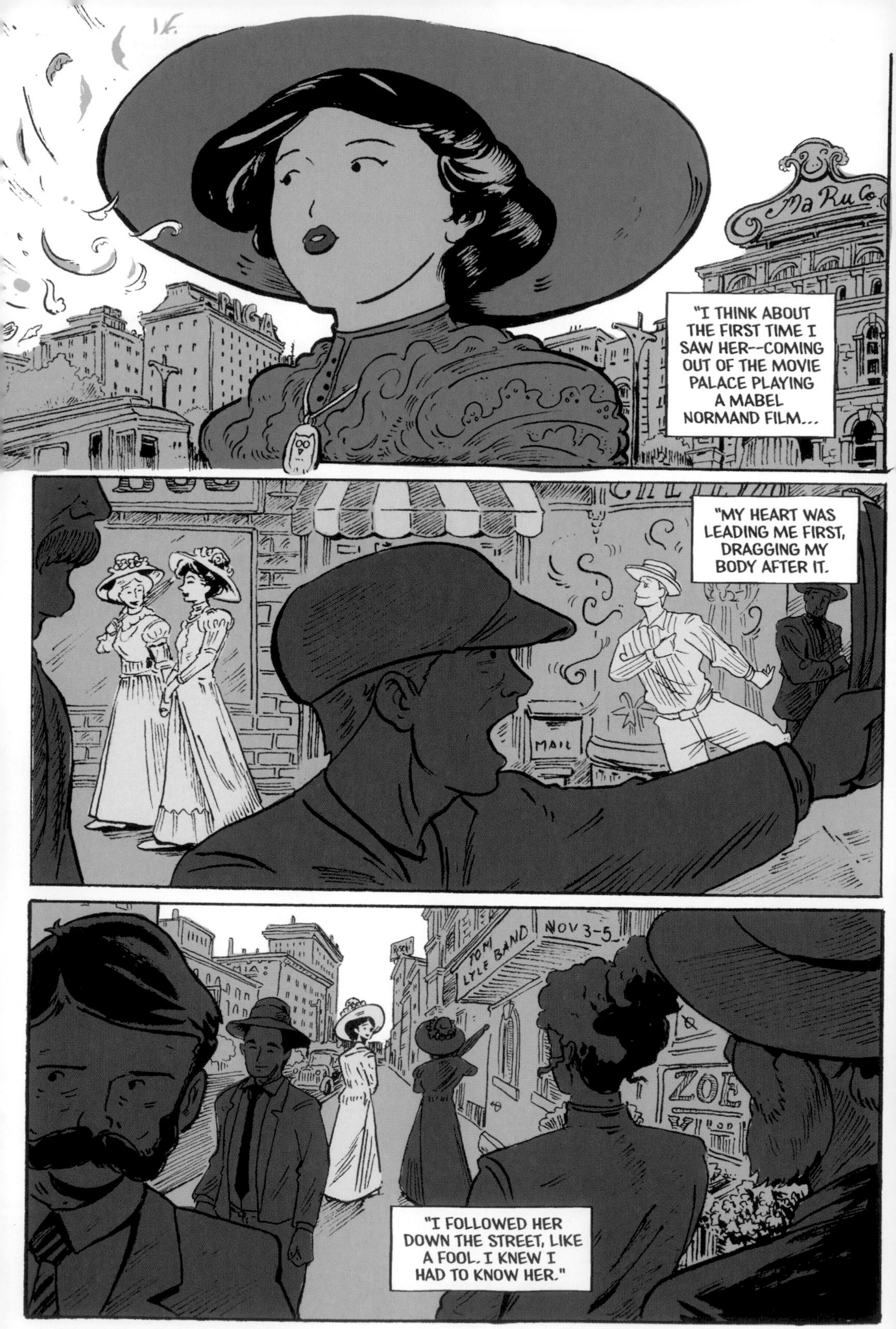
"I THINK ABOUT THE FIRST TIME I SAW HER--COMING OUT OF THE MOVIE PALACE PLAYING A MABEL NORMAND FILM...
"MY HEART WAS LEADING ME FIRST, DRAGGING MY BODY AFTER IT.
MAIL
NOV 3-5
TOM LYLE BAND
ZOE
"I FOLLOWED HER DOWN THE STREET, LIKE A FOOL. I KNEW I HAD TO KNOW HER."

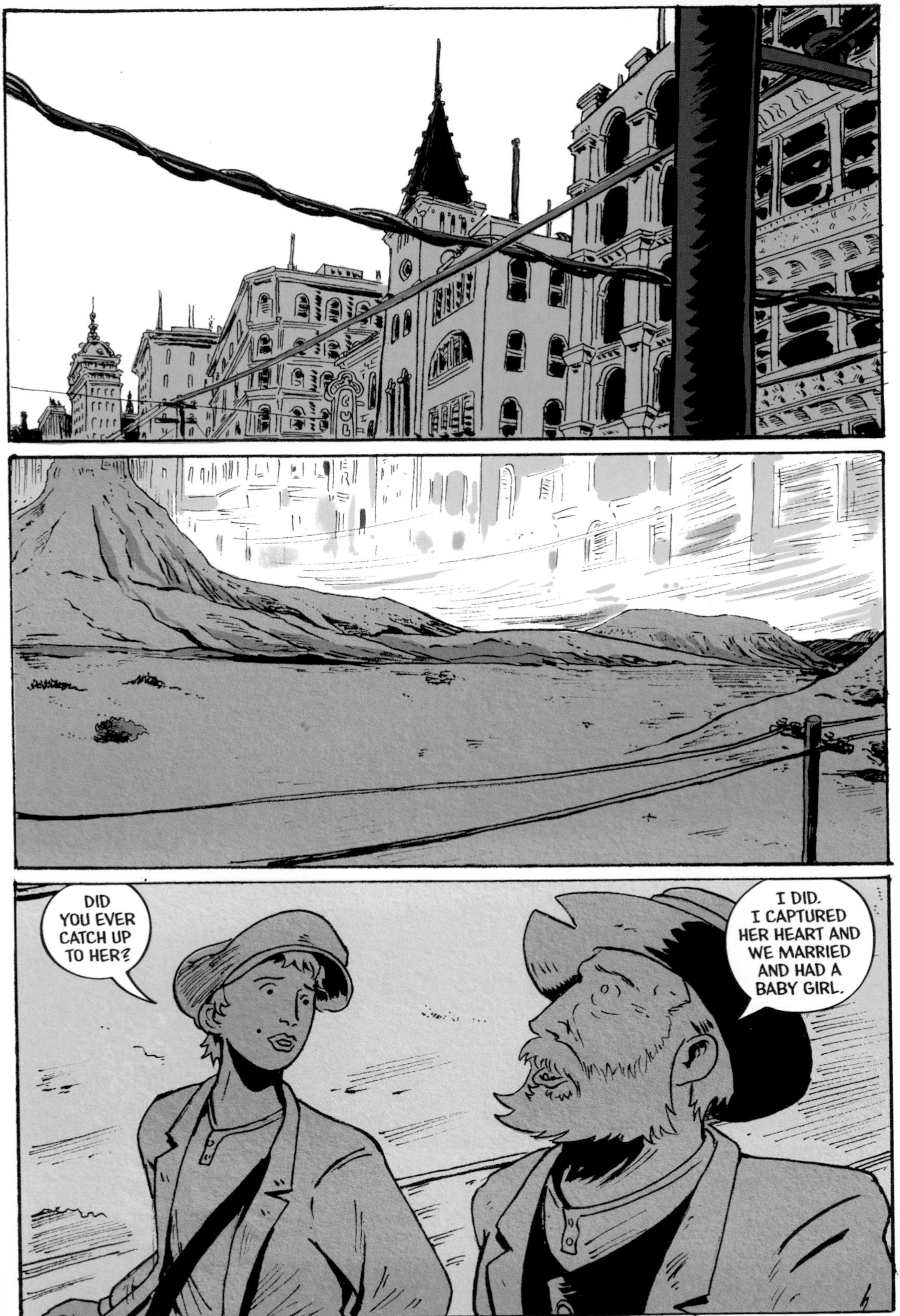
DID YOU EVER CATCH UP TO HER?
I DID. I CAPTURED HER HEART AND WE MARRIED AND HAD A BABY GIRL.

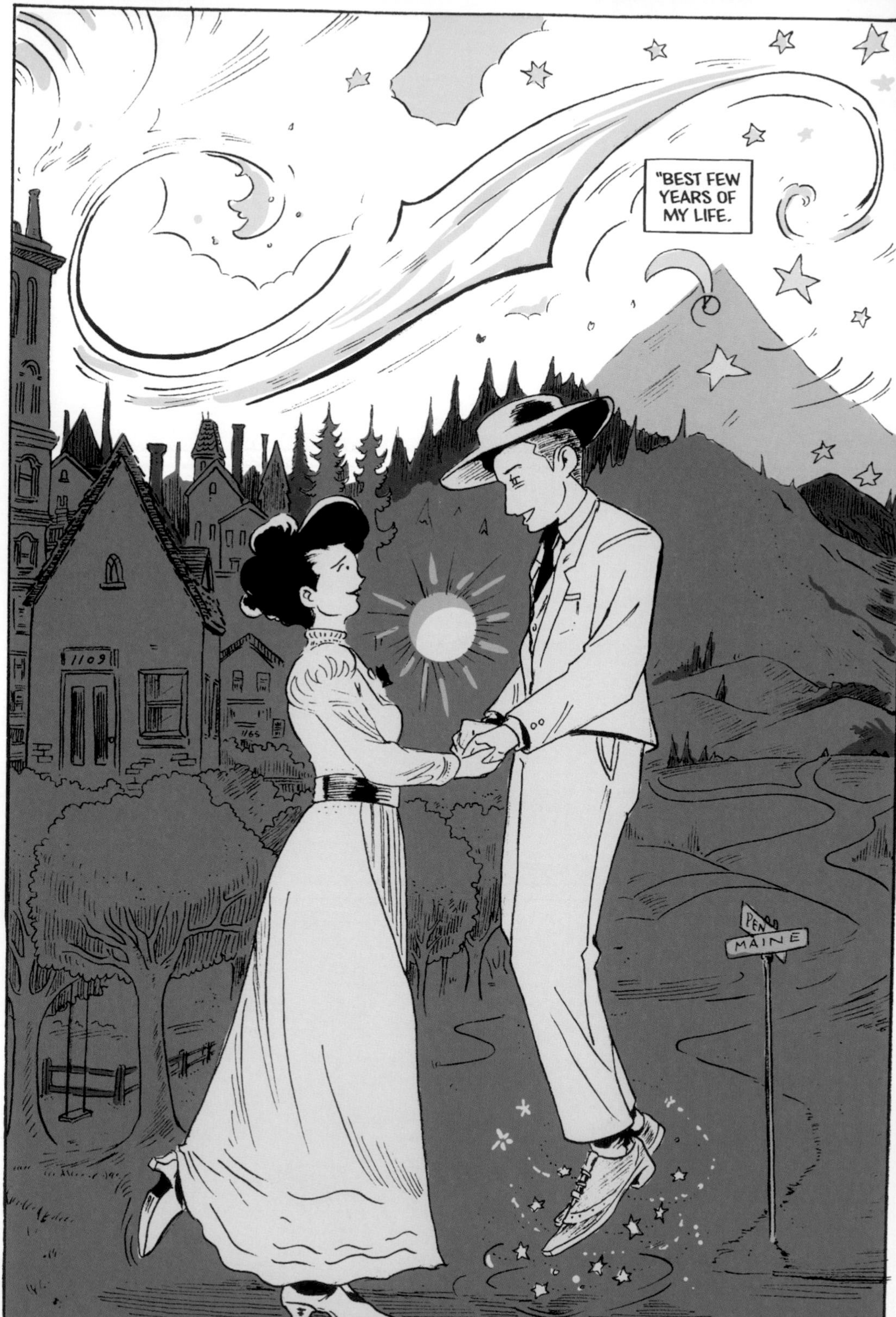
"BEST FEW YEARS OF MY LIFE.
1109
1165
PEN
MAINE

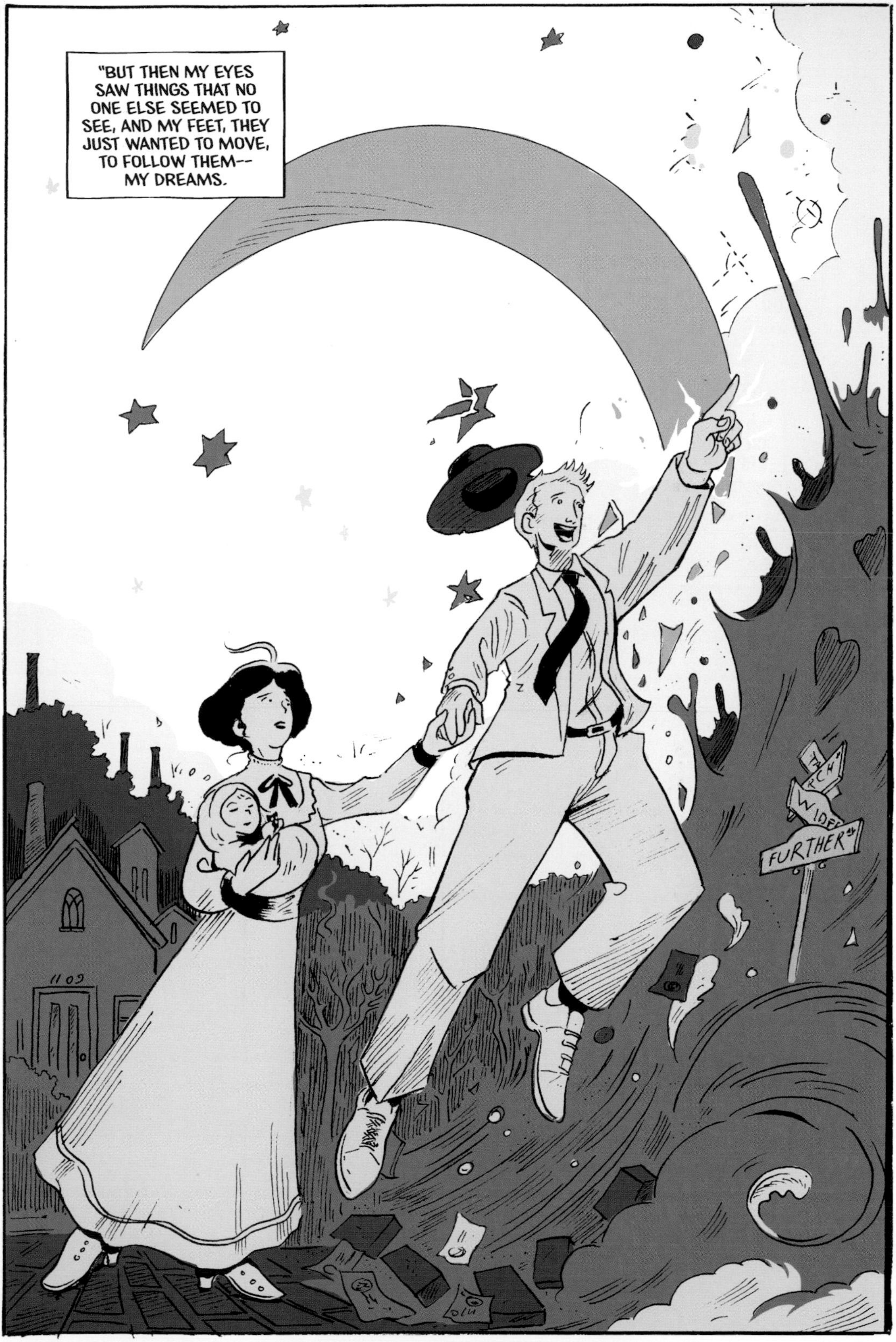
"BUT THEN MY EYES SAW THINGS THAT NO ONE ELSE SEEMED TO SEE, AND MY FEET, THEY JUST WANTED TO MOVE, TO FOLLOW THEM-- MY DREAMS.
FURTHER

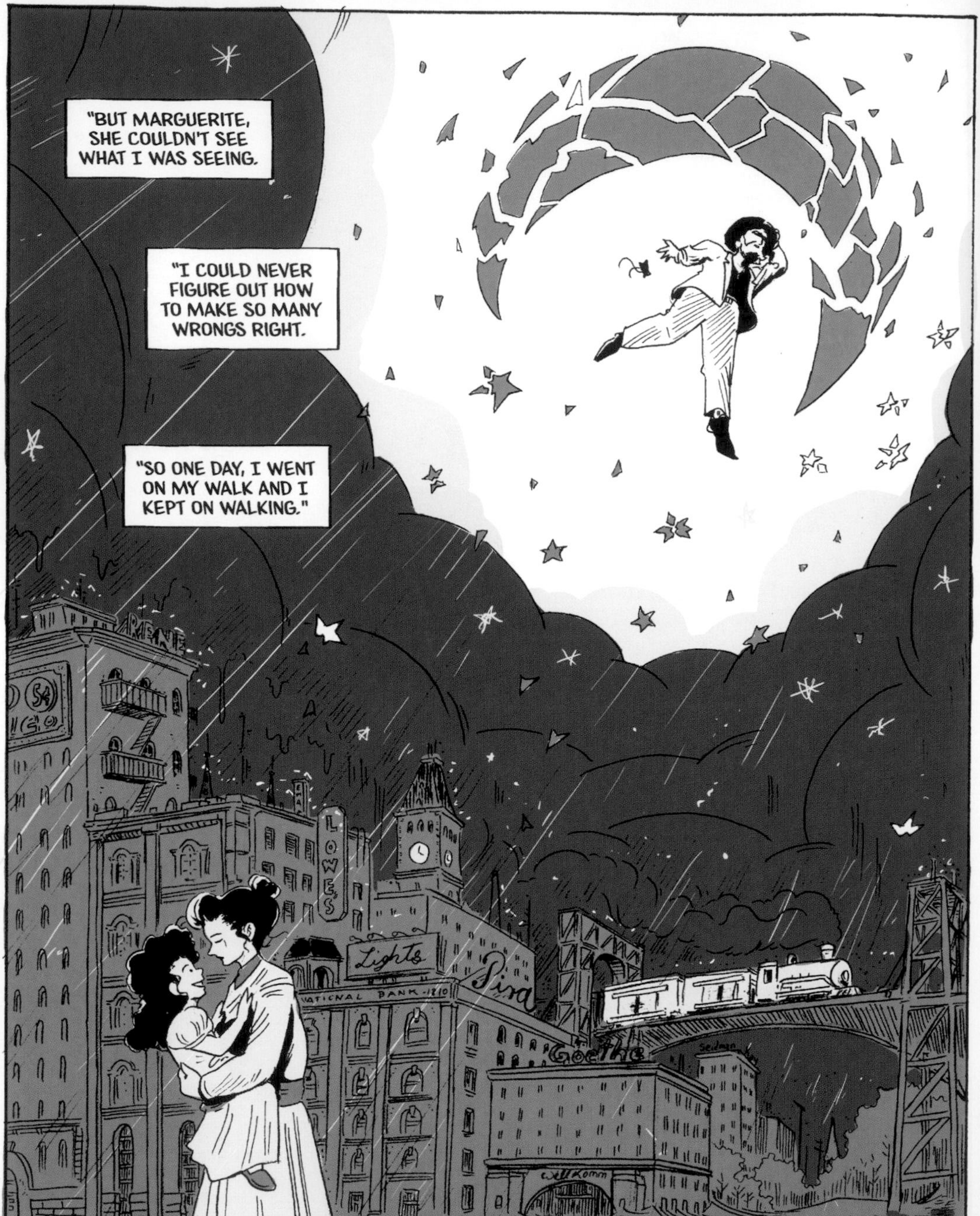
"BUT MARGUERITE, SHE COULDN'T SEE WHAT I WAS SEEING.
"I COULD NEVER FIGURE OUT HOW TO MAKE SO MANY WRONGS RIGHT.
"SO ONE DAY, I WENT ON MY WALK AND I KEPT ON WALKING."
LOWES
Lights
Goethe

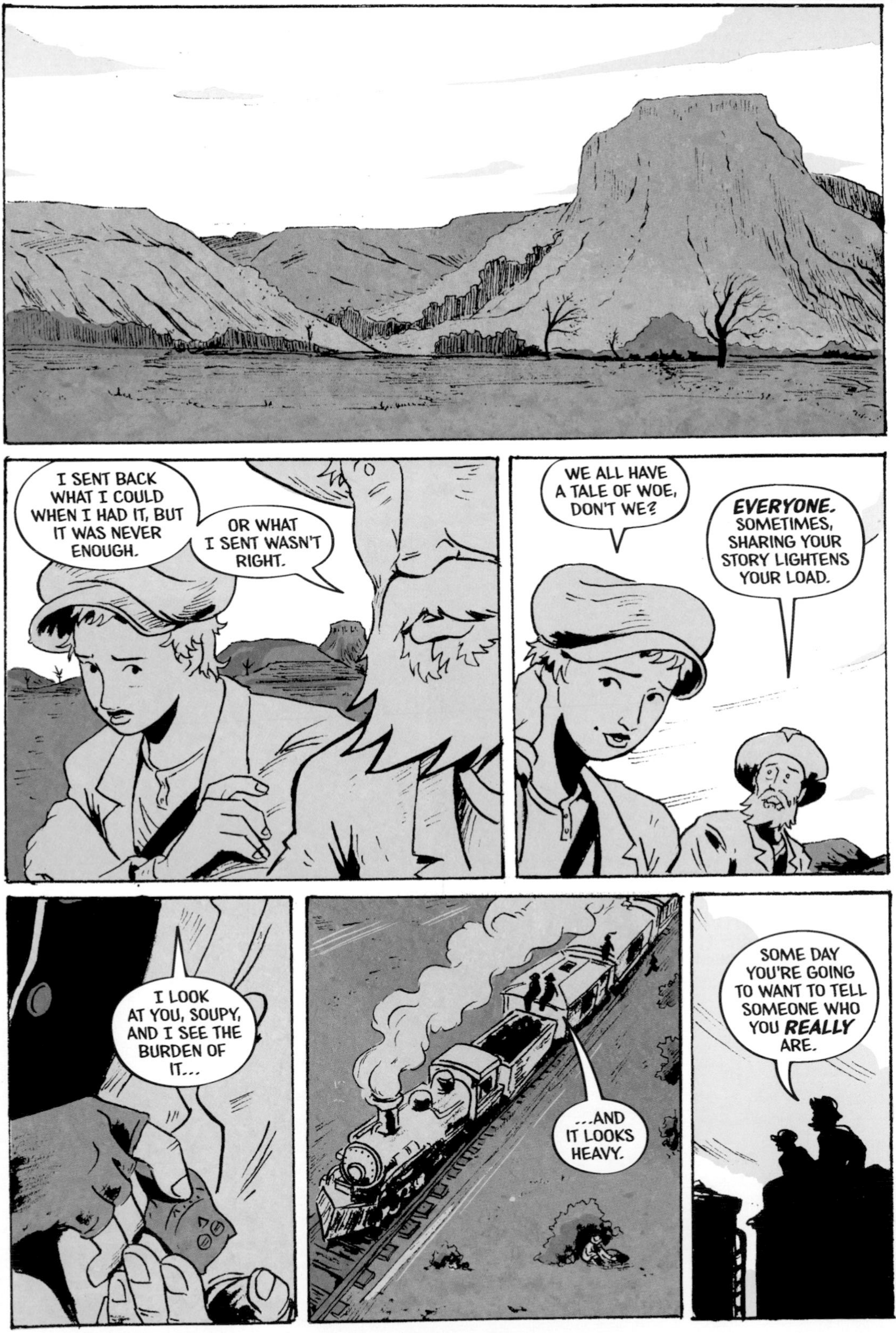
I SENT BACK WHAT I COULD WHEN I HAD IT, BUT IT WAS NEVER ENOUGH.
OR WHAT I SENT WASN'T RIGHT.
WE ALL HAVE A TALE OF WOE, DON'T WE?
EVERYONE. SOMETIMES, SHARING YOUR STORY LIGHTENS YOUR LOAD.
I LOOK AT YOU, SOUPY, AND I SEE THE BURDEN OF IT...
...AND IT LOOKS HEAVY.
SOME DAY YOU'RE GOING TO WANT TO TELL SOMEONE WHO YOU *REALLY* ARE.

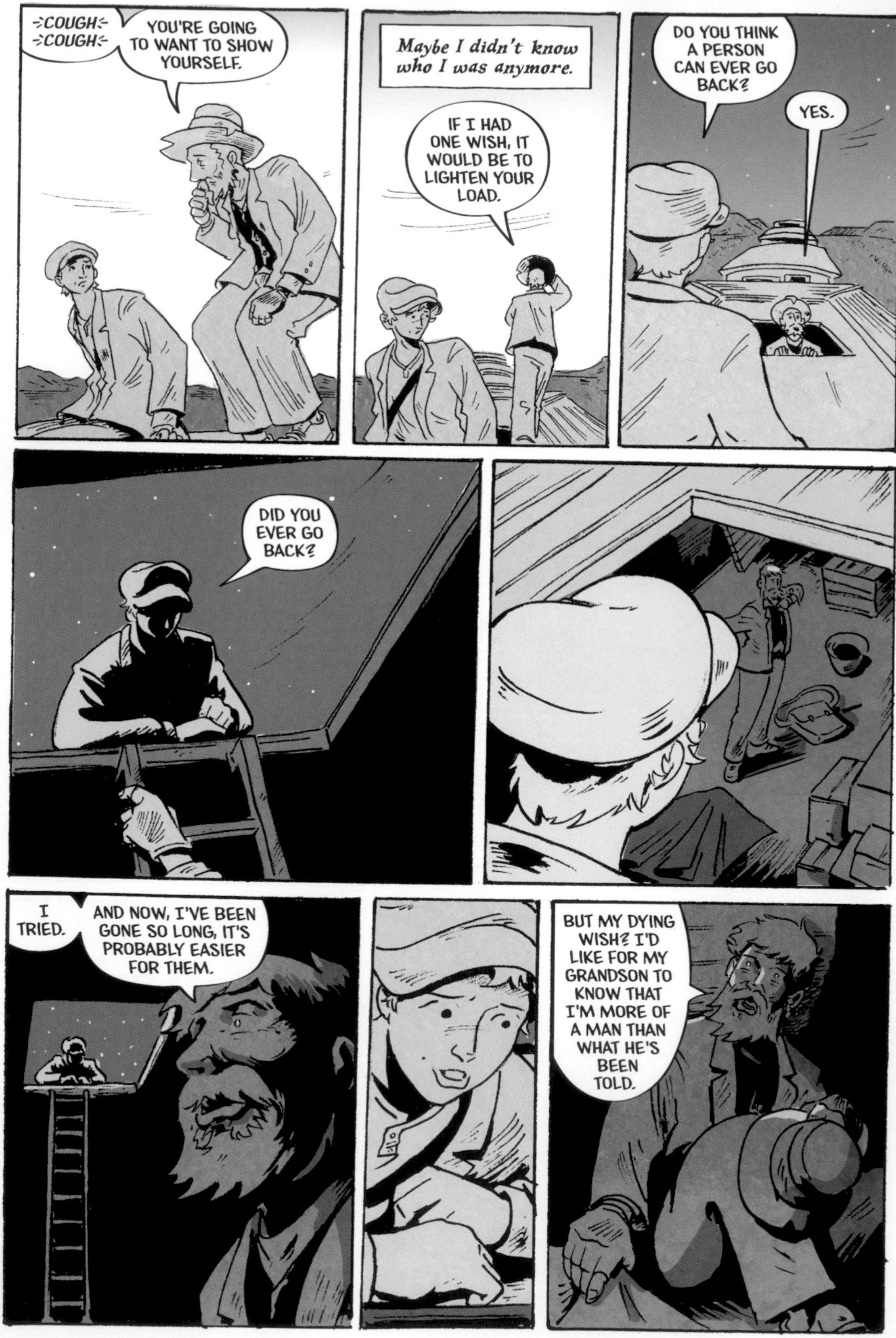

COUGH
COUGH
YOU'RE GOING TO WANT TO SHOW YOURSELF.
Maybe I didn't know who I was anymore.
IF I HAD ONE WISH, IT WOULD BE TO LIGHTEN YOUR LOAD.
DO YOU THINK A PERSON CAN EVER GO BACK?
YES.
DID YOU EVER GO BACK?
I TRIED.
AND NOW, I'VE BEEN GONE SO LONG, IT'S PROBABLY EASIER FOR THEM.
BUT MY DYING WISH? I'D LIKE FOR MY GRANDSON TO KNOW THAT I'M MORE OF A MAN THAN WHAT HE'S BEEN TOLD.

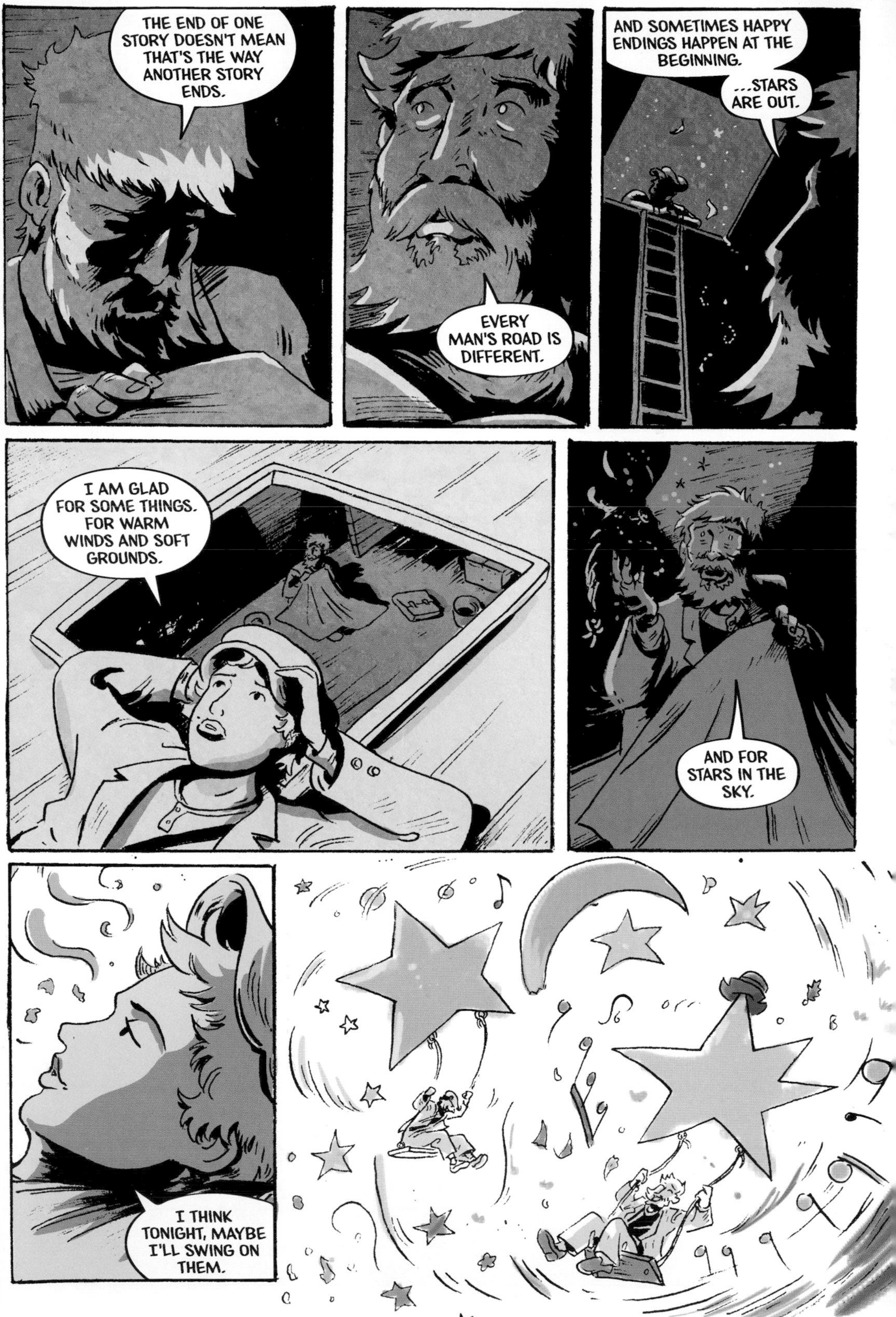
THE END OF ONE STORY DOESN'T MEAN THAT'S THE WAY ANOTHER STORY ENDS.
EVERY MAN'S ROAD IS DIFFERENT.
AND SOMETIMES HAPPY ENDINGS HAPPEN AT THE BEGINNING.
...STARS ARE OUT.
I AM GLAD FOR SOME THINGS. FOR WARM WINDS AND SOFT GROUNDS.
AND FOR STARS IN THE SKY.
I THINK TONIGHT, MAYBE I'LL SWING ON THEM.

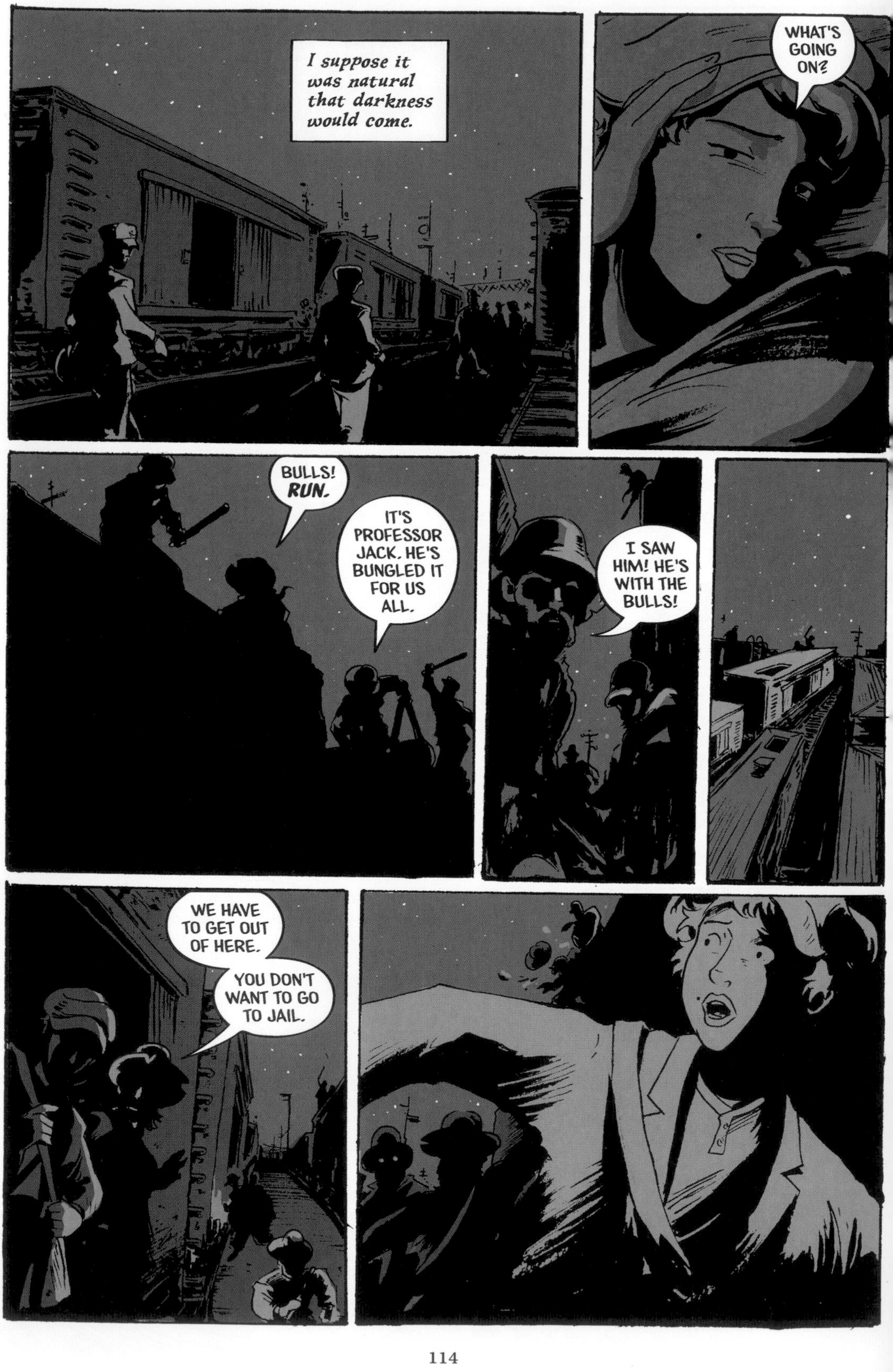
I suppose it was natural that darkness would come.
WHAT'S GOING ON?
BULLS! RUN.
IT'S PROFESSOR JACK. HE'S BUNGLED IT FOR US ALL.
I SAW HIM! HE'S WITH THE BULLS!
WE HAVE TO GET OUT OF HERE.
YOU DON'T WANT TO GO TO JAIL.

FOLLOW ME.

I KNOW A WAY OUT AND A PLACE TO GO.

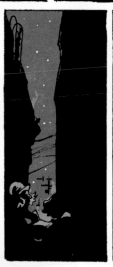

I'M NOT GOING WITH YOU.

IF YOU DON'T COME WITH ME, YOU'LL GET CAUGHT.

YOU EVER BEEN TO JAIL?

NO.

DON'T START NOW.

If I got caught, they would find out that I was a girl.

THEY SAY YOU CAUSED THIS TROUBLE.

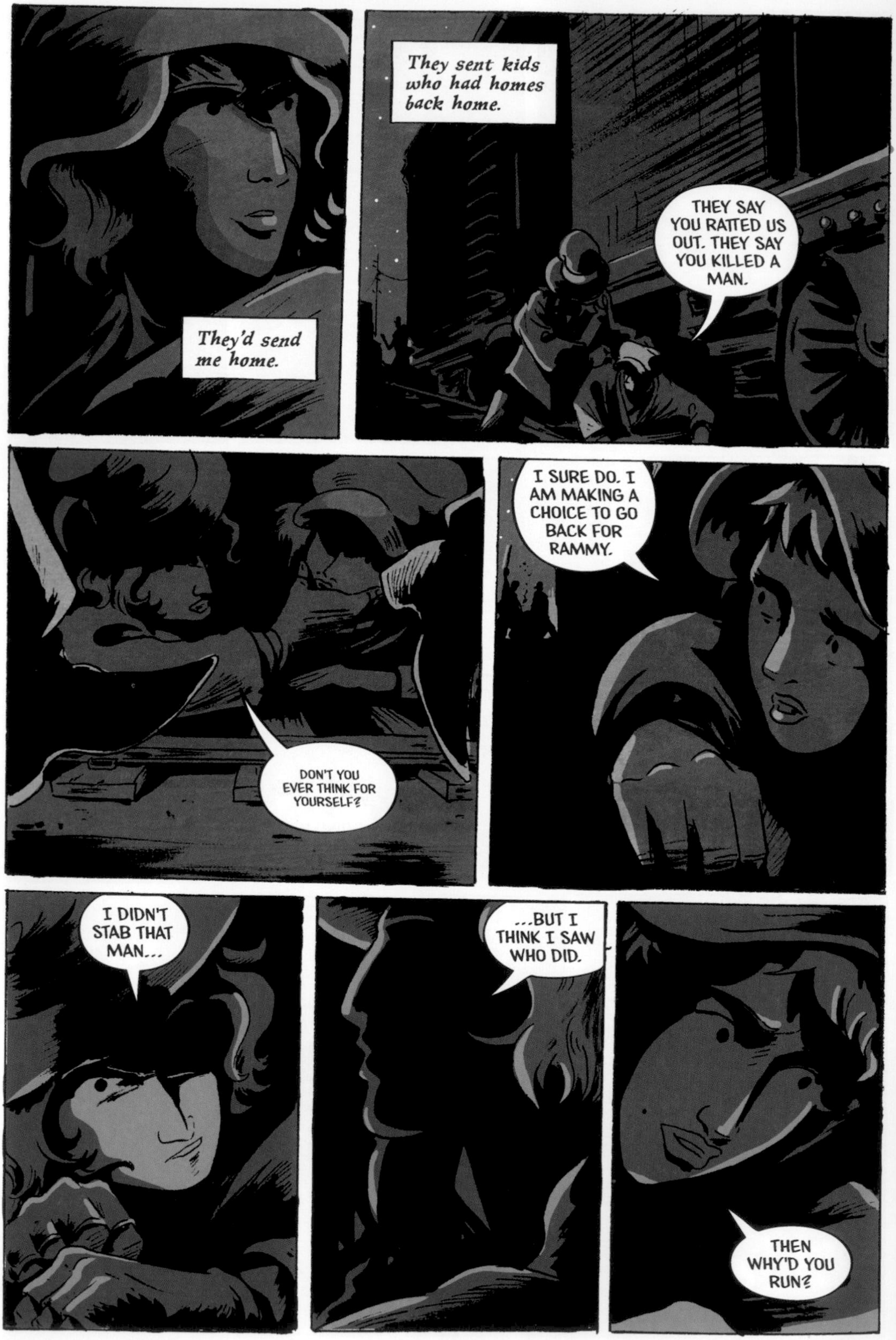
They'd send me home.
They sent kids who had homes back home.
THEY SAY YOU RATTED US OUT. THEY SAY YOU KILLED A MAN.
DON'T YOU EVER THINK FOR YOURSELF?
I SURE DO. I AM MAKING A CHOICE TO GO BACK FOR RAMMY.
I DIDN'T STAB THAT MAN...
...BUT I THINK I SAW WHO DID.
THEN WHY'D YOU RUN?

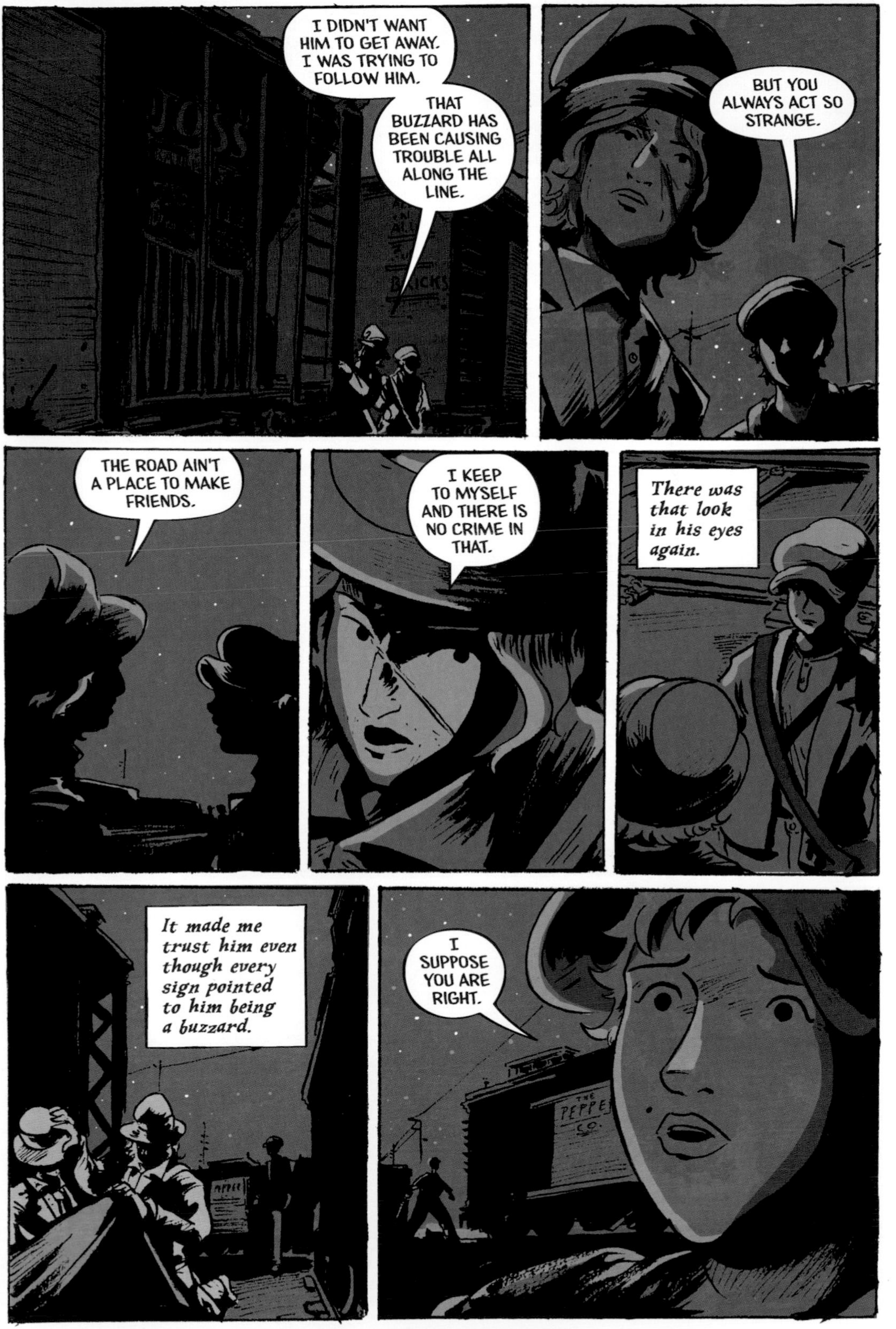
I DIDN'T WANT HIM TO GET AWAY. I WAS TRYING TO FOLLOW HIM.
THAT BUZZARD HAS BEEN CAUSING TROUBLE ALL ALONG THE LINE.
BUT YOU ALWAYS ACT SO STRANGE.
THE ROAD AIN'T A PLACE TO MAKE FRIENDS.
I KEEP TO MYSELF AND THERE IS NO CRIME IN THAT.
There was that look in his eyes again.
It made me trust him even though every sign pointed to him being a buzzard.
I SUPPOSE YOU ARE RIGHT.

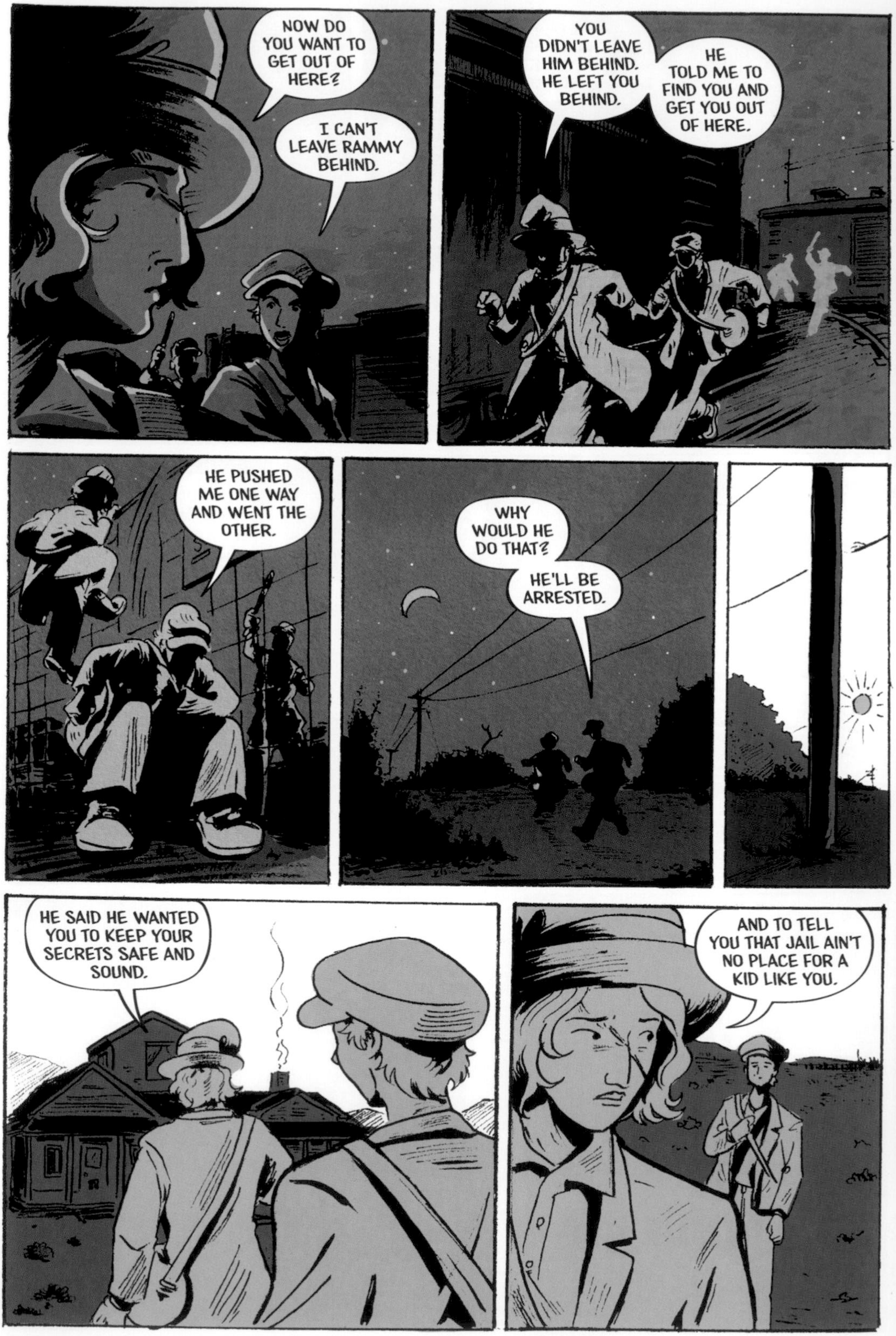
NOW DO YOU WANT TO GET OUT OF HERE?
I CAN'T LEAVE RAMMY BEHIND.
YOU DIDN'T LEAVE HIM BEHIND. HE LEFT YOU BEHIND.
HE TOLD ME TO FIND YOU AND GET YOU OUT OF HERE.
HE PUSHED ME ONE WAY AND WENT THE OTHER.
WHY WOULD HE DO THAT?
HE'LL BE ARRESTED.
HE SAID HE WANTED YOU TO KEEP YOUR SECRETS SAFE AND SOUND.
AND TO TELL YOU THAT JAIL AIN'T NO PLACE FOR A KID LIKE YOU.

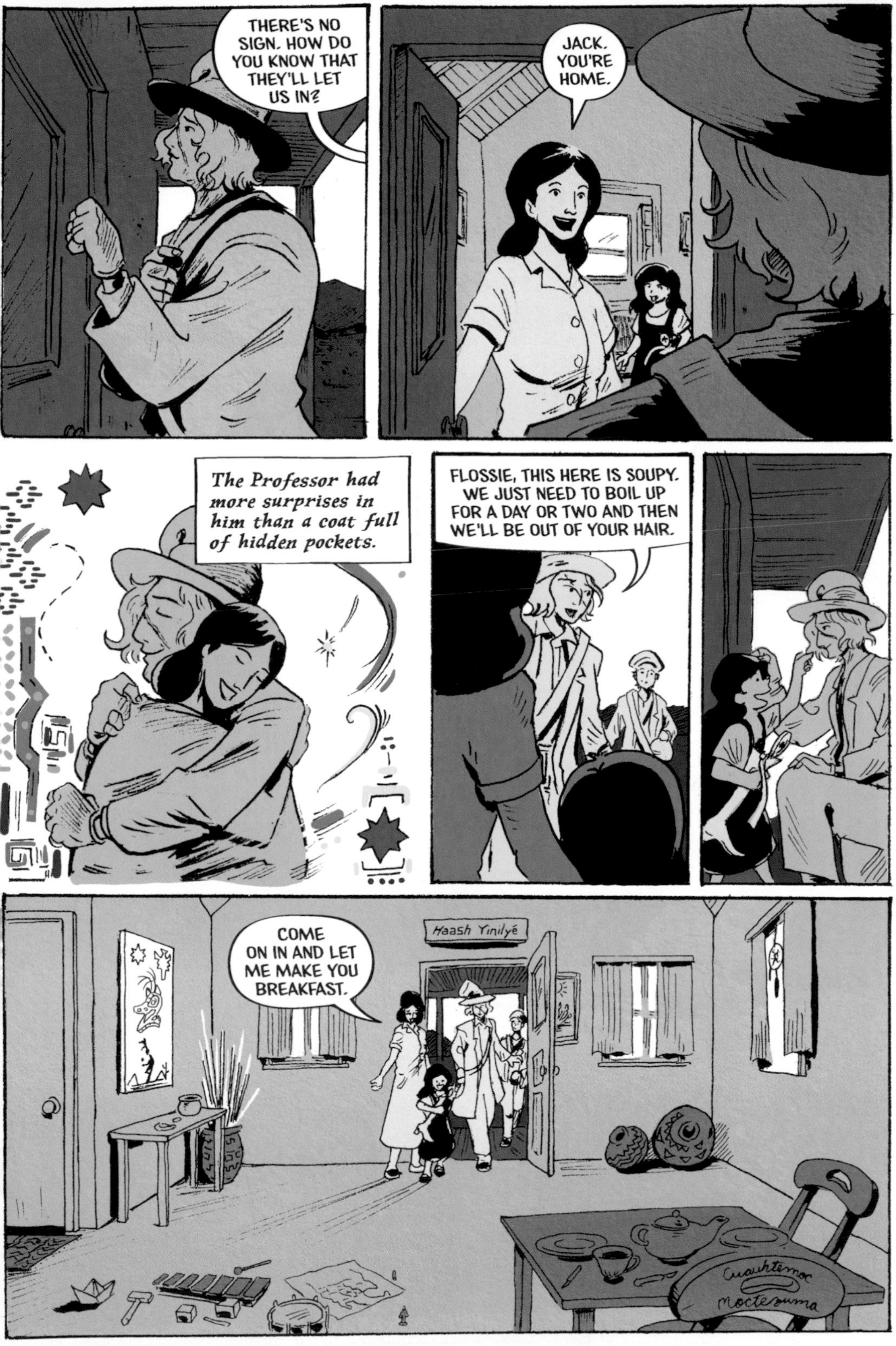
THERE'S NO SIGN. HOW DO YOU KNOW THAT THEY'LL LET US IN?
JACK. YOU'RE HOME.
The Professor had more surprises in him than a coat full of hidden pockets.
FLOSSIE, THIS HERE IS SOUPY. WE JUST NEED TO BOIL UP FOR A DAY OR TWO AND THEN WE'LL BE OUT OF YOUR HAIR.
Haash Yinilyé
COME ON IN AND LET ME MAKE YOU BREAKFAST.
Cuauhtemoc
Moctesuma

The house was warm.

There was love in this home.

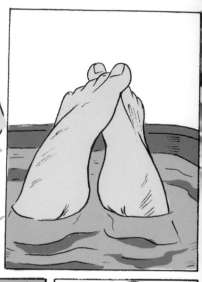

Flossie loved her brother Jack.

And so she cared for me.

I could see myself growing to be happy here.

I could see myself staying forever.

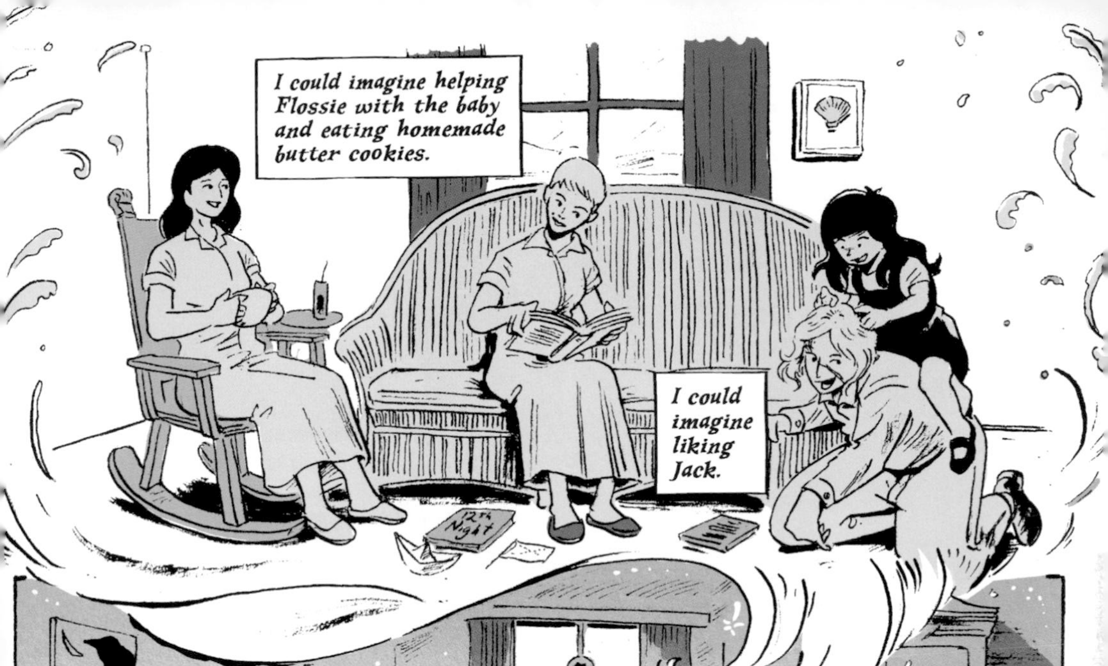
I could imagine helping Flossie with the baby and eating homemade butter cookies.
12th Night
I could imagine liking Jack.

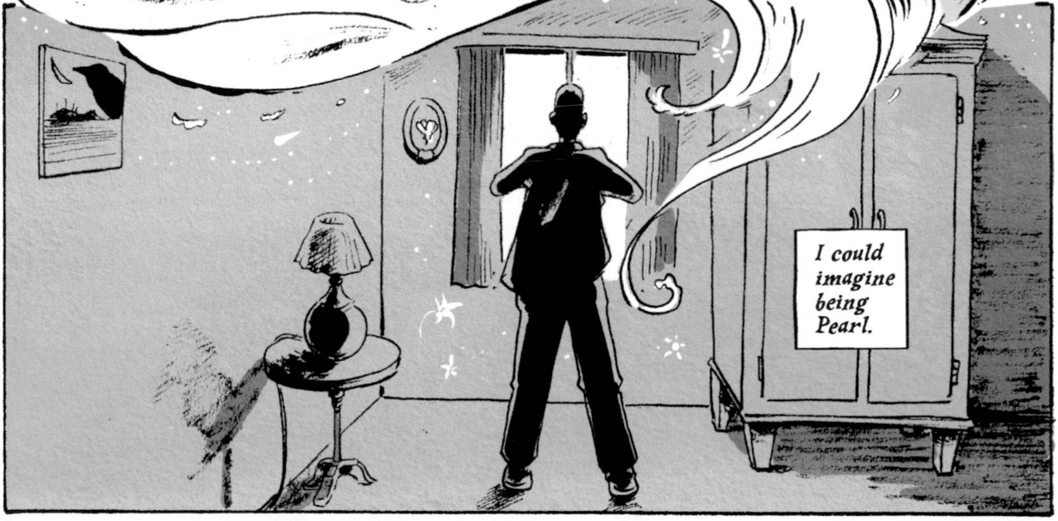
I could imagine being Pearl.

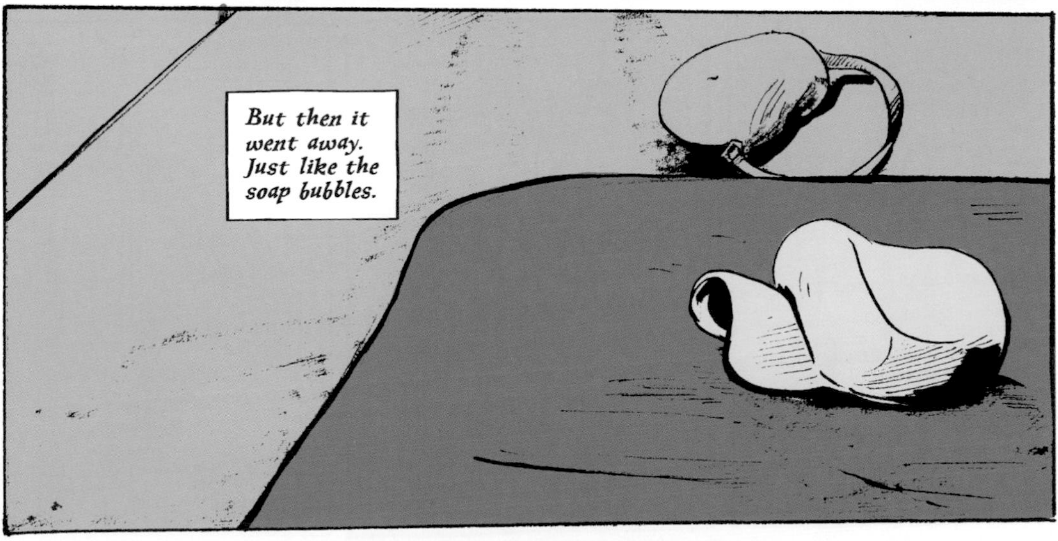
But then it went away. Just like the soap bubbles.

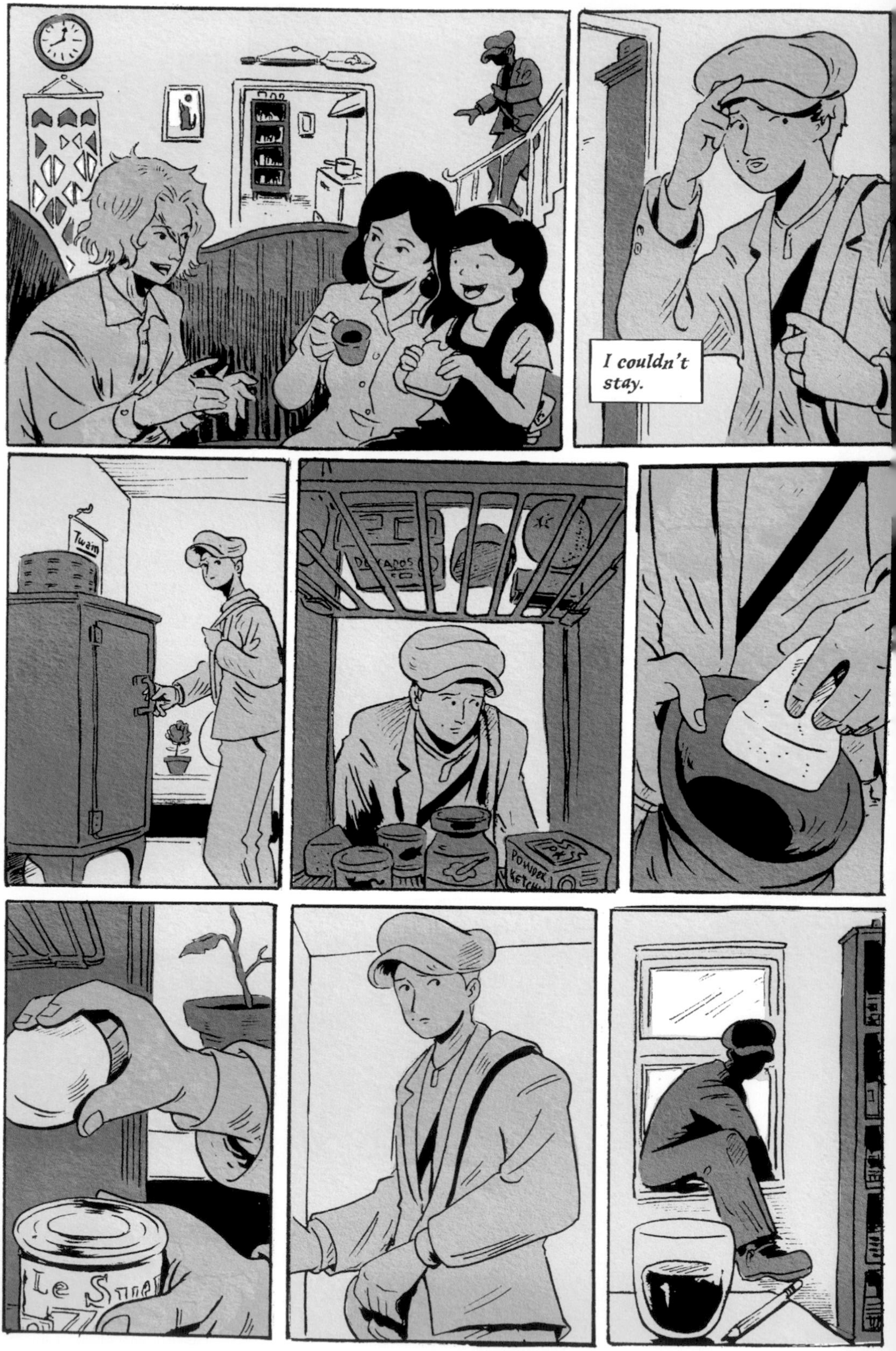
I couldn't stay.
Twain

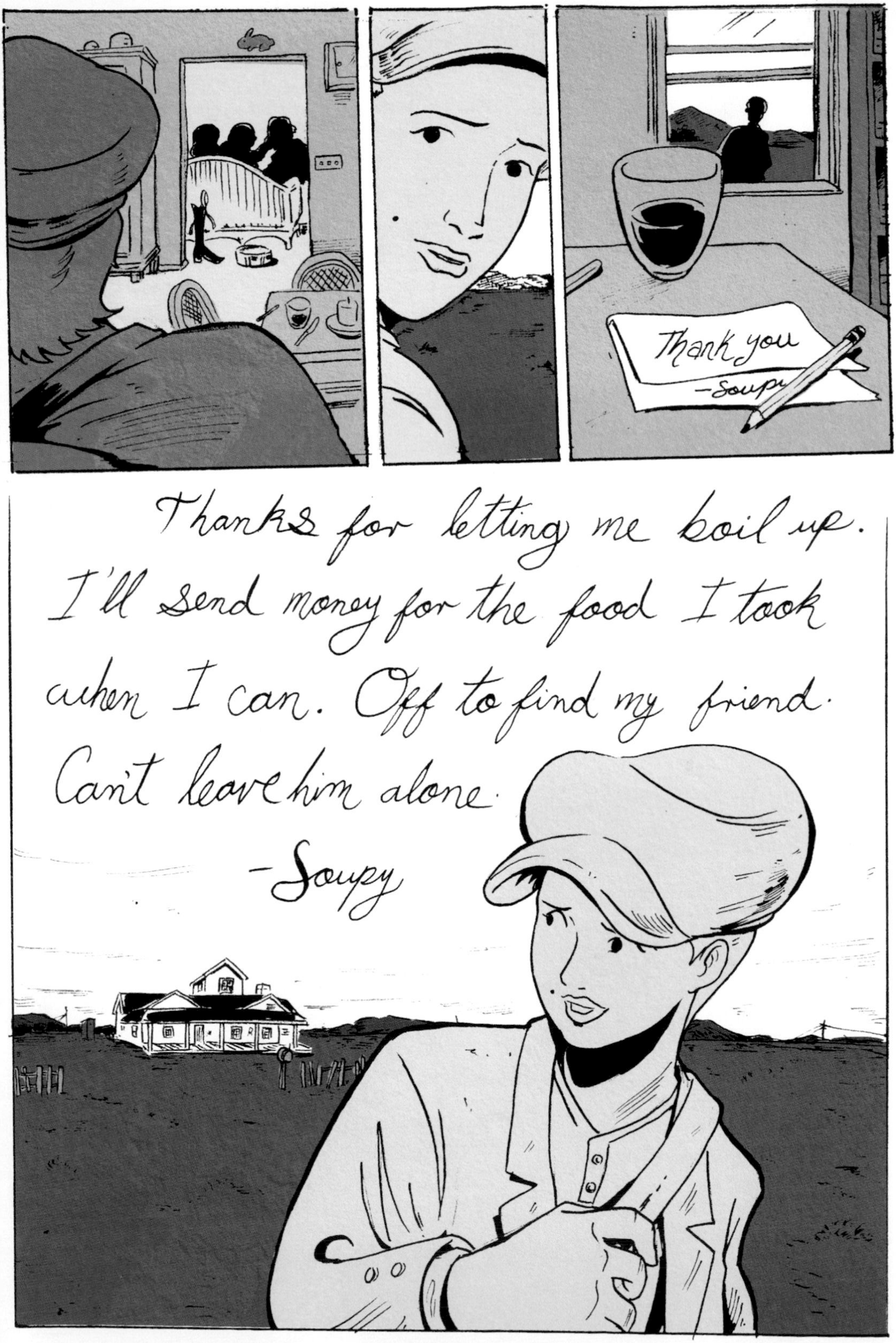
Thank you
-Soupy
Thanks for letting me boil up. I'll send money for the food I took when I can. Off to find my friend. Can't leave him alone.
-Soupy

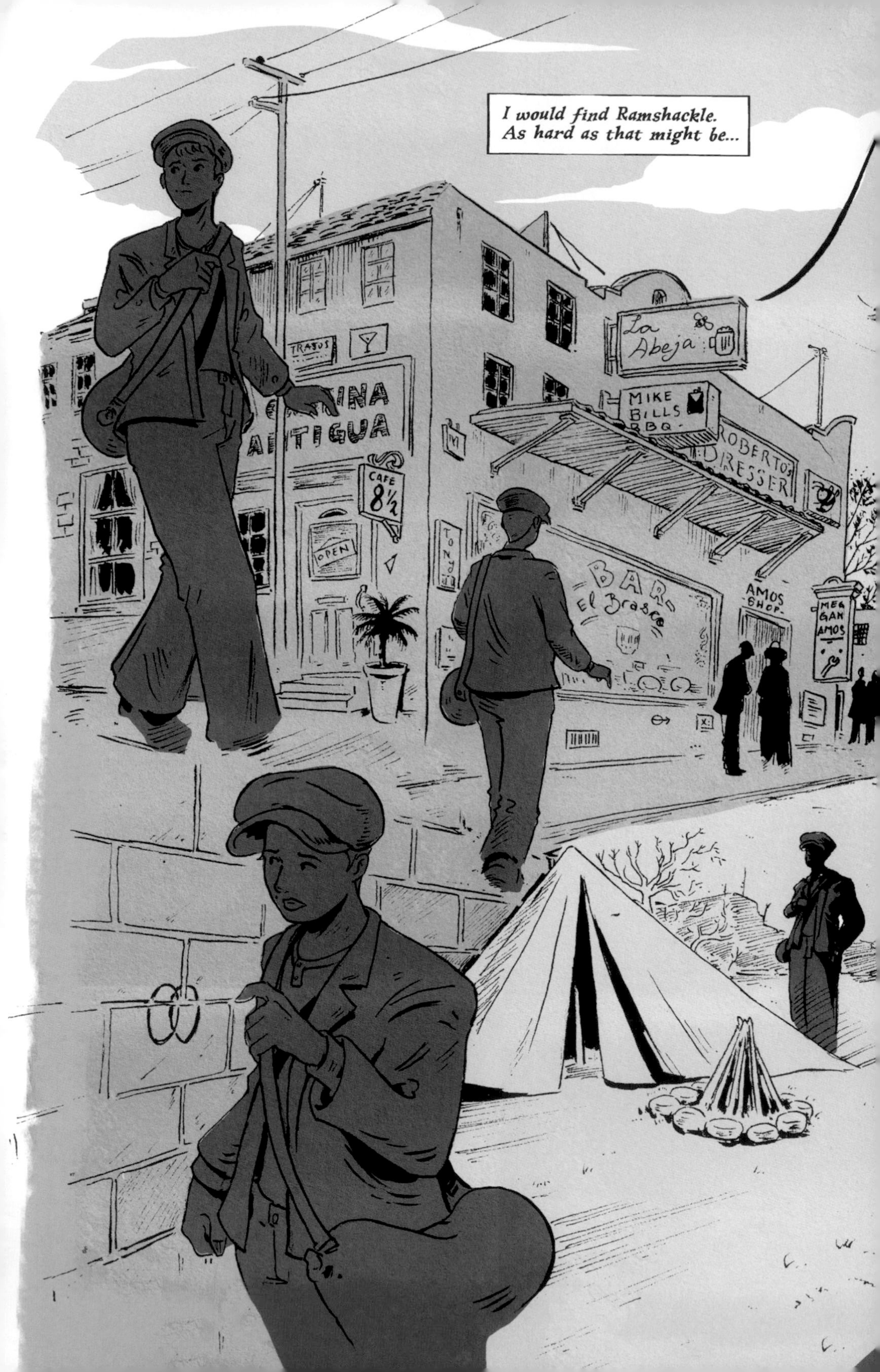
I would find Ramshackle.
As hard as that might be...
La Abeja
MIKE BILLS BBQ
ROBERTO's DRESSER
CAFE 8½
OPEN
TONY
BAR El Brasco
AMOS SHOP
MEG GAN AMOS

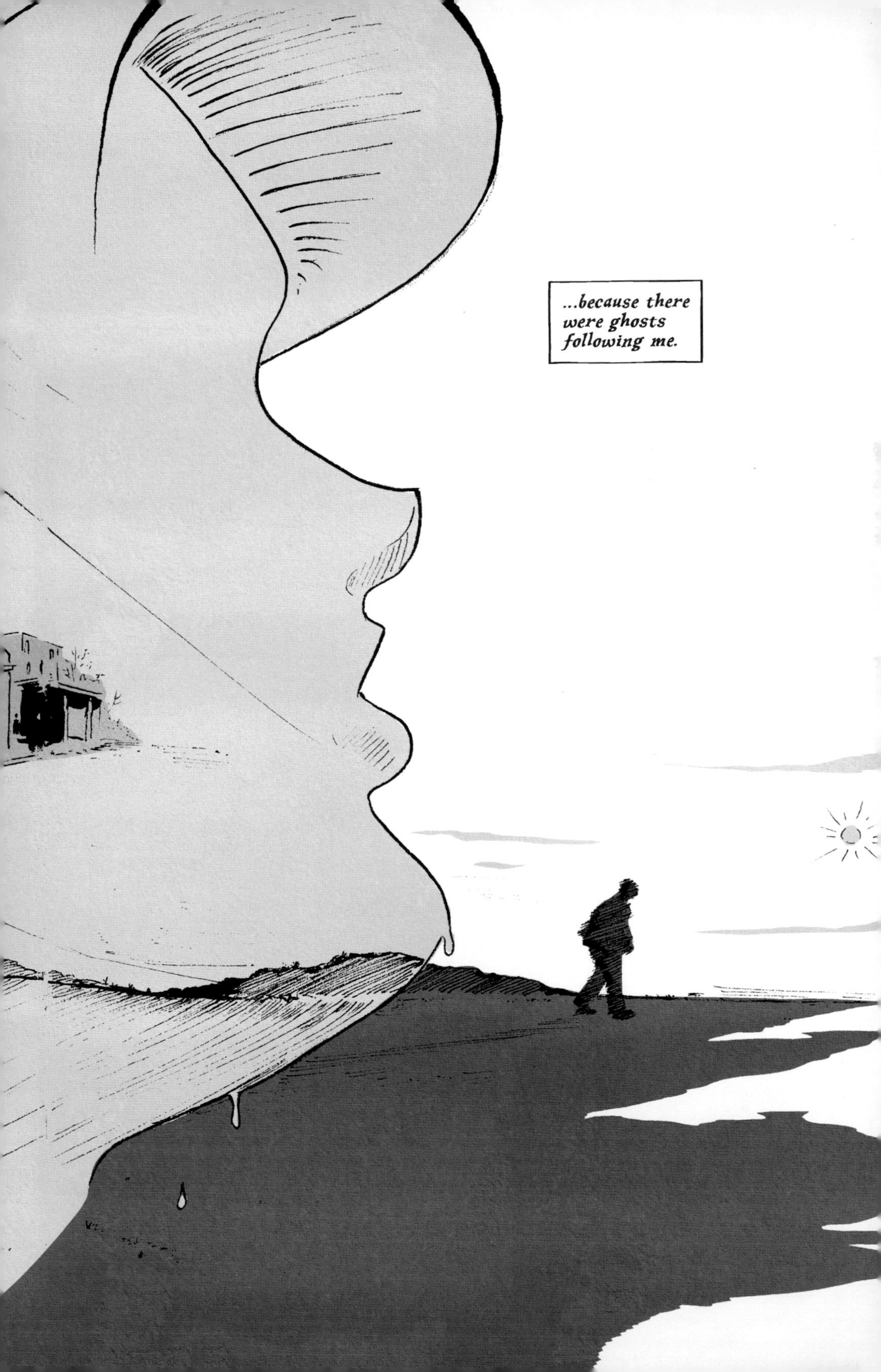
...because there were ghosts following me.

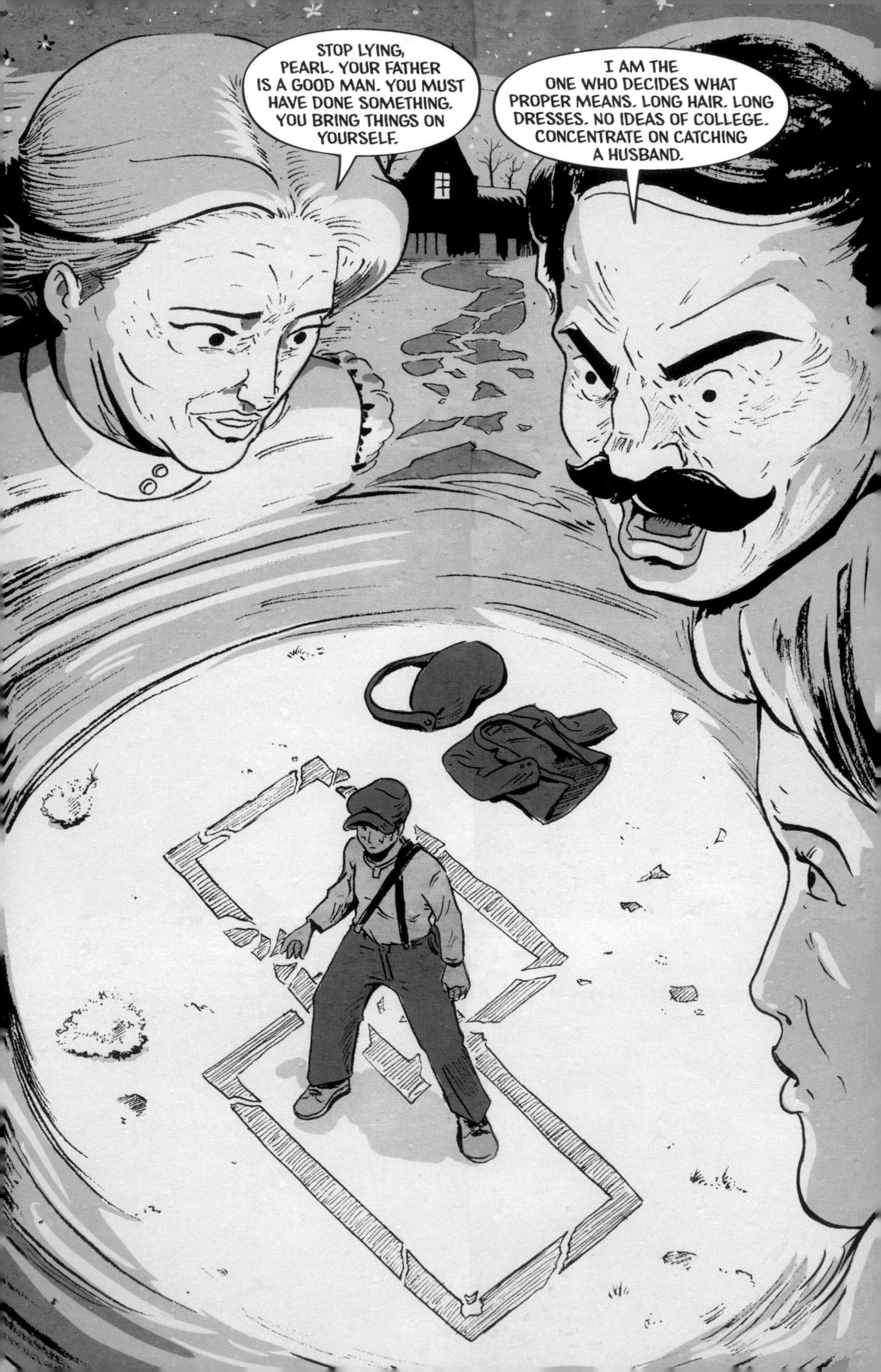
STOP LYING, PEARL. YOUR FATHER IS A GOOD MAN. YOU MUST HAVE DONE SOMETHING. YOU BRING THINGS ON YOURSELF.
I AM THE ONE WHO DECIDES WHAT PROPER MEANS. LONG HAIR. LONG DRESSES. NO IDEAS OF COLLEGE. CONCENTRATE ON CATCHING A HUSBAND.

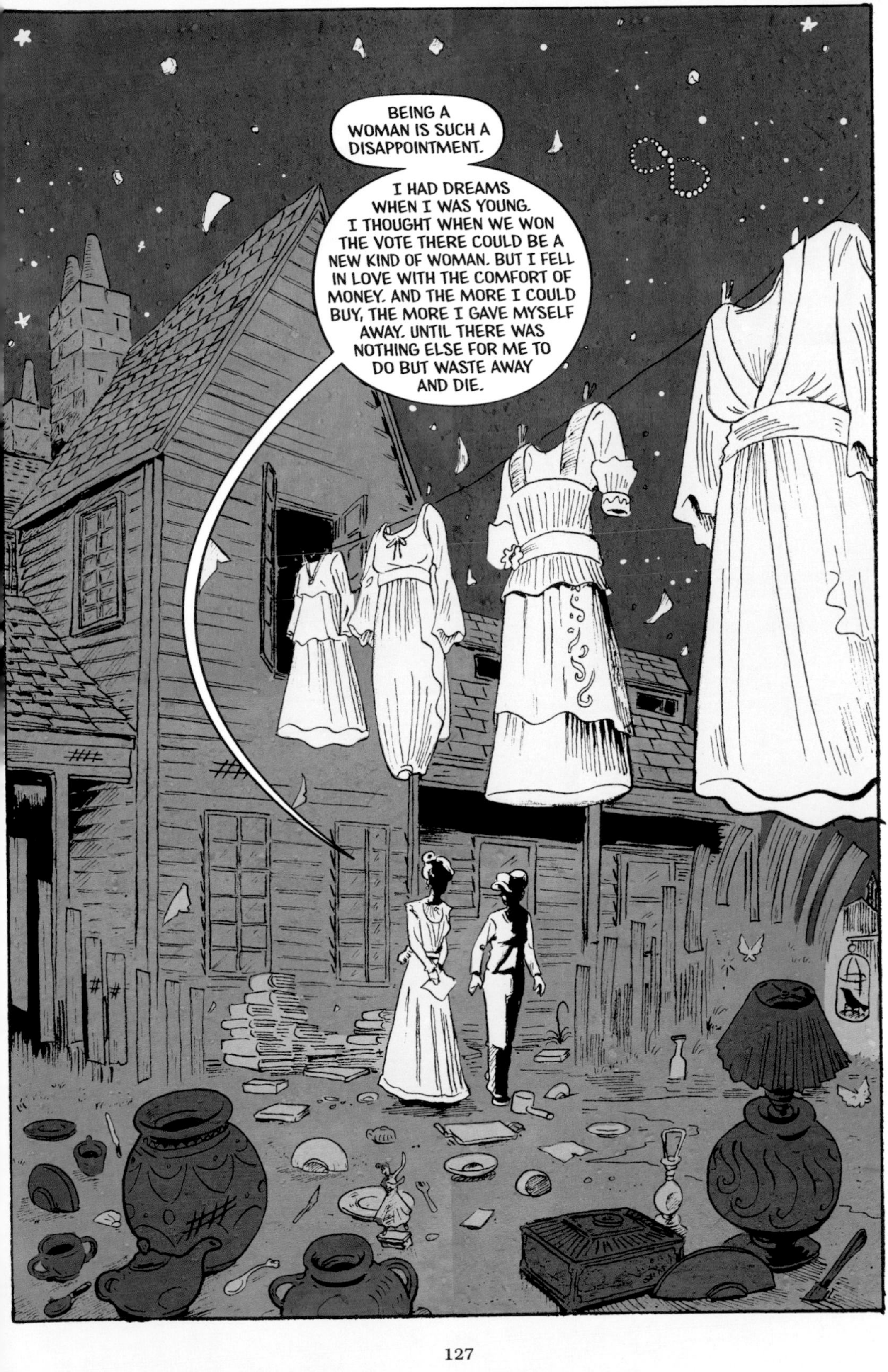
BEING A WOMAN IS SUCH A DISAPPOINTMENT.
I HAD DREAMS WHEN I WAS YOUNG. I THOUGHT WHEN WE WON THE VOTE THERE COULD BE A NEW KIND OF WOMAN. BUT I FELL IN LOVE WITH THE COMFORT OF MONEY. AND THE MORE I COULD BUY, THE MORE I GAVE MYSELF AWAY. UNTIL THERE WAS NOTHING ELSE FOR ME TO DO BUT WASTE AWAY AND DIE.

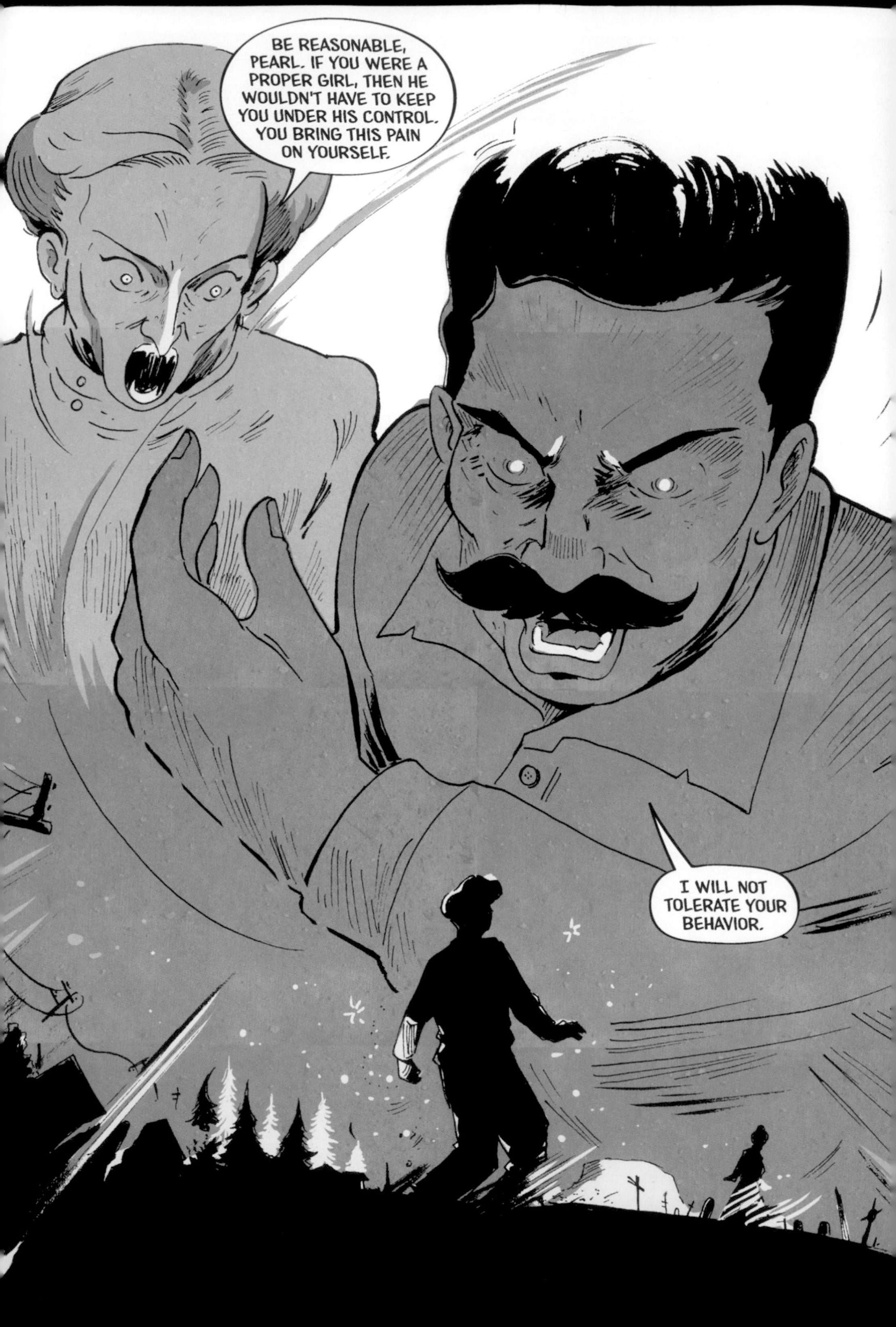
BE REASONABLE, PEARL. IF YOU WERE A PROPER GIRL, THEN HE WOULDN'T HAVE TO KEEP YOU UNDER HIS CONTROL. YOU BRING THIS PAIN ON YOURSELF.
I WILL NOT TOLERATE YOUR BEHAVIOR.

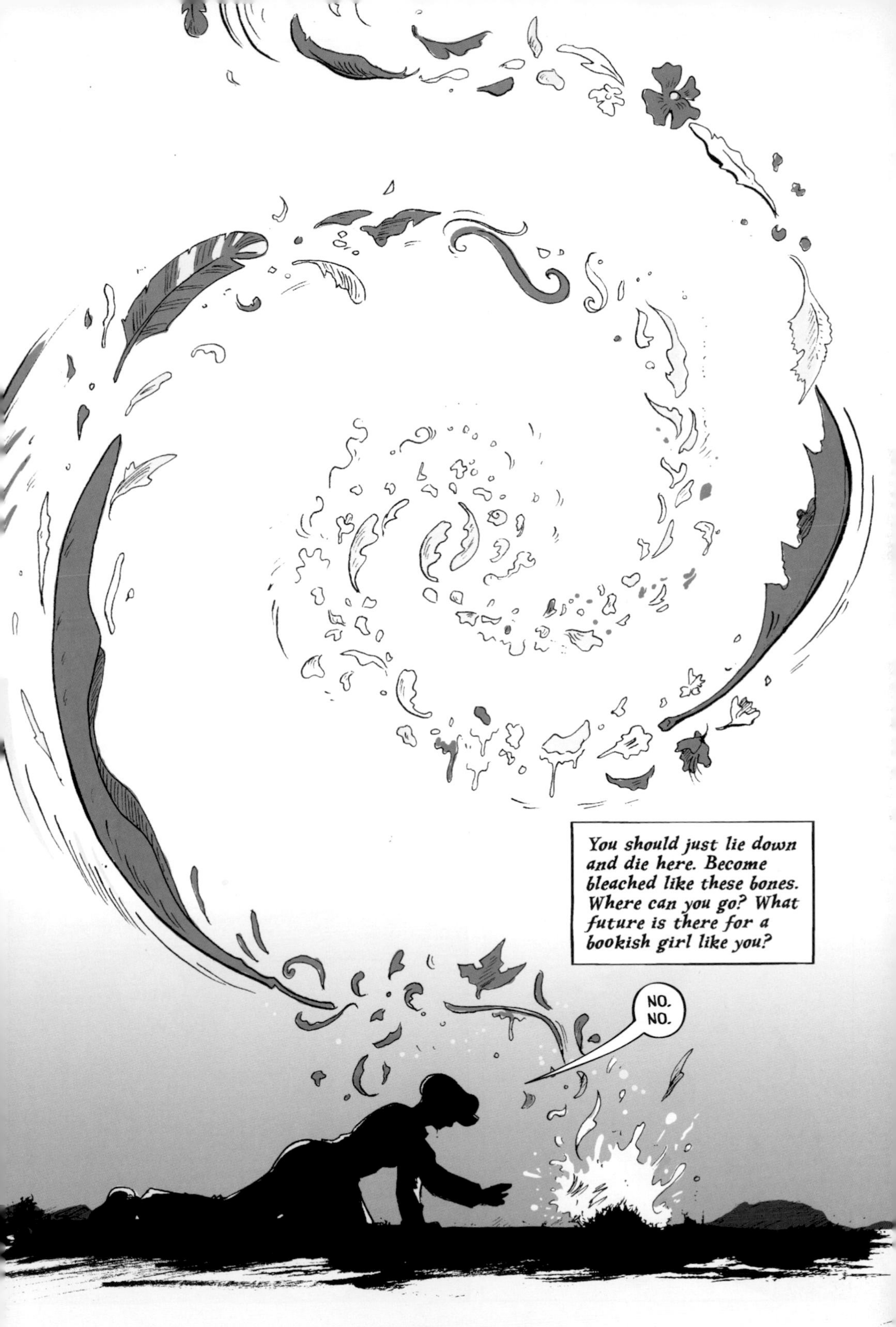
You should just lie down and die here. Become bleached like these bones. Where can you go? What future is there for a bookish girl like you?
NO. NO.

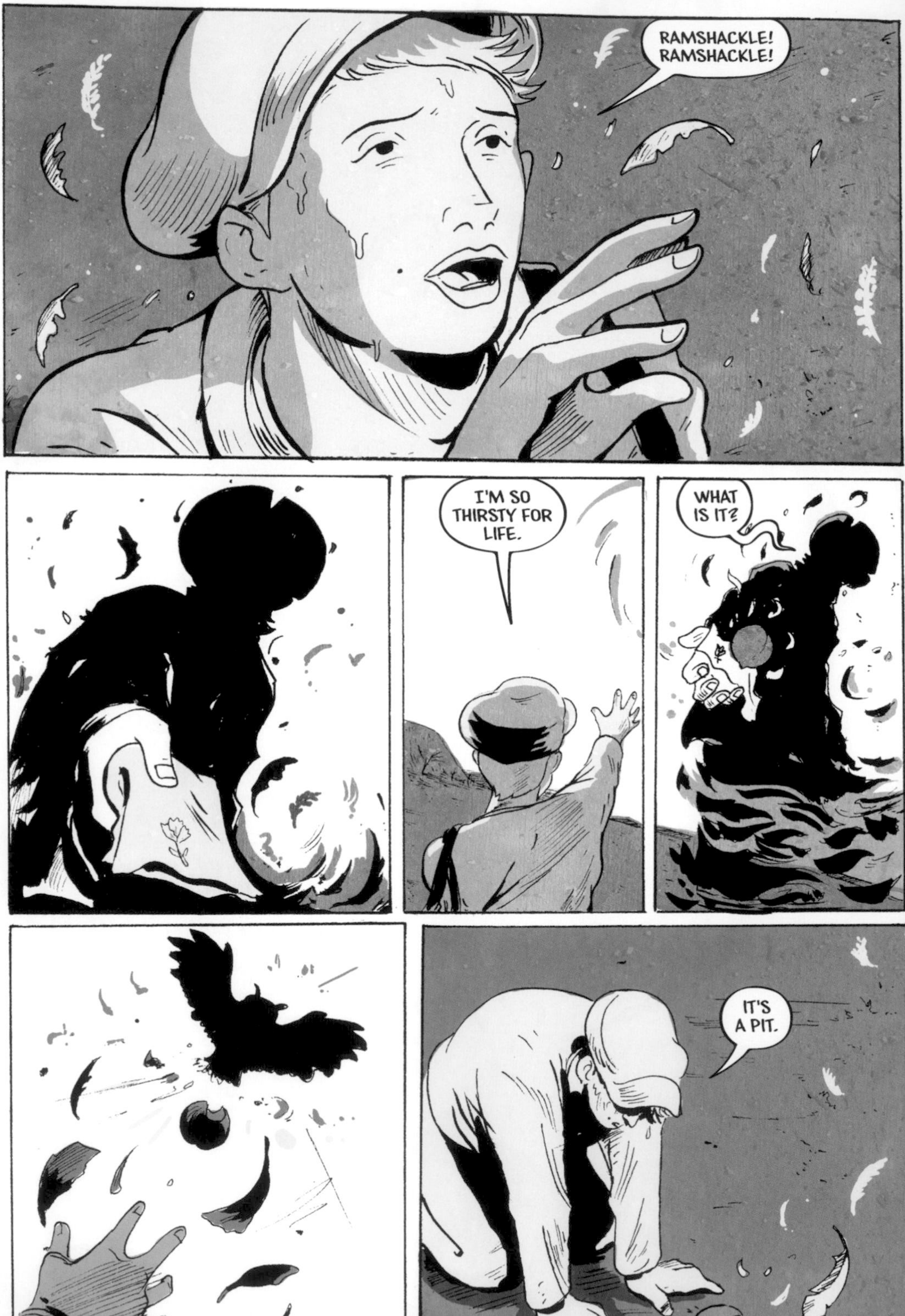
RAMSHACKLE! RAMSHACKLE!
I'M SO THIRSTY FOR LIFE.
WHAT IS IT?
IT'S A PIT.

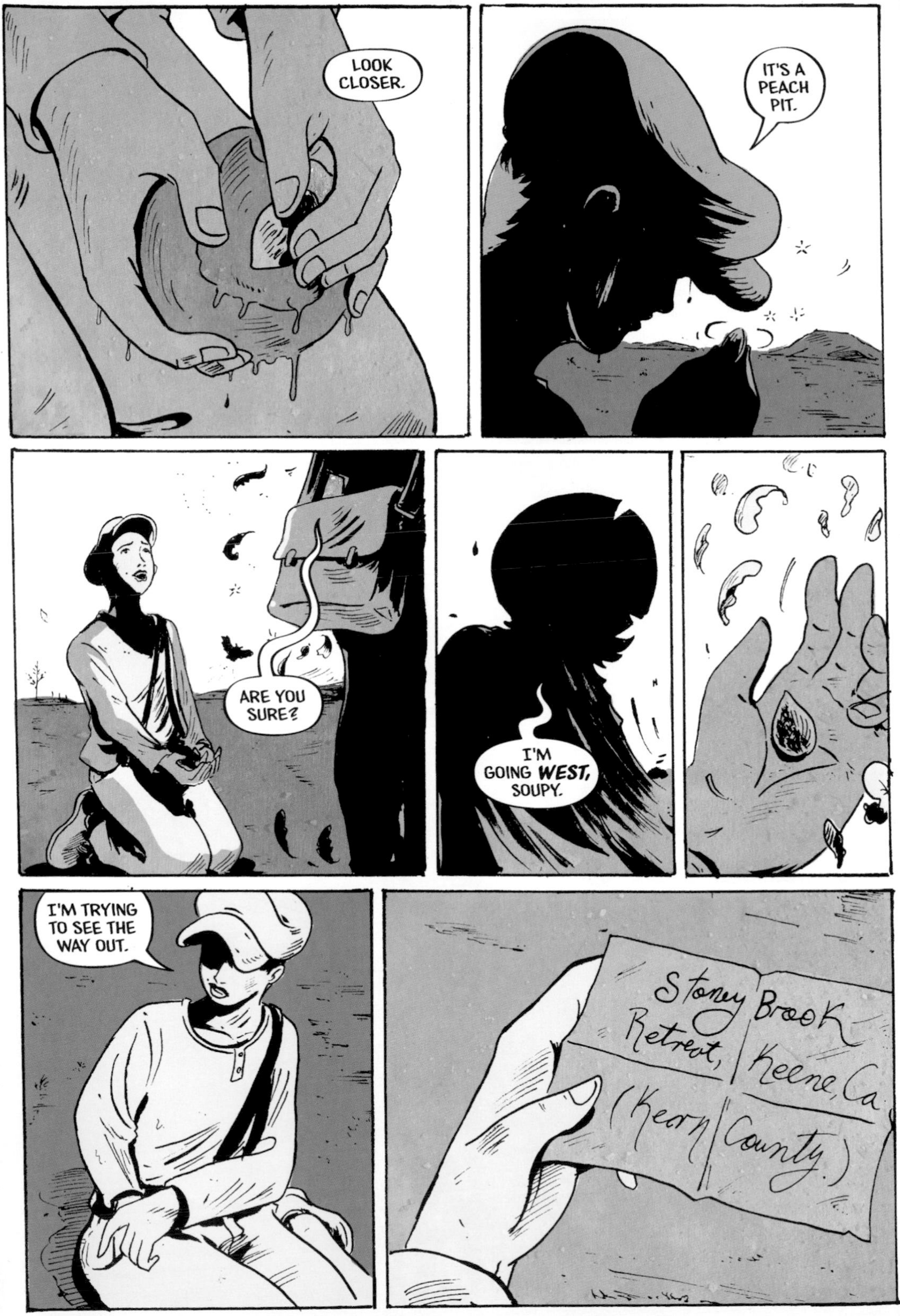
LOOK CLOSER.
IT'S A PEACH PIT.
ARE YOU SURE?
I'M GOING WEST, SOUPY.
I'M TRYING TO SEE THE WAY OUT.
Stoney Brook Retreat, Keene, Ca (Kern County)

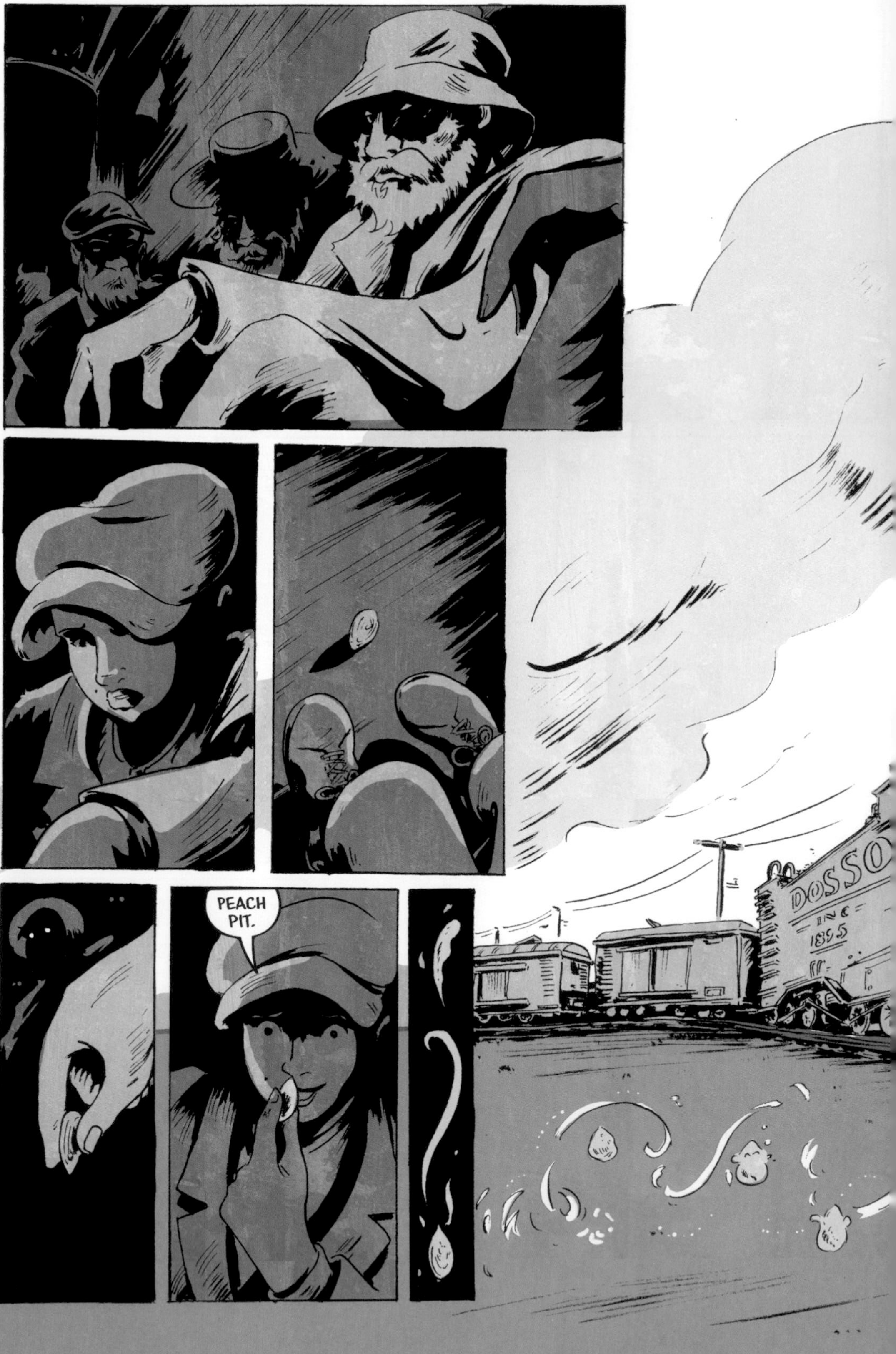
PEACH PIT.
DOSSO
INC
1895

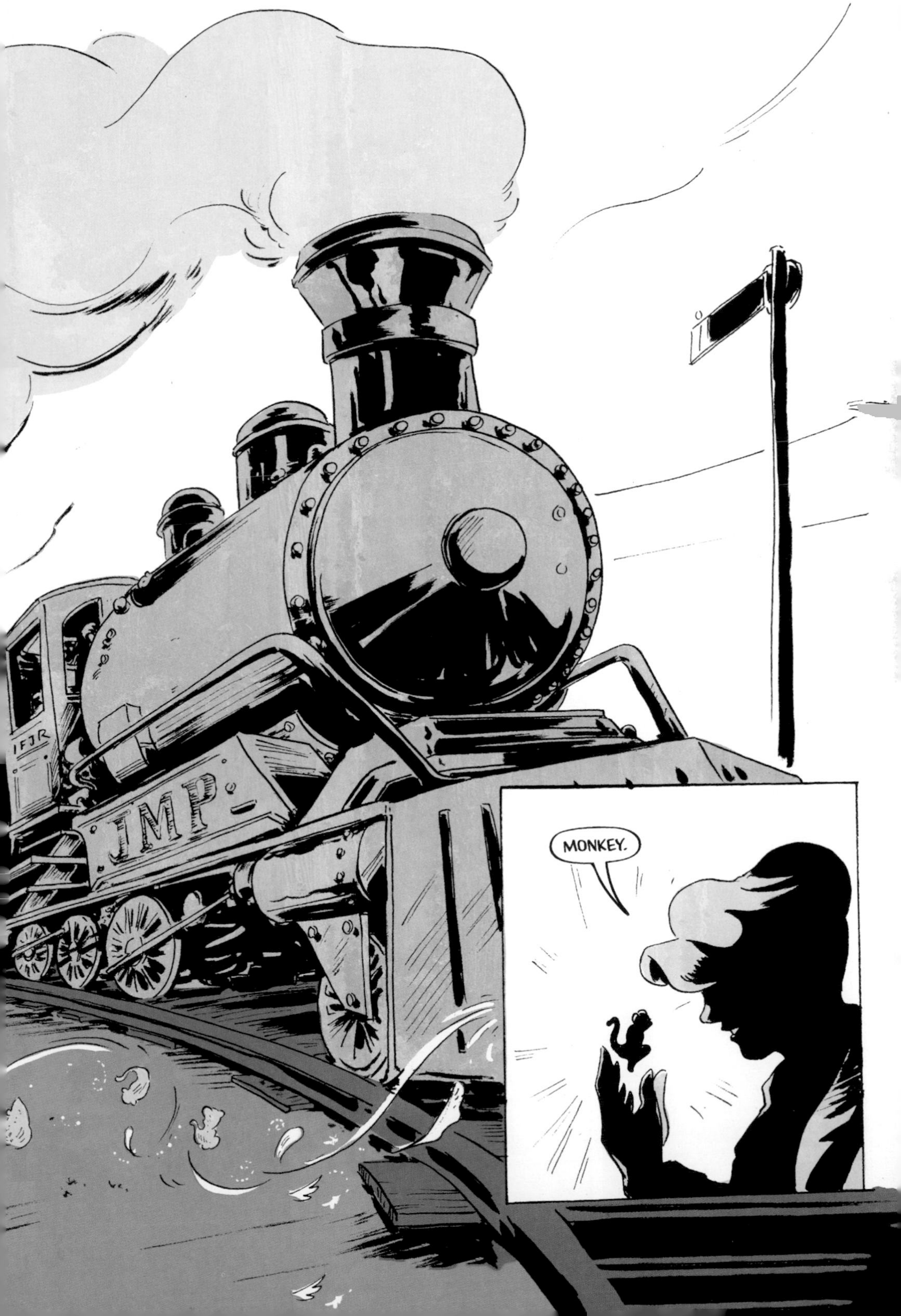
IFJR
JMP
MONKEY.

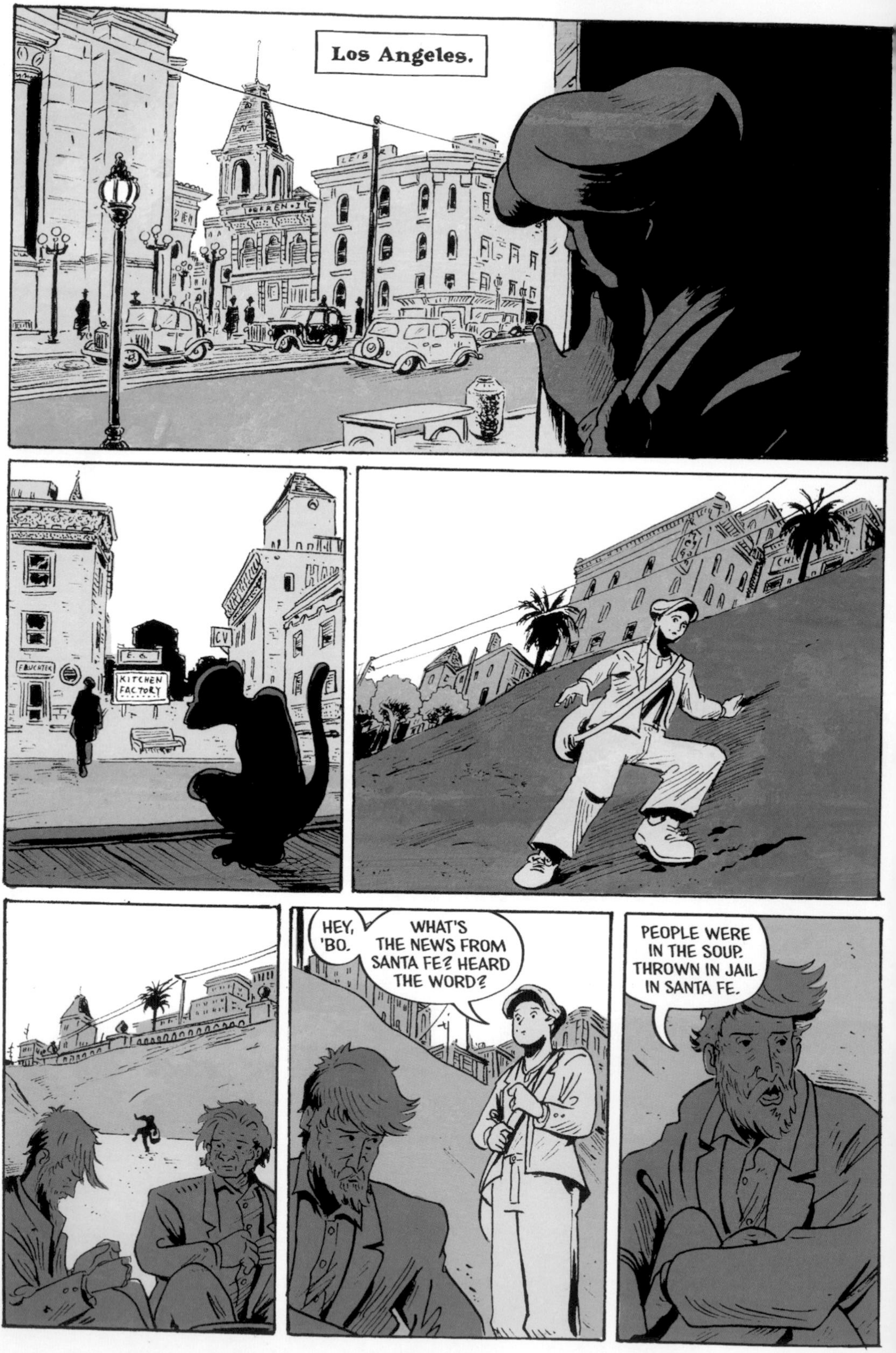
Los Angeles.
KITCHEN FACTORY
HEY, 'BO.
WHAT'S THE NEWS FROM SANTA FE? HEARD THE WORD?
PEOPLE WERE IN THE SOUP. THROWN IN JAIL IN SANTA FE.

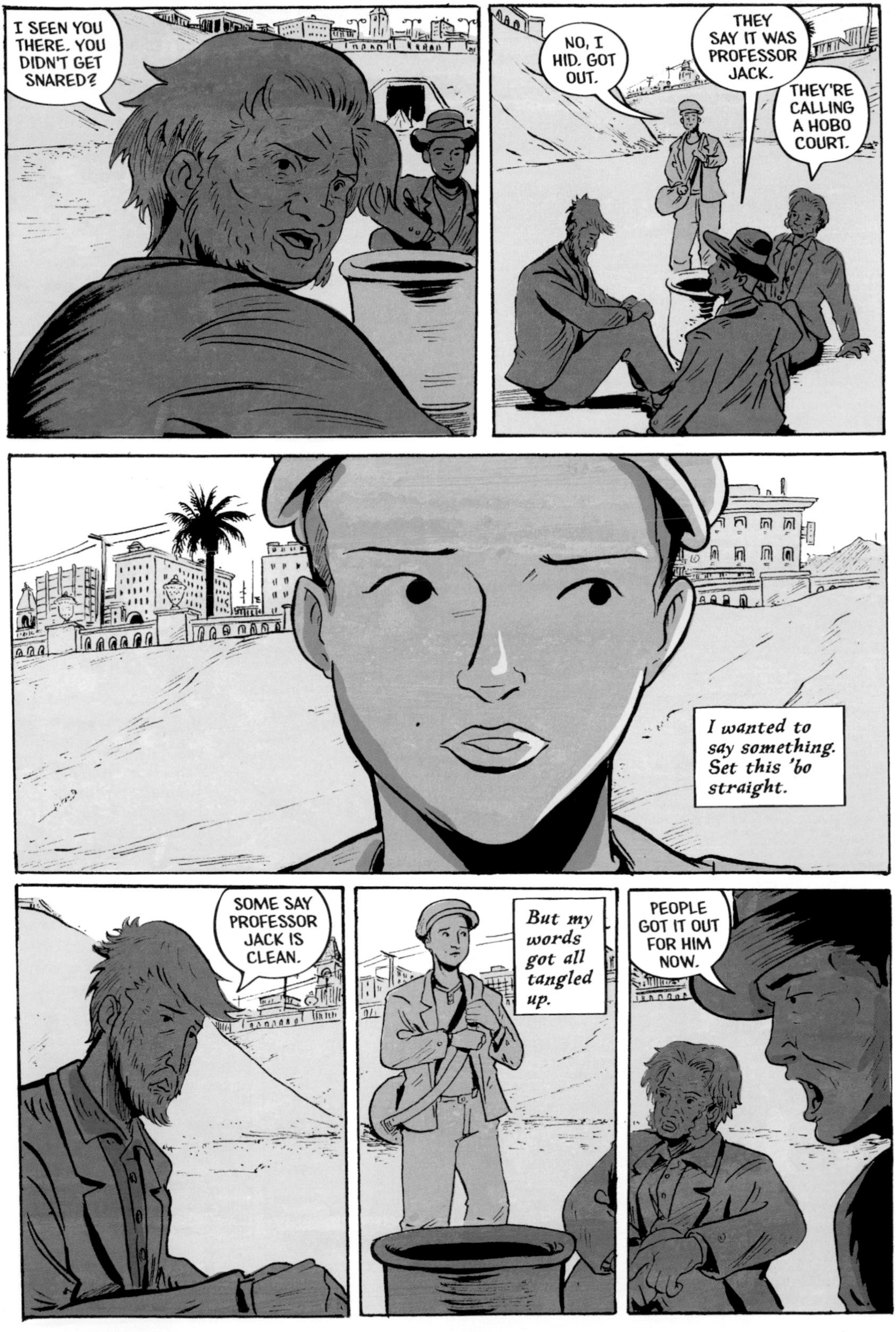
I SEEN YOU THERE. YOU DIDN'T GET SNARED?
NO, I HID. GOT OUT.
THEY SAY IT WAS PROFESSOR JACK.
THEY'RE CALLING A HOBO COURT.
I wanted to say something. Set this 'bo straight.
SOME SAY PROFESSOR JACK IS CLEAN.
But my words got all tangled up.
PEOPLE GOT IT OUT FOR HIM NOW.

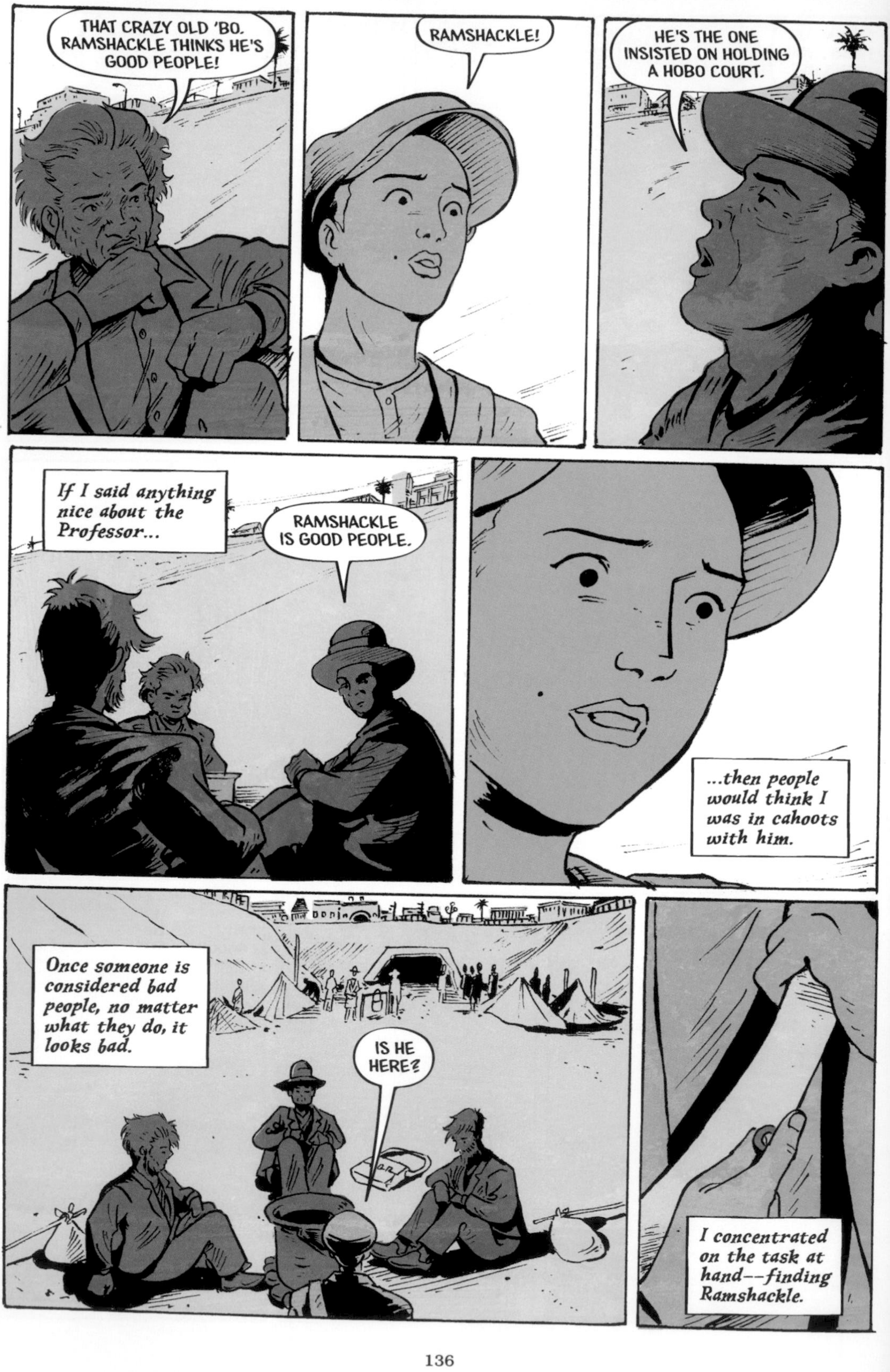
THAT CRAZY OLD 'BO. RAMSHACKLE THINKS HE'S GOOD PEOPLE!
RAMSHACKLE!
HE'S THE ONE INSISTED ON HOLDING A HOBO COURT.
If I said anything nice about the Professor...
RAMSHACKLE IS GOOD PEOPLE.
...then people would think I was in cahoots with him.
Once someone is considered bad people, no matter what they do, it looks bad.
IS HE HERE?
I concentrated on the task at hand--finding Ramshackle.

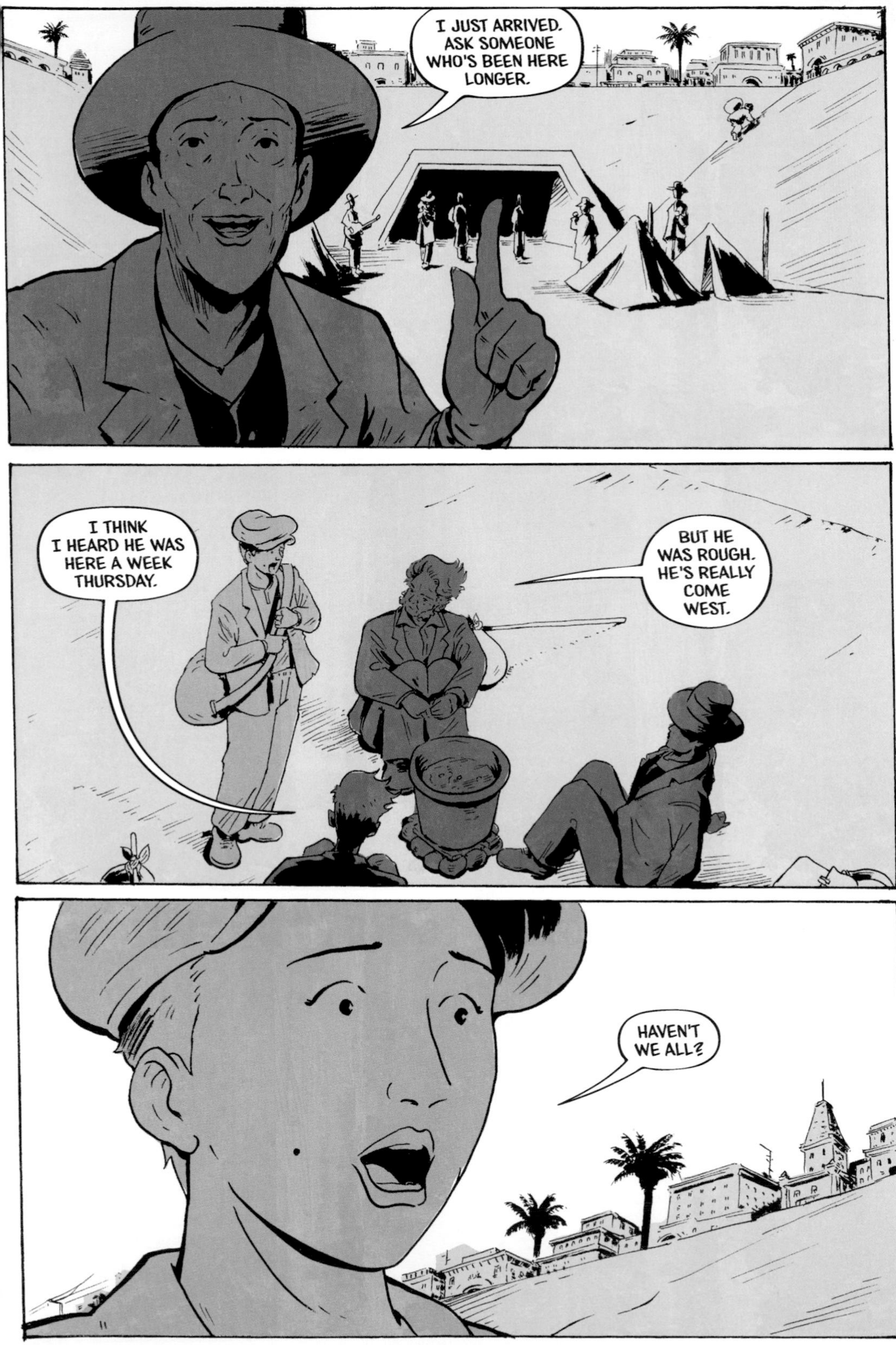
I JUST ARRIVED. ASK SOMEONE WHO'S BEEN HERE LONGER.
I THINK I HEARD HE WAS HERE A WEEK THURSDAY.
BUT HE WAS ROUGH. HE'S REALLY COME WEST.
HAVEN'T WE ALL?

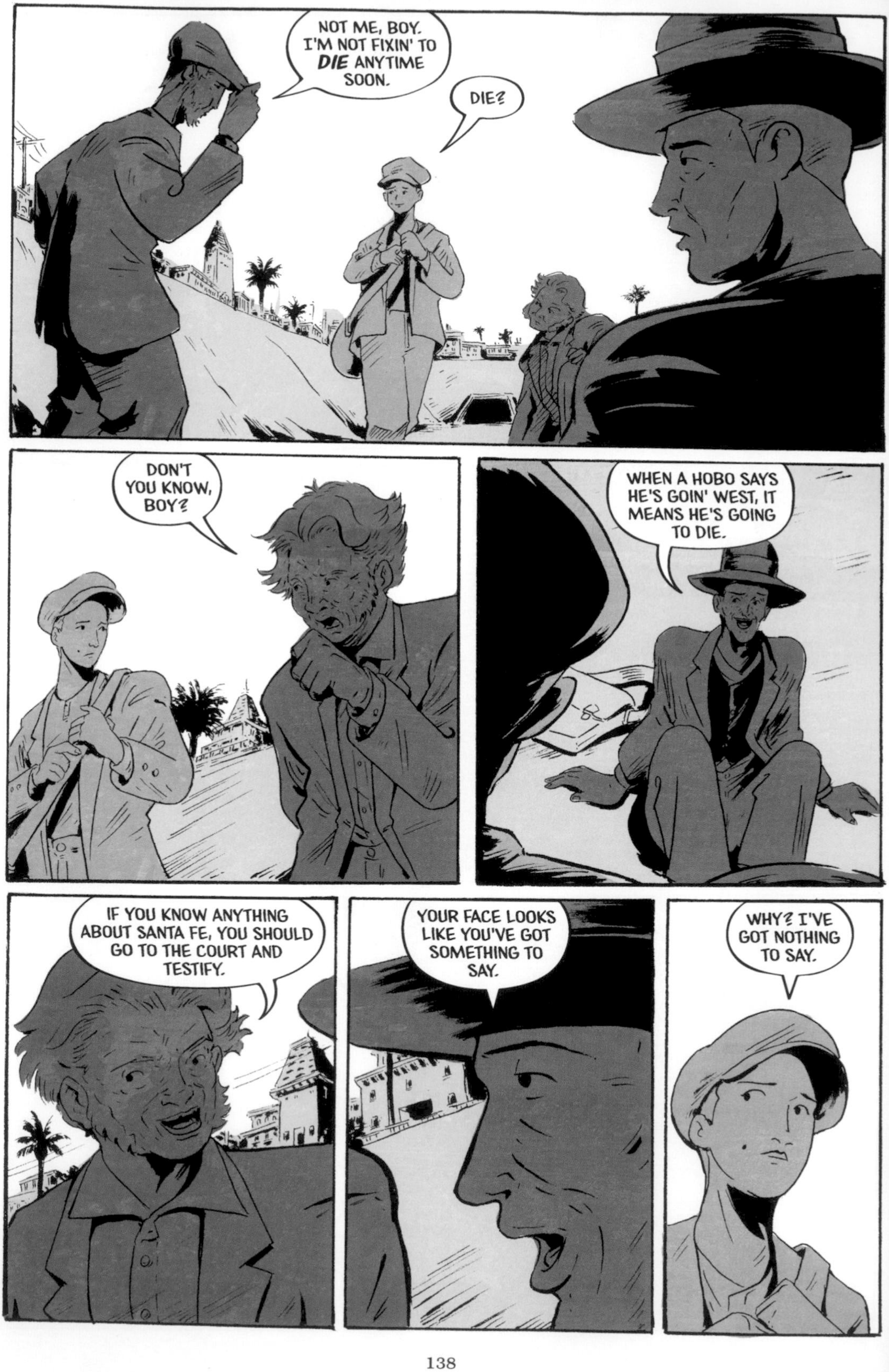
NOT ME, BOY. I'M NOT FIXIN' TO DIE ANYTIME SOON.
DIE?
DON'T YOU KNOW, BOY?
WHEN A HOBO SAYS HE'S GOIN' WEST, IT MEANS HE'S GOING TO DIE.
IF YOU KNOW ANYTHING ABOUT SANTA FE, YOU SHOULD GO TO THE COURT AND TESTIFY.
YOUR FACE LOOKS LIKE YOU'VE GOT SOMETHING TO SAY.
WHY? I'VE GOT NOTHING TO SAY.

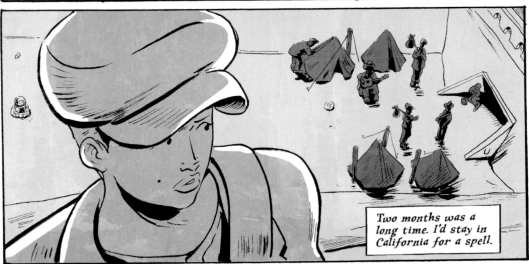

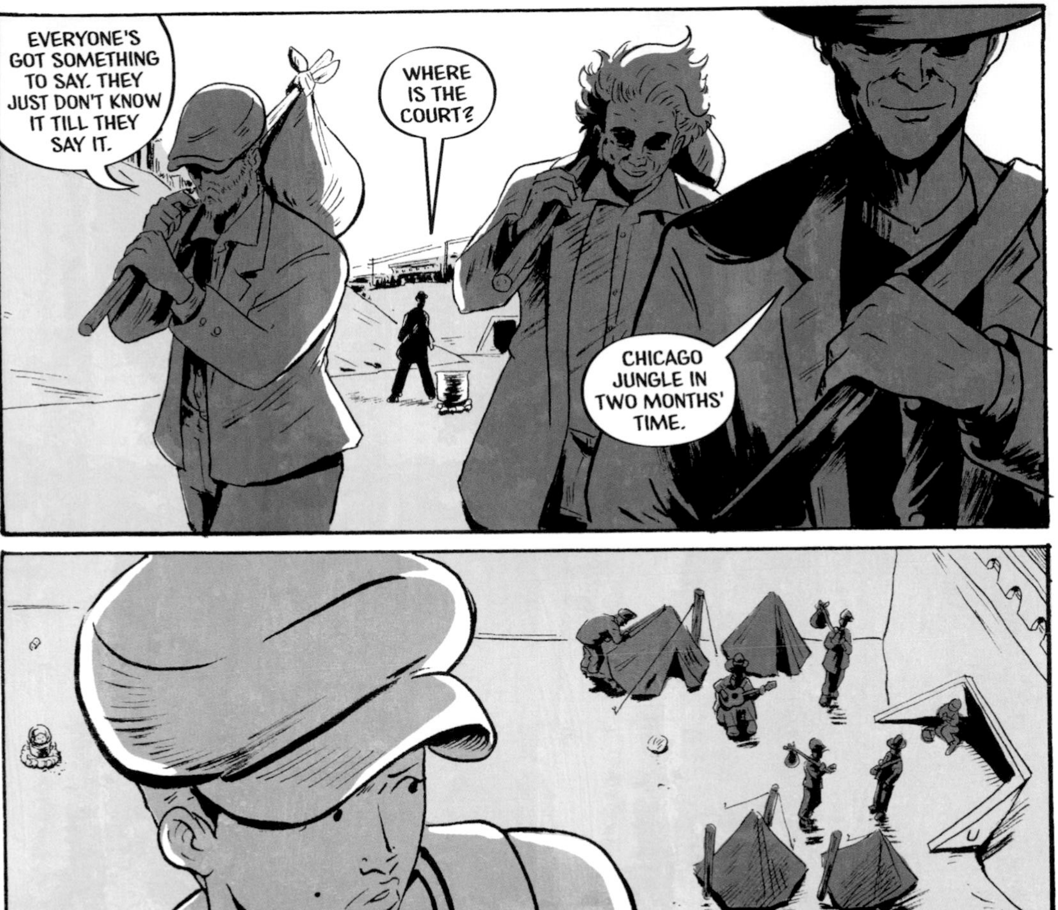
EVERYONE'S GOT SOMETHING TO SAY. THEY JUST DON'T KNOW IT TILL THEY SAY IT.
WHERE IS THE COURT?
CHICAGO JUNGLE IN TWO MONTHS' TIME.
Two months was a long time. I'd stay in California for a spell.
ARROZ
206
Wilshire

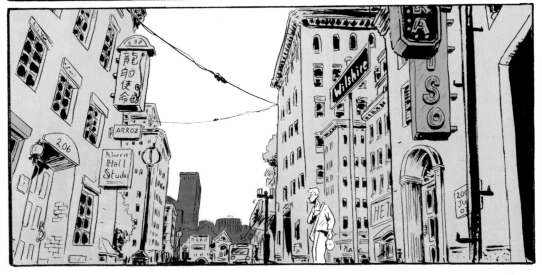

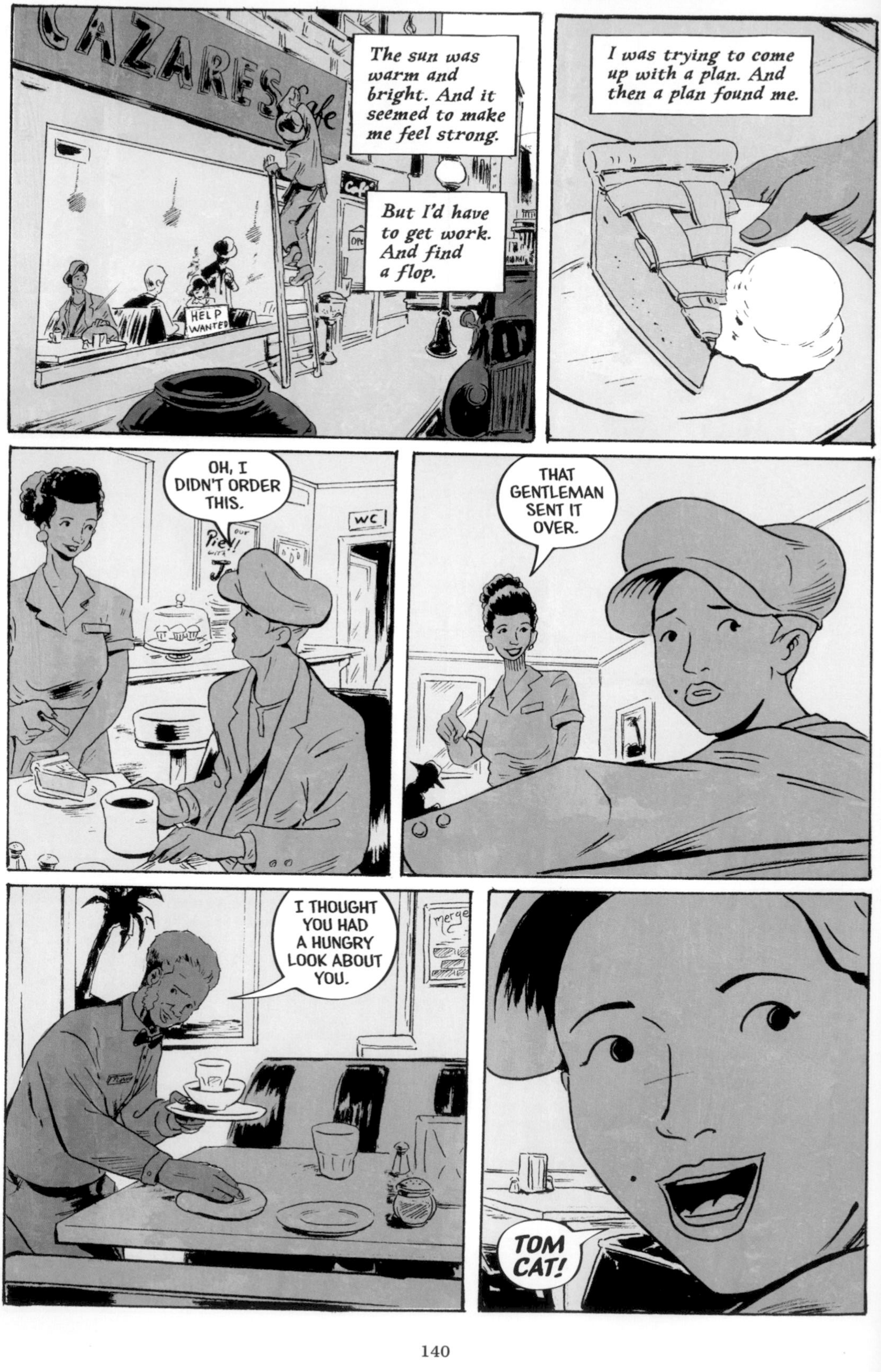
CAZARES Cafe
The sun was warm and bright. And it seemed to make me feel strong.
But I'd have to get work. And find a flop.
HELP WANTED
I was trying to come up with a plan. And then a plan found me.
OH, I DIDN'T ORDER THIS.
WC
THAT GENTLEMAN SENT IT OVER.
I THOUGHT YOU HAD A HUNGRY LOOK ABOUT YOU.
TOM CAT!

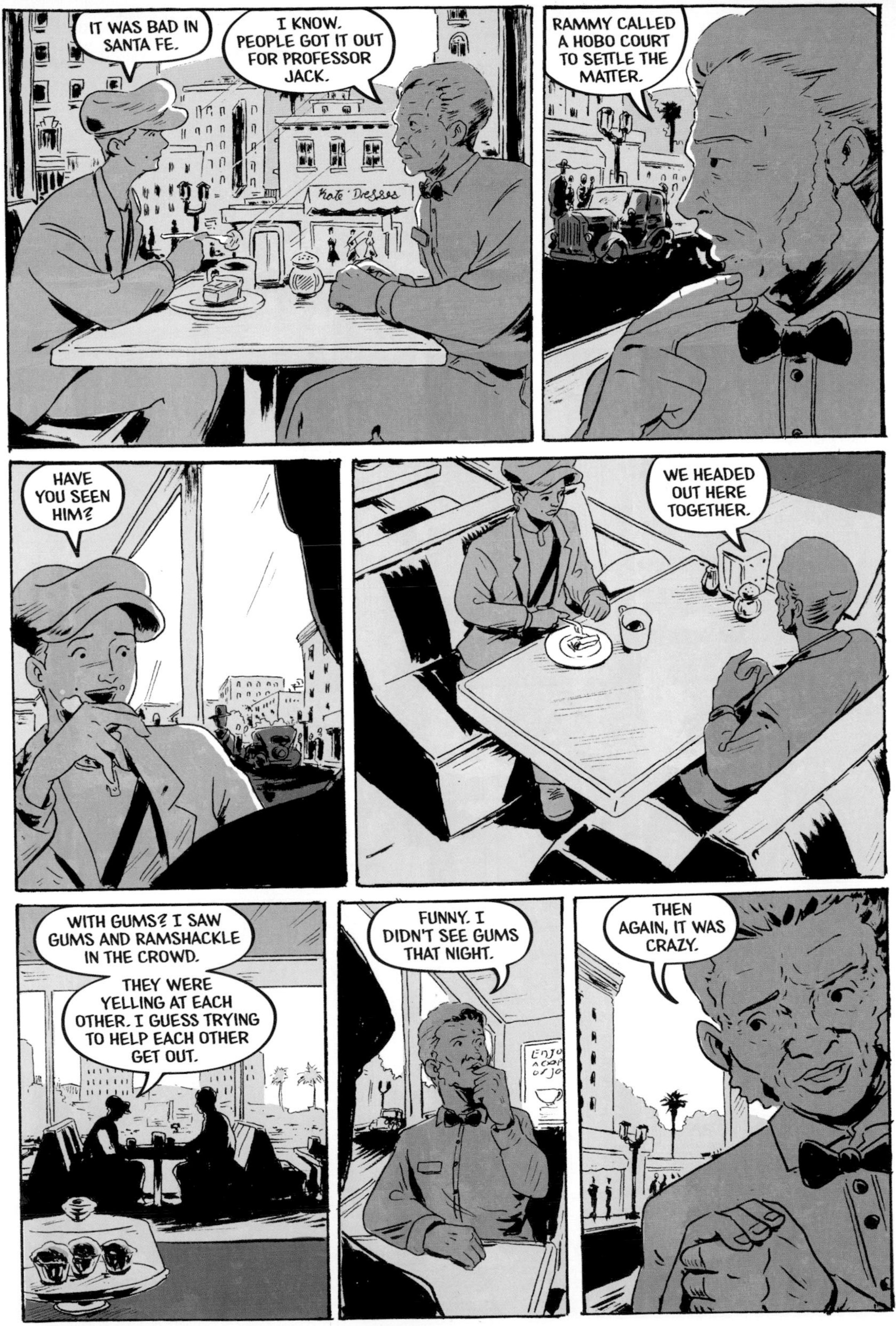
IT WAS BAD IN SANTA FE.
I KNOW. PEOPLE GOT IT OUT FOR PROFESSOR JACK.
Kate Dresses
RAMMY CALLED A HOBO COURT TO SETTLE THE MATTER.
HAVE YOU SEEN HIM?
WE HEADED OUT HERE TOGETHER.
WITH GUMS? I SAW GUMS AND RAMSHACKLE IN THE CROWD.
THEY WERE YELLING AT EACH OTHER. I GUESS TRYING TO HELP EACH OTHER GET OUT.
FUNNY. I DIDN'T SEE GUMS THAT NIGHT.
THEN AGAIN, IT WAS CRAZY.

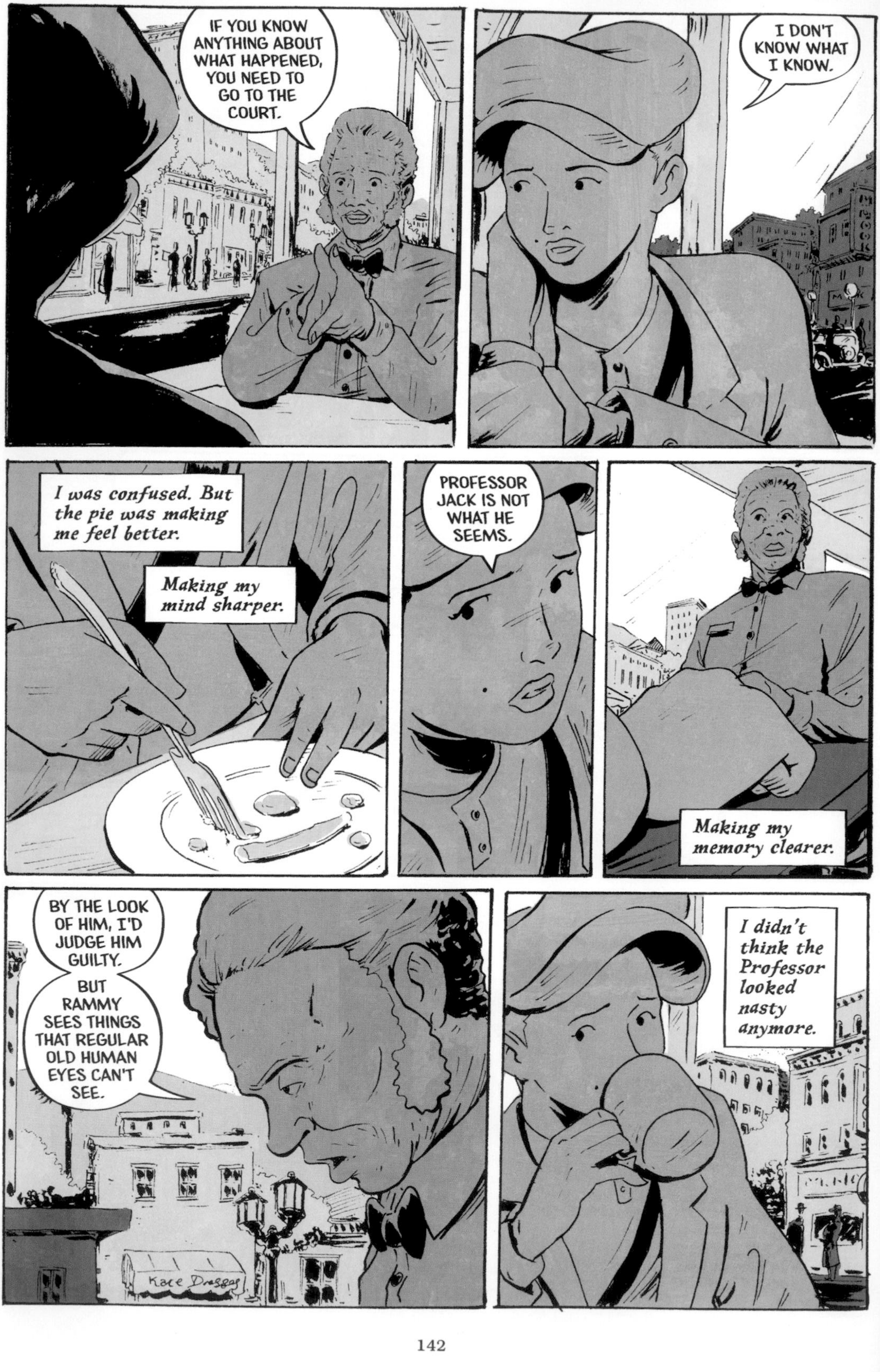
IF YOU KNOW ANYTHING ABOUT WHAT HAPPENED, YOU NEED TO GO TO THE COURT.
I DON'T KNOW WHAT I KNOW.
I was confused. But the pie was making me feel better.
Making my mind sharper.
PROFESSOR JACK IS NOT WHAT HE SEEMS.
Making my memory clearer.
BY THE LOOK OF HIM, I'D JUDGE HIM GUILTY.
BUT RAMMY SEES THINGS THAT REGULAR OLD HUMAN EYES CAN'T SEE.
I didn't think the Professor looked nasty anymore.

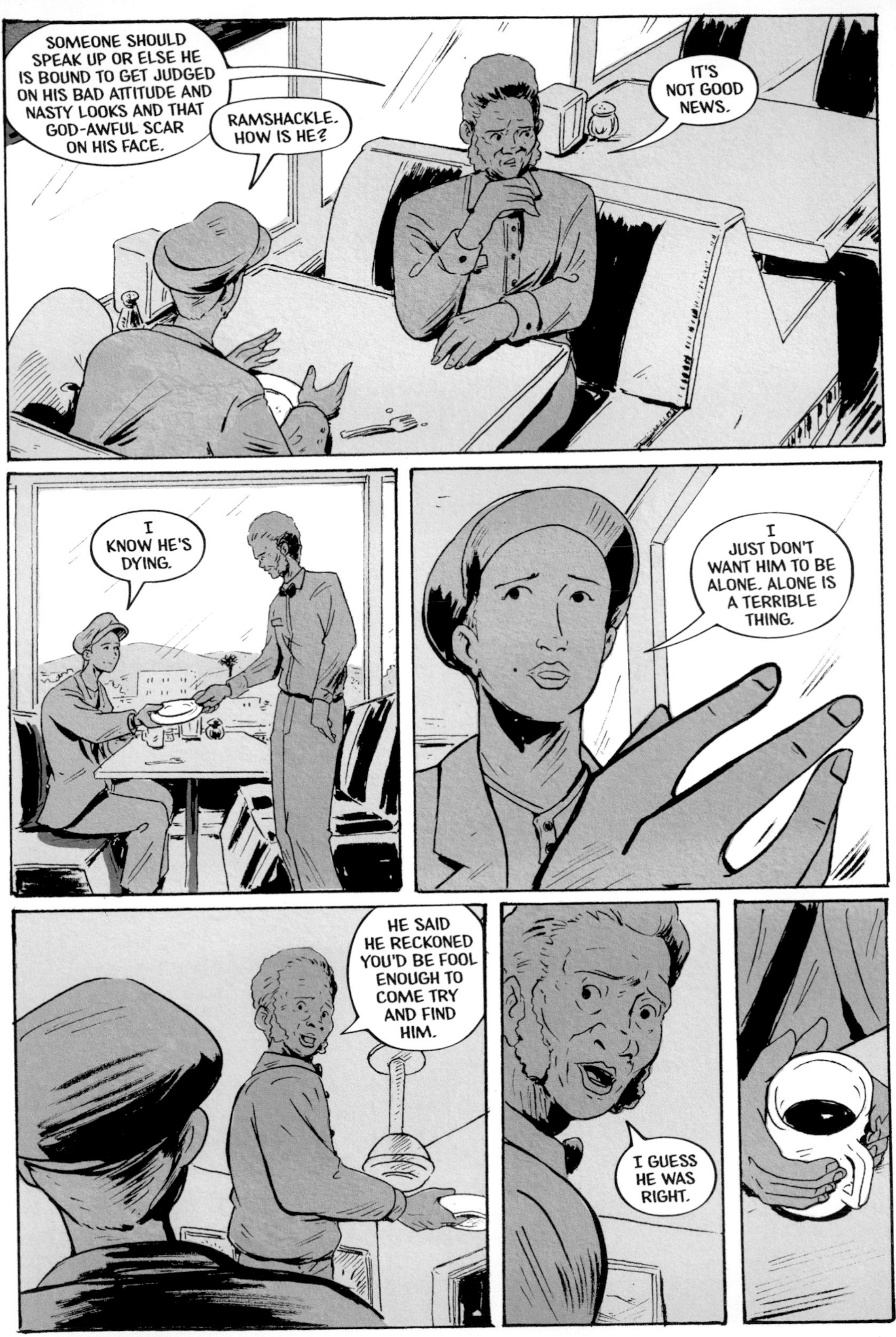
SOMEONE SHOULD SPEAK UP OR ELSE HE IS BOUND TO GET JUDGED ON HIS BAD ATTITUDE AND NASTY LOOKS AND THAT GOD-AWFUL SCAR ON HIS FACE.
RAMSHACKLE. HOW IS HE?
IT'S NOT GOOD NEWS.
I KNOW HE'S DYING.
I JUST DON'T WANT HIM TO BE ALONE. ALONE IS A TERRIBLE THING.
HE SAID HE RECKONED YOU'D BE FOOL ENOUGH TO COME TRY AND FIND HIM.
I GUESS HE WAS RIGHT.

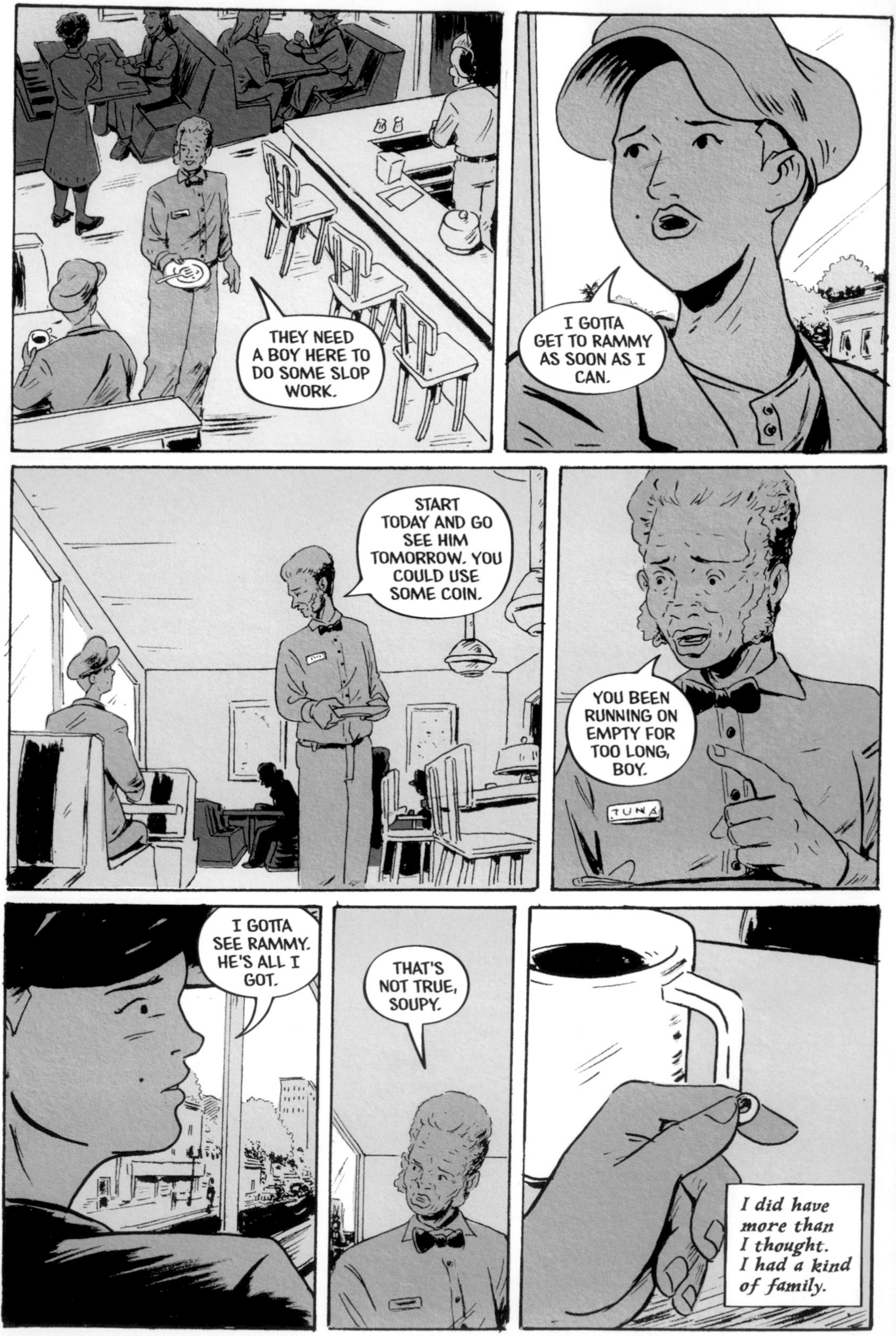
THEY NEED A BOY HERE TO DO SOME SLOP WORK.
I GOTTA GET TO RAMMY AS SOON AS I CAN.
START TODAY AND GO SEE HIM TOMORROW. YOU COULD USE SOME COIN.
YOU BEEN RUNNING ON EMPTY FOR TOO LONG, BOY.
TUNA
I GOTTA SEE RAMMY. HE'S ALL I GOT.
THAT'S NOT TRUE, SOUPY.
I did have more than I thought. I had a kind of family.

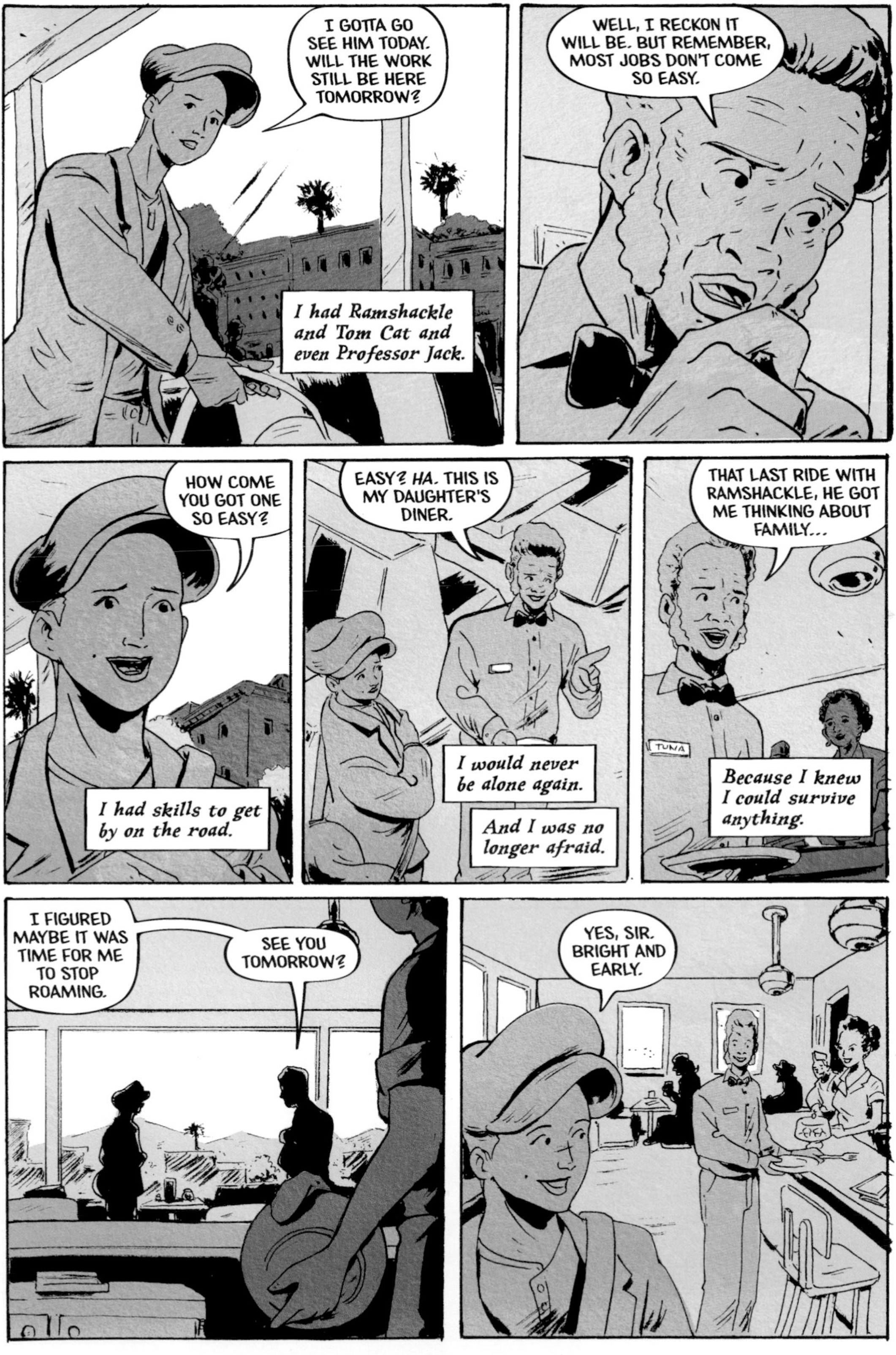
I GOTTA GO SEE HIM TODAY. WILL THE WORK STILL BE HERE TOMORROW?
I had Ramshackle and Tom Cat and even Professor Jack.
WELL, I RECKON IT WILL BE. BUT REMEMBER, MOST JOBS DON'T COME SO EASY.
HOW COME YOU GOT ONE SO EASY?
I had skills to get by on the road.
EASY? HA. THIS IS MY DAUGHTER'S DINER.
I would never be alone again.
And I was no longer afraid.
THAT LAST RIDE WITH RAMSHACKLE, HE GOT ME THINKING ABOUT FAMILY...
TUNA
Because I knew I could survive anything.
I FIGURED MAYBE IT WAS TIME FOR ME TO STOP ROAMING.
SEE YOU TOMORROW?
YES, SIR. BRIGHT AND EARLY.

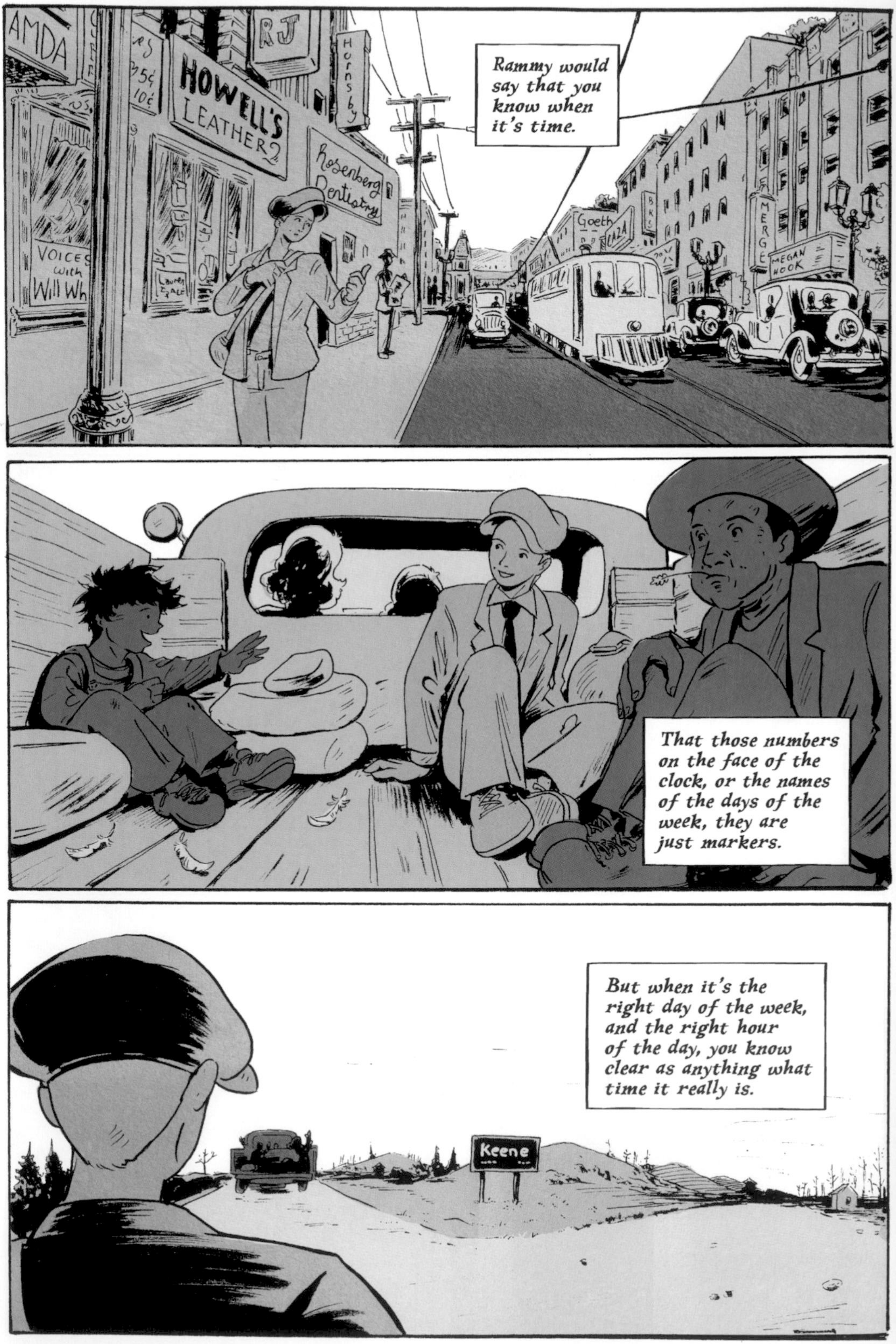
AMDA
RJ
HOWELL'S LEATHER
Hornsby
Rosenberg Dentistry
Rammy would say that you know when it's time.
MEGAN HOOK
That those numbers on the face of the clock, or the names of the days of the week, they are just markers.
But when it's the right day of the week, and the right hour of the day, you know clear as anything what time it really is.
Keene

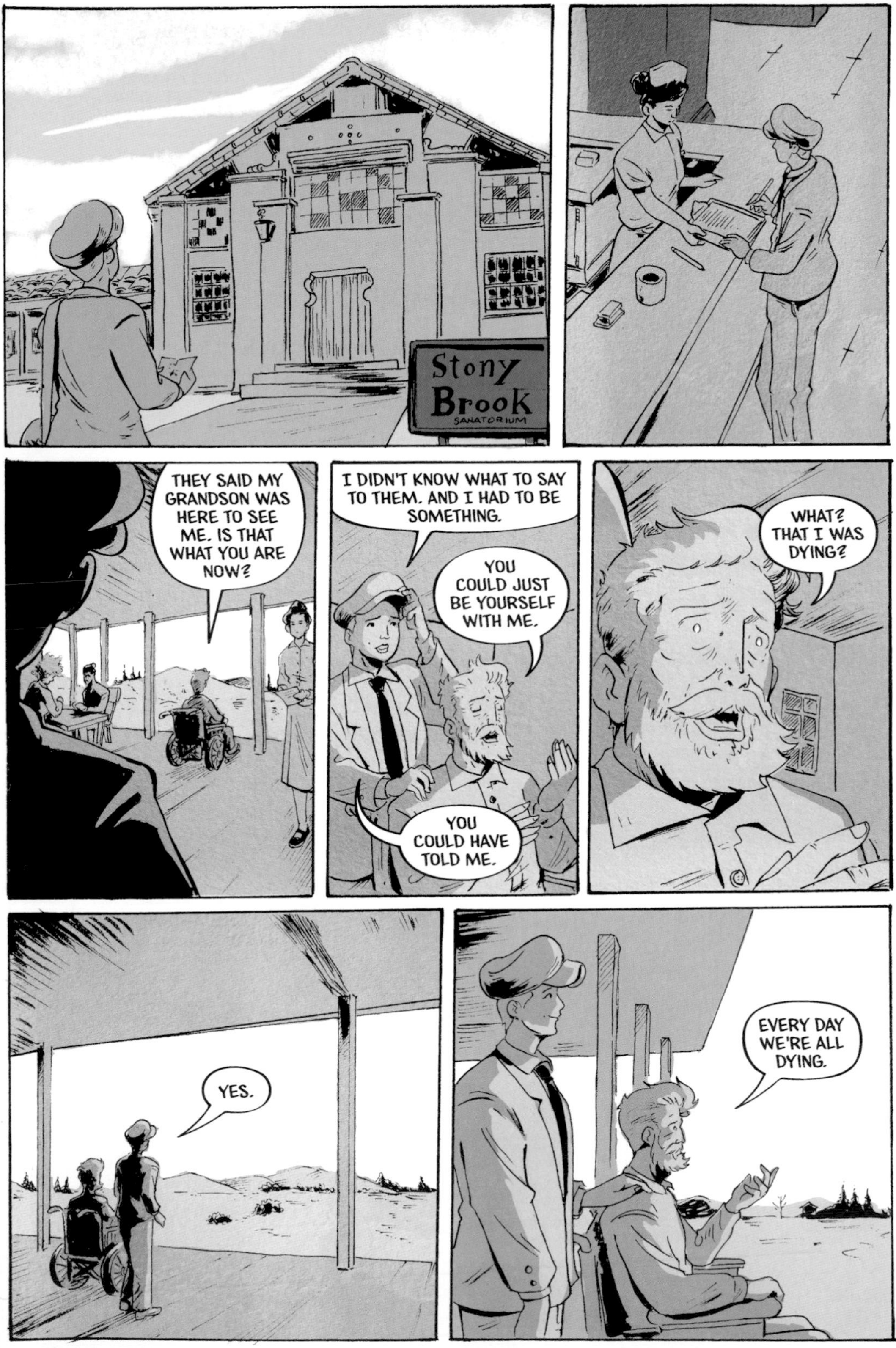
Stony Brook
SANATORIUM
THEY SAID MY GRANDSON WAS HERE TO SEE ME. IS THAT WHAT YOU ARE NOW?
I DIDN'T KNOW WHAT TO SAY TO THEM. AND I HAD TO BE SOMETHING.
YOU COULD JUST BE YOURSELF WITH ME.
YOU COULD HAVE TOLD ME.
WHAT? THAT I WAS DYING?
YES.
EVERY DAY WE'RE ALL DYING.

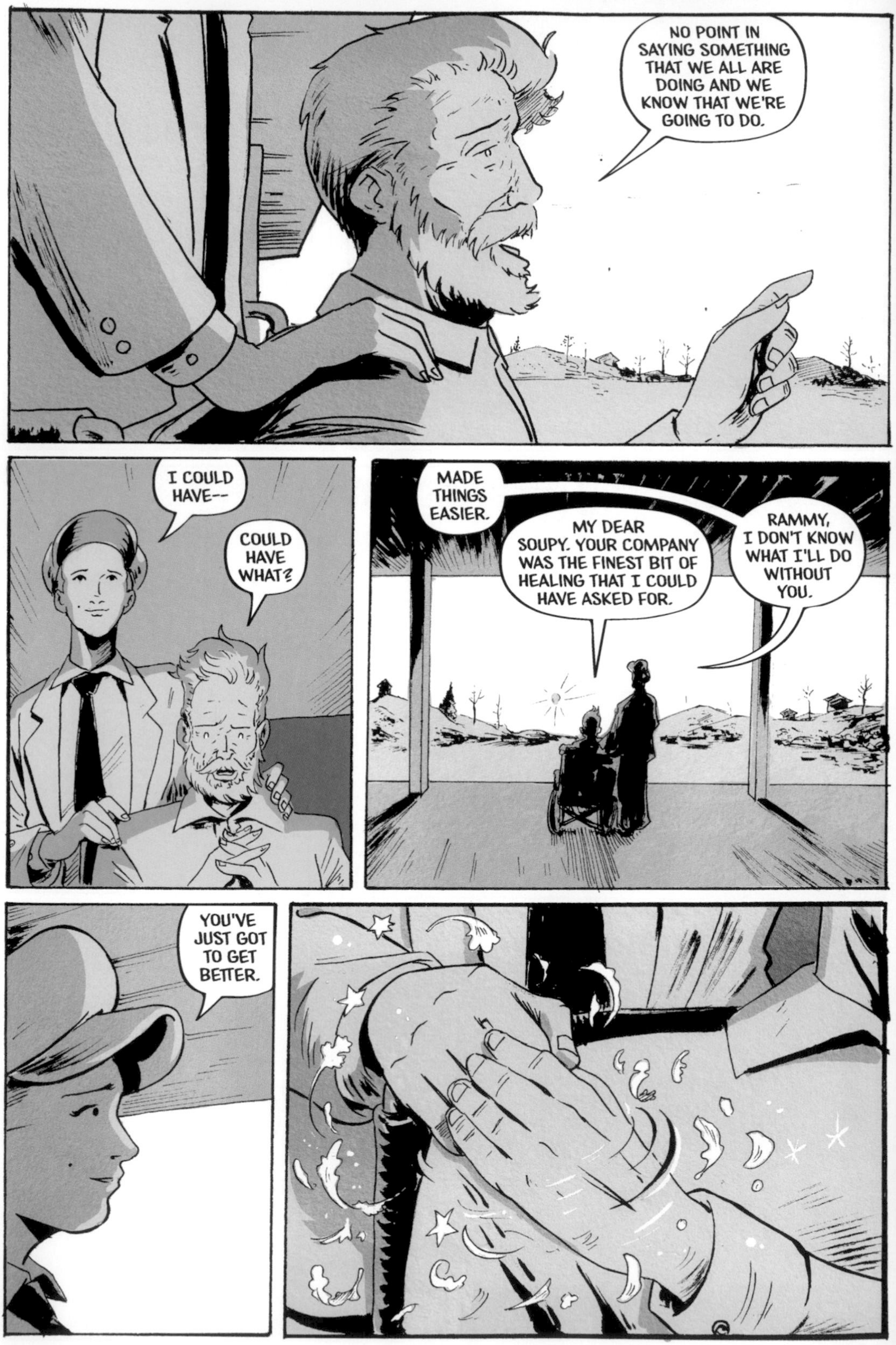
NO POINT IN SAYING SOMETHING THAT WE ALL ARE DOING AND WE KNOW THAT WE'RE GOING TO DO.
I COULD HAVE--
COULD HAVE WHAT?
MADE THINGS EASIER.
MY DEAR SOUPY. YOUR COMPANY WAS THE FINEST BIT OF HEALING THAT I COULD HAVE ASKED FOR.
RAMMY, I DON'T KNOW WHAT I'LL DO WITHOUT YOU.
YOU'VE JUST GOT TO GET BETTER.

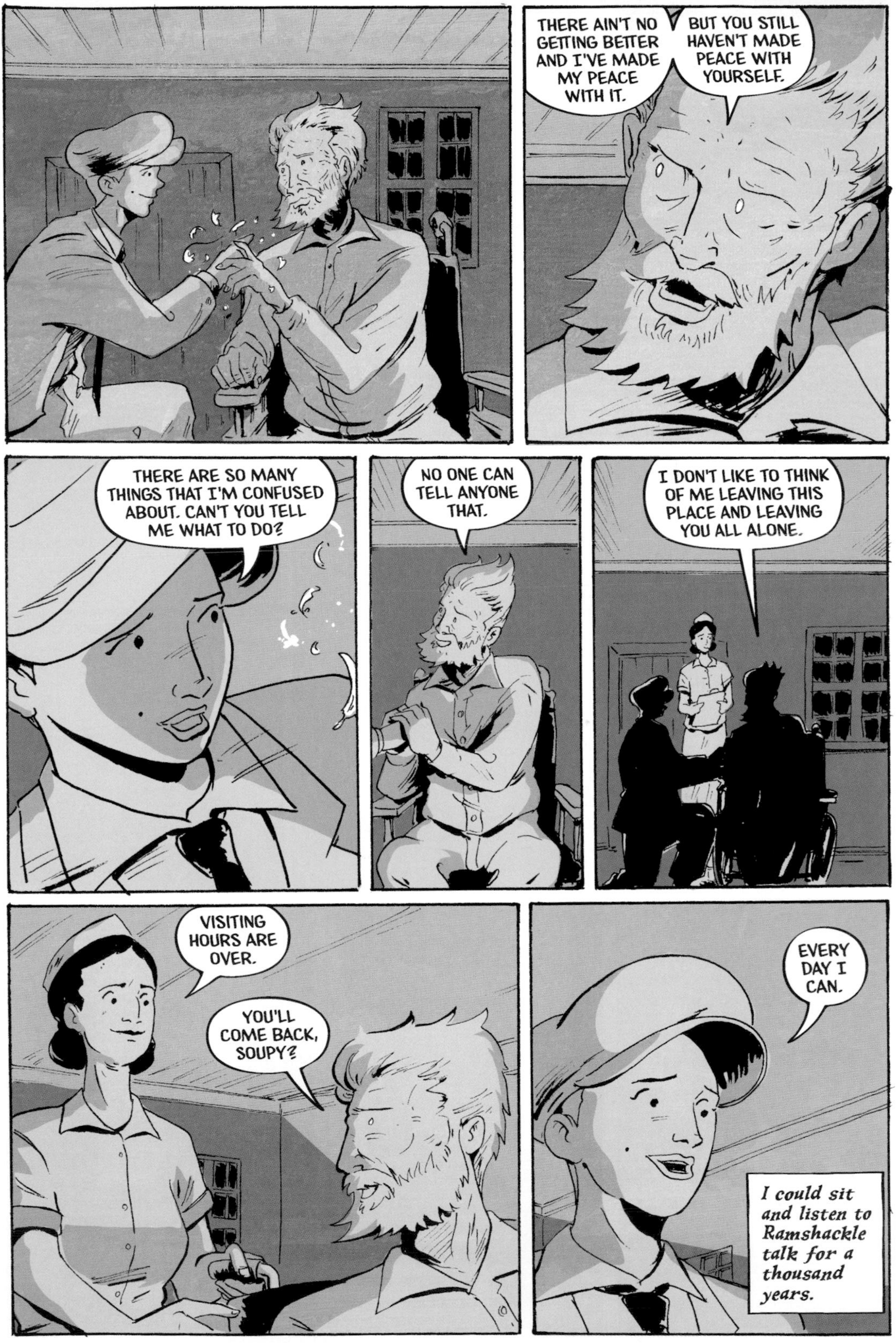
THERE AIN'T NO GETTING BETTER AND I'VE MADE MY PEACE WITH IT.
BUT YOU STILL HAVEN'T MADE PEACE WITH YOURSELF.
THERE ARE SO MANY THINGS THAT I'M CONFUSED ABOUT. CAN'T YOU TELL ME WHAT TO DO?
NO ONE CAN TELL ANYONE THAT.
I DON'T LIKE TO THINK OF ME LEAVING THIS PLACE AND LEAVING YOU ALL ALONE.
VISITING HOURS ARE OVER.
YOU'LL COME BACK, SOUPY?
EVERY DAY I CAN.
I could sit and listen to Ramshackle talk for a thousand years.

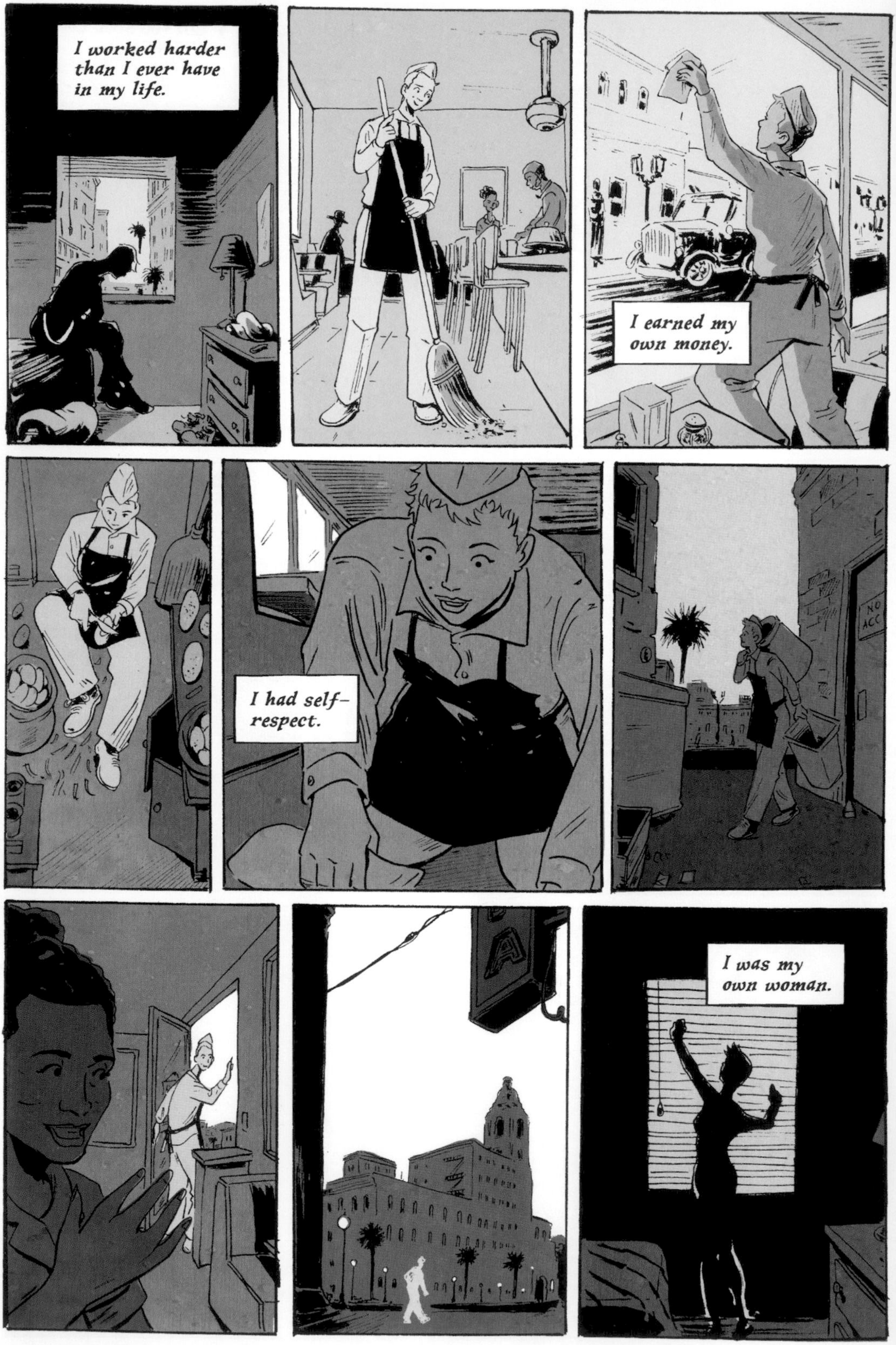
I worked harder than I ever have in my life.
I earned my own money.
I had self-respect.
I was my own woman.

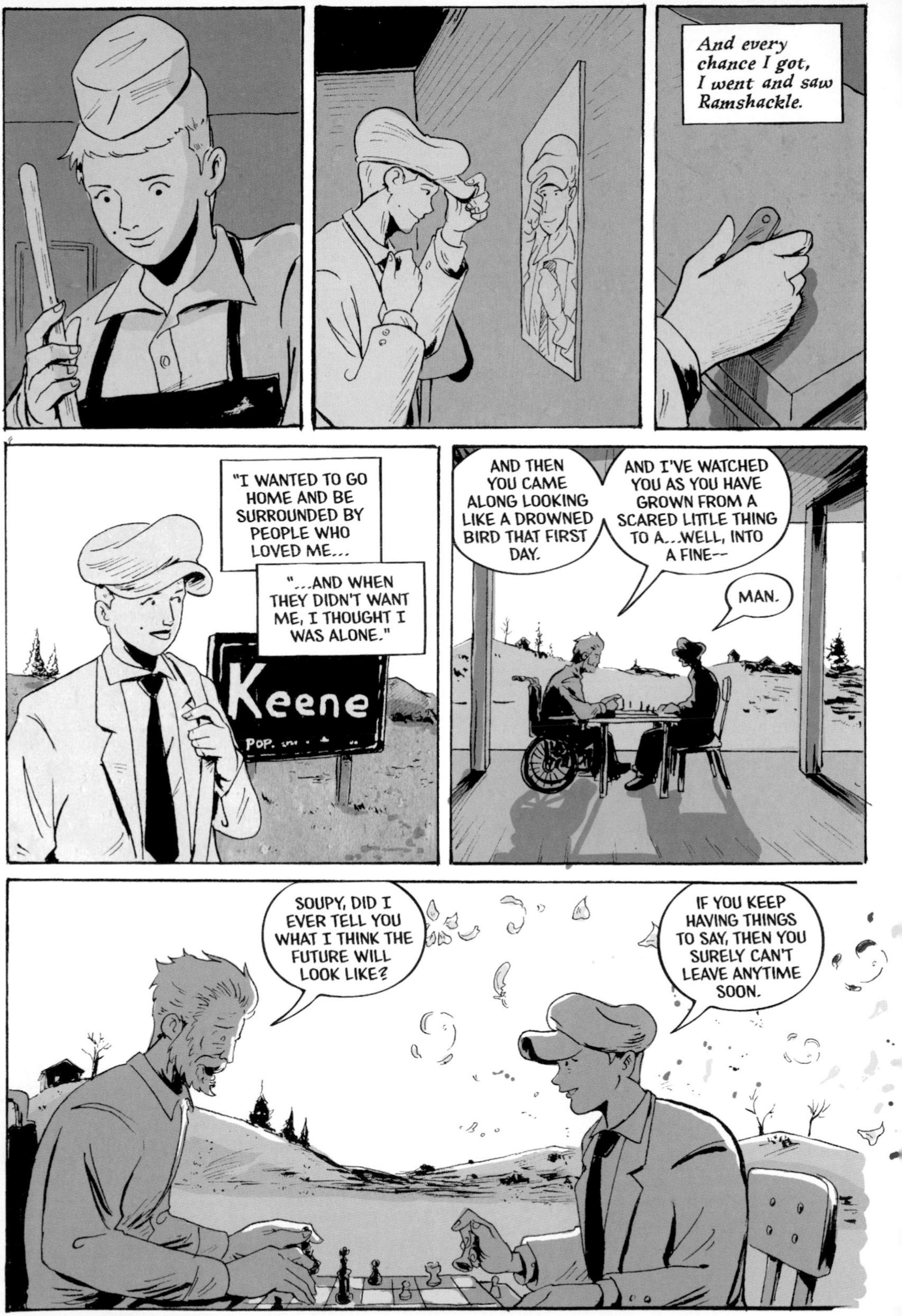
And every chance I got, I went and saw Ramshackle.
"I WANTED TO GO HOME AND BE SURROUNDED BY PEOPLE WHO LOVED ME...
"...AND WHEN THEY DIDN'T WANT ME, I THOUGHT I WAS ALONE."
Keene
POP.
AND THEN YOU CAME ALONG LOOKING LIKE A DROWNED BIRD THAT FIRST DAY.
AND I'VE WATCHED YOU AS YOU HAVE GROWN FROM A SCARED LITTLE THING TO A...WELL, INTO A FINE--
MAN.
SOUPY, DID I EVER TELL YOU WHAT I THINK THE FUTURE WILL LOOK LIKE?
IF YOU KEEP HAVING THINGS TO SAY, THEN YOU SURELY CAN'T LEAVE ANYTIME SOON.

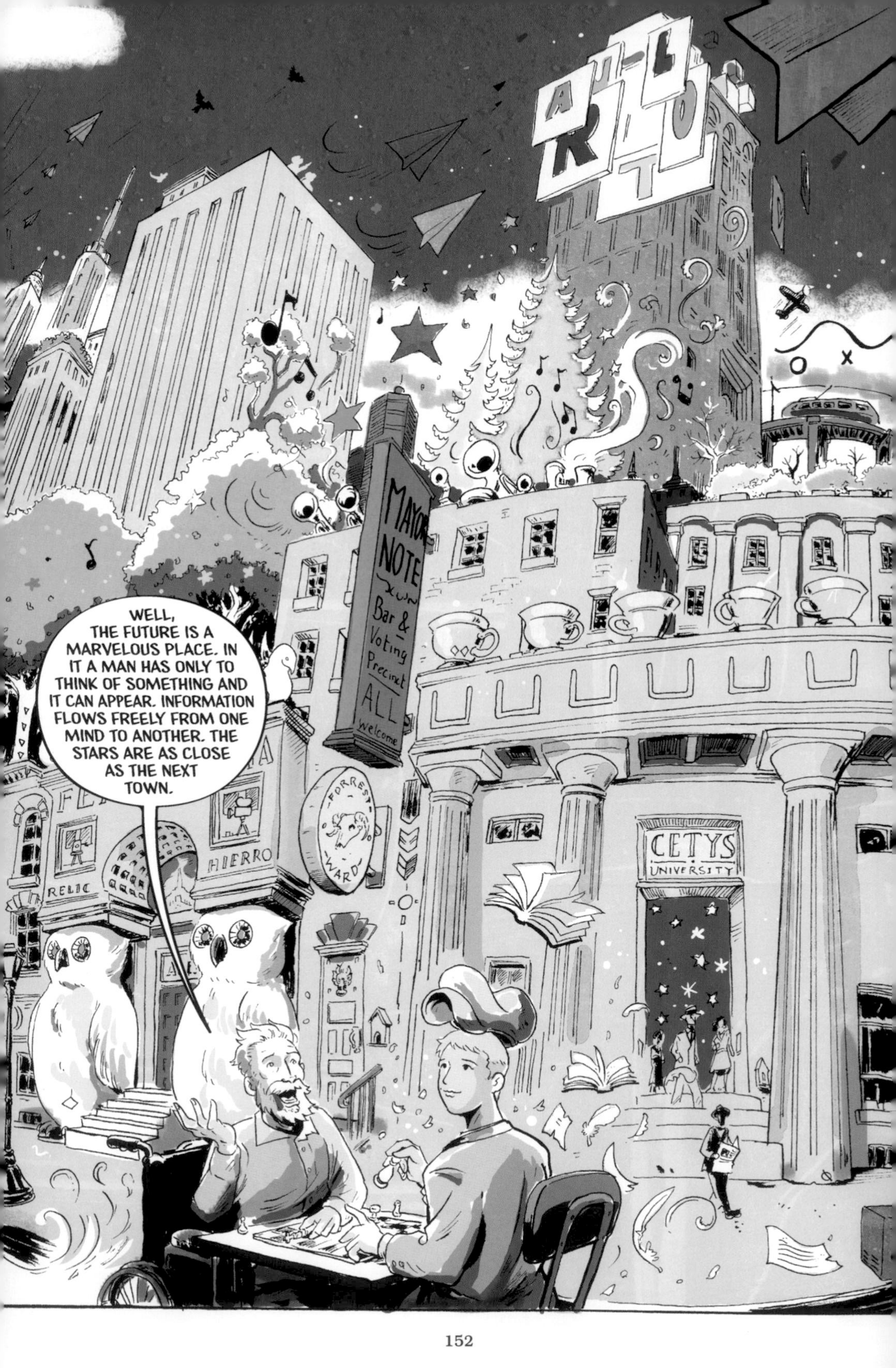
WELL, THE FUTURE IS A MARVELOUS PLACE. IN IT A MAN HAS ONLY TO THINK OF SOMETHING AND IT CAN APPEAR. INFORMATION FLOWS FREELY FROM ONE MIND TO ANOTHER. THE STARS ARE AS CLOSE AS THE NEXT TOWN.
MAYOR NOTE
Bar & Voting Precinct
ALL welcome
FORREST WARD
CETYS UNIVERSITY
HIERRO
RELIC

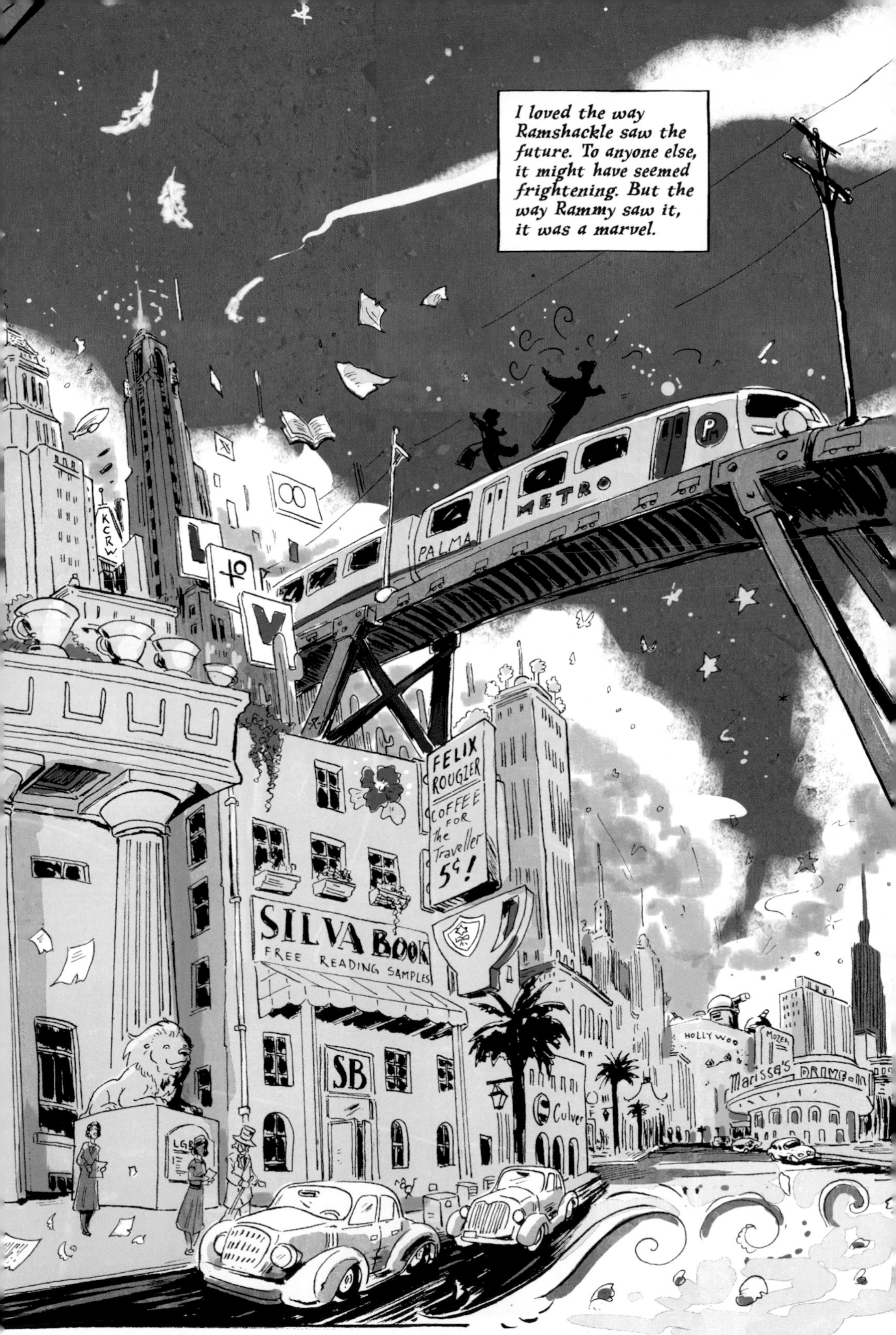
I loved the way Ramshackle saw the future. To anyone else, it might have seemed frightening. But the way Rammy saw it, it was a marvel.
KCRW
METRO
PALMA
FELIX ROUGIER
COFFEE FOR the Traveller 5¢!
SILVA BOOK
FREE READING SAMPLES
SB
Culver
HOLLYWOO
Marissa's
DRIVE-IN

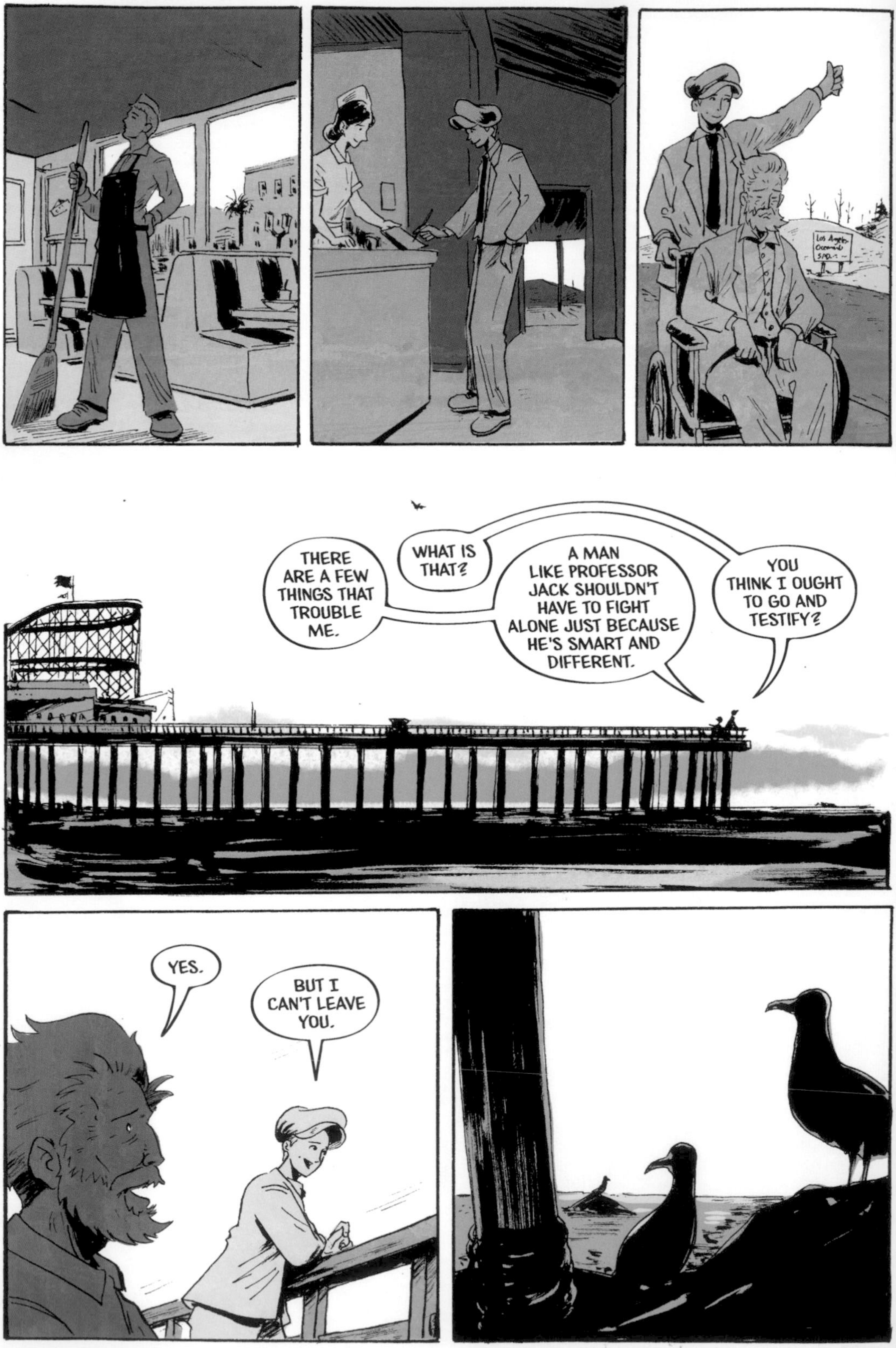
THERE ARE A FEW THINGS THAT TROUBLE ME.
WHAT IS THAT?
A MAN LIKE PROFESSOR JACK SHOULDN'T HAVE TO FIGHT ALONE JUST BECAUSE HE'S SMART AND DIFFERENT.
YOU THINK I OUGHT TO GO AND TESTIFY?
YES.
BUT I CAN'T LEAVE YOU.

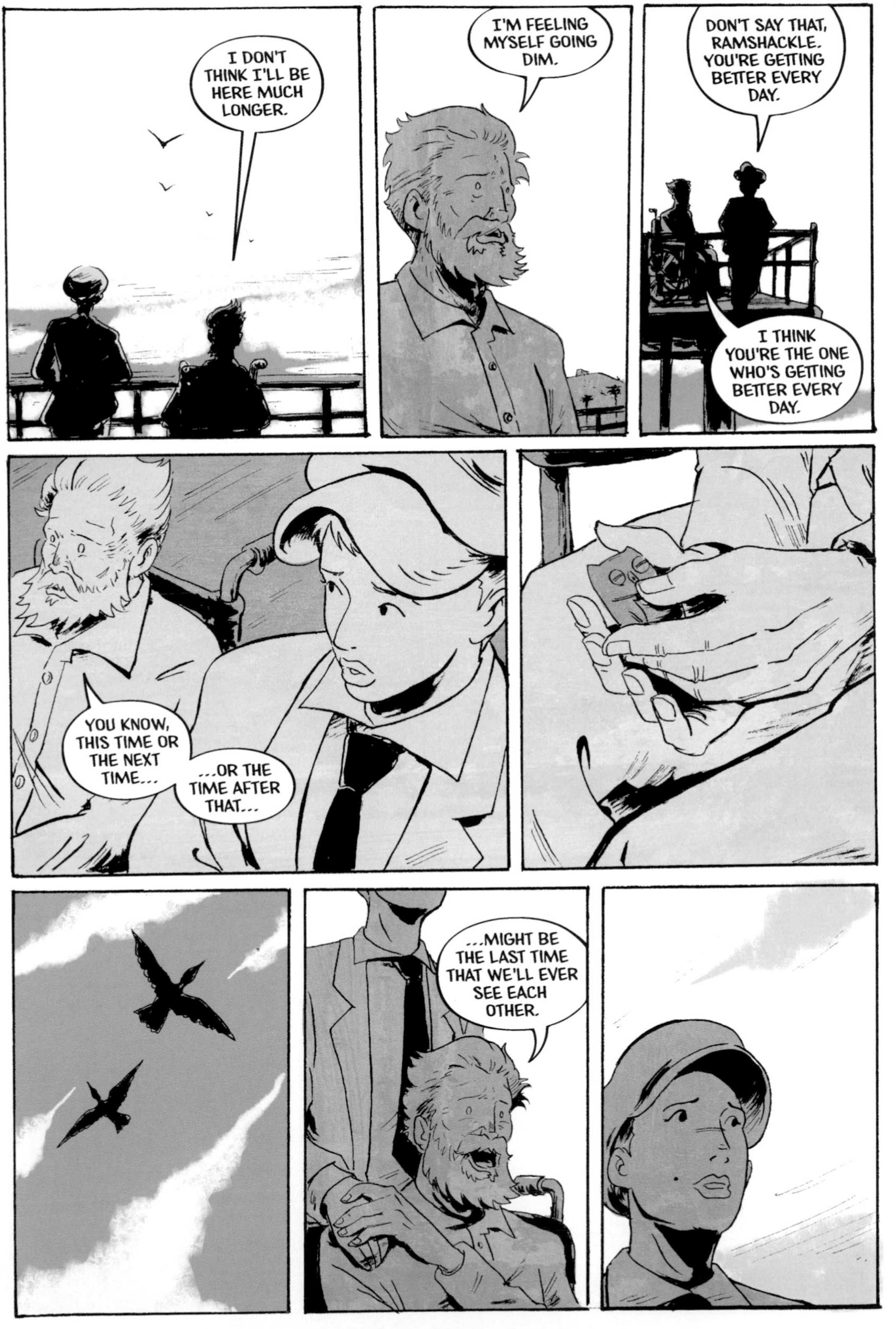
I DON'T THINK I'LL BE HERE MUCH LONGER.
I'M FEELING MYSELF GOING DIM.
DON'T SAY THAT, RAMSHACKLE. YOU'RE GETTING BETTER EVERY DAY.
I THINK YOU'RE THE ONE WHO'S GETTING BETTER EVERY DAY.
YOU KNOW, THIS TIME OR THE NEXT TIME...
...OR THE TIME AFTER THAT...
...MIGHT BE THE LAST TIME THAT WE'LL EVER SEE EACH OTHER.

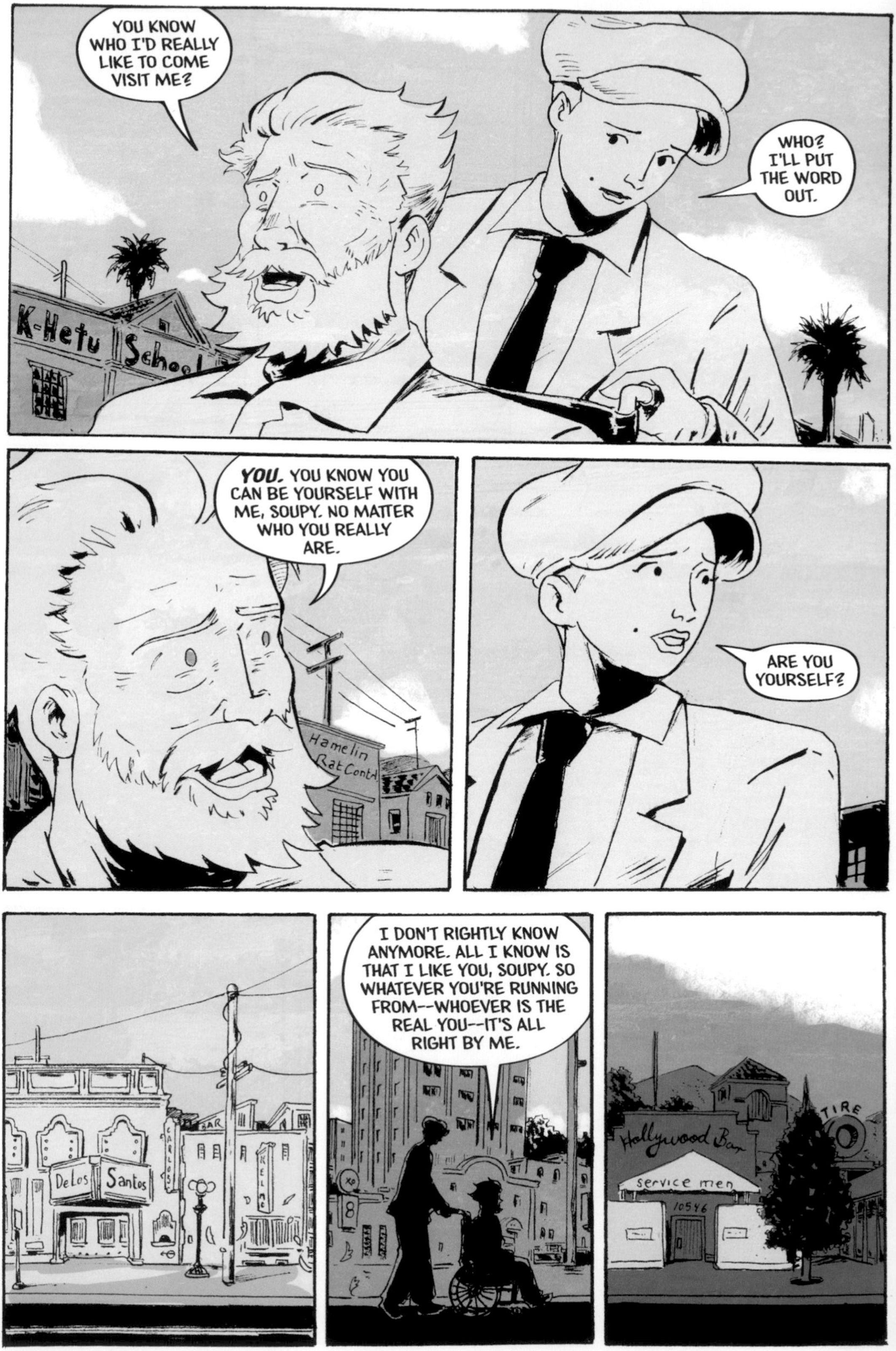
YOU KNOW WHO I'D REALLY LIKE TO COME VISIT ME?
WHO? I'LL PUT THE WORD OUT.
K-Hetu School
YOU. YOU KNOW YOU CAN BE YOURSELF WITH ME, SOUPY. NO MATTER WHO YOU REALLY ARE.
Hamelin Rat Contr
ARE YOU YOURSELF?
De Los Santos
BAR
I DON'T RIGHTLY KNOW ANYMORE. ALL I KNOW IS THAT I LIKE YOU, SOUPY. SO WHATEVER YOU'RE RUNNING FROM--WHOEVER IS THE REAL YOU--IT'S ALL RIGHT BY ME.
Hollywood Bar
service men
10546
TIRE

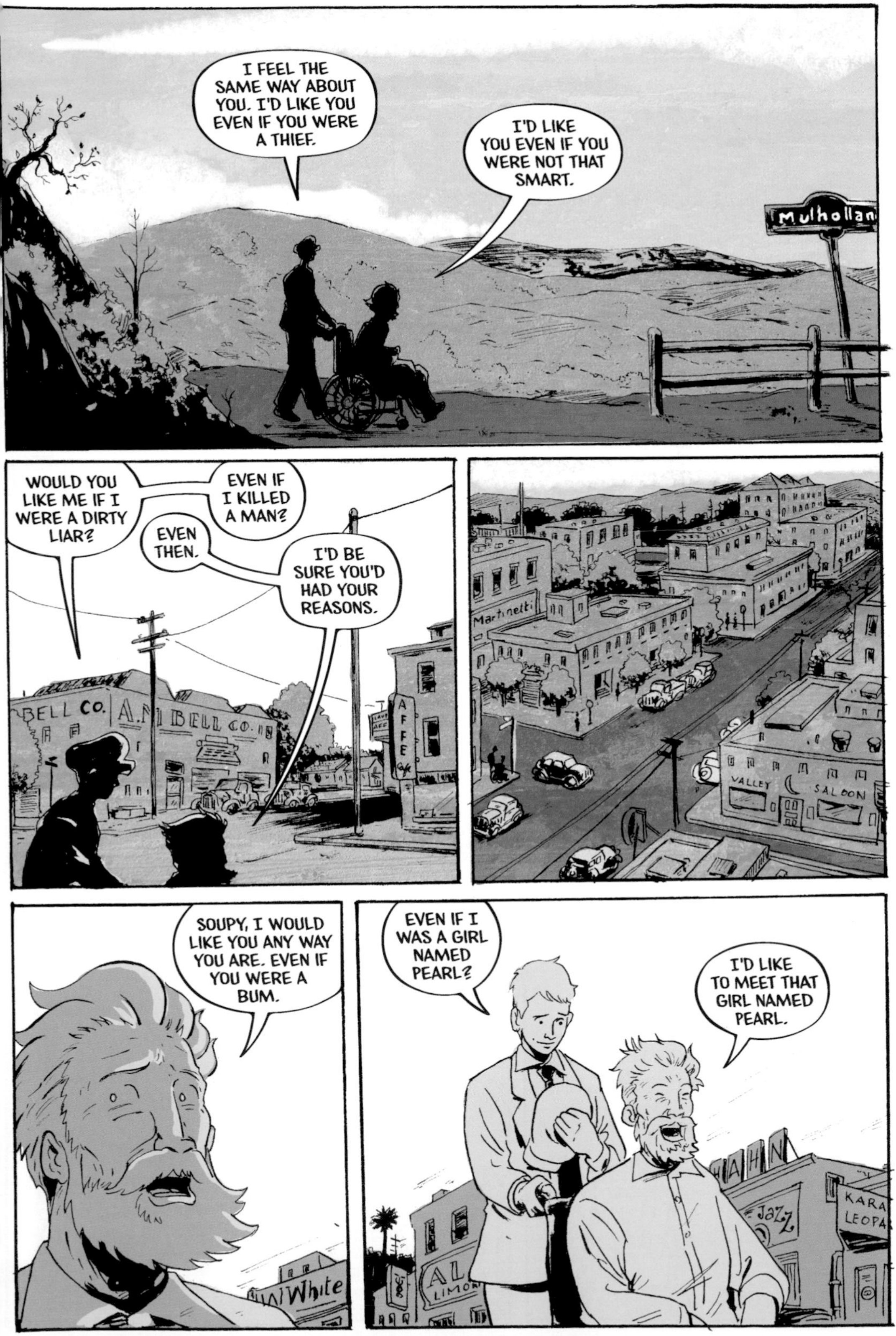
I FEEL THE SAME WAY ABOUT YOU. I'D LIKE YOU EVEN IF YOU WERE A THIEF.
I'D LIKE YOU EVEN IF YOU WERE NOT THAT SMART.
Mulhollan
WOULD YOU LIKE ME IF I WERE A DIRTY LIAR?
EVEN IF I KILLED A MAN?
EVEN THEN.
I'D BE SURE YOU'D HAD YOUR REASONS.
BELL CO.
BELL CO.
AFFE
Martinetti
VALLEY
SALOON
SOUPY, I WOULD LIKE YOU ANY WAY YOU ARE. EVEN IF YOU WERE A BUM.
White
EVEN IF I WAS A GIRL NAMED PEARL?
I'D LIKE TO MEET THAT GIRL NAMED PEARL.
Jazz
KARA
LEOPA

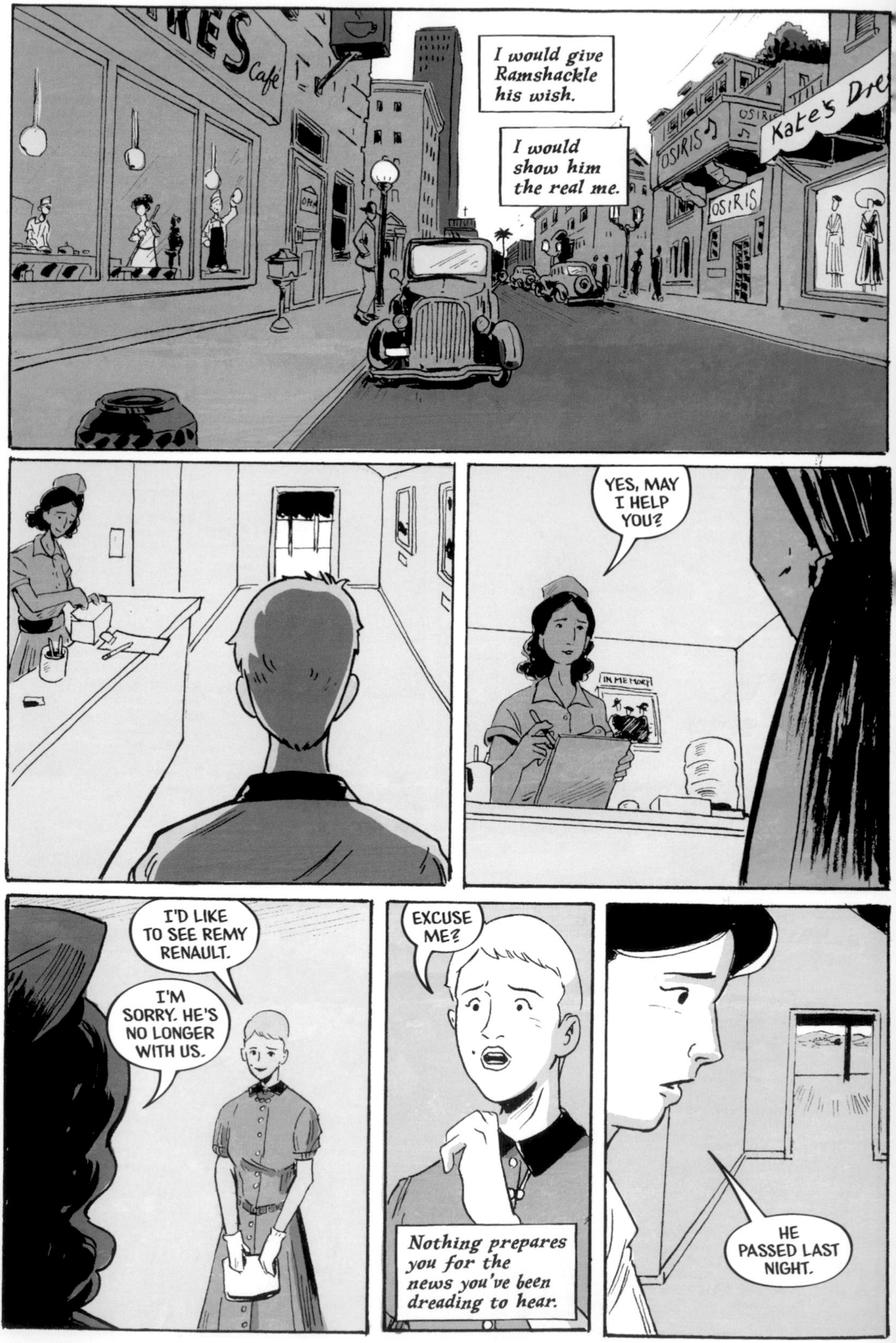

I would give Ramshackle his wish.
I would show him the real me.
Café
OPEN
OSIRIS ♪
OSIRIS
OSIRIS
Kate's Dre
YES, MAY I HELP YOU?
IN MEMORY
I'D LIKE TO SEE REMY RENAULT.
I'M SORRY. HE'S NO LONGER WITH US.
EXCUSE ME?
Nothing prepares you for the news you've been dreading to hear.
HE PASSED LAST NIGHT.

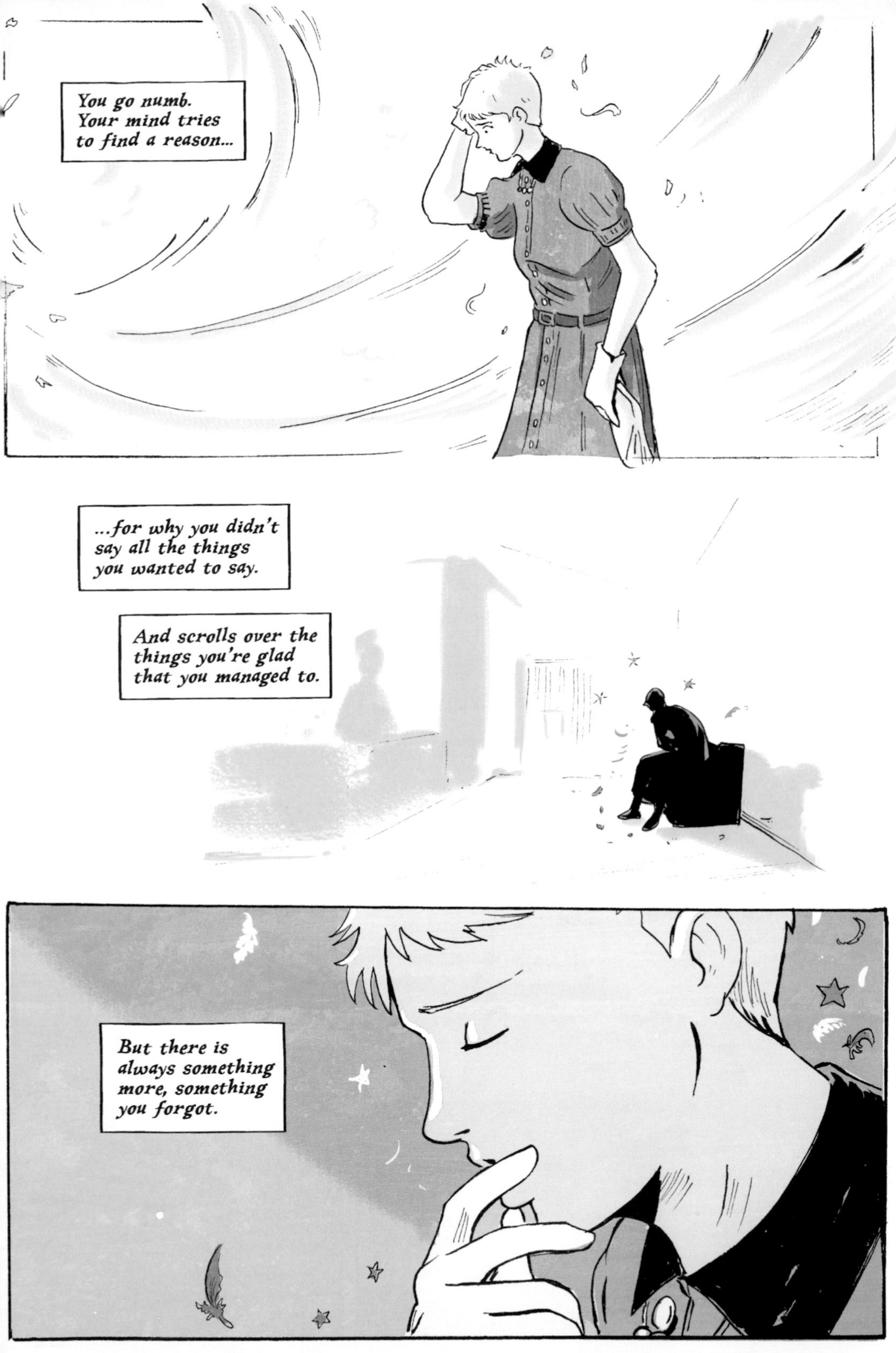
You go numb. Your mind tries to find a reason...
...for why you didn't say all the things you wanted to say.
And scrolls over the things you're glad that you managed to.
But there is always something more, something you forgot.

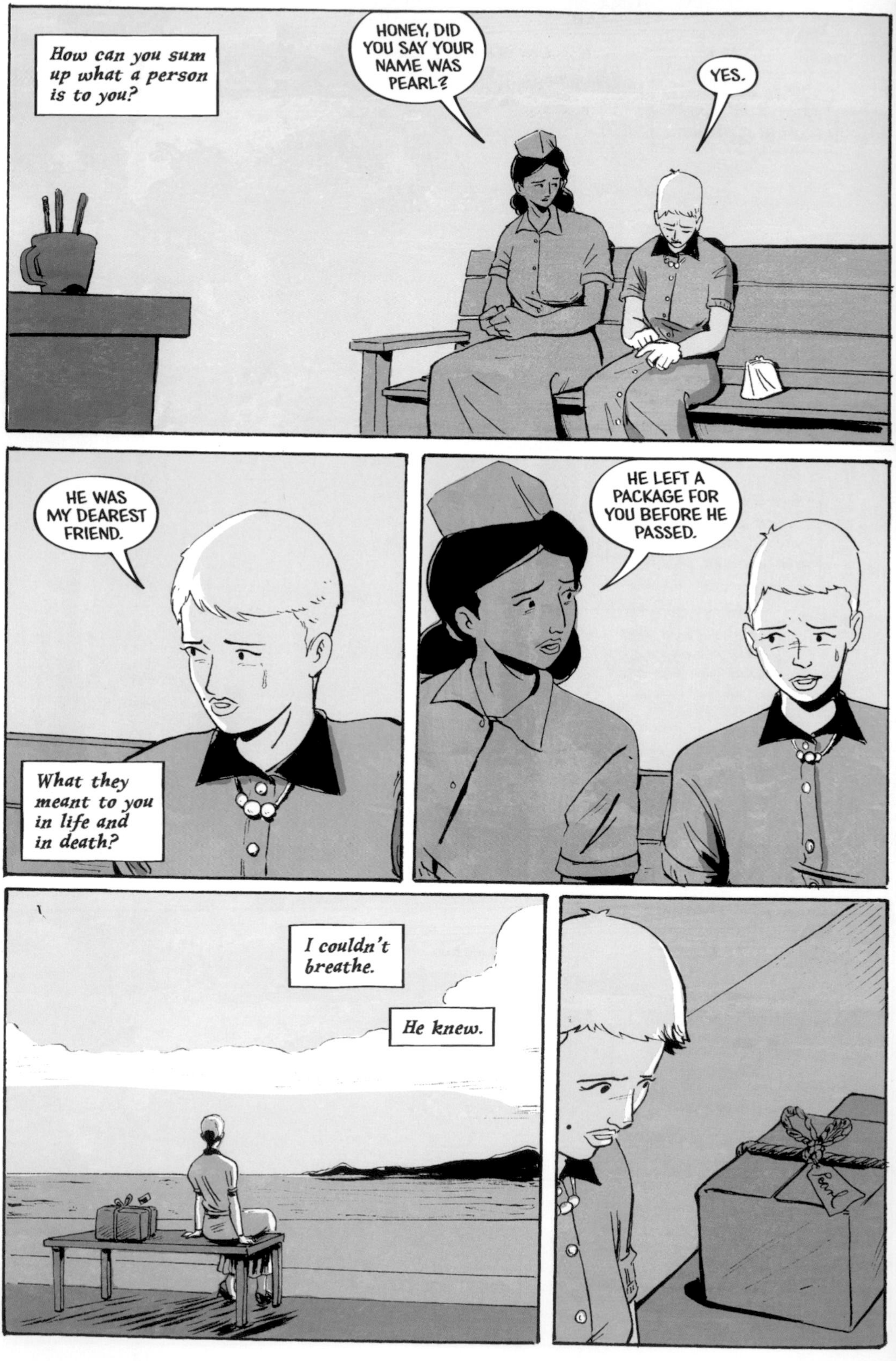
How can you sum up what a person is to you?
HONEY, DID YOU SAY YOUR NAME WAS PEARL?
YES.
HE WAS MY DEAREST FRIEND.
What they meant to you in life and in death?
HE LEFT A PACKAGE FOR YOU BEFORE HE PASSED.
I couldn't breathe.
He knew.

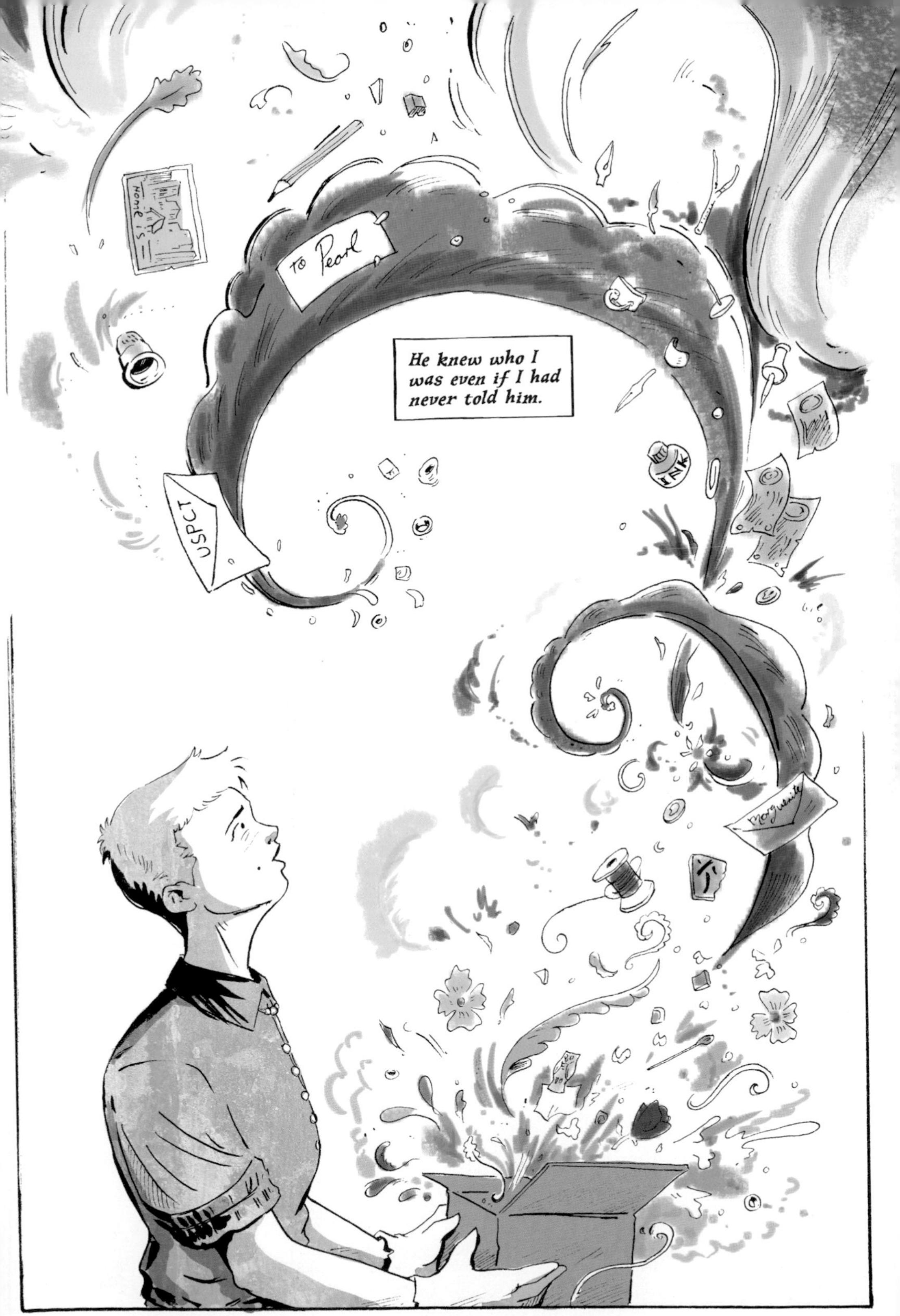
to Pearl
He knew who I was even if I had never told him.
USPCT
INK
Marguerite

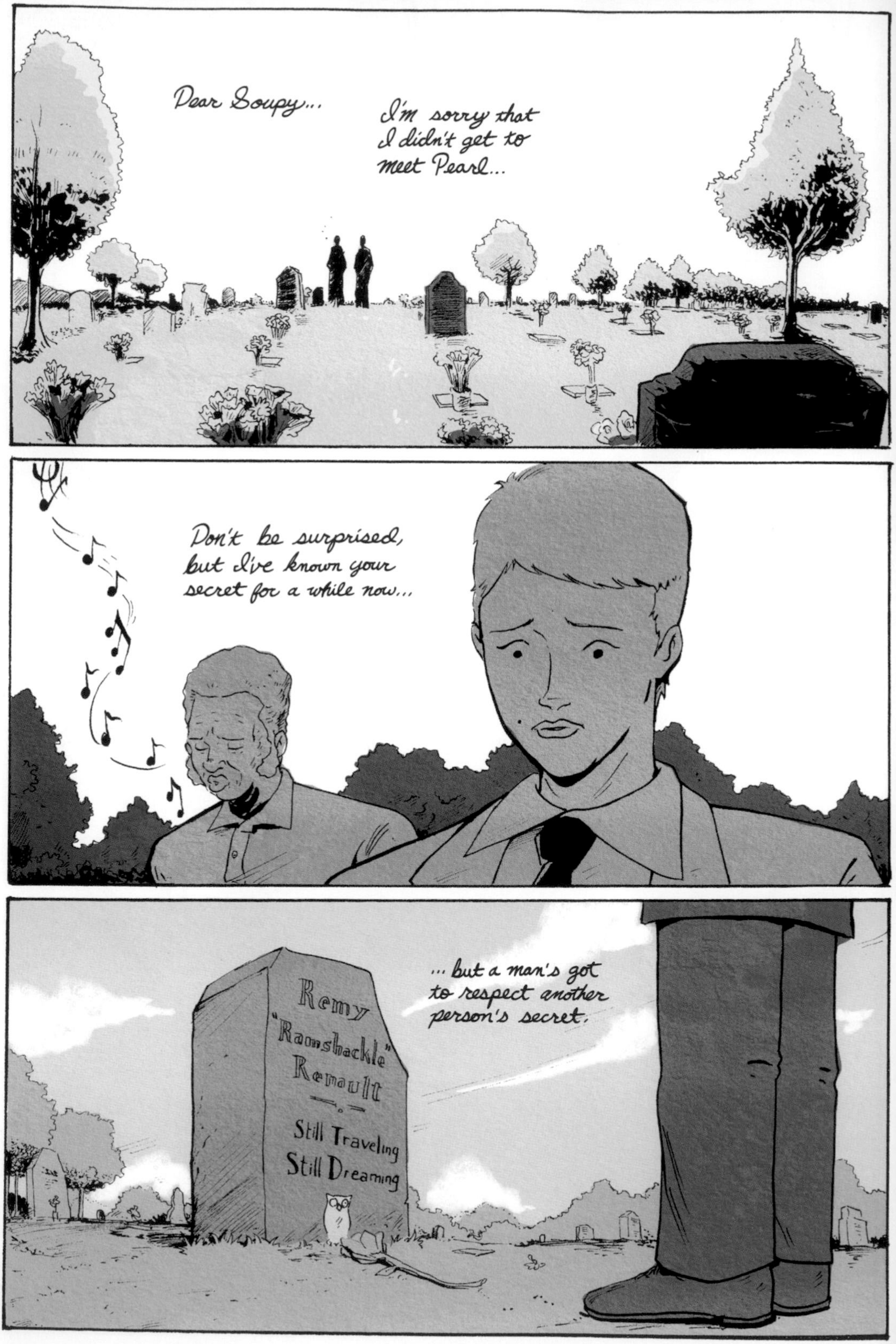
Dear Soupy...
I'm sorry that I didn't get to meet Pearl...
Don't be surprised, but I've known your secret for a while now...
... but a man's got to respect another person's secret.
Remy "Ramshackle" Renault
Still Traveling Still Dreaming

I don't think I'll be here much longer.

I can't seem to catch my breath...

...and everything seems glassy, but not in that way that I love.

ONE, PLEASE, ON THE *GOLDEN STATE*. ALL THE WAY TO CHICAGO.

I've had a good life, so don't you mourn me too much.

I've seen sunsets and stars.

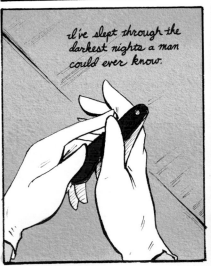

I've slept through the darkest nights a man could ever know.

I've had grief and joy.

I've loved and I've hated.

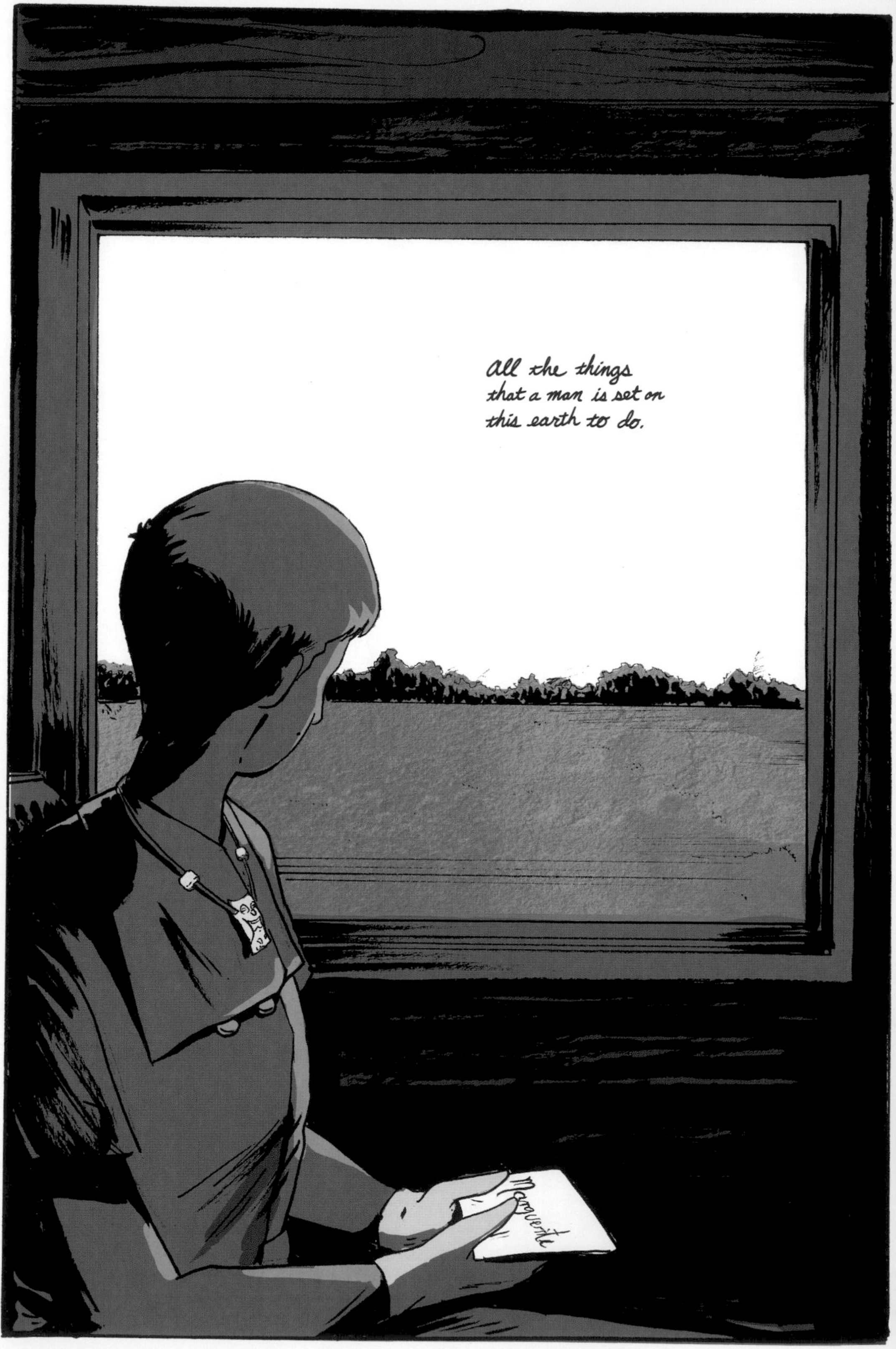
All the things
that a man is set on
this earth to do.
Marguerite

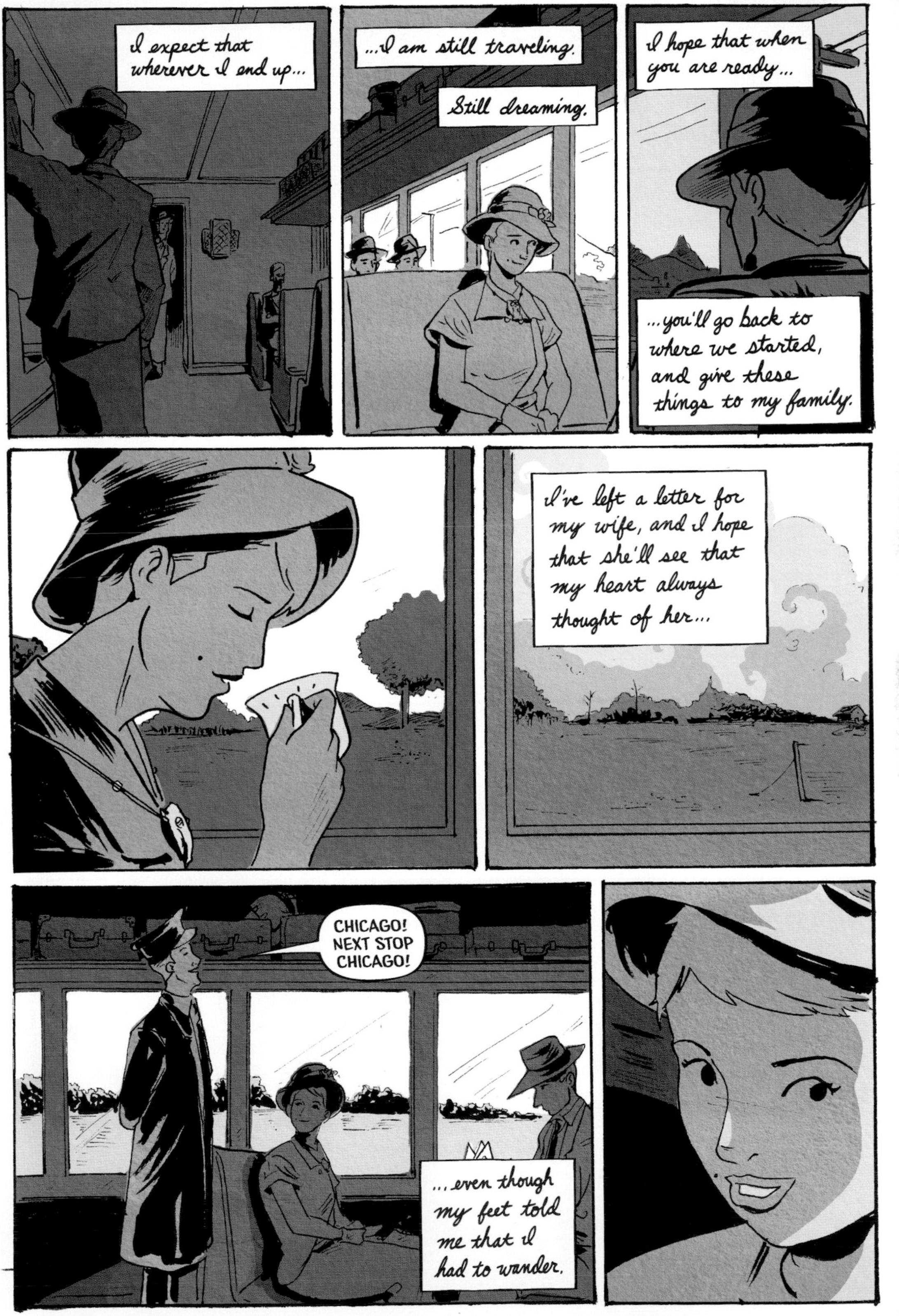
I expect that wherever I end up...
...I am still traveling.
Still dreaming.
I hope that when you are ready...
...you'll go back to where we started, and give these things to my family.
I've left a letter for my wife, and I hope that she'll see that my heart always thought of her...
CHICAGO! NEXT STOP CHICAGO!
...even though my feet told me that I had to wander.

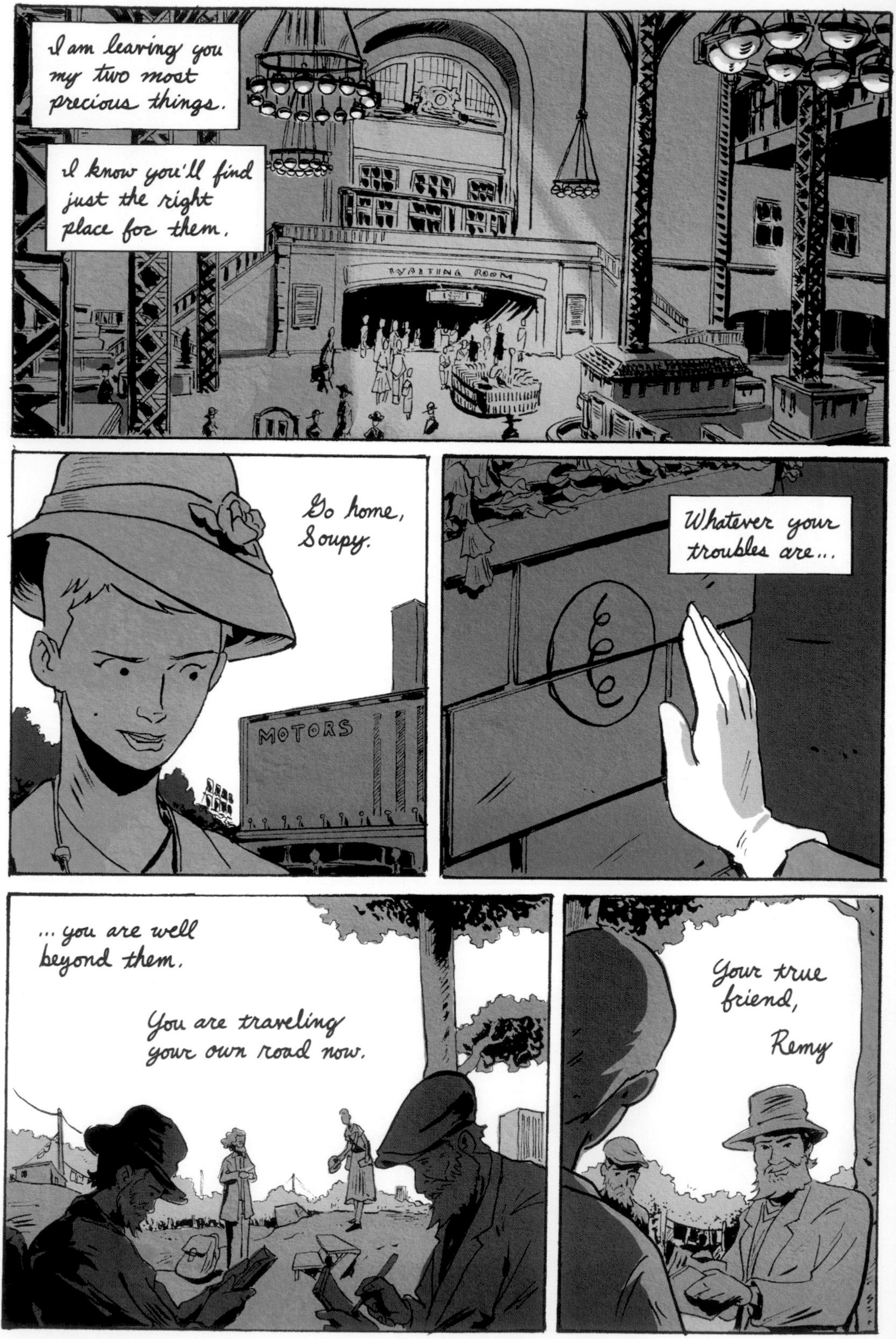
I am leaving you my two most precious things.
I know you'll find just the right place for them.
Go home, Soupy.
MOTORS
Whatever your troubles are...
... you are well beyond them.
You are traveling your own road now.
Your true friend,
Remy

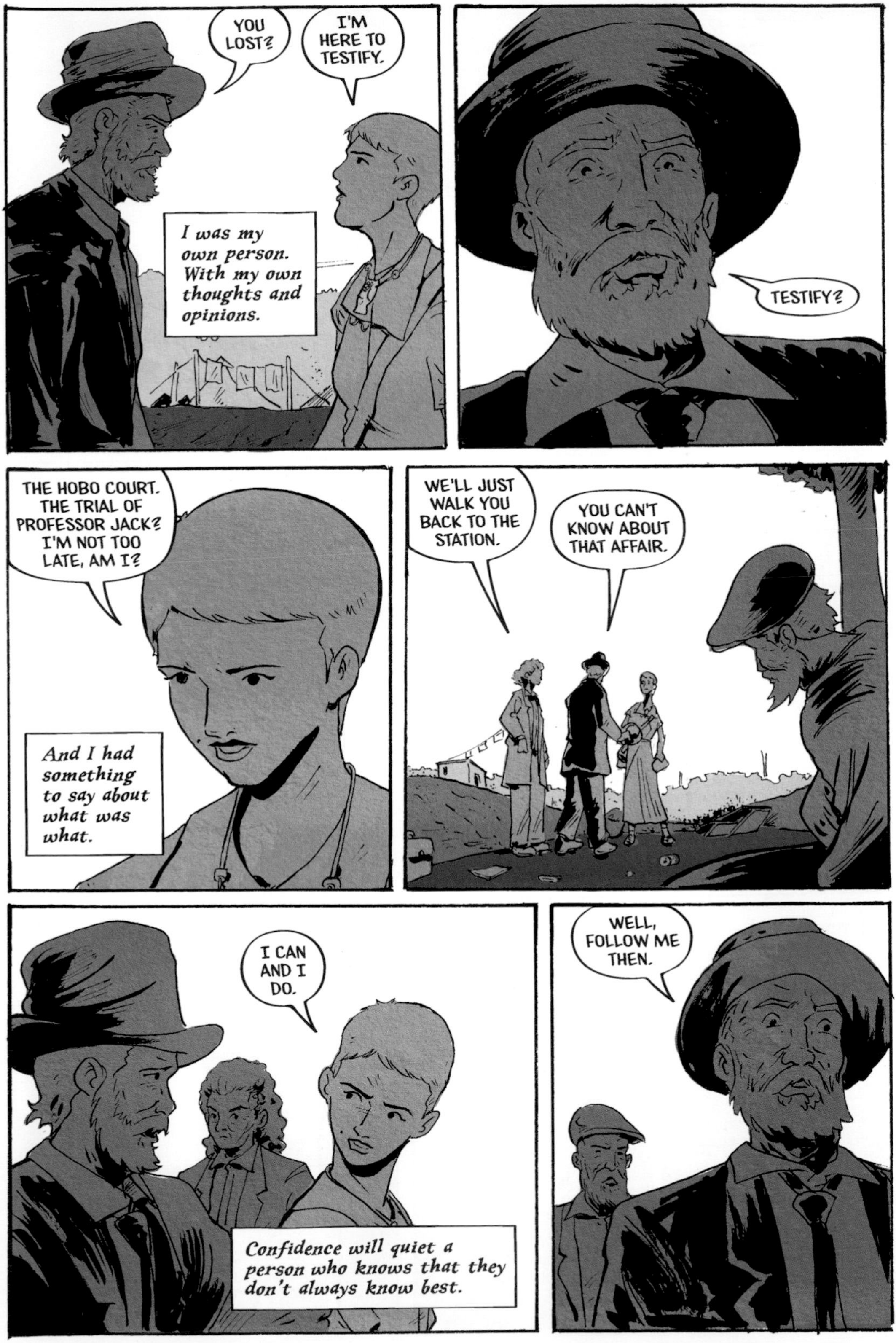
YOU LOST?
I'M HERE TO TESTIFY.
I was my own person. With my own thoughts and opinions.
TESTIFY?
THE HOBO COURT. THE TRIAL OF PROFESSOR JACK? I'M NOT TOO LATE, AM I?
And I had something to say about what was what.
WE'LL JUST WALK YOU BACK TO THE STATION.
YOU CAN'T KNOW ABOUT THAT AFFAIR.
I CAN AND I DO.
Confidence will quiet a person who knows that they don't always know best.
WELL, FOLLOW ME THEN.

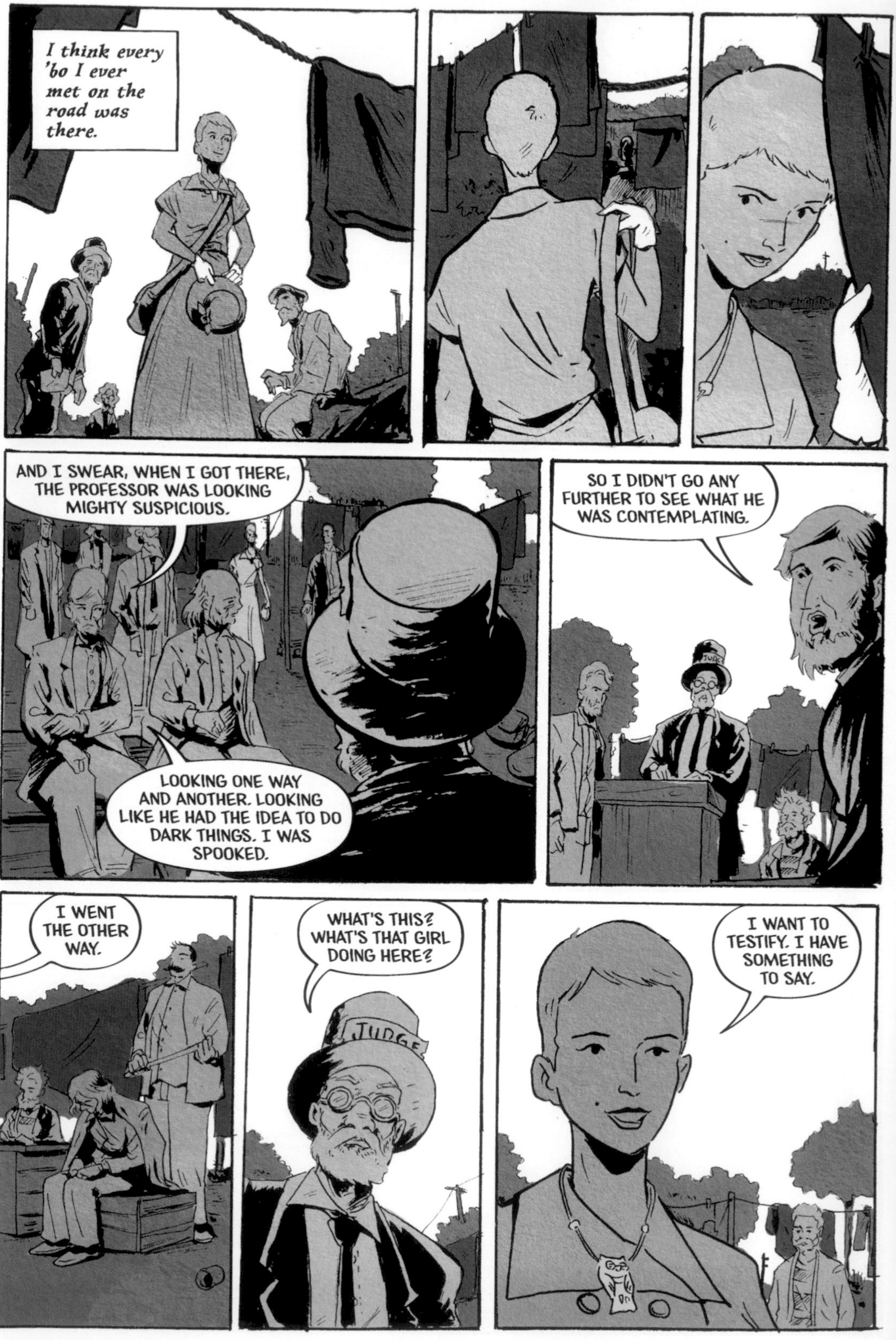
I think every 'bo I ever met on the road was there.
AND I SWEAR, WHEN I GOT THERE, THE PROFESSOR WAS LOOKING MIGHTY SUSPICIOUS.
LOOKING ONE WAY AND ANOTHER. LOOKING LIKE HE HAD THE IDEA TO DO DARK THINGS. I WAS SPOOKED.
SO I DIDN'T GO ANY FURTHER TO SEE WHAT HE WAS CONTEMPLATING.
I WENT THE OTHER WAY.
WHAT'S THIS? WHAT'S THAT GIRL DOING HERE?
JUDGE
I WANT TO TESTIFY. I HAVE SOMETHING TO SAY.

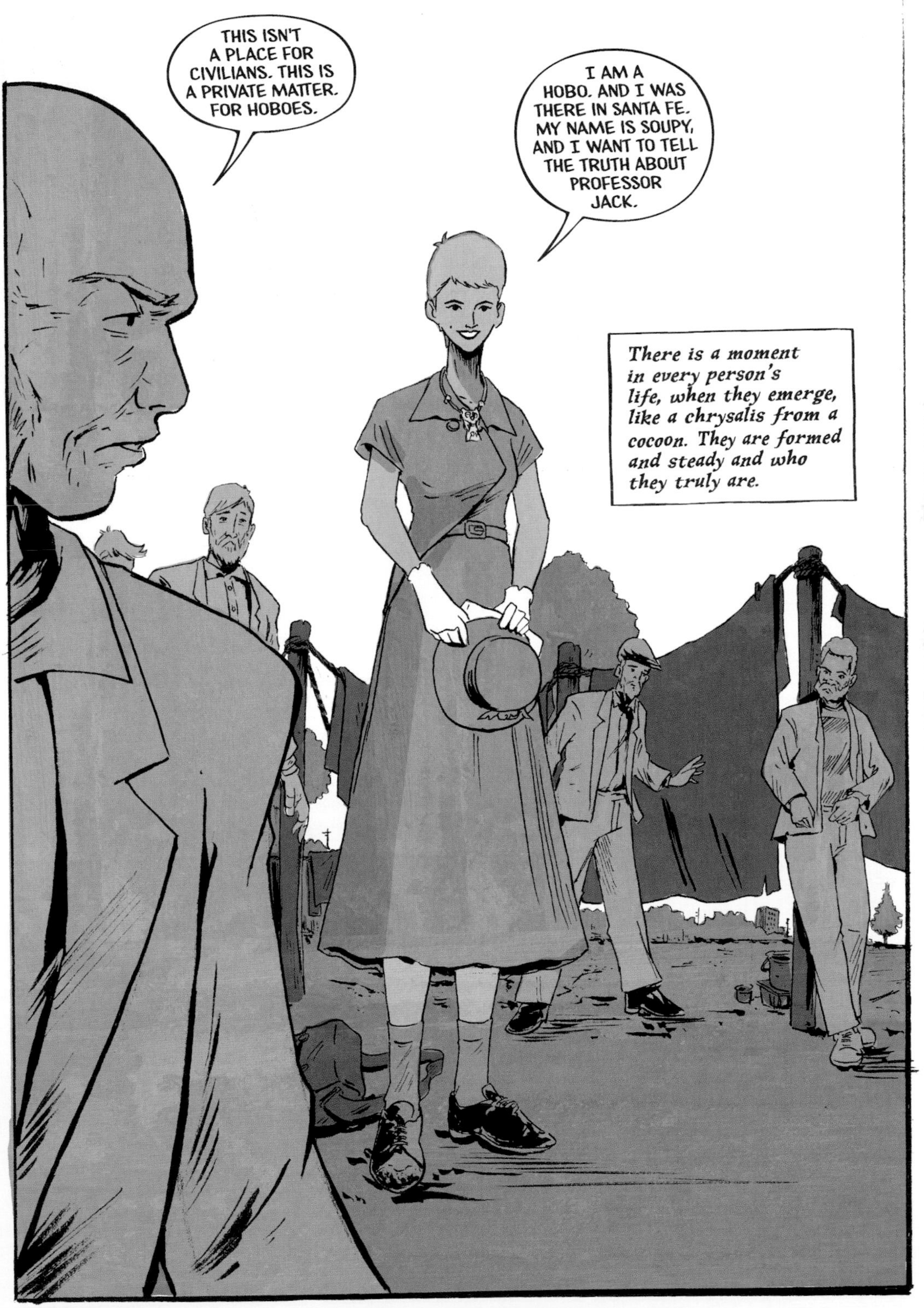
THIS ISN'T A PLACE FOR CIVILIANS. THIS IS A PRIVATE MATTER. FOR HOBOES.
I AM A HOBO. AND I WAS THERE IN SANTA FE. MY NAME IS SOUPY, AND I WANT TO TELL THE TRUTH ABOUT PROFESSOR JACK.
There is a moment in every person's life, when they emerge, like a chrysalis from a cocoon. They are formed and steady and who they truly are.

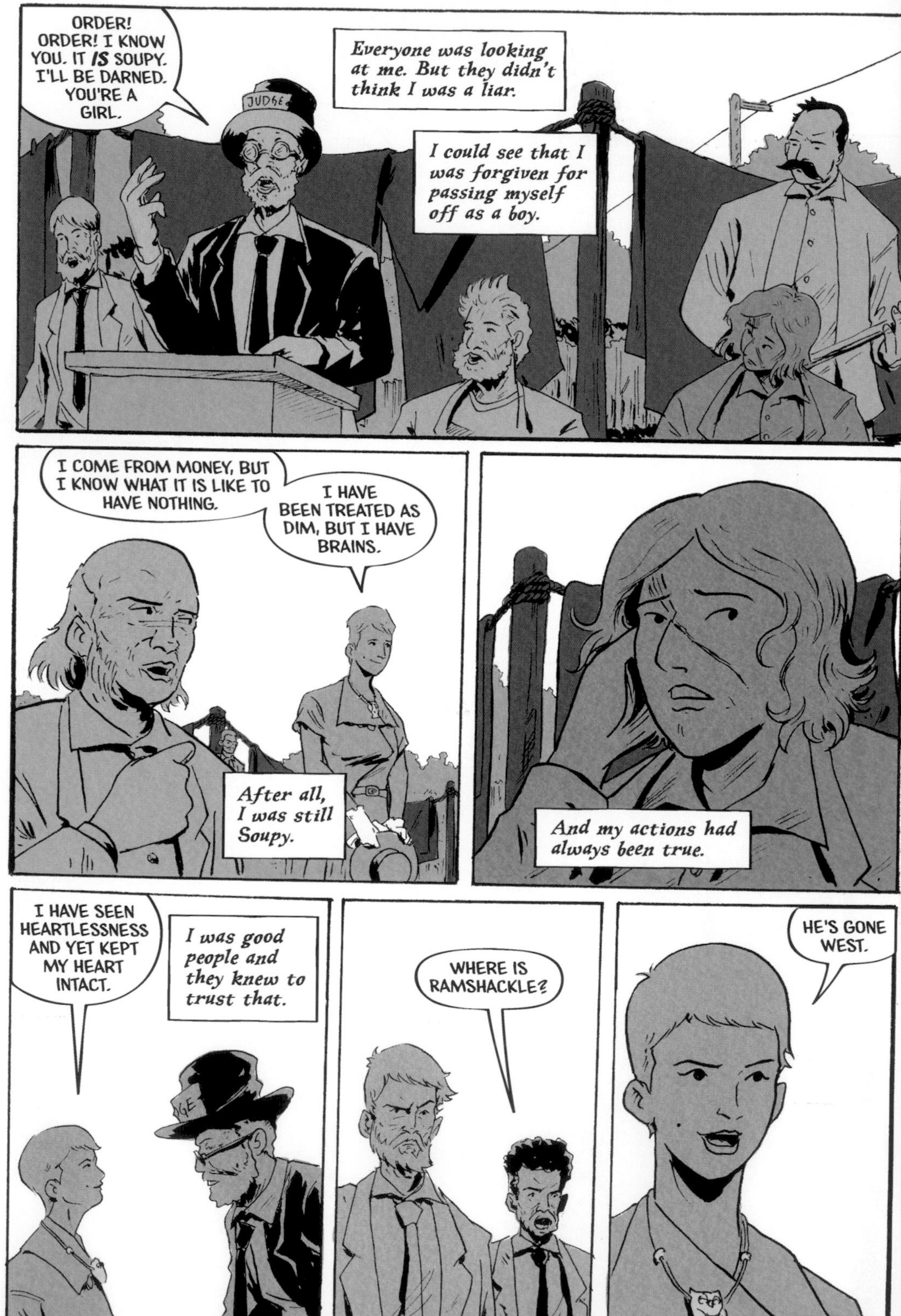
ORDER! ORDER! I KNOW YOU. IT *IS* SOUPY. I'LL BE DARNED. YOU'RE A GIRL.
JUDGE
Everyone was looking at me. But they didn't think I was a liar.
I could see that I was forgiven for passing myself off as a boy.
I COME FROM MONEY, BUT I KNOW WHAT IT IS LIKE TO HAVE NOTHING.
I HAVE BEEN TREATED AS DIM, BUT I HAVE BRAINS.
After all, I was still Soupy.
And my actions had always been true.
I HAVE SEEN HEARTLESSNESS AND YET KEPT MY HEART INTACT.
I was good people and they knew to trust that.
WHERE IS RAMSHACKLE?
HE'S GONE WEST.

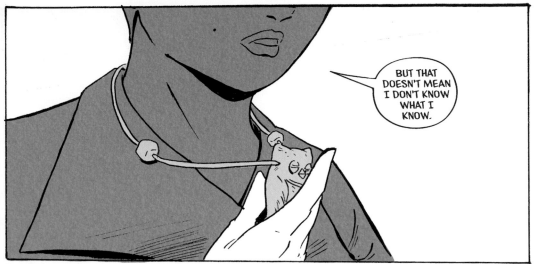

BUT THAT DOESN'T MEAN I DON'T KNOW WHAT I KNOW.

I'M MIGHTY SAD TO HEAR THAT. HE WAS GOOD PEOPLE.

WELL, IF YOU'VE GOT SOMETHING TO SAY, THEN YOU'D BEST GET ON THE STAND AND SAY IT.

The hardest part and what surprised me the most...

DO YOU SWEAR TO TELL THE TRUTH?

I DO.

...was how Professor Jack looked at me.

SPEAK YOUR PIECE.

Like somehow I'd hurt his feelings.

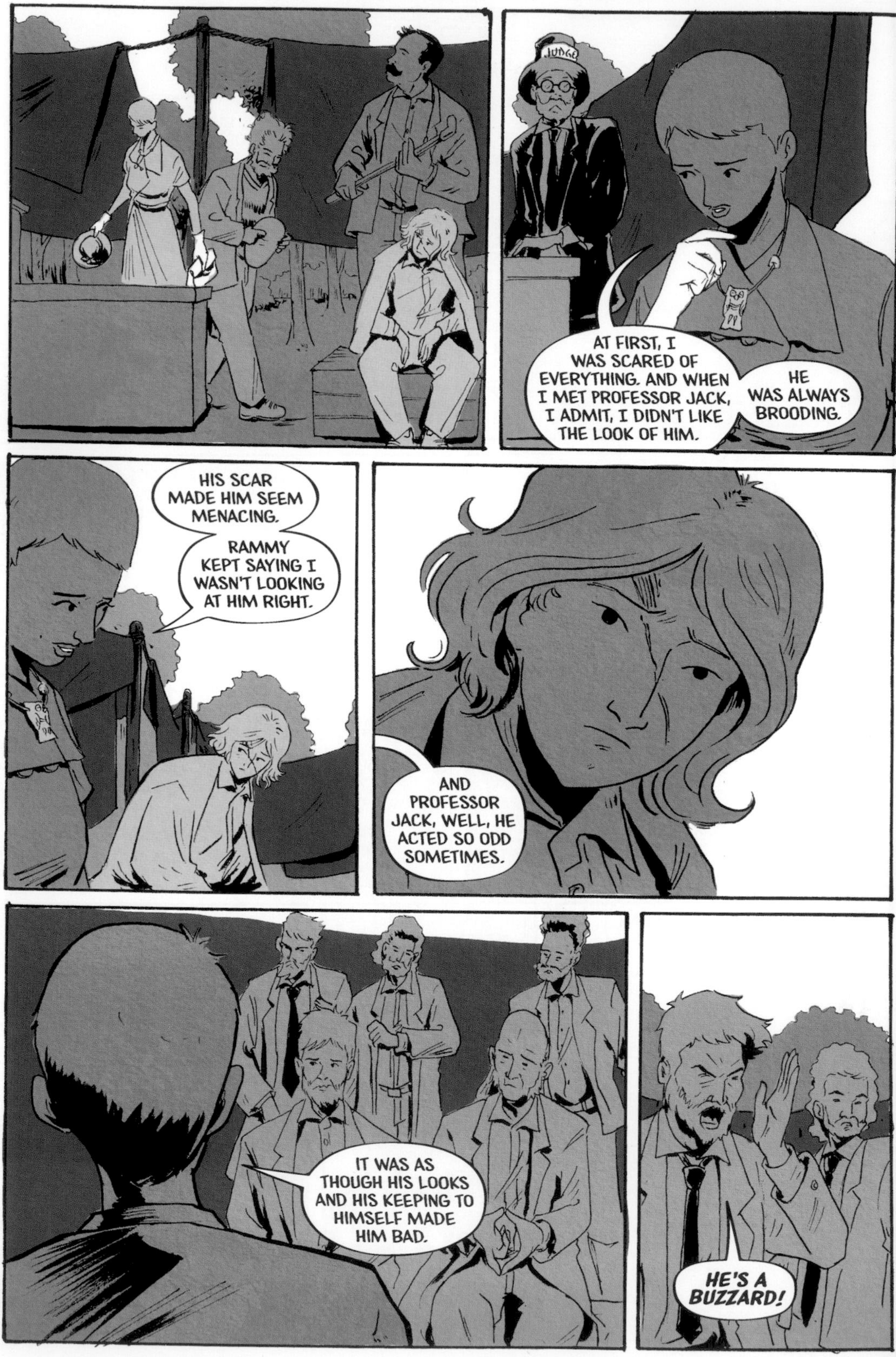
JUDGE
AT FIRST, I WAS SCARED OF EVERYTHING. AND WHEN I MET PROFESSOR JACK, I ADMIT, I DIDN'T LIKE THE LOOK OF HIM.
HE WAS ALWAYS BROODING.
HIS SCAR MADE HIM SEEM MENACING.
RAMMY KEPT SAYING I WASN'T LOOKING AT HIM RIGHT.
AND PROFESSOR JACK, WELL, HE ACTED SO ODD SOMETIMES.
IT WAS AS THOUGH HIS LOOKS AND HIS KEEPING TO HIMSELF MADE HIM BAD.
HE'S A BUZZARD!

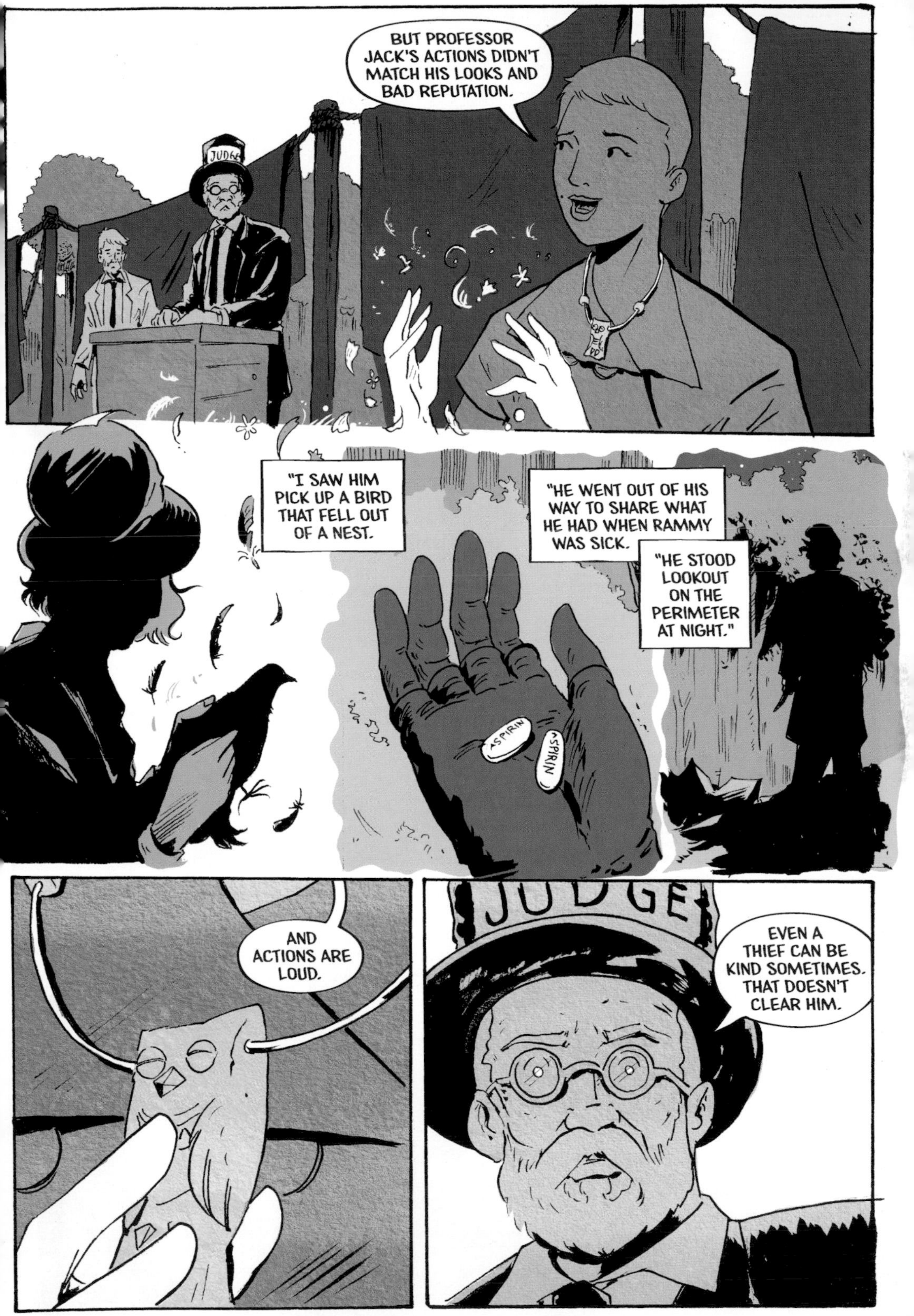
BUT PROFESSOR JACK'S ACTIONS DIDN'T MATCH HIS LOOKS AND BAD REPUTATION.
JUDGE
"I SAW HIM PICK UP A BIRD THAT FELL OUT OF A NEST.
"HE WENT OUT OF HIS WAY TO SHARE WHAT HE HAD WHEN RAMMY WAS SICK.
ASPIRIN
ASPIRIN
"HE STOOD LOOKOUT ON THE PERIMETER AT NIGHT."
AND ACTIONS ARE LOUD.
JUDGE
EVEN A THIEF CAN BE KIND SOMETIMES. THAT DOESN'T CLEAR HIM.

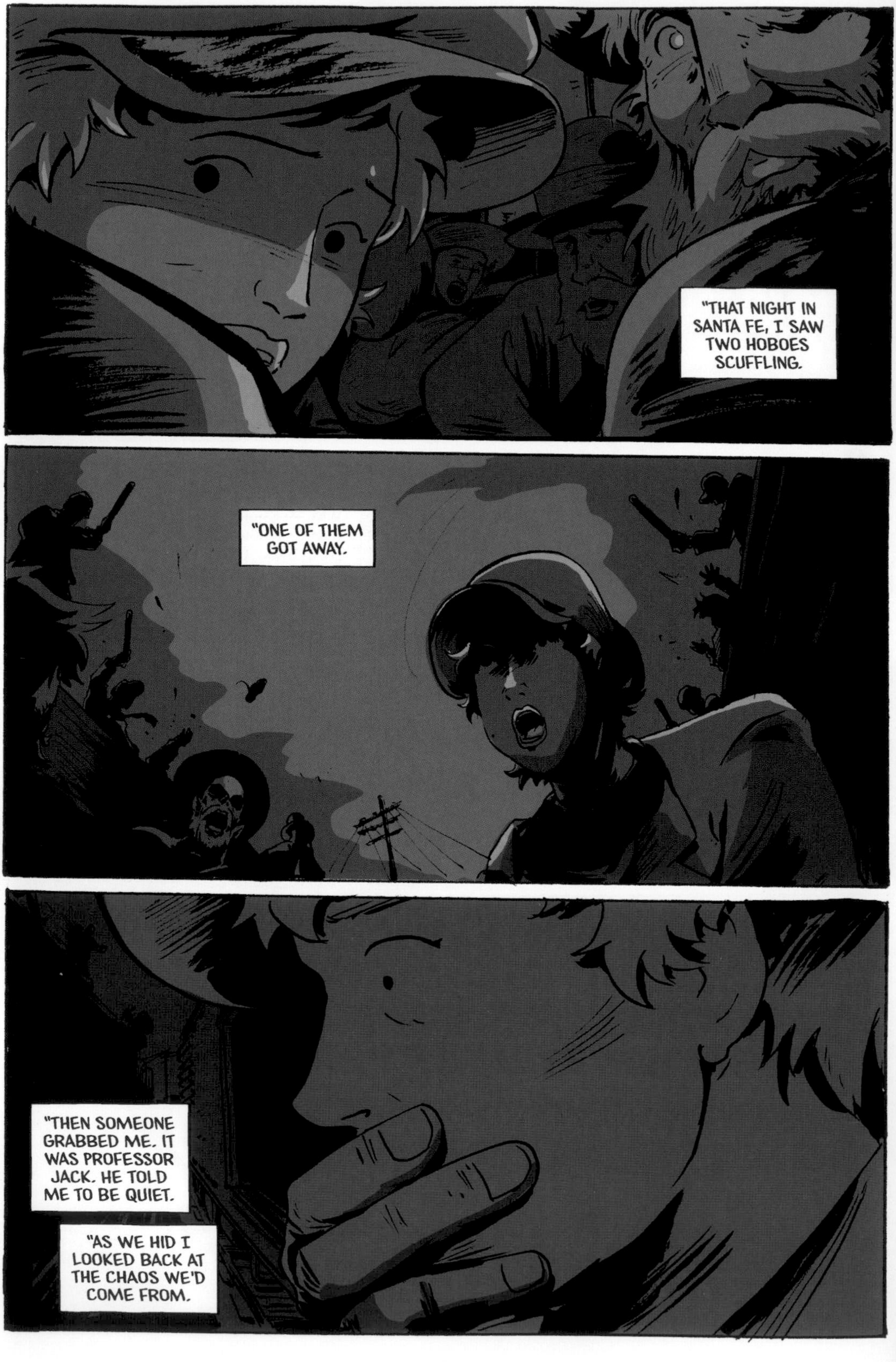
"THAT NIGHT IN SANTA FE, I SAW TWO HOBOES SCUFFLING.
"ONE OF THEM GOT AWAY.
"THEN SOMEONE GRABBED ME. IT WAS PROFESSOR JACK. HE TOLD ME TO BE QUIET.
"AS WE HID I LOOKED BACK AT THE CHAOS WE'D COME FROM.

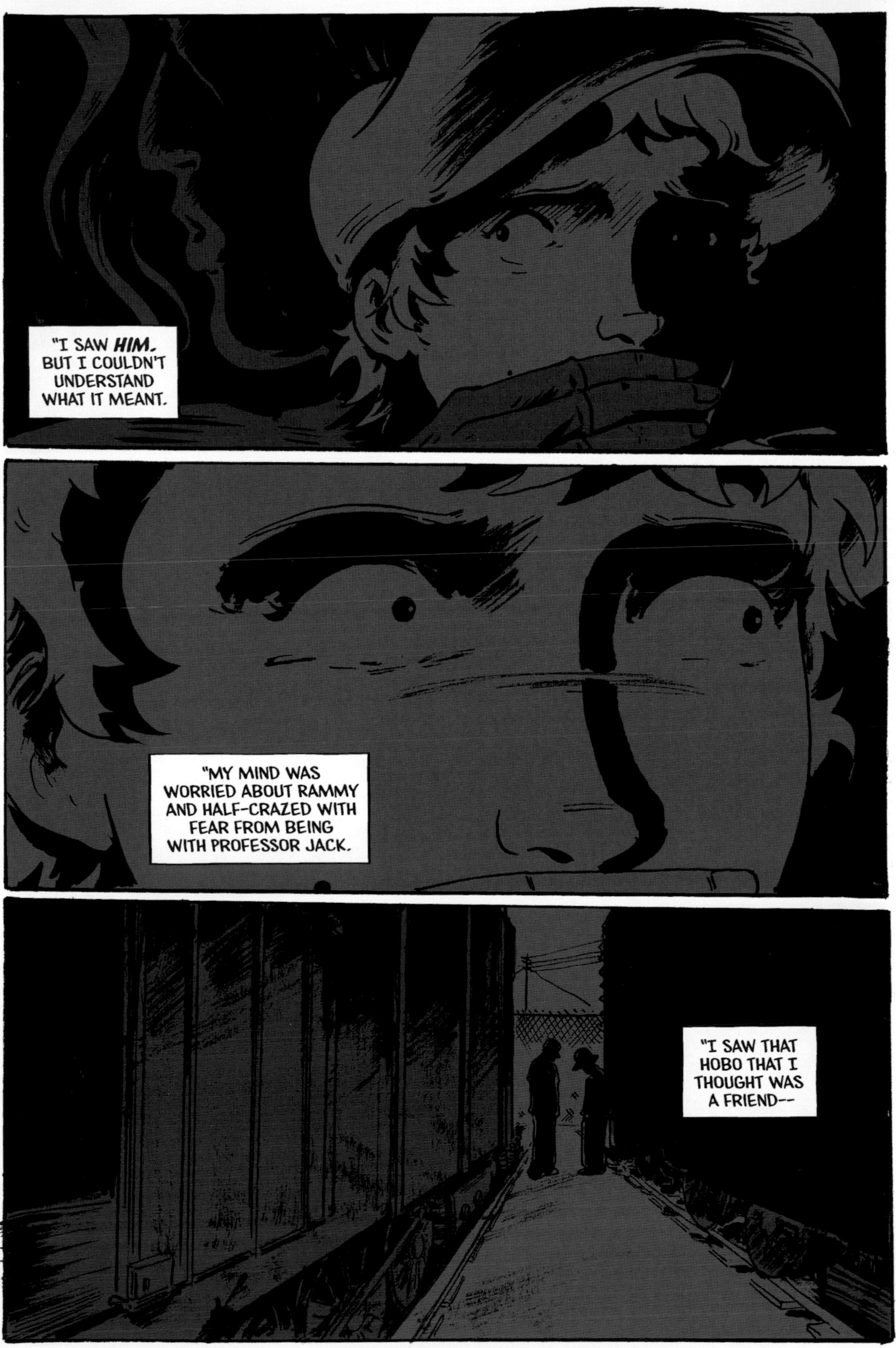
"I SAW ***HIM.*** BUT I COULDN'T UNDERSTAND WHAT IT MEANT.
"MY MIND WAS WORRIED ABOUT RAMMY AND HALF-CRAZED WITH FEAR FROM BEING WITH PROFESSOR JACK.
"I SAW THAT HOBO THAT I THOUGHT WAS A FRIEND--

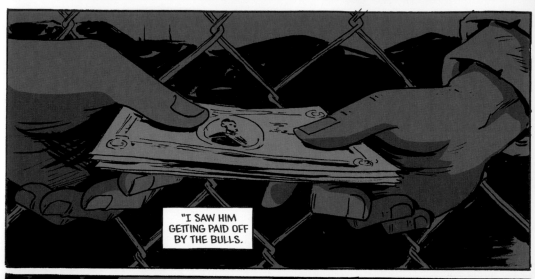

"I SAW HIM GETTING PAID OFF BY THE BULLS.

"I THOUGHT HE WAS ME AND RAMMY'S FRIEND.

"BUT NOW I KNOW THAT RAMMY KEPT GUMS CLOSE SO THAT HE COULD KEEP AN EYE ON HIM, AND SO THAT GUMS COULDN'T DO ME NO HARM."

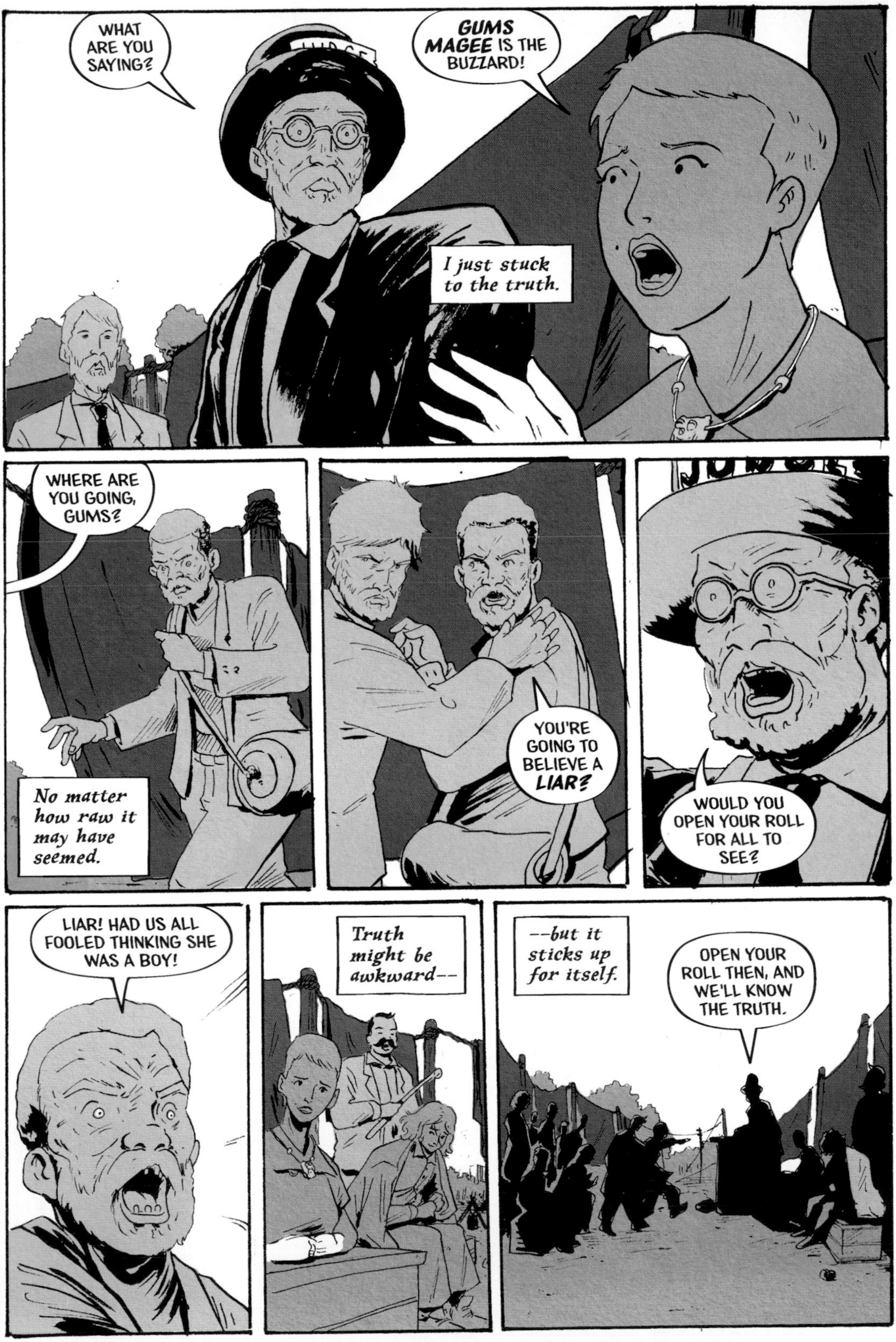

WHAT ARE YOU SAYING?
GUMS MAGEE IS THE BUZZARD!
I just stuck to the truth.
WHERE ARE YOU GOING, GUMS?
No matter how raw it may have seemed.
YOU'RE GOING TO BELIEVE A LIAR?
WOULD YOU OPEN YOUR ROLL FOR ALL TO SEE?
LIAR! HAD US ALL FOOLED THINKING SHE WAS A BOY!
Truth might be awkward--
--but it sticks up for itself.
OPEN YOUR ROLL THEN, AND WE'LL KNOW THE TRUTH.

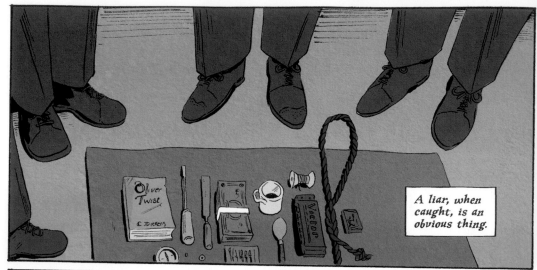

A liar, when caught, is an obvious thing.

I DECLARE THE PROFESSOR TO BE GOOD PEOPLE.

GUMS MAGEE IS BANNED FROM ALL JUNGLES EVERYWHERE.

SPREAD THE WORD.

Or, rather, once you see what a liar looks like, you can't unsee it.

THANK YOU, SOUPY.

YOU MIGHT HAVE TOLD ME YOU WERE A GIRL.

I COULDN'T.

I DIDN'T EVEN WANT TO BE A PERSON.

178

RAMSHACKLE SAID THAT YOU WERE ALL HIS FAMILY AND HE'D LIKE YOU TO HAVE SOMETHING OF WHAT HE COLLECTED.

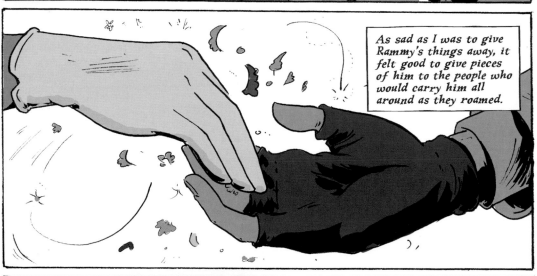

As sad as I was to give Rammy's things away, it felt good to give pieces of him to the people who would carry him all around as they roamed.

Wherever he was, I knew he would like that.

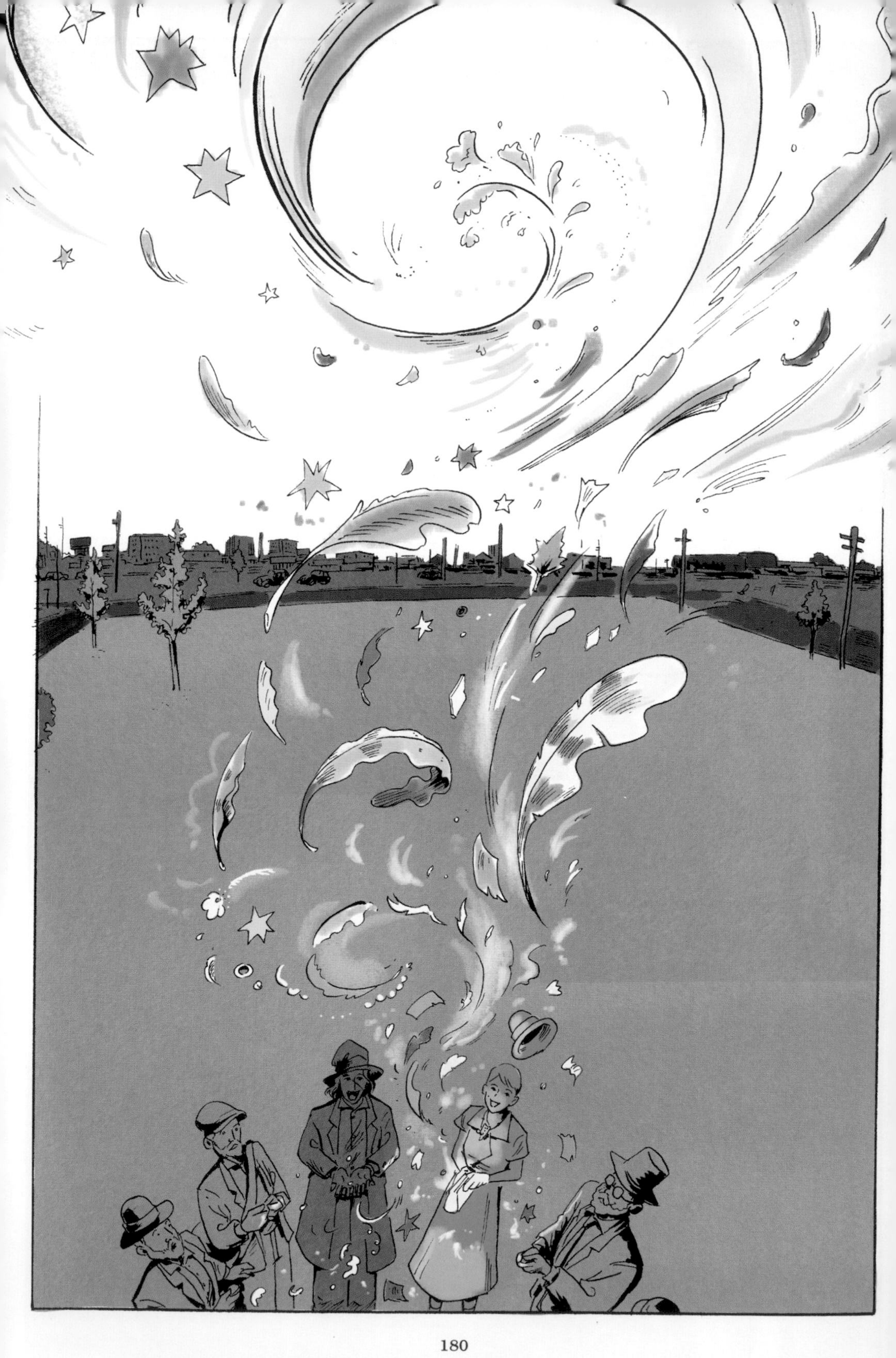

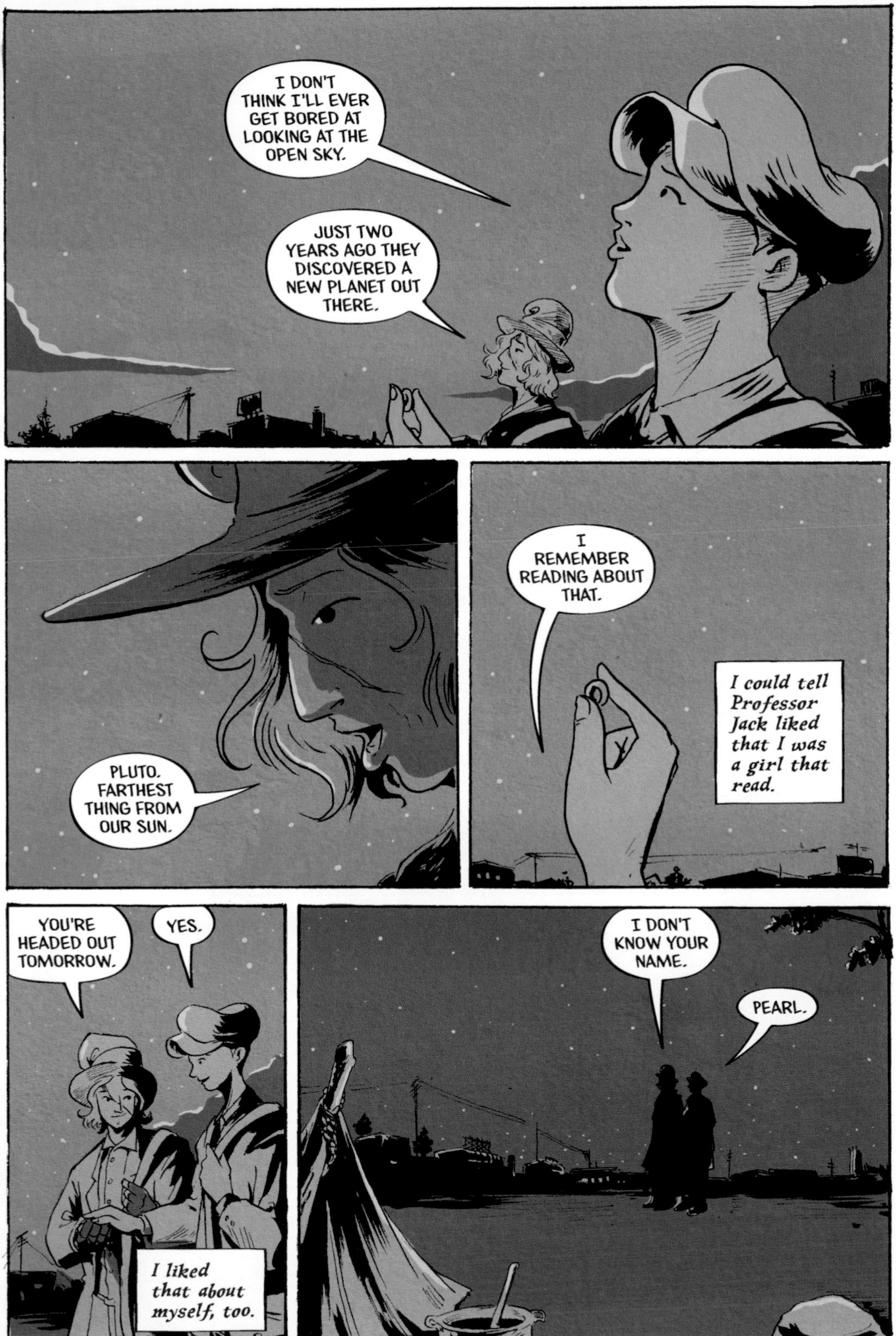
I DON'T THINK I'LL EVER GET BORED AT LOOKING AT THE OPEN SKY.
JUST TWO YEARS AGO THEY DISCOVERED A NEW PLANET OUT THERE.
PLUTO. FARTHEST THING FROM OUR SUN.
I REMEMBER READING ABOUT THAT.
I could tell Professor Jack liked that I was a girl that read.
YOU'RE HEADED OUT TOMORROW.
YES.
I liked that about myself, too.
I DON'T KNOW YOUR NAME.
PEARL.

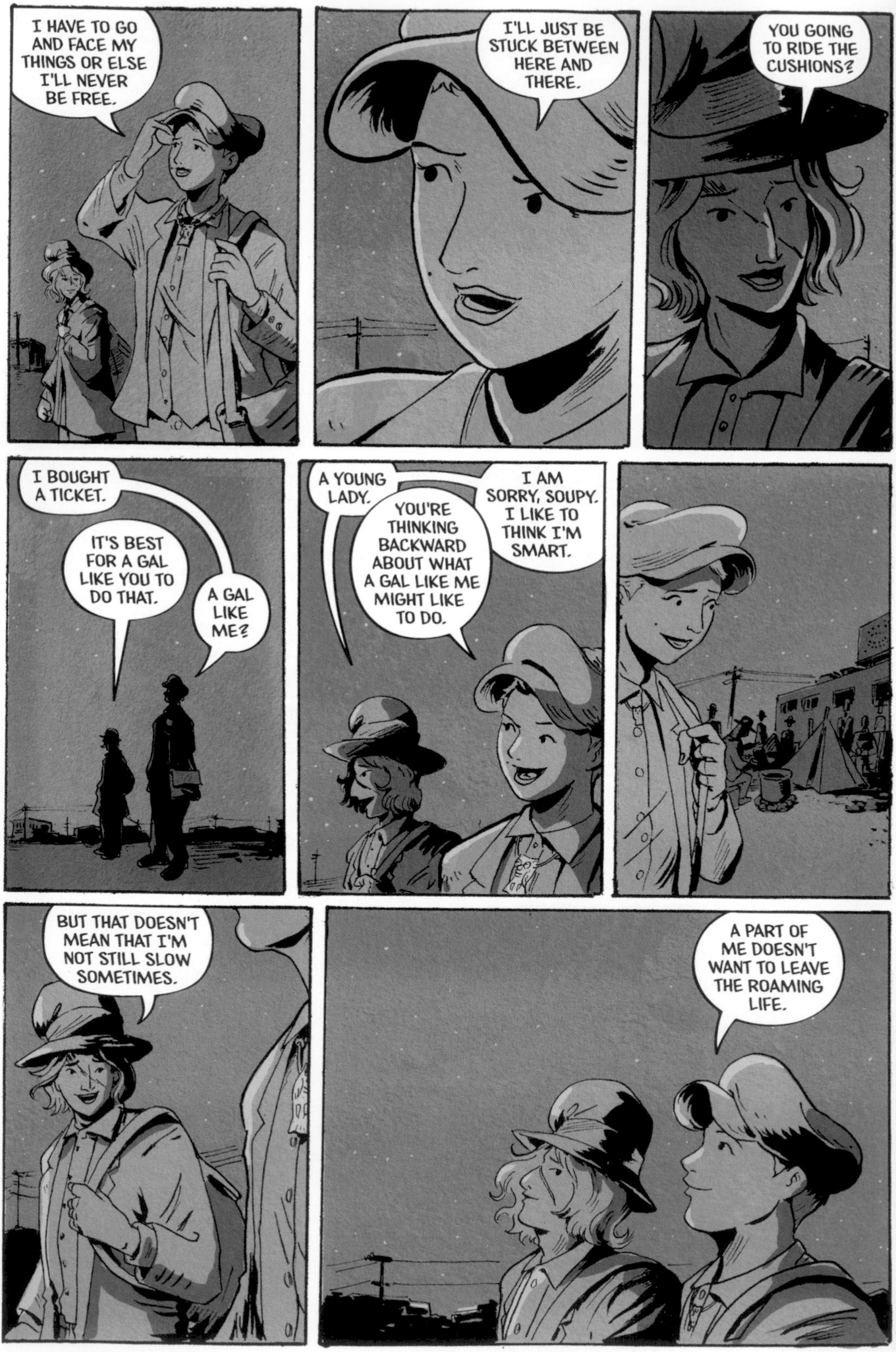
I HAVE TO GO AND FACE MY THINGS OR ELSE I'LL NEVER BE FREE.
I'LL JUST BE STUCK BETWEEN HERE AND THERE.
YOU GOING TO RIDE THE CUSHIONS?
I BOUGHT A TICKET.
IT'S BEST FOR A GAL LIKE YOU TO DO THAT.
A GAL LIKE ME?
A YOUNG LADY.
YOU'RE THINKING BACKWARD ABOUT WHAT A GAL LIKE ME MIGHT LIKE TO DO.
I AM SORRY, SOUPY. I LIKE TO THINK I'M SMART.
BUT THAT DOESN'T MEAN THAT I'M NOT STILL SLOW SOMETIMES.
A PART OF ME DOESN'T WANT TO LEAVE THE ROAMING LIFE.

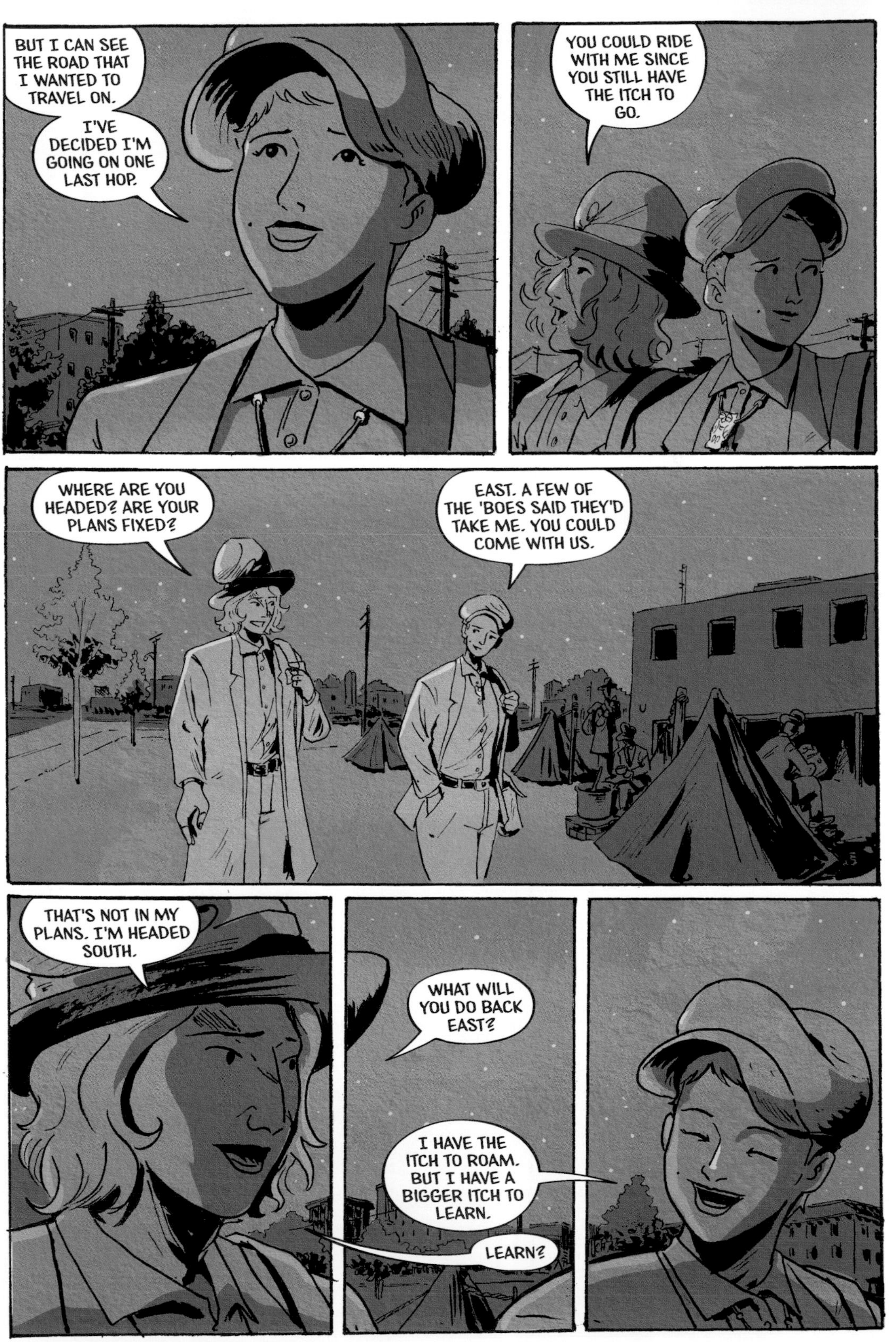
BUT I CAN SEE THE ROAD THAT I WANTED TO TRAVEL ON.
I'VE DECIDED I'M GOING ON ONE LAST HOP.
YOU COULD RIDE WITH ME SINCE YOU STILL HAVE THE ITCH TO GO.
WHERE ARE YOU HEADED? ARE YOUR PLANS FIXED?
EAST. A FEW OF THE 'BOES SAID THEY'D TAKE ME. YOU COULD COME WITH US.
THAT'S NOT IN MY PLANS. I'M HEADED SOUTH.
WHAT WILL YOU DO BACK EAST?
I HAVE THE ITCH TO ROAM. BUT I HAVE A BIGGER ITCH TO LEARN.
LEARN?

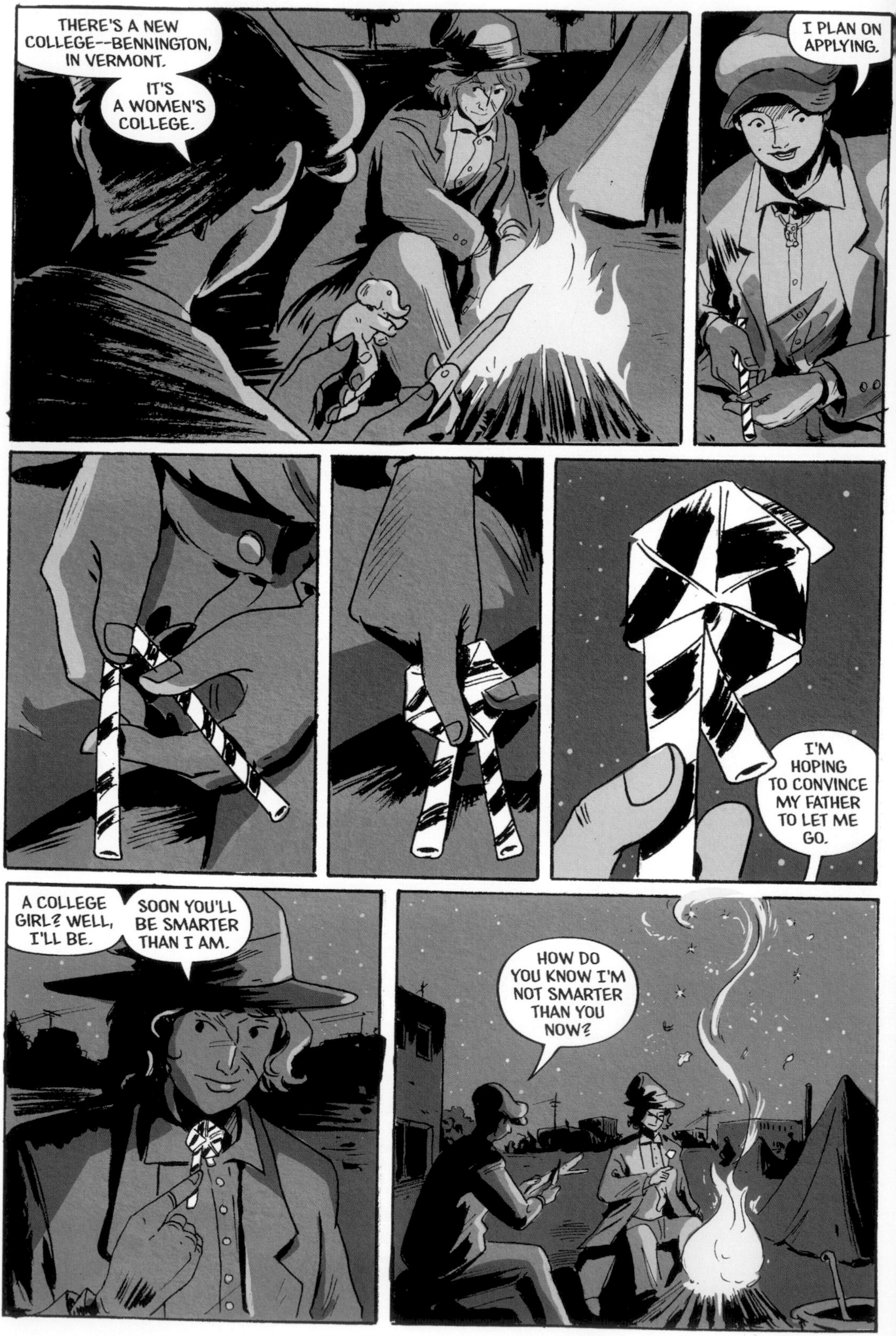
THERE'S A NEW COLLEGE--BENNINGTON, IN VERMONT.
IT'S A WOMEN'S COLLEGE.
I PLAN ON APPLYING.
I'M HOPING TO CONVINCE MY FATHER TO LET ME GO.
A COLLEGE GIRL? WELL, I'LL BE.
SOON YOU'LL BE SMARTER THAN I AM.
HOW DO YOU KNOW I'M NOT SMARTER THAN YOU NOW?

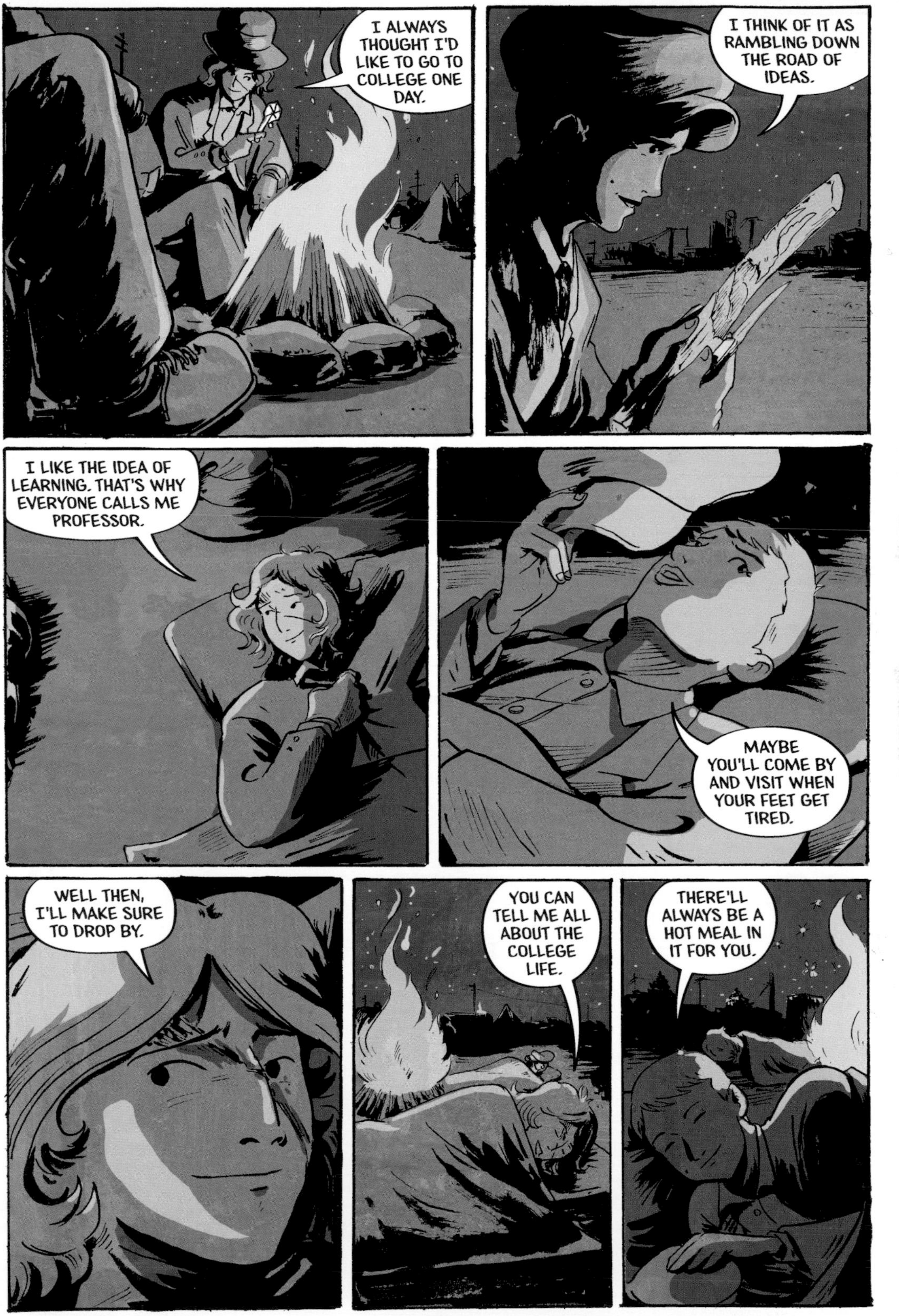
I ALWAYS THOUGHT I'D LIKE TO GO TO COLLEGE ONE DAY.
I THINK OF IT AS RAMBLING DOWN THE ROAD OF IDEAS.
I LIKE THE IDEA OF LEARNING. THAT'S WHY EVERYONE CALLS ME PROFESSOR.
MAYBE YOU'LL COME BY AND VISIT WHEN YOUR FEET GET TIRED.
WELL THEN, I'LL MAKE SURE TO DROP BY.
YOU CAN TELL ME ALL ABOUT THE COLLEGE LIFE.
THERE'LL ALWAYS BE A HOT MEAL IN IT FOR YOU.

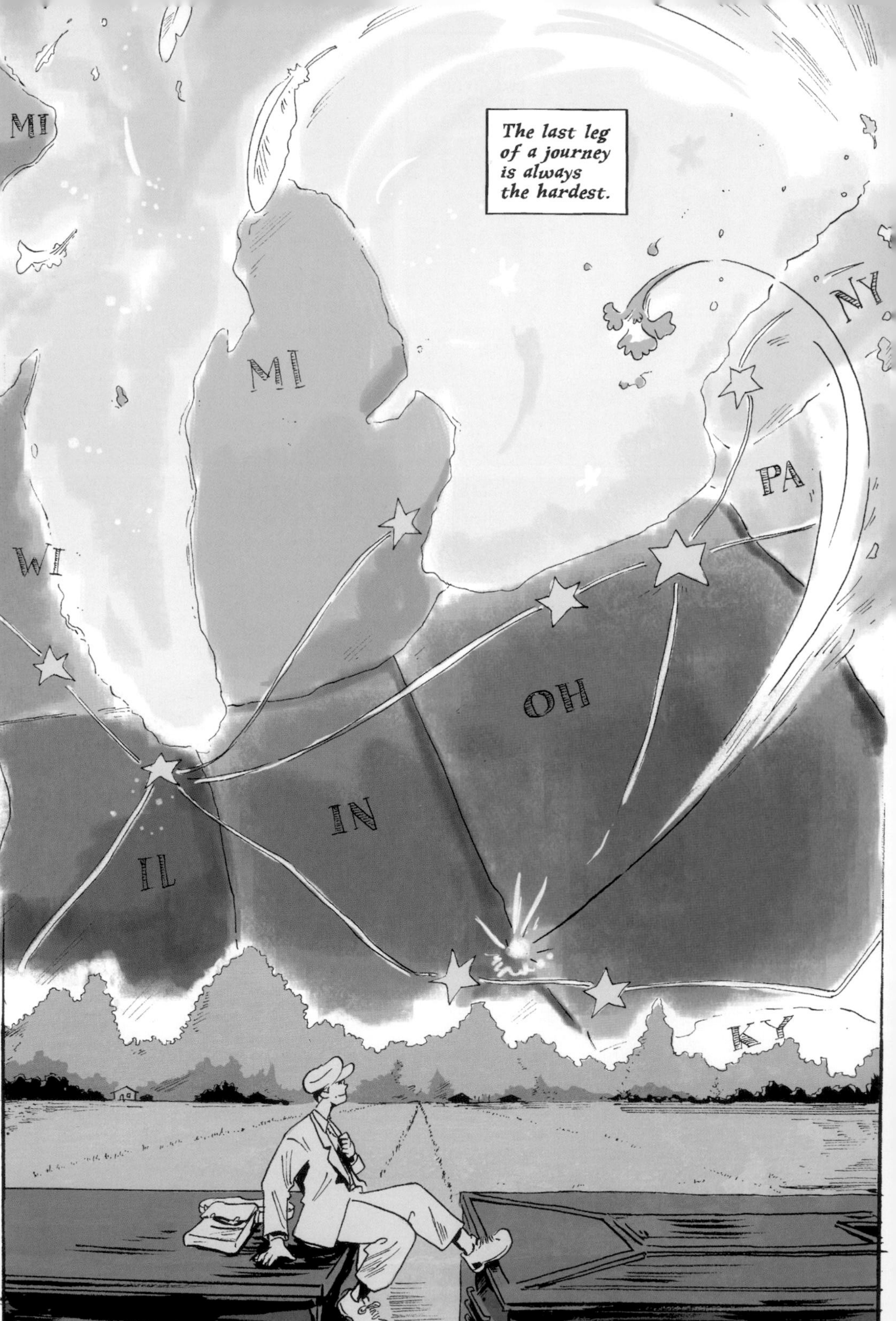
The last leg of a journey is always the hardest.
MI
MI
WI
NY
PA
OH
IN
IL
KY

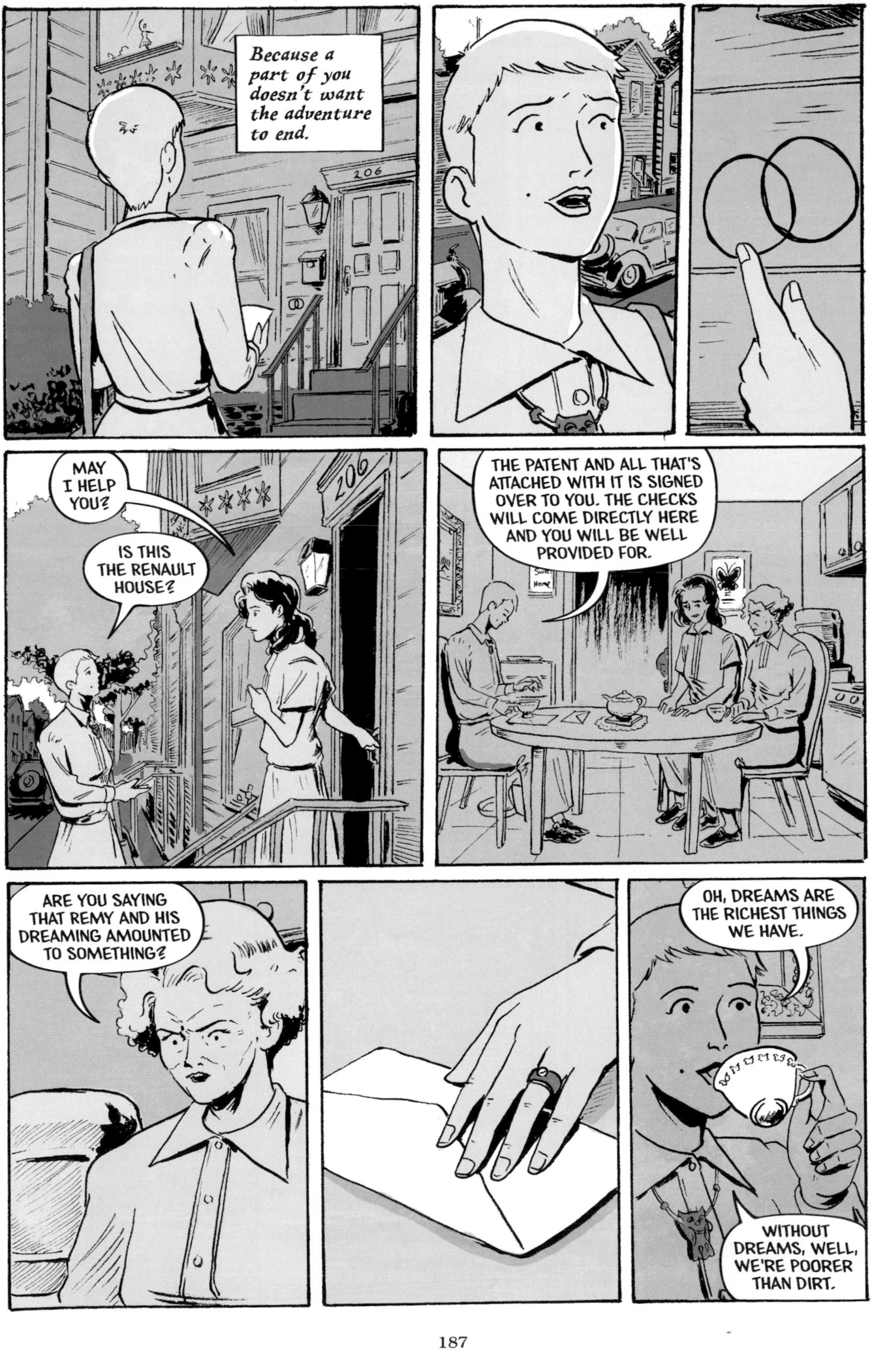

Because a part of you doesn't want the adventure to end.
206
MAY I HELP YOU?
IS THIS THE RENAULT HOUSE?
THE PATENT AND ALL THAT'S ATTACHED WITH IT IS SIGNED OVER TO YOU. THE CHECKS WILL COME DIRECTLY HERE AND YOU WILL BE WELL PROVIDED FOR.
ARE YOU SAYING THAT REMY AND HIS DREAMING AMOUNTED TO SOMETHING?
OH, DREAMS ARE THE RICHEST THINGS WE HAVE.
WITHOUT DREAMS, WELL, WE'RE POORER THAN DIRT.

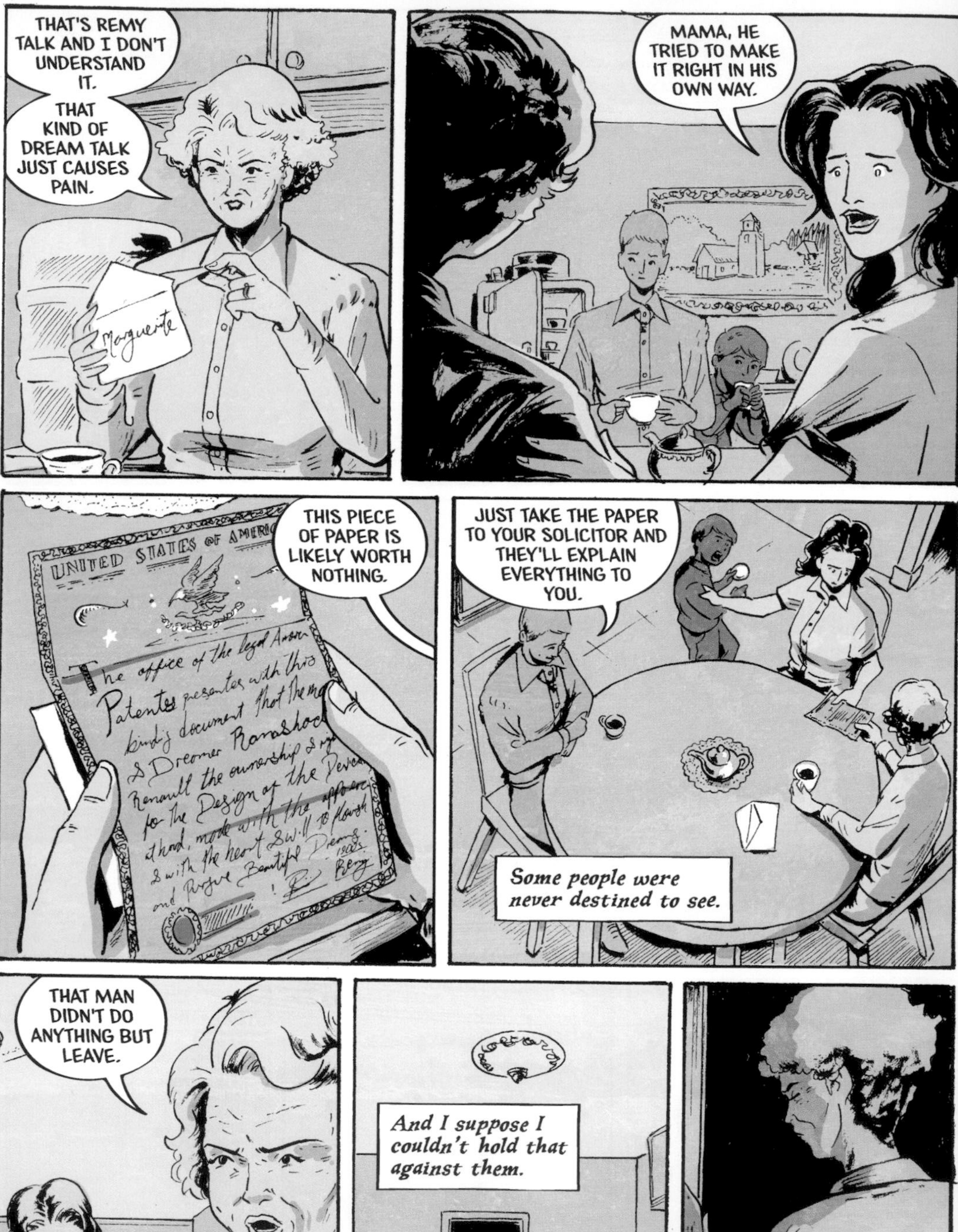
THAT'S REMY TALK AND I DON'T UNDERSTAND IT.
THAT KIND OF DREAM TALK JUST CAUSES PAIN.
Marguerite
MAMA, HE TRIED TO MAKE IT RIGHT IN HIS OWN WAY.
THIS PIECE OF PAPER IS LIKELY WORTH NOTHING.
JUST TAKE THE PAPER TO YOUR SOLICITOR AND THEY'LL EXPLAIN EVERYTHING TO YOU.
Some people were never destined to see.
THAT MAN DIDN'T DO ANYTHING BUT LEAVE.
And I suppose I couldn't hold that against them.
NOW IF YOU'LL EXCUSE ME, I'M TIRED.

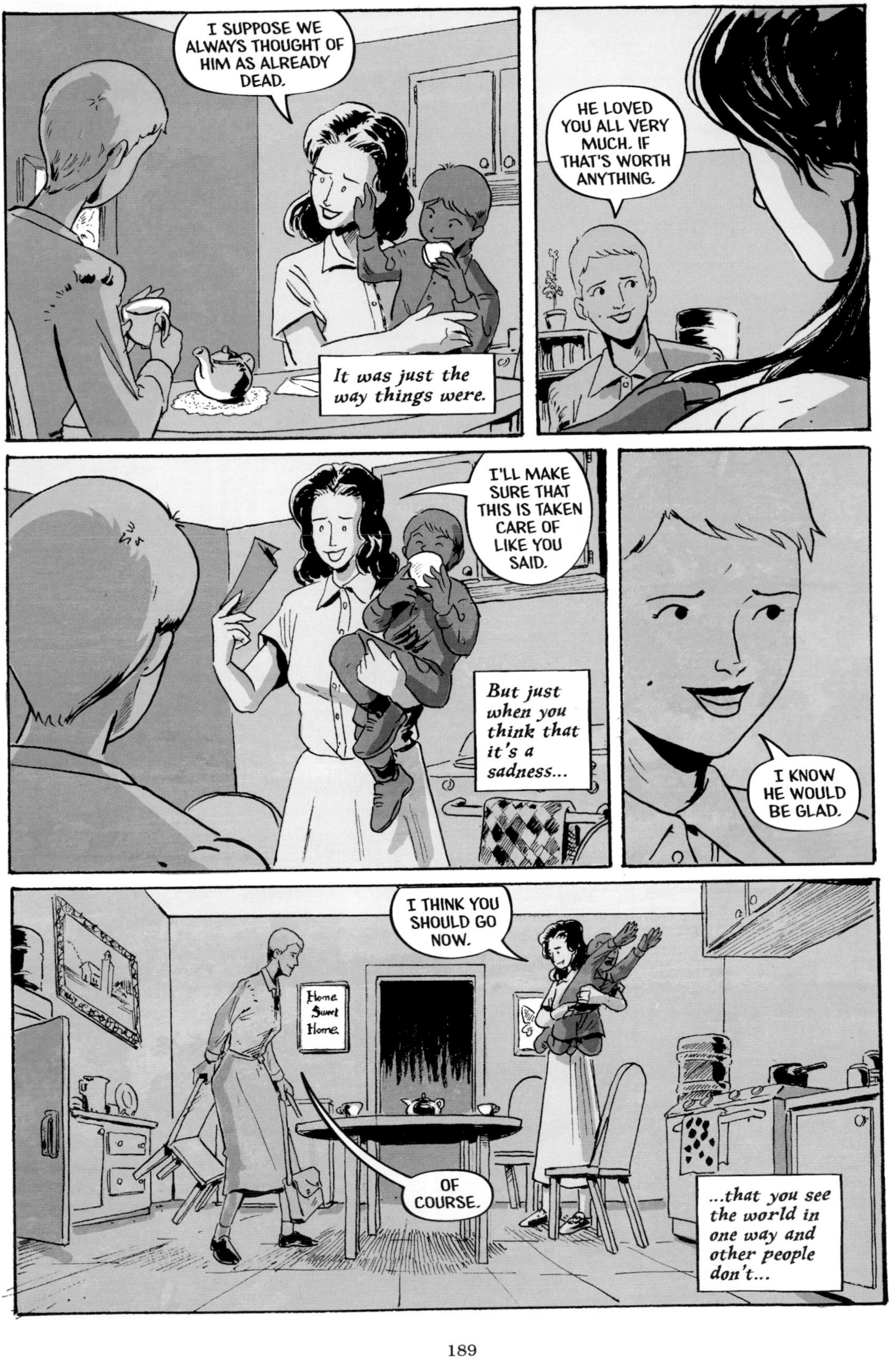
I SUPPOSE WE ALWAYS THOUGHT OF HIM AS ALREADY DEAD.
It was just the way things were.
HE LOVED YOU ALL VERY MUCH. IF THAT'S WORTH ANYTHING.
I'LL MAKE SURE THAT THIS IS TAKEN CARE OF LIKE YOU SAID.
But just when you think that it's a sadness...
I KNOW HE WOULD BE GLAD.
I THINK YOU SHOULD GO NOW.
Home Sweet Home
OF COURSE.
...that you see the world in one way and other people don't...

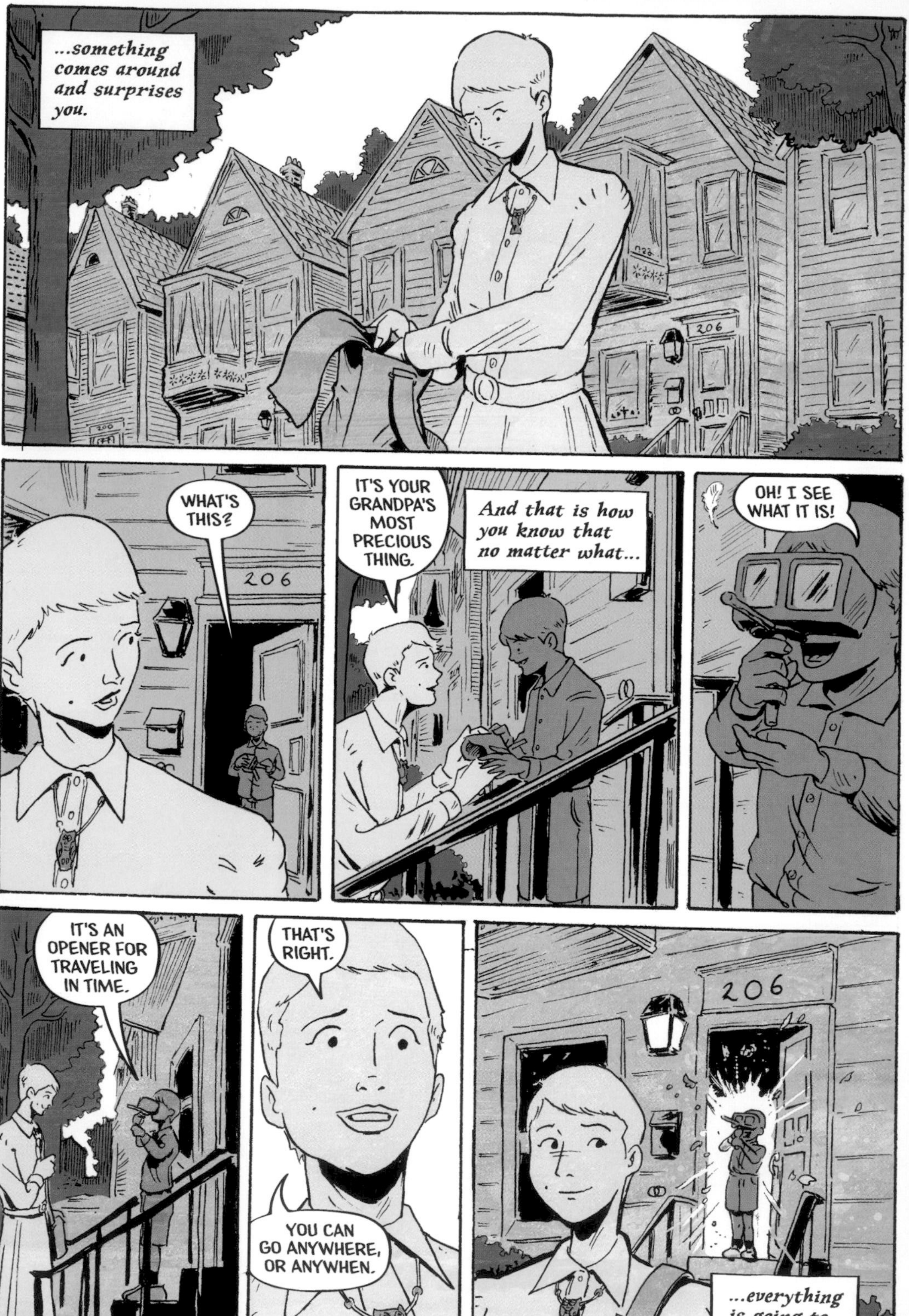
...something comes around and surprises you.
WHAT'S THIS?
IT'S YOUR GRANDPA'S MOST PRECIOUS THING.
And that is how you know that no matter what...
OH! I SEE WHAT IT IS!
IT'S AN OPENER FOR TRAVELING IN TIME.
THAT'S RIGHT.
YOU CAN GO ANYWHERE, OR ANYWHEN.
206
...everything is going to be all right.

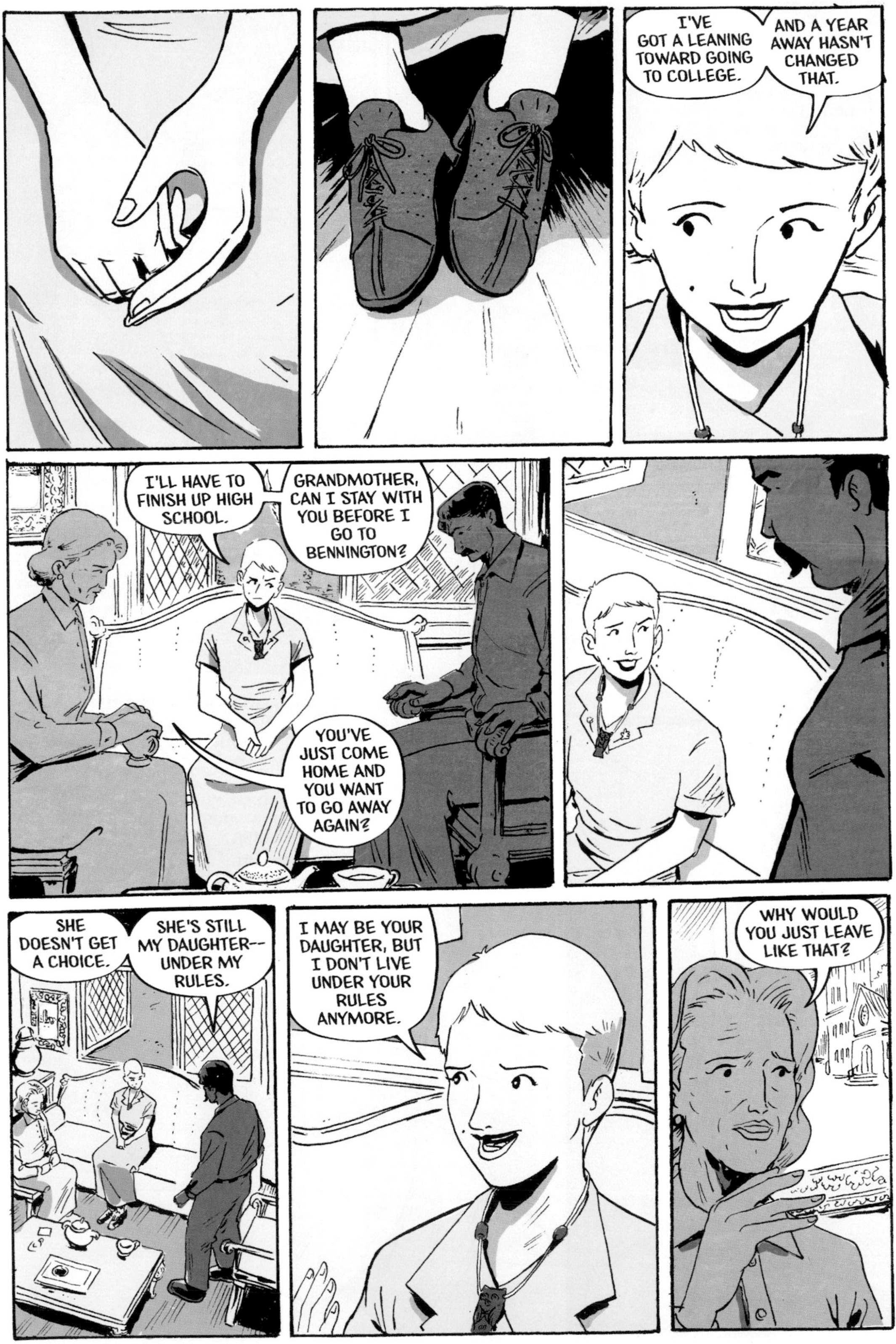
I'VE GOT A LEANING TOWARD GOING TO COLLEGE.
AND A YEAR AWAY HASN'T CHANGED THAT.
I'LL HAVE TO FINISH UP HIGH SCHOOL.
GRANDMOTHER, CAN I STAY WITH YOU BEFORE I GO TO BENNINGTON?
YOU'VE JUST COME HOME AND YOU WANT TO GO AWAY AGAIN?
SHE DOESN'T GET A CHOICE.
SHE'S STILL MY DAUGHTER--UNDER MY RULES.
I MAY BE YOUR DAUGHTER, BUT I DON'T LIVE UNDER YOUR RULES ANYMORE.
WHY WOULD YOU JUST LEAVE LIKE THAT?

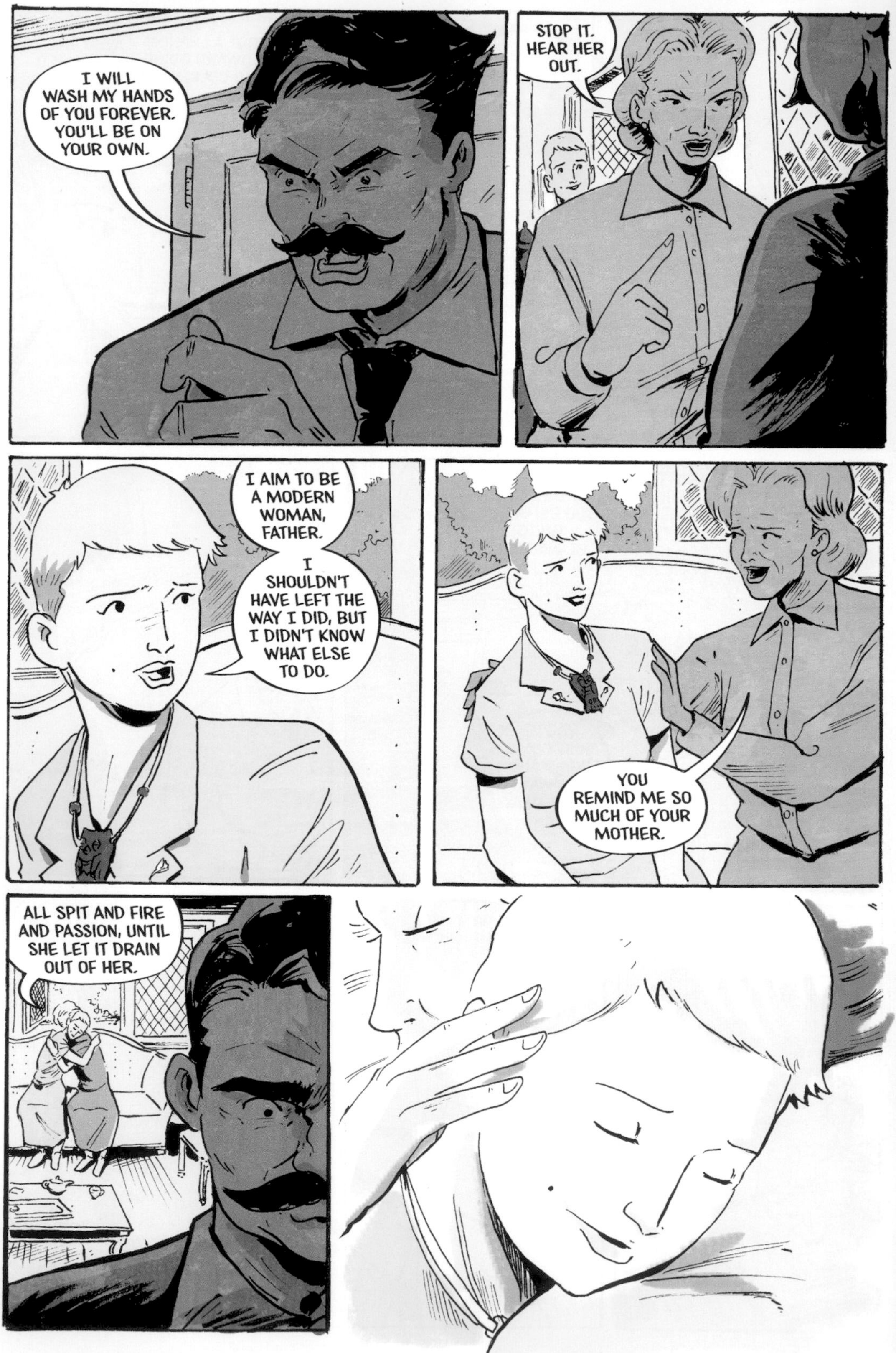
I WILL WASH MY HANDS OF YOU FOREVER. YOU'LL BE ON YOUR OWN.
STOP IT. HEAR HER OUT.
I AIM TO BE A MODERN WOMAN, FATHER.
I SHOULDN'T HAVE LEFT THE WAY I DID, BUT I DIDN'T KNOW WHAT ELSE TO DO.
YOU REMIND ME SO MUCH OF YOUR MOTHER.
ALL SPIT AND FIRE AND PASSION, UNTIL SHE LET IT DRAIN OUT OF HER.

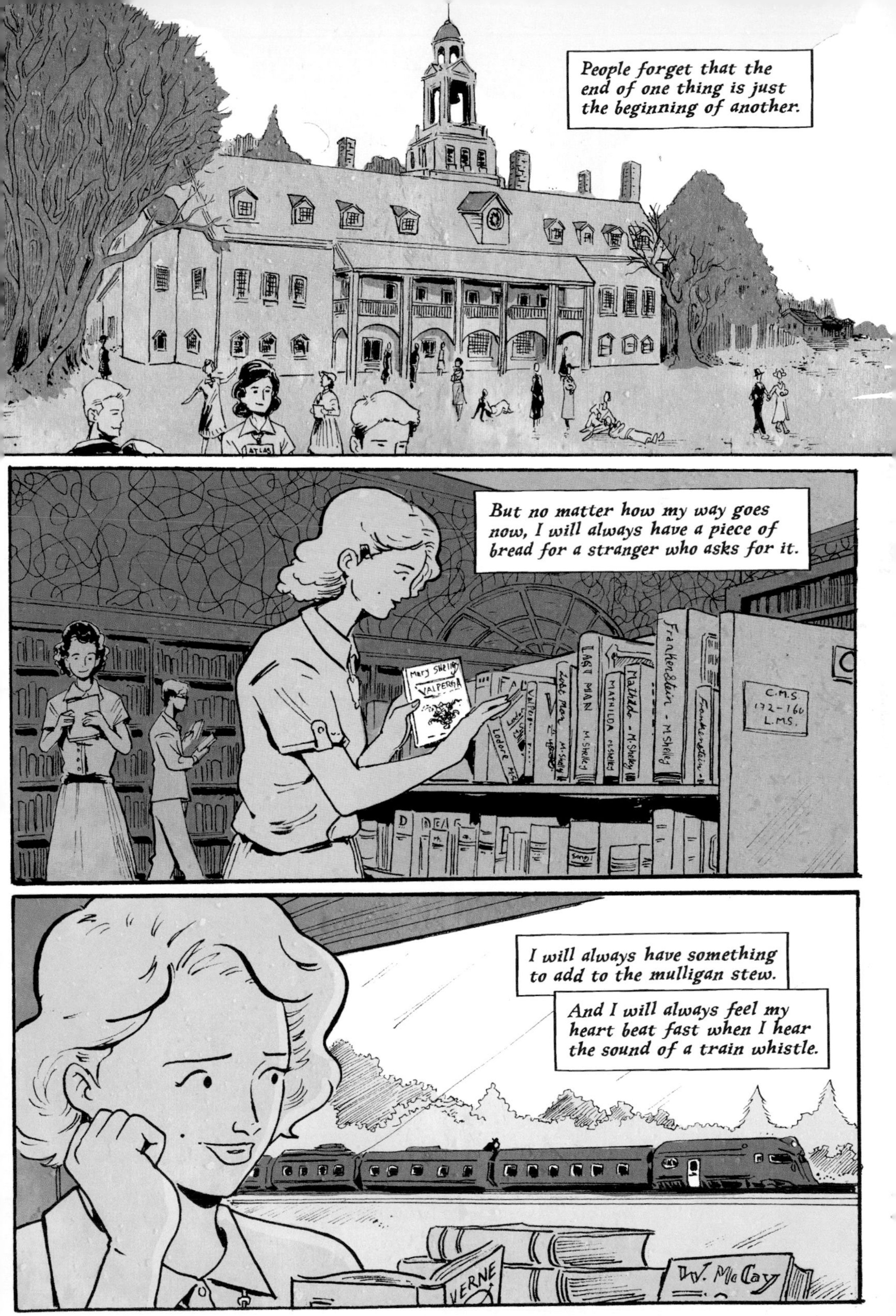
People forget that the end of one thing is just the beginning of another.
ATLAS
But no matter how my way goes now, I will always have a piece of bread for a stranger who asks for it.
Mary Shelley
VALPERGA
LAST MAN
MATHILDA
M. Shelley
Frankenstein
C.M.S.
172-160
L.MS.
I will always have something to add to the mulligan stew.
And I will always feel my heart beat fast when I hear the sound of a train whistle.
VERNE
W. McCay

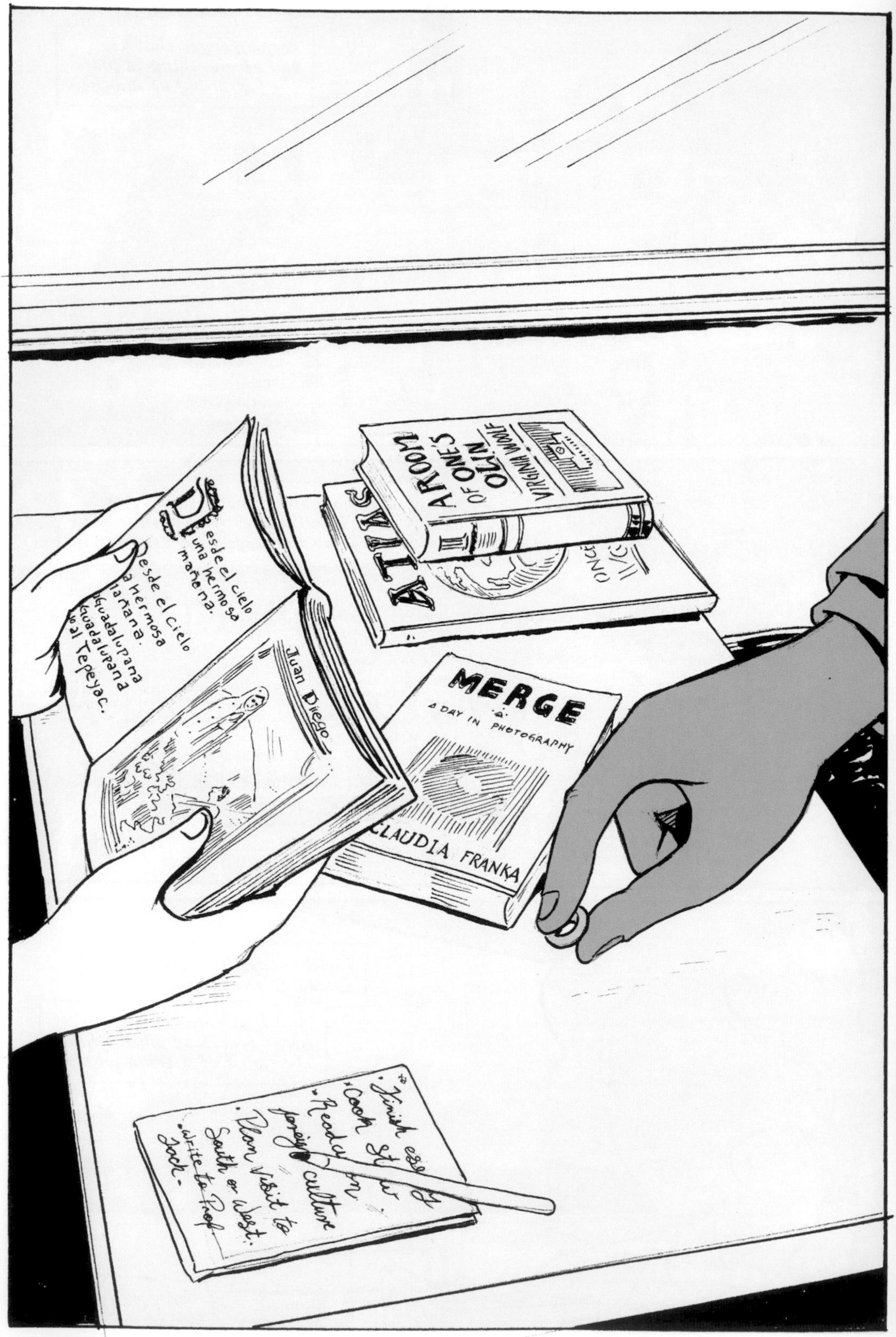
Desde el cielo
una hermosa
mañana.
Desde el cielo
Juan Diego
A ROOM OF ONE'S OWN
VIRGINIA WOOLF
ATLAS
MERGE
A DAY IN PHOTOGRAPHY
CLAUDIA FRANKA
culture
Plan visit to
South or West.
write to Prof

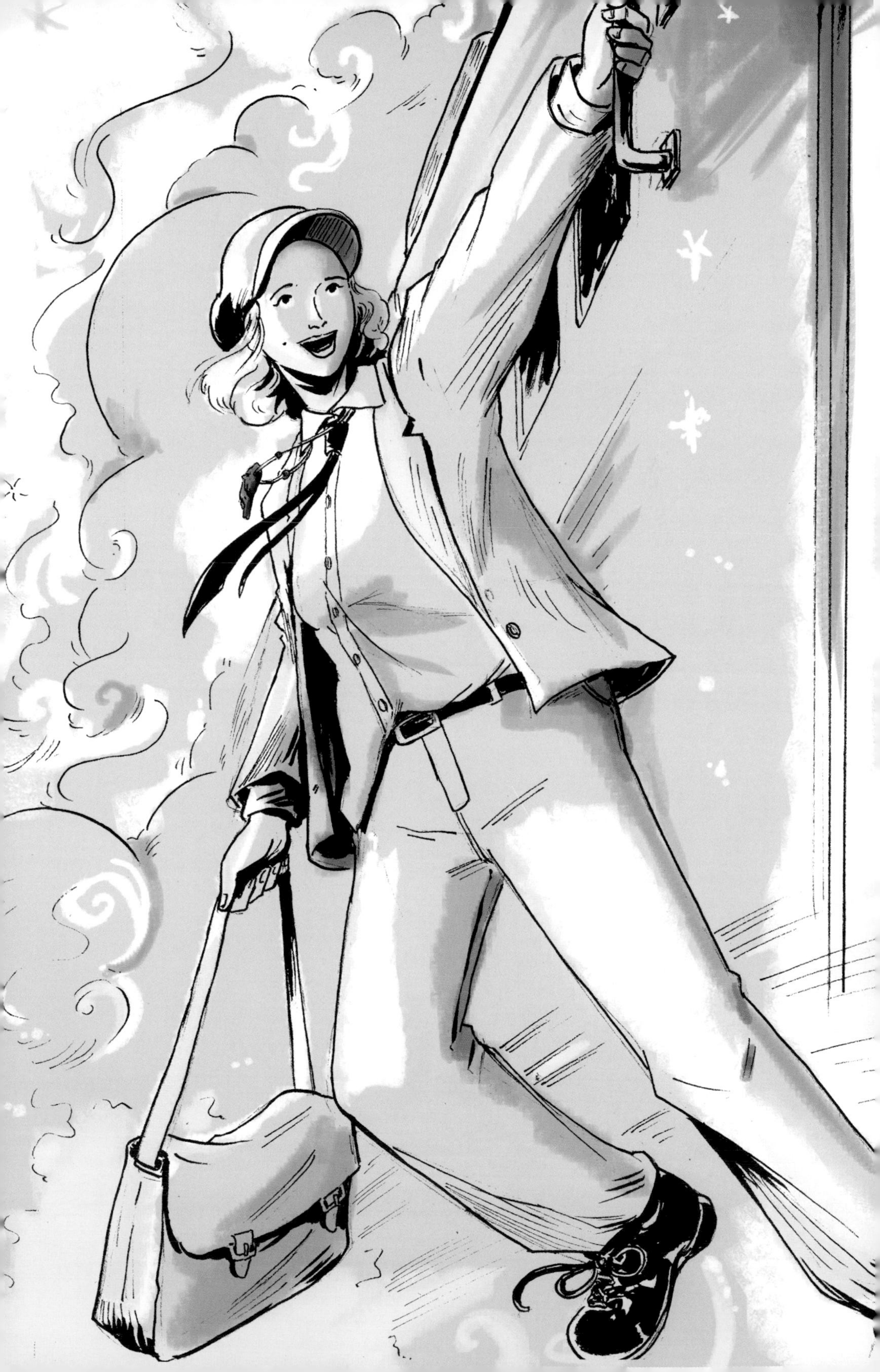

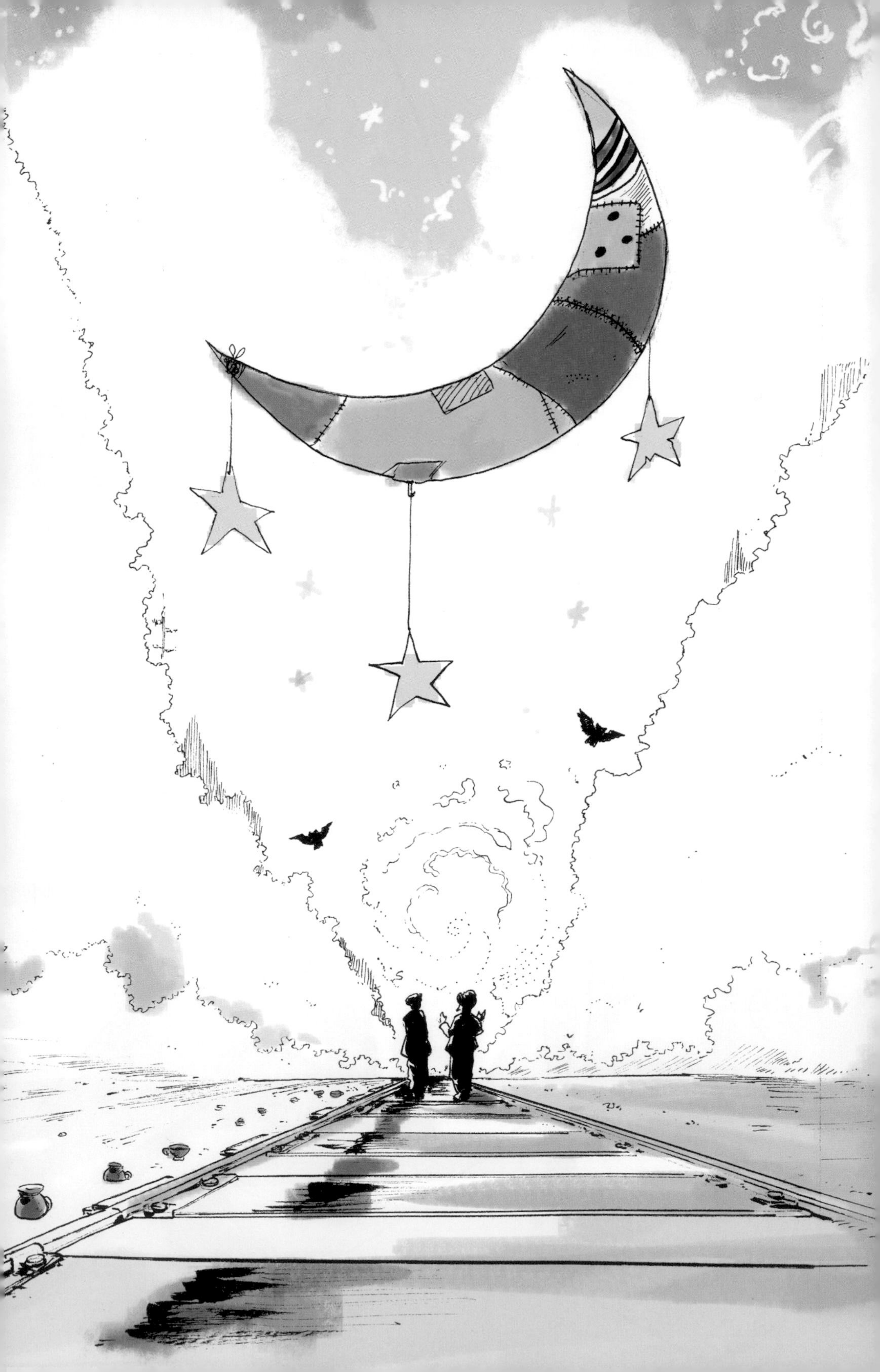

Check out the books that Soupy is reading and the stories that inspired Cecil and Jose!

Farthest North by **Fridtjof Nansen**

Valperga; or, The Life and Adventures of Castruccio, Prince of Lucca and *Frankenstein; or, The Modern Prometheus* by **Mary Shelley**

Little Nemo in Slumberland by **Winsor McCay**

Journey to the Center of the Earth by **Jules Verne**

A Room of One's Own by **Virginia Woolf**

The tale of Juan Diego and the Virgin of Guadalupe

Citizen Hobo by **Todd DePastino**

Tramping with Tramps by **Josiah Flynt**

Hoboes by **Mark Wyman**

I Was Looking for a Street by **Charles Willeford**

Beggars of Life by **Jim Tully**

You Can't Win by **Jack Black**

HOBO SIGNS

During the Great Depression, hoboes developed a visual code they used to communicate. Though some were unable to read, all could recognize and remember the symbols. Hoboes would write this code with chalk or coal to provide directions, information, and warnings to others coming down the line. Symbols could indicate many different things. Here are some that show up in *Soupy Leaves Home*.

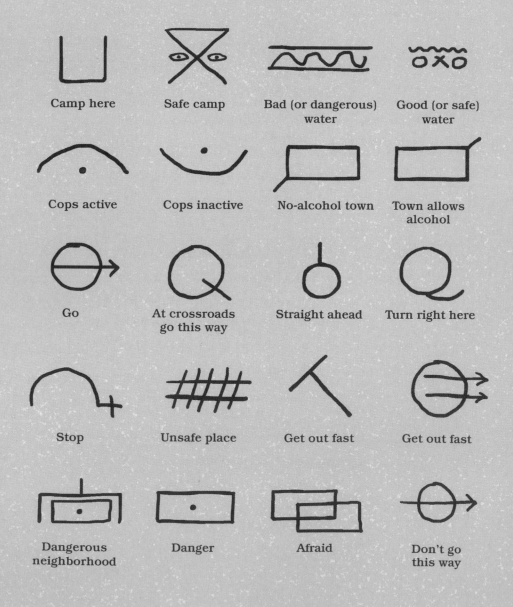

Camp here

Safe camp

Bad (or dangerous) water

Good (or safe) water

Cops active

Cops inactive

No-alcohol town

Town allows alcohol

Go

At crossroads go this way

Straight ahead

Turn right here

Stop

Unsafe place

Get out fast

Get out fast

Dangerous neighborhood

Danger

Afraid

Don't go this way

Worth robbing

Catch train
here

Don't give up

Man with gun

You'll get cursed
out here

Railroad

Trolley

Kindly woman

Be ready to
defend yourself

Turn left here

Good road
to follow

Sit-down meal

Courthouse or
police station

Keep away

Unsafe area

Will care for sick

Tramps here

Be quiet

Jail

Chain gang

Hold your tongue

Hoboes arrested
on sight

Doctor does
not charge

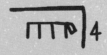
Beware—
four dogs

Cowards—will give
to get rid of you

Sleep in
the loft

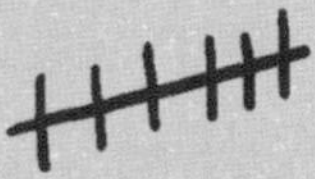

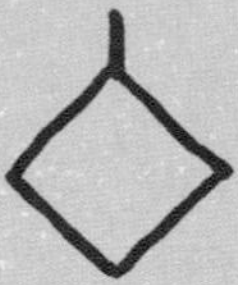

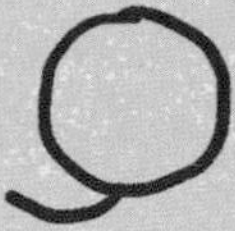

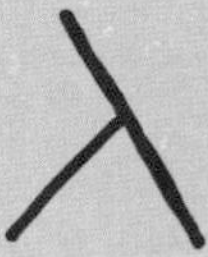

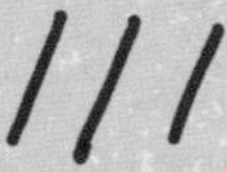

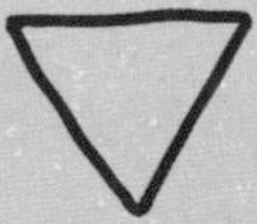

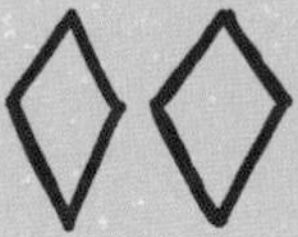

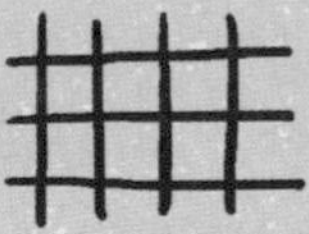

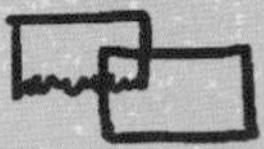

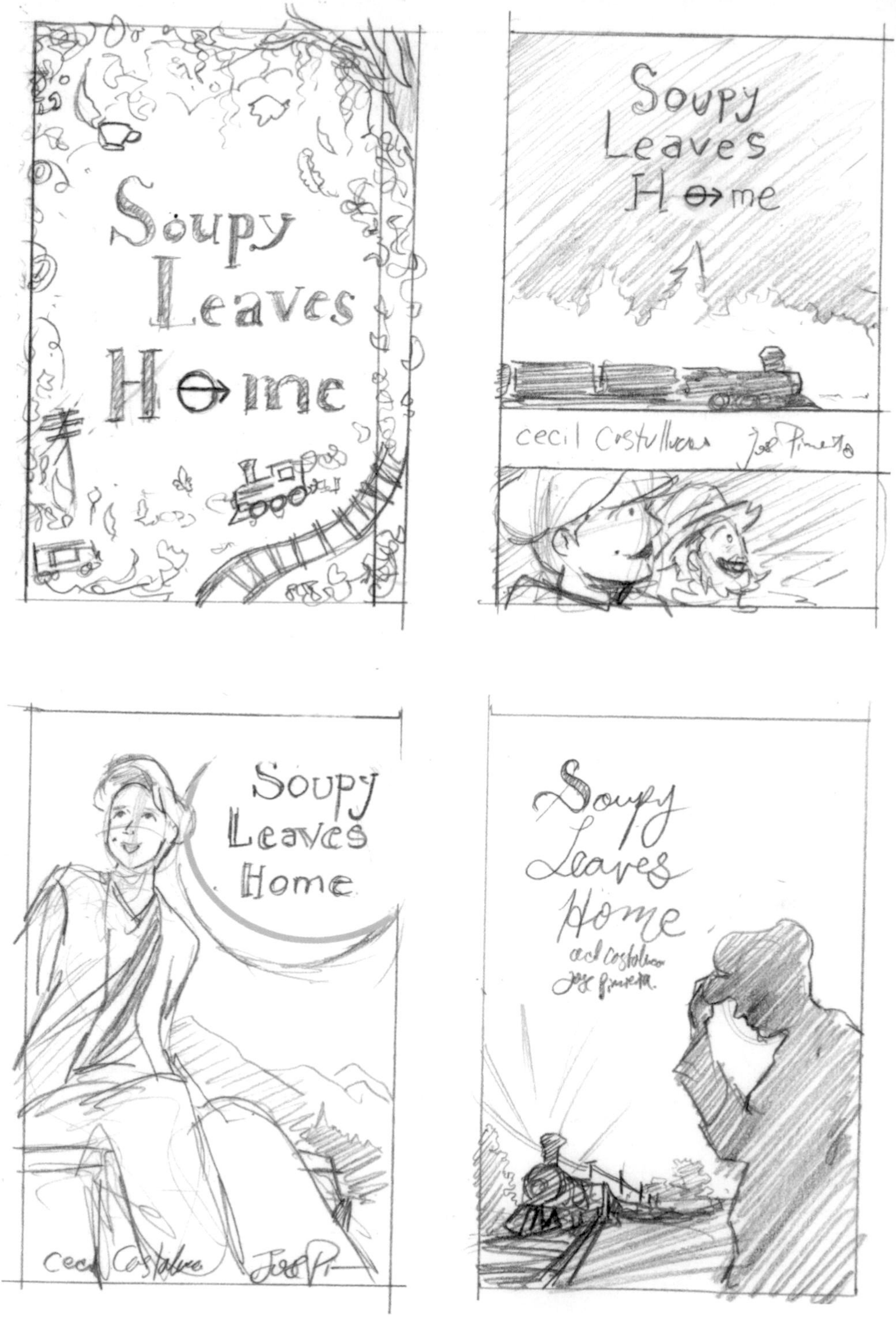
Soupy Leaves Home
Soupy Leaves Home
Soupy Leaves Home
Soupy Leaves Home

Cover sketches and final pencils (*facing*) by Jose

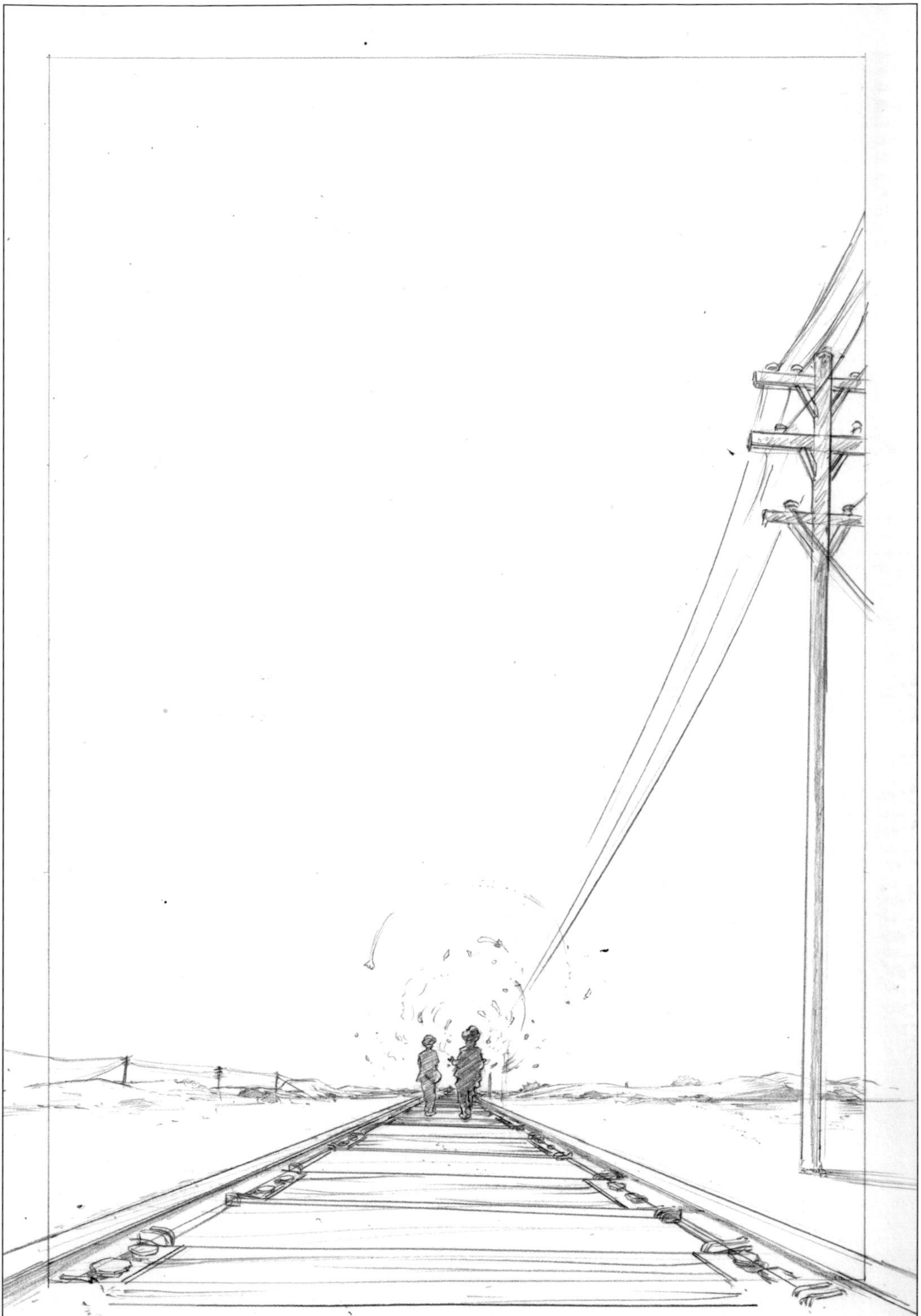

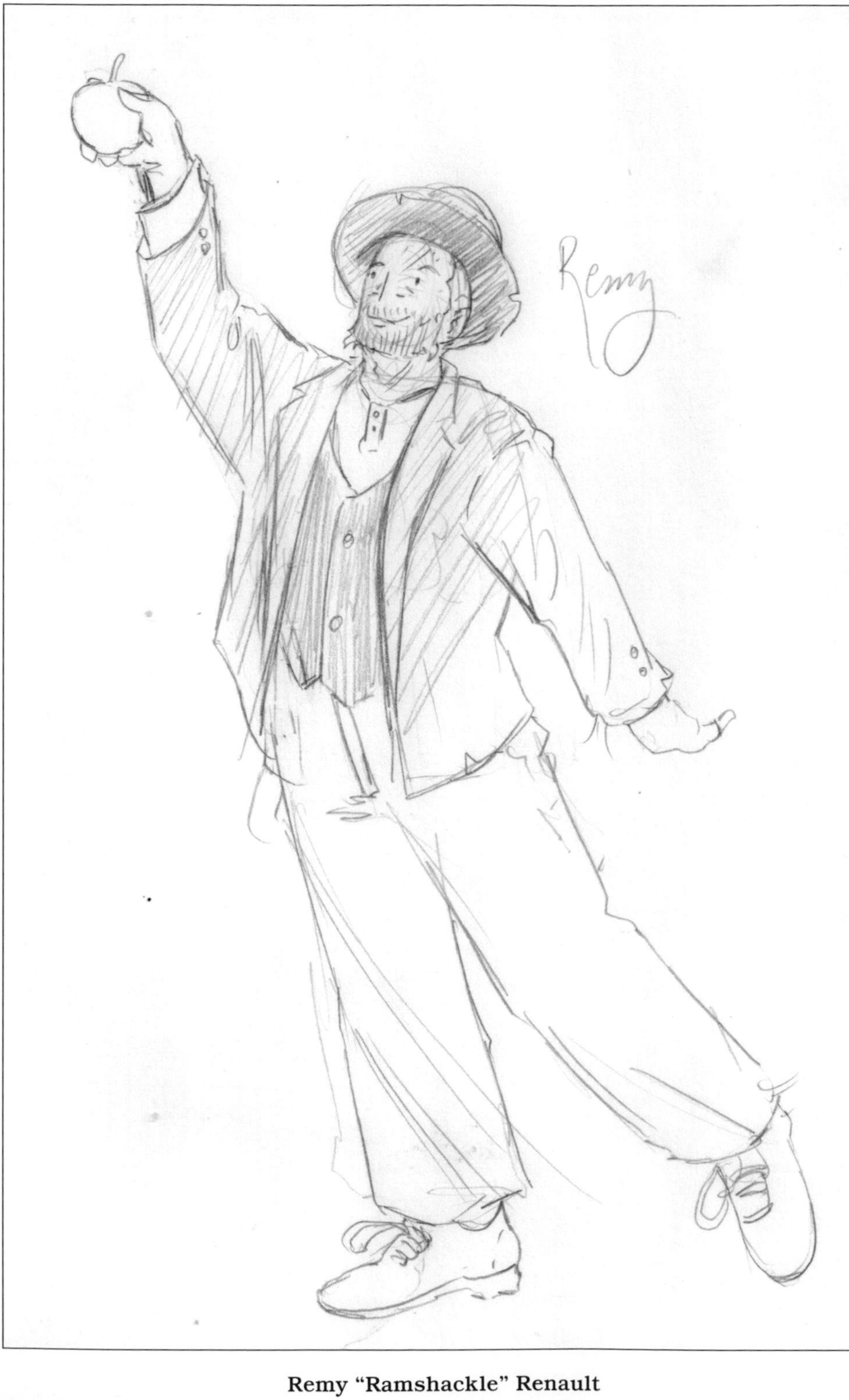
Remy

Remy “Ramshackle” Renault

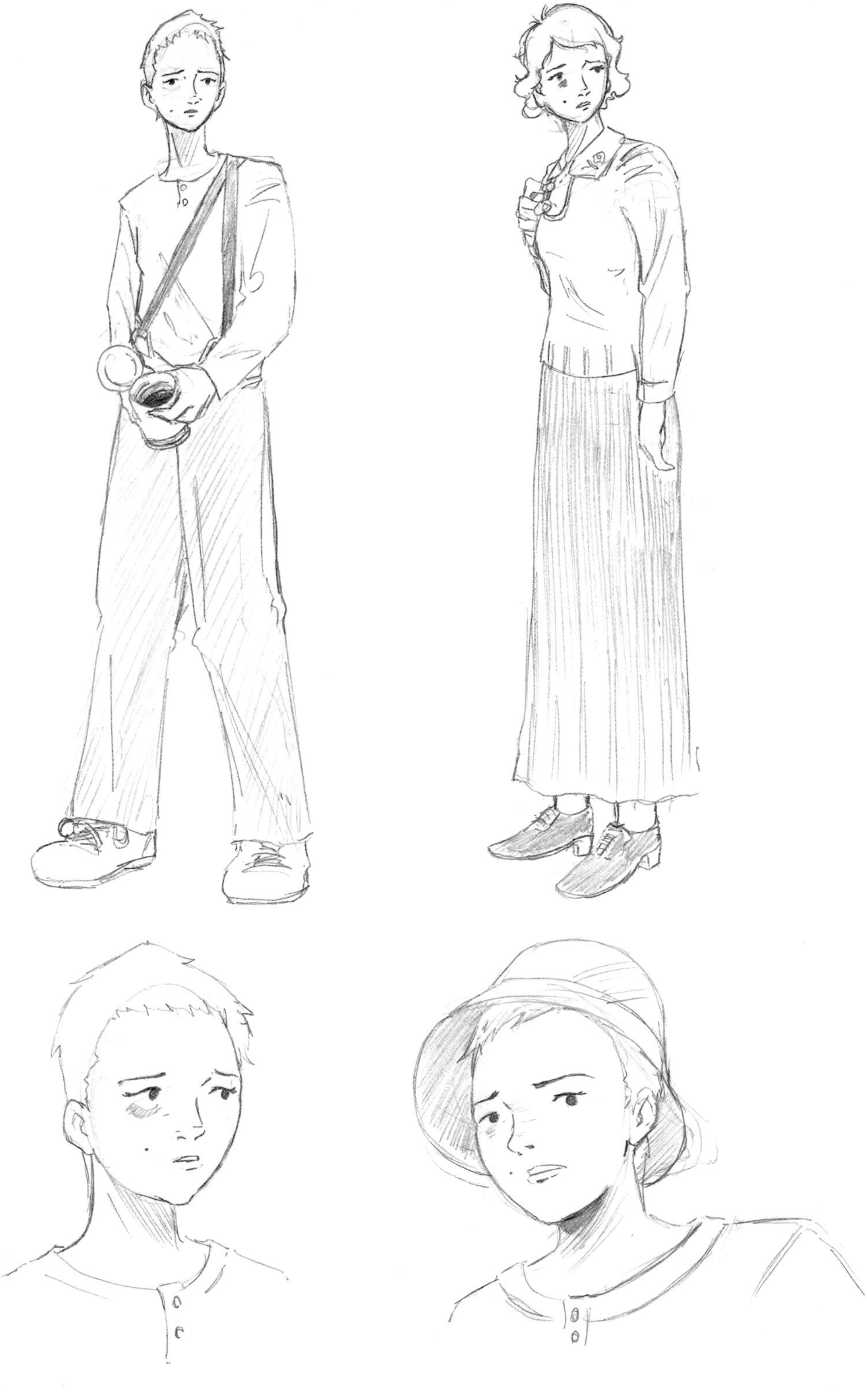

Pearl “Soupy” Plankette

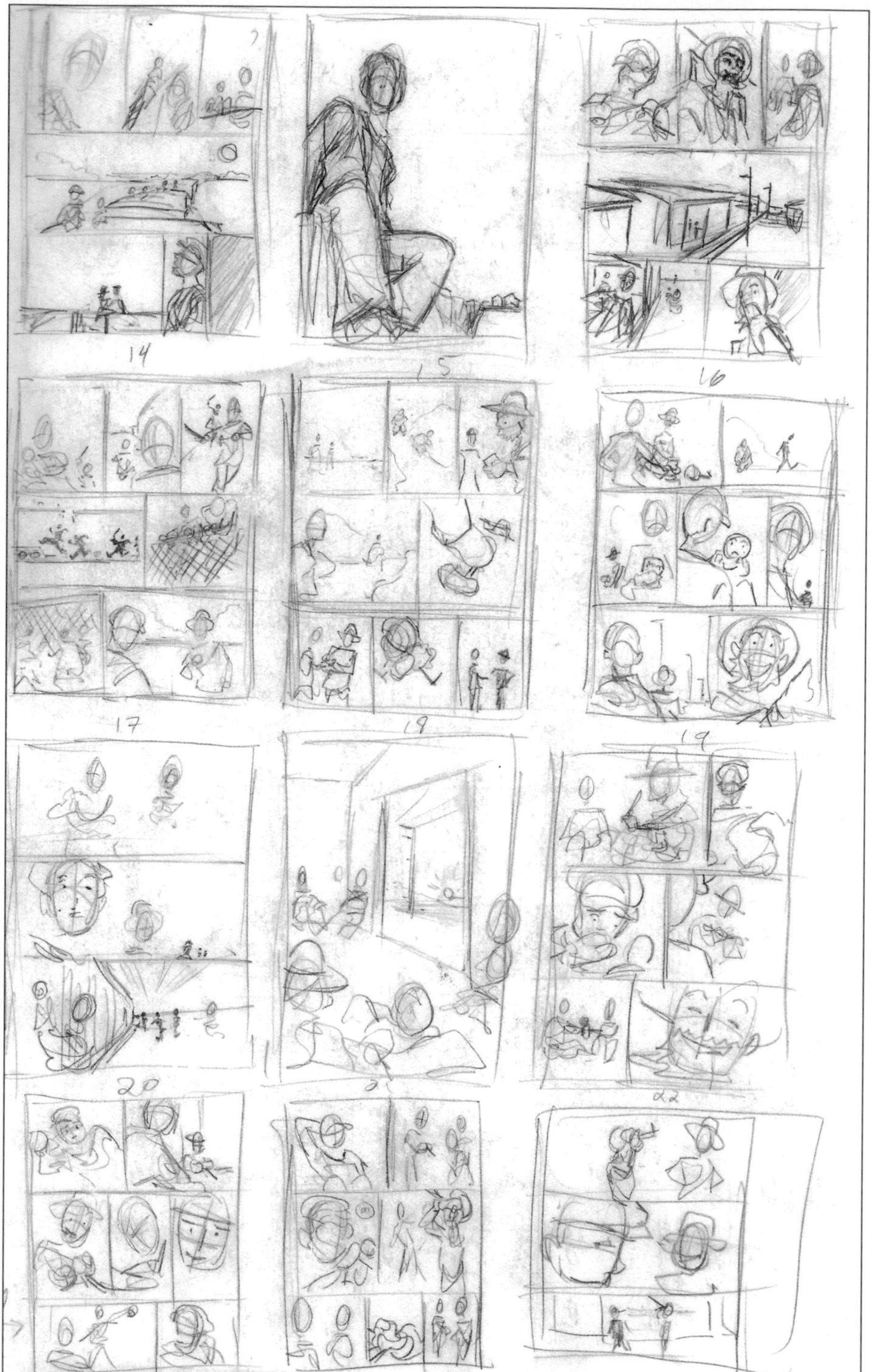

Layouts for pages 17-28 and 121-132, 136-145, 147-149 (*facing*) by Jose

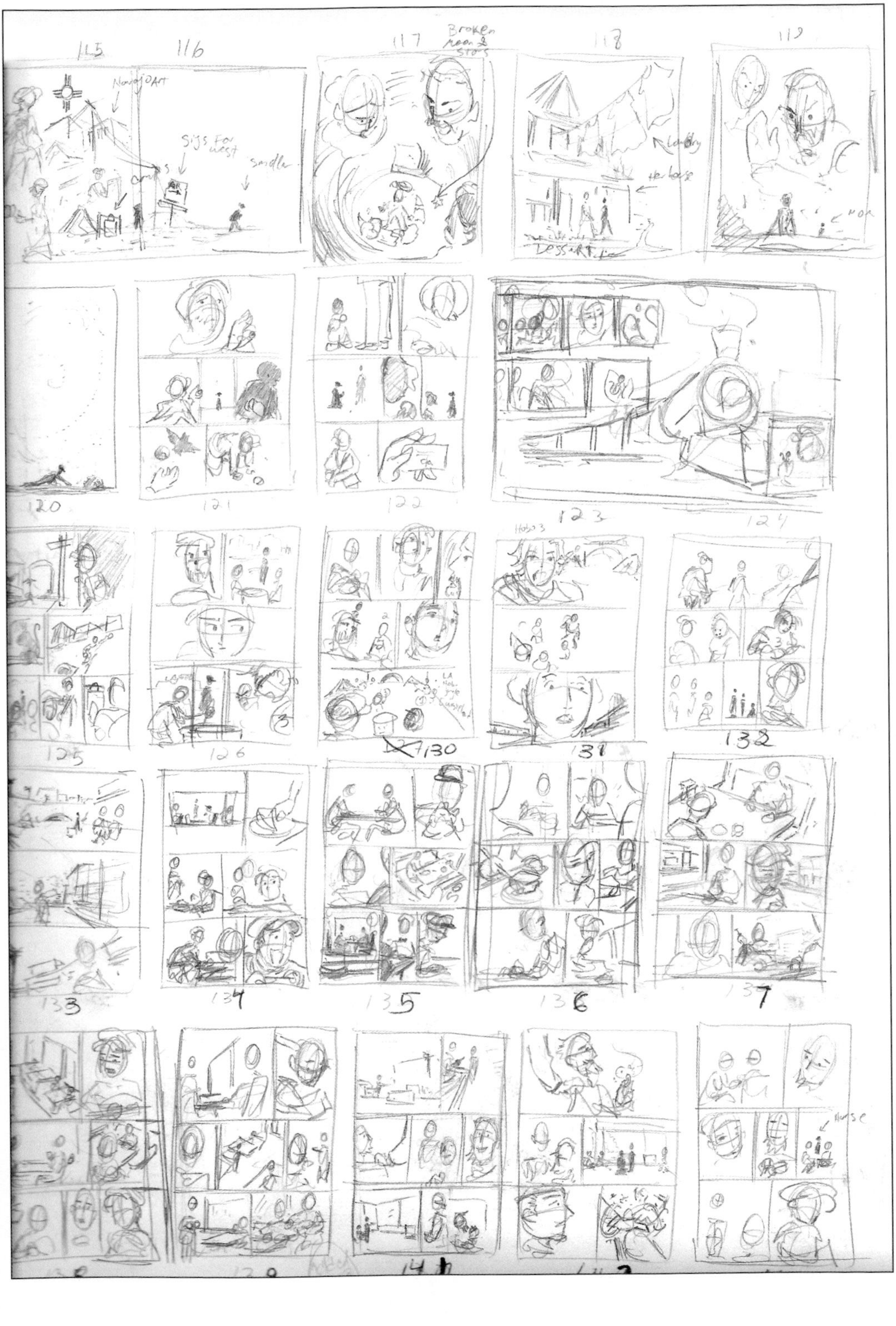

115
116
117
Broken
118
119
Laundry
120
121
122
123
124
125
126
130
132
133
134
135
136
137
Nurse

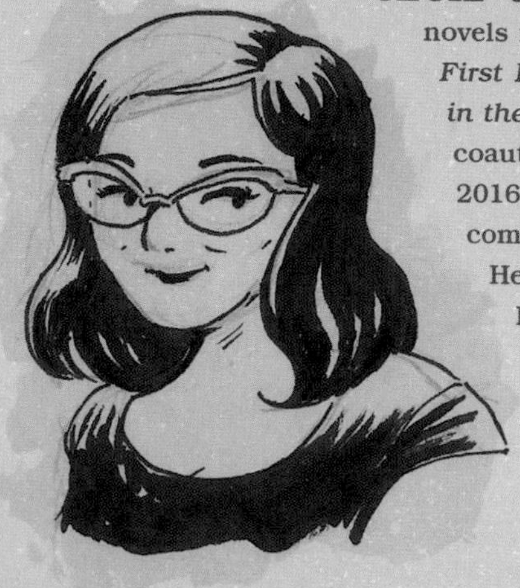

CECIL CASTELLUCCI is the author of books and graphic novels for young adults including *Boy Proof*, *The Plain Janes*, *First Day on Earth*, *The Year of the Beasts*, *Tin Star*, *Stone in the Sky*, and the Eisner-nominated *Odd Duck*. In 2015 she coauthored *Moving Target: A Princess Leia Adventure*, and in 2016 she worked on *Shade, the Changing Girl*, an ongoing comic for Gerard Way's Young Animal imprint at DC Comics. Her picture book *Grandma's Gloves* won the California Book Awards Gold Medal. Her short stories have been published in *Strange Horizons*, YARN, Tor.com, and various anthologies, including *Teeth*, *After*, and *Interfictions 2*. She is the children's correspondence coordinator for The Rumpus, a two-time MacDowell Fellow, and the founding YA editor at the *Los Angeles Review of Books*. She lives in Los Angeles.

JOSE PIMIENTA grew up in Mexicali, Mexico, watching a lot of cartoons and listening to as much music as possible. After finishing high school, he studied visual storytelling in Georgia, where he made friends and drank a lot of coffee. Eventually, he headed back to Southern California, where he currently resides. He draws on a regular basis and still listens to as much music as he can. He also enjoys recreational walks and whistling. Sometimes he goes by "Joe."

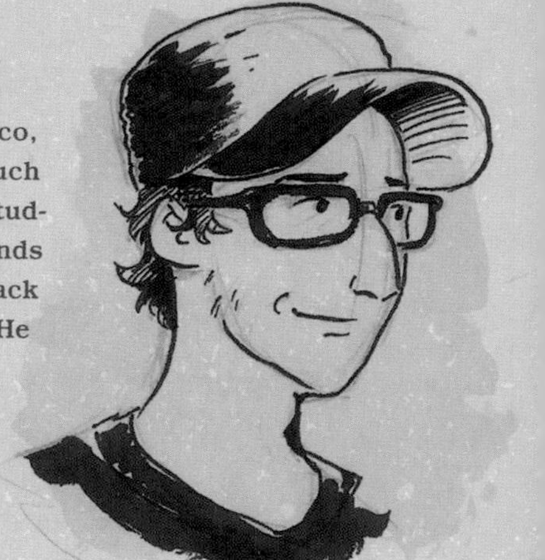

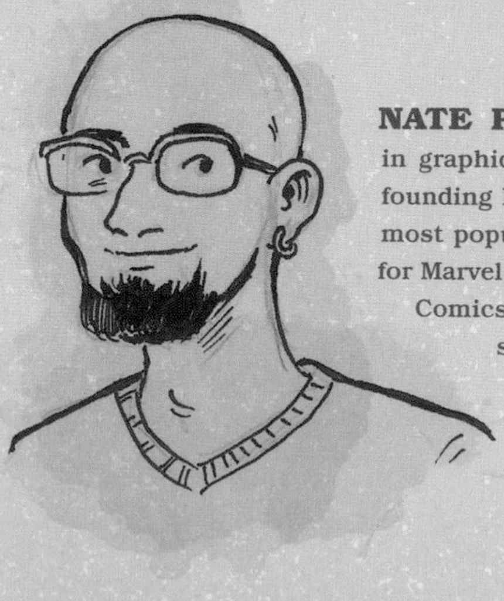

NATE PIEKOS graduated with a bachelor of arts degree in graphic design from Rhode Island College in 1998. Since founding Blambot.com, he has created some of the industry's most popular fonts and has used them to letter comic books for Marvel Comics, DC Comics, Dark Horse Comics, and Image Comics, as well as dozens of independent publishers. In his spare time, Nate plays guitar, cooks, and draws web comics. He's married and lives in the woods of Rhode Island.